W9-CHS-069

"I loved *Warprize*! Keir is a hero to savor."
—nationally bestselling author
Claire Delacroix

"Vaughan's brawny barbarian romance re-creates the delicious feeling of adventure and the thrill of exploring mysterious cultures created by Robert E. Howard in his Conan books and makes for a satisfying escapist read with its enjoyable romance between a plucky, near-naked heroine and a truly heroic hero."

—*Booklist*

Dear Reader,

Mom instilled a love of reading in me at an early age, but it was Dad that introduced me to the worlds of fantasy. While I will read just about any book, put a sword in a warrior's hand, hint at magic and an epic journey, and I can't wait to get my hands on that story.

For what you hold in your hands, at the very moment that you read this, is the closest that I will ever get to casting a magic spell. No messy ingredients, no frogs, no eyes of newt, no secret room deep in a dungeon or high in a spire. No sparkly dress, no magic wand, no magic mirror. No, the only source of my power are the pages you hold and the words written thereon. As you read them, I hope the magic starts to work between my words and your imagination.

If I've woven my spell with a bit of art and skill, then you will be lost in the Kingdom of Xy, entranced with Xylara's choices and the consequences for her and the Kingdom. And there are more tales to be told, more spells to be woven, more adventures to be had. But all stories must "begin at the beginning" and so it is with this one.

So please, let me tell you a story . . .

—Elizabeth

WARPRIZE

ELIZABETH VAUGHAN

tor paranormal romance

A TOM DOHERTY ASSOCIATES BOOK
NEW YORK

WARPRIZE

Copyright © 2005 by Elizabeth Vaughan

Edited by Anna Genoese

A Tor Book
Published by Tom Doherty Associates, LLC
175 Fifth Avenue
New York, NY 10010

www.tor.com

Tor® is a registered trademark of Tom Doherty Associates, LLC.

ISBN-13: 978-0-765-35736-6
ISBN-10: 0-765-35736-4

First Edition: June 2005
Second Edition: November 2006

Printed in the United States of America

0 9 8 7 6 5 4 3 2 1

To my parents, Park and Patricia Vaughan

Acknowledgments

There are so many people I need to thank, who have extended their friendship, love and support to me during the creation of the book. Of all the gifts that writing has given me, your presence in my life is the greatest gift of all.

Spencer Luster, who told me to 'put up or shut up'. My writer's group, which includes Spencer, Helen Kourous, Robert Wenzlaff, Marc Tassin, and Keith Flick. Kathleen Crow, who refused to let my dream die. Kandace Klumper, for quiet words of encouragement and a good swift kick when necessary. Lisa Black, who always wanted more. Patricia Merritt, who is my partner in evil. JoAnn Thompson, who believes in me when I don't. Mary Fry, Roberto Ledesma and David Browder, who cheerfully read and commented on my early drafts. Phil Fry, Cathie Hansen and Deb Spychalski, for putting up with me for the last two years. Jane Lackey, for her long suffering patience. Linda Baker, Don Bingle, and Janet Deaver Pack who showed me that it could happen. Annette Leggett, always running through the forest with sharp objects. The Maumee Valley

Chapter of the RWA, who welcomed me with open arms. Tom Redding, who suffered through the galleys. Merrilee Heifetz, Anna Genoese and Fiorella DeLima, whose hard work and contributions to this book made me look damn good.

But most of all, credit must go to Jean Rabe, who pushed me into the pool, and to Meg Davis, who found me there.

1

I pulled the shard out just as his wound began spurting blood.

"Goddess, no." I dropped the knife, pressed my hands against his stomach, into the blood, and threw my full weight onto the wound. Biting my lip, I pressed harder still, desperate to stop the bleeding. "Hold him, boys."

The apprentices gathered around the table grabbed tight to his arms and legs, all of them wide-eyed and pale as they tried to keep him from moving. The wooden table beneath my aged patient creaked and complained at the added weight as the room echoed with the sound of our leather shoes slapping against the stone floor and my patient's frantic panting.

A quick glance around the large kitchen told me that there were no other healers in sight. They were all in the main hall, tending the others. Just the apprentices, clustered around the table. Blood bubbled up between my fingers, warm and thick. The metallic smell was strong and settled in my mouth. There was something wrong with the smell, but I was too busy to think on it. One of the lads frantically waved a fresh bandage before my eyes, and I snatched it, crammed it into the wound, and pressed down. I had to get it stopped. The bandage turned to scarlet before my eyes.

The man under my hands groaned and thrashed, trying to get away from the pain. One of the smaller lads was flung away. The patient's freed arm swiped through the air, catching me on the cheek. Vision blurred for a precious instant as my head rocked back with the blow. My hair came loose, and one long brown curl floated down to lie in the blood that surrounded my hands. The felled boy scrambled up and threw himself back into the fray, grabbing the flailing arm and wrestling it down. "Sorry, Lara," he told me.

"Hold him." My voice was a croak. I was too harsh on the lads who were trying their best. Their bloodless faces were pale blurs. I heard the one next to me swallowing rapidly. Pray to the Goddess that he'd not spew on the wound. My shoulders tightened as I tried to increase the pressure, trying to staunch the red flow. "I need help here." I raised my voice to carry into the main hall that was filled with wounded and other healers.

"Lara? What's happened?" A quiet, calm voice came from behind me.

It was Eln, thank the Goddess.

The warrior surged up again, and the table squeaked in protest. We stayed with him, trying to keep him still, trying to keep the pressure on. He cried out suddenly, then sagged back, exhausted. I gulped in breath to answer. "The shard came out clean but he's bleeding."

A head popped in next to mine as Eln craned his scrawny neck to have a look. My teacher for years, he always moved like a gray lake-crane. He made a noncommittal noise, then pulled a deep breath in through his nose. I gritted my teeth. Sometimes he decides that I need a lesson in the midst of saving a life, even though I've held my mastery for years. Eln's head pulled back, but I could feel him standing behind me.

"Not my patient, and not my place to say." Eln's voice was quiet, but cut through the moans of the warrior. "But what happens after you stop the bleeding?"

I slammed my eyes shut. My patient shifted again, and we moved with him, automatically.

"Stubborn child . . ." Eln's voice was a whisper, but I heard it. "You may have gained your mastery but you haven't truly learned, have you?"

I did not want to concede to his wisdom, did not want to face what the scent of waste in the blood meant, the scent I'd failed to identify a moment before. But experience had been a hard teacher, harder then Eln had ever been. With a nod, and a strangled sob, I released the pressure on the wound. The apprentices froze, not understanding.

"Come, boys." Eln spoke quietly. "Come with me."

I ignored them all as they filed out. One stopped, and looked at me.

"Why'd ya stop?"

Kneeling to wash my hands in a bucket on the floor, I looked up into his wide young eyes. "Eln will tell you, child. Go now."

Eln would not miss a chance to give a lesson, a chance to explain the slow, painful death of a belly wound that stank of waste. Explain that a good healer knew when to let a patient go, that death wasn't always an enemy. Explain that good healers didn't stubbornly refuse to acknowledge their limits. I wished them the best of it, for it was a lesson I'd never learned.

Coward that I was, I took a moment to rinse my tunic and trous of the worst of the blood. That might save me some abuse from Anna when I returned to the castle. She claimed that I didn't own a piece of clothing that didn't have blood on it at one time or another. The cool, wet cloth felt good against my hot and sweaty skin.

I took a fresh bowl of water and a clean cloth and bathed the man's face. The bleeding had turned sluggish. It would not be long now. The man sighed and relaxed, muscles releasing their tension under my touch.

Aye, Eln would offer a lesson. But I would offer comfort to a dying man.

The water seemed to ease him, and I put the cloth down for

a moment, and steadied myself. I forced myself to rinse my hands again, working the nails to get the blood off. I took a moment to clean the one stray lock of hair and tuck it up again. My hair was a constant irritation, the curls were never content to stay neat on top of my head.

The kitchen had cleared again. It was the best room in the old barracks to use for the worst of the wounded. The large tables served well, and every counter and cupboard was filled with jars and bowls of ointments and remedies. I stared at their bright colors and the false promise of the claims that they could cure all ails. But nothing lay there that could save this man.

A noise drew my attention down. His eyes fluttered open. Once again I took up the water and cloth. As I worked, he focused on me, a question in his stare. I smiled.

"You are in the healing house, warrior. You took a wound. Rest now."

He licked his lips, narrowed his eyes. "Lance . . . tip broke off . . . belly."

I nodded. No need to speak. He knew.

He closed his eyes, then opened them again and for the first time he seemed to really look at me. "Fought with your father, Lady." He gasped as the effort cost him breath. His voice was soft and tight.

I paused. Few were left that could claim to have known my father. "I am sorry, but I don't know you."

He didn't seem to hear me. One corner of his mouth turned up. "You've his eyes, child. All fey blue and wise." His arm trembled as he tried to raise his hand. I caught it and held it in mine. His eyes got a strange light in them, perhaps an echo of his younger self. "Now there was a king, your father. What a warrior he was." He looked over my shoulder, seeing into the mists of memory.

"I miss him." I said quietly.

A wave of pain crossed his face. "Aye, Lady," was the breathless response. "So do we all." He seemed to gather strength somehow, and he squeezed my hand and gave a slight tug. I lowered my hand to his mouth. With a rasping breath, he spoke. "My hand to yours. Bless you, Xylara, Daughter of the House of Xy, Daughter of Xyron, Warrior King." He pressed his dry lips to the back of my hand.

It had been long since I'd heard those old words. I kissed his forehead. "My hand to yours. Blessings upon you, Warrior of the House of Xy."

He smiled, slipping into death even as his hand slipped from mine.

"You care too much." It was Eln again.

His voice floated over the stone tubs that had been set aside to wash instruments. I ignored him for the moment, concentrating on getting things clean and ready for the next wave of wounded. Experience taught that the lulls in the fighting were to be used, not wasted.

"A good healer is dispassionate. Objective."

The warrior's body had been taken up for burial. He had been the last of the severely wounded. I had a small cluster of unhappy apprentices outside, boiling bandages and linens. Not their favorite chore, but a vital one.

Eln had started brewing more orchid root at the fire. The sweet scent was a comfort. Others were tending the large kettles of fever's foe outside. Everyone, no matter how tired, worked and waited. For the sounds of more battle, more wounded. I closed my eyes, giving in to my exhaustion and prayed for an end to the war that waged outside the city walls. Prayed that the Firelanders would stop using their lances. Prayed that I'd be skilled enough that no more of my patients would die.

Eln rattled the jars and bottles, and I opened my eyes and watched him. My old teacher, his long arms stretching out, putting them in some kind of order. Slow and steady, moving carefully on tall legs, considering each step. The straight, gray hair that flowed down his back only added to the image of a lake-crane. He gave me a look out of the corner of his eye, and shook his head. "How can one so slight be so stubborn?"

"Eln, how long was I your apprentice?"

He stared pointedly at my bruised cheek. "Long enough to learn." He regarded me with a solemn look.

"And I have been a master for how long?" I rinsed more of the instruments and set them on a cloth to dry.

He pursed his lips, and pretended to study one of the jars. "Long enough to learn to talk back."

I snorted. "During that period, how many times have you said that to me?"

"More than I can count, but that does not make it any less true." He started to gather up the things we would need to check the wounded and tend them. "If you are so wise, Lara, then why do I see guilt in your eyes?"

I glanced out the kitchen window. The afternoon shadows were growing. "I should not have tried to cut it out. Should have left it alone. If I had . . ."

"If." Eln came to stand next to me. "If you had left it in, was his death not as sure? You tried. That was all you could do. All any of us can do when we are overwhelmed like this."

I dried my hands, and blinked back tears I didn't have time for. "We'd better get to work."

Out in the common room, men lay sleeping on cots and pallets, crammed close together. We moved quickly, checking bandages, dispensing medications and powders. Apprentices scurried back and forth, bringing water and cloths, supplies and instruments. Our medicines were greeted with the usual laments over the taste. We ignored the complaints, as we moved around the room, seeing to each man. There were even more upstairs, on the second floor.

Our job was made difficult by the enemy's use of a thrown lance. Four foot long, tipped with sharp metal barbs which were designed to break off in the wound. When thrown from horseback, they tore flesh and muscle in ways that could easily cripple a man, and made healing difficult. Our warriors had seen nothing like it before. Nor had they ever dealt with an army that fought only from horseback. Devil riders, they called them, men and women who could sit on a galloping horse and shoot arrow after arrow, with deadly accuracy. We'd heard rumors that they ate their dead, and tore the hearts out of their kills. That they were black, and yellow, and blue, and that their eyes glowed with madness.

I ignored the talk, and concentrated on my work. The men were grateful, and it tore my heart, how a kind word and a cool cloth would lift their spirits. A few recognized me as a Daughter of the Blood, but most simply welcomed me as the healer that I was. Just as well. I was not particularly proud of my 'royal' heritage at the moment.

We worked our way through the men, cleaning and checking wounds. Tomorrow, we would welcome a small legion of servants who came every morning, for the general bathing, bedding, and slop pots. Volunteers from the city folk, some castle servants, since the need was so great. The healers and apprentices couldn't do everything.

It was late by the time I knelt next to the last patient. "It's well?" He rasped, peering at the gash in his calf as I replaced the bandage.

"Very well."

"It don't look well." He reached out a finger to touch it. I smacked his hand. He pulled it back, as shocked as a child.

"It will not be well if you poke at it." I frowned at him, and finished covering the wound. "Leave it be."

"Aye, Lady." He bobbed his head, looking sheepish, giving me a toothless grin.

I rose from the floor, and stifled a cry as the muscles in my back protested. I was feeling all of my twenty-five years. I picked up my supplies and moved off, trying to stretch out the tightness in my back as I went downstairs. Eln was in the kitchen, washing up. He grimaced at me as I grabbed up some soap and a cloth. "Finished?"

I nodded.

"I've no one to send to escort you."

I shrugged. "It's not the first time I've walked to the castle alone."

"It's not proper." He paused for a moment. "I suppose you are going to those tents now?" I could hear the resignation in his tone.

I avoided him for the moment and plunged my hands into one of the buckets. The familiar scents of the herbs and mixtures were welcome and I took a deep breath. The bitter smell of fever's foe came in through the window.

"The King has told you not to go there, Lara. I thought that maybe . . ." His voice trailed off, hinting at the doubt in his eyes.

"The King? Let me worry about him, Eln." I gathered my hair up and tried to tame it back in a braid. "Death and injury aren't limited to us Xyians. I can't stop the fighting, can't bring peace, but I won't neglect wounded men. We take oaths when we gain our mastery. Remember?"

He sighed, and thrust a jar toward me. "There's extra of the fever's foe. It will go bad if it's not used."

Fever's foe takes months to go bad. This jar was from last week's batch. I hid my smile and put the jar in the basket I had pulled from the corner, carefully cushioning all the other bottles inside. "My thanks."

"I wish I could do more." He made a move to follow.

I picked up the basket and grabbed the jug of liniment that I'd mixed the night before. "Eln, I don't expect you to come with me."

"I have sworn the same oaths." He tilted his head. "Xylara . . ."

"You can't get away with disobeying the King, Eln." I flashed him a smile. "He's not your half-brother."

He laughed ruefully. "That is so."

I smiled, headed outside, and paused to let my eyes adjust to the twilight. Summer was still with us, but barely. There was a hint of chill in the evenings now, the first sign of the winter snows to come. I shifted my basket and the jug and wished that I had thought to grab my cloak. It would be late before I would finish my work in the tents deep in the castle gardens.

The barracks sprawled against the southern wall of the

city. I had a fairly long walk ahead of me. Even as I stepped out, my eyes were drawn up.

I have seen it nearly every day since I was a little girl, but the sight of the castle of Water's Fall never failed to amaze. The huge tower was built into the mountainside. Even in the starlight, its gray rugged granite was a stark contrast to the greenery around it. The various waterfalls that gave the city and castle its name trickled and roared down the cliffs, making a striking picture. Ten generations, the House of Xy had labored to build and expand and improve the castle at the head of the valley and its city. I bit my lip, trying to remember which ancestor had named the place. Xyson? Or was it Xyred?

I crossed the ward to the small gate that would let me out onto the main street. There was an older guard there, and he raised a hand in greeting as I passed him. I nodded back, then plunged into the hustle and bustle of the avenue. This late, everyone was starting to head for home. Rather than head north to the main thoroughfare, I went south. It was the more direct route, although it would take me past the farmers' markets. Hopefully the crowds would have dwindled, having made their purchases earlier in the day. I strode along as quickly as I could, watching where I stepped. For all the ordinances about refuse, one was never sure what might be tossed out into the street at any given moment. Of course there were fines, but the Guard had little time to worry over that issue. They had more than enough problems on their hands.

It had not been a good summer for us. Spring had brought with it what we'd thought would be the normal raiding along the border by the people we called the Firelanders. But the warriors we faced this time were led by a warlord they called the Cat. His armies had descended on our southern borders, devastating the countryside and the towns and villages that lay there. Usually the Firelanders looted and pillaged on the border and then disappear into their wide grasslands without a trace. But this warlord had different ideas. He was seizing towns, and holding them, forcing the folk to swear fealty to him. It was said that he would kill all the men if the people resisted, torture the women and children, and burn the town to the ground. All through the summer, he'd fought his way up the valley, securing the lands behind him.

Water's Fall had filled with those fleeing the conflict. King Xymund had assured his council and the lords that this upstart would be crushed under the might of the armies of Xy. But over the months, our army had been pushed back by the warlord's thundering horses and flights of arrows. The healing temple overflowed with the injured and displaced. Many were taken in by families in the city who opened their homes. With the influx of people, the city was a crowded, unhappy place. Eln said that the crowding would bring more illness with it, and I feared he was right.

The farmers' market wasn't its normal noisy boisterous self, with vendors calling out the virtue of their wares. There was a dullness to it, fear that hovered in the very air. Still the clamor from the poulterer's was as loud as ever. Geese, tied to the stall in every way possible, honked and gabbled and beat their wings. Chickens and ducks, their legs trussed together, floundered on the ground nearby, their clucking adding to the cacophony. There were feathers everywhere, and the smell of drying blood.

Even with the armies of the warlord drawing close to the city, Xymund, Lord High King, had evidenced great mercy to his opponents. He had publicly decreed that wounded prisoners taken on the field were to be housed and cared for as our own. But his private hypocrisy was the few prisoners that had been taken were isolated in the deepest part of the gardens that lay within the castle walls, surrounded by guards and given the barest of necessities. As the days passed, it was clear that Xymund regretted his public stance. It was only the need to live up to his honorable image that kept those men alive.

Certainly no other healer dared to venture there. The King seemed to feel that caring for these men was treason of the highest order. I'd fought hard to be Eln's apprentice, fought harder to claim journeyman's status, and then defied my father himself to claim my mastery. Xymund could bully the entire guild, but I'd sworn oaths to deprive no one in need of my services, and I'd ventured to the tent, with no support, and much opposition. I'd ignored them all, and dared any and all to say me nay, but in my heart of hearts, I wasn't sure if I cared for their wounds out of a higher ideal, or simply as a way to anger my elder half-brother.

My elder half-brother had, in turn, suggested, asked, demanded, ordered, and forbidden my visits. I disregarded him. He had cursed, ranted and shouted to no avail. He'd kept the pressure up, making it a daily battle for me to render aid to those men. Pressure had been brought to bear, and I'd come close a time or two to wavering. But each time I'd reconsider my defiance, there'd be another wounded Firelander dragged to the tent and dumped on the floor. I could not turn my back. Not when I had it within my power to heal and ease their pain.

Nevertheless, Xymund had made one thing very clear. None of the prisoners was to know that I was a Daughter of the Blood. If anyone learned that fact, he said that he would chain me in my room for the duration of the war.

Even I could see the sense in that.

I walked through the city, dodging animals and people, carts and wagons. It was very crowded on the streets. People of all shapes and sizes were moving about their business before the markets closed for the night and the Watch was about. At one intersection a cart had lost its wheel, its cargo spilled onto the street. Men were shouting at one another, trying to clear the way. I turned down one of the side streets, trying to avoid the mess. Here, the buildings were built tight to one another and leaned out over the streets, blocking the light. I was glad to turn back onto one of the wide main streets and get on my way.

As I went, I could sense a difference. There seemed to be a feeling of suppressed panic in the air. Men stood at corners, talking softly in clusters. The bargaining had a frantic sense to it. I wondered if there had been some news of the Cat. I took another detour of sorts, moving down an alley to come out in the spice markets. I paused before entering the flow of traffic, looking for colorful flags on poles and spotted Kalisa's cart, tucked in the entrance of another alley.

Bent half double with age, her back humped up, her fingers crooked and swollen, Kalisa was one of the few shorter than I was. Normally, she also had the brightest smile and the best cheese in the city. But there was no smile for me today.

"Lara." Whatever else, her eyes and mind were still sharp. "Don't you have an escort? It's not safe, child." She tipped her head and looked me over.

"Kalisa, I've never had any trouble—"

"Aye, were times what they were, I'd agree. Not now." She scowled at me, even as her hands pulled out a small wheel of hard cheese. "Rumor has it that our king has hired mercenaries to guard his carcass, heathen foreigners who wander the streets terrorizing women."

I set my jug and basket down between my feet. "The same rumor that says that the Firelanders are blue, red, and black, and belch fire from their mouths?"

She handed me a slice of her sharpest cheese, and a thin cracker, which I took eagerly. The taste flooded my mouth, making me aware of my hunger. It had been long since breakfast, and it tasted wonderful. Kalisa tilted her head to be able to look into my eyes. "Have you not heard?" Her face as serious as I had ever seen.

"Heard what?"

"The army has pulled back within the city walls. King's command. Did you not hear the horns?" She cut another slice. "Heard tell that the Lord Marshall is having fits."

The cracker and cheese was suddenly dry in my mouth. "Pulled back? But . . ."

Her white head shook as she handed me another piece of cheese. "Child, you need to look up from your work once in a while, eh?"

"The last I heard, things were going well." I swallowed hard. "At the very gates?"

"Everyone's frantic. Stripped my cart almost bare, they did. And the Watch is doubled tonight. You best be getting home." Kalisa nudged me. "Aye and look there."

I looked to where her gnarled finger, held low behind the cart, pointed into the crowd. I looked up to see Lord Durst riding by, with his son and heir, Degnan. They wore their usual haughty, sullen expressions. No fear that they would recognize me in the press, but then my odd ways were an open secret. Xymund usually said something when one of the nobility came for a visit. What were they doing here?

Kalisa had no doubts. "Cowards fled their lands for this safety. Left all behind, so I hear."

I scowled at her. "Such talk could get you beaten, old woman."

She snorted. "Everyone's saying that Xymund's not the warrior your father was, and rightly so if rumor is true, that he's a bast—" I frowned at her and she broke off her words. "Never mind. I've enough cheese to fill my cart tomorrow, but after that I've none to sell." She shook her head at my questioning look. "Anser and Mya have fled with the herds, and I've no milk to work. Talk is that with those heathens outside, the harvest is thin and food will be scarce. They say that some merchants are already raising their prices."

I crammed the rest of the cheese into my mouth and dug for my pouch.

Kalisa waved me off. "Never you mind, child. My thanks for that jar of joint cream you gave me. It works well." She held up her hands and flexed them.

I smiled, pleased to see that she had more movement in her fingers. "I will bring you another jar, Kalisa. I promise."

"I'd rather you stayed safe in that castle. Off with you now. That grandson of mine will be along to get me home soon enough." She started to pack up her cart as I continued on, lost in my thoughts.

Lord Marshall Warren had seemed very confident of his ability to hold the warlord's men at bay. I had no mind for tactics and troop movements, but Father had thought Warren an excellent general and had every faith in him. Something must have gone wrong. That explained the mood of the city, with the enemy at the very gates. I picked up my pace.

Before I knew it, the castle walls were before me, comforting symbols of strength. The gate guards called a greeting, well used to my routine at this point. Once through the gate, I turned down toward the path that led into the overgrowth.

Xymund's mother had been a great one for flowers and plants. She'd spent many hours directing the gardeners in their work, creating elaborate pleasure gardens. That may be why the rumors had started, that Xymund was a bastard, a result of an affair that his mother had. It didn't help that she'd come from a distant kingdom to marry our father, since my people have a deep distrust of all things foreign. Father had thought the potential alliance was worth facing their intolerance, but from the stories I'd heard, it had not been easy on him or the Queen.

Of course my father denied the rumors, acknowledged Xymund as his son and heir, and swore that he was the spitting image of his grandfather, but the story never died. Older Xyians were quick to point out that Xymund and his father looked nothing alike, a fact that stuck Xymund like a knife. Even after he was acknowledged as heir, even after ascending the throne, it was a scab that he seemed to pick at constantly.

Xymund's mother had passed and my mother, youngest daughter of a Xyian lord, had no interest in the work necessary to see the pleasure gardens maintained. The kitchen gardens were well-kept, mind, since they were of practical value. But she saw no point in frivolous pursuits. It was one of the few things I knew about my mother, as she'd died giving birth to me.

The path wound through the trees and bushes, and through a great rose briar that had grown wild. I could see that some of the rose hips were ready to be picked. I didn't stop, but made a note to get some later.

The overgrowth made the path dark and close. Finally, I broke through to the cleared area that held a large canvas tent. It was here that the enemy wounded were housed.

The first sentry did not even challenge me, just waved me through. He was leaning on his spear, looking like he was trying to nap. I continued on, puffing a little. I was tired. It always seemed to take longer for these visits than I had planned. There was a High Court tonight, but my presence would not be missed. Or noted. I rarely attended them.

The second sentry stood post outside the tent. I was pleased to see Heath standing there, and quickened my pace.

He was not pleased to see me. One hand holding his spear, the other planted firmly on his hip. His round face was marred by a frown, surrounded by curls much the color of mine.

"Lara." He grimaced. "You are not supposed to be here." He jerked his head in the direction of the tent. "And I don't think they really appreciate what you are doing."

I stopped next to him, holding my burdens, and looked up at him. At first I maintained a serious countenance then slowly allowed a smile to spread over my face. As I stood there before my childhood friend, his frown faded as a smile crept over his face in answer to mine. I lowered my eyes and tried not to laugh. I stepped up to him, and he put a hand behind my neck, and pulled my forehead to rest against his. We'd done it since we were kids, a greeting just between the two of us. Of course, he now had to lower his head and stoop a bit to make it work, tall as he was.

Anna said I was just right—not too tall, not too short. But some days I wished for an extra inch or two.

I stepped back and grinned.

Heath glanced to the heavens in a great show of patience, as if looking for guidance, then returned his attention to me. "If anyone asks, you ordered me to step aside."

I deepened my smile. "My thanks, Heath."

"I could never say no to you, little bird." He sighed as he lifted the tent flap. "I already had the men heat the water kettles for you." He got that look on his face again. "My shift ends in three hours. Arneath comes on duty after me and you need to be out by then."

I wrinkled my nose and Heath grimaced right back at me. There was something about Arneath that made my skin itch. He'd been made head of the Palace Guard recently by Xymund, over the heads of more qualified men. I avoided him whenever I could.

"I'll be out in time."

Heath rolled his eyes. "I've heard that before. Have a care, little bird." With that, he lifted the tent flap.

I stepped into the tent.

The first thing to hit me was the smell. Herbs, blood, and death. The men were crammed in close, with more pallets than cots. There were no apprentices here, no helpers to air the place out or fresh linens or help with bathing. I made do with what I had, which was precious little.

When I had first come into their midst, no one would let me touch them, much less speak to me. Their language was fluid and fast, and I'd a hard time trying to pick up the meaning. It had taken persistence and sheer stubbornness on my part, but eventually a few allowed me to tend them. While they were all so different, ranging from fair complexions to deep tan, to almost yellow, one thing held true. They all bled red, and they all responded to my medicines. Thanks to the Goddess, a few spoke the trade tongue rather well and were willing to translate.

I let my eyes adjust, greeted the two guards stationed inside, and moved further into the tent. There was a silence when I stepped in, the tension palpable. Once they saw it was me, their relief was subtle, but clear. It was the signal that they would be permitted to bathe, and wash clothes and bedding as best they could. Unlike my Xyian patients, these men preferred being clean. There was even some sort of prayer that they murmured as they poured the water.

"Lara."

I turned and saw Rafe making his way to me, a smaller man, thin, with fair skin and deep black hair and brown eyes. His face seemed always lit with a smile. One of the youngest, he had been the first to let me treat him, and to help me learn the language. There were still gaps in my understanding, words that I missed, or used incorrectly. But I was understood most of the time. These men did not seem to believe that I could treat them. I certainly had not been able to help them deal with the strange headaches they suffered from. But I had proved myself as to other hurts.

"Rafe, I hope that you are feeling better." I spoke slowly, trying to get the correct sounds out of my mouth. I looked carefully at the wound that ran down the side of his face. It appeared to be healing well.

Rafe quirked his mouth. "You still sound like a child at lessons."

He followed as I moved to the center of the tent, where there was a small table. I sat down my supplies, rummaged in my basket and produced a jar, which I handed to him. "Rub this on the gash, Rafe. It will reduce the scar."

He took the jar, but frowned. "Why so? It is an honorable scar."

"It will still be honorable if it heals flat and tight." These men had very strange ideas about injuries. Rafe scowled, but kept the jar.

The men about us were already stirring, but Rafe shifted his weight, making no move to go bathe. A shadow passed over his face.

"Is something wrong?" I asked.

He hesitated and replied softly. "There is a new man here," and jerked his head toward the back of the tent. I could see some men clustered around one of the cots. "If you would please . . ."

I took my basket and headed in that direction. Best to see what I had to deal with now, before I started to see to the others.

As I approached, some of the men drifted away. But two large men remained standing by the cot. With my eyes fixed firmly on my patient, I lowered the basket to the ground, knelt, and got a good look.

He was an enormous black man, spilling over the sides and ends of the cot. Black as night, black as wrought iron. The rumors were true. I caught my breath, and for one fleeting moment wondered if he would belch fire. But common sense came to the fore, as I took in his condition. Wrapped in a cloak and blankets, his eyes were open but unseeing. Sweat dripped from his forehead and close-cropped black hair, hair like I'd never seen before. Whatever his color, it seemed he suffered as any other.

The rough bandage was down close to the groin and my mouth went dry. Please, Goddess, not another gut wound. I reached out my hand and one of the men grabbed my wrist.

"What are you doing?" His voice was hard and clipped, but I could understand him. Dark, black eyes bored into me as his grip tightened. His broad, round face was grim, and while not as dark as the man on the cot, he was darker then most. I couldn't help a brief thought—*would I get to see a blue one*?—before the man wrenched my arm again.

"I am a healer." I focused on his eyes.

He snarled. "You are a *bragnect*."

I did not know the word, but suspected that it was one that was not taught to children. Careful not to return the anger, I did not pull away. "I can help him." I kept my gaze steady on his face. "I will help him."

He paused, studying me.

A sound came from the darkness. "Please, Joden. She is a healer." Rafe came up behind us, his voice soft and serious. "We fought her off at first, but she can help."

Joden glanced at him. "This? This is a warrior-priest?"

Rafe shook his head. "Even better, she is a healer." He used the word from my language, rather than his own. "When she first came, she seemed mad and we tried to drive her away, but she has persisted." He turned his face slightly, to display his scar. "See? She has helped many, Joden. I will swear it to the open sky, if you wish."

Joden looked from me to the wounded man. He released my wrist with a huff of disdain. "If you harm Simus, I will kill you."

I gestured with my hands. "Get him off this cot and onto a pallet." Joden started to pull the blankets away. "Uncover him, and use wet cloths to wipe his face, arms, and chest. We must get the fever down. Leave the wound and the bandage to me."

One of the younger men stepped forward to help. This one

had skin that was a lighter color than Joden's, but his black hair fell in braids.

"Rafe?" I sat back on my heels. "I mean no offense, but does he heal as others do? Will my medicines aid him, as they do the others?" He looked puzzled, as did the men around him. I cleared my throat. "I've never worked on one such as he."

"There is no difference . . ." He began. I lay my hand on his forehead, and Rafe's gaze followed my gesture. "Do you mean his skin?"

I nodded, and pulled my hand back, giving it a quick glance to see if any of the color had come off on my fingers.

Rafe snorted. "There's no difference beyond looks," He cast a sly eye over at Joden. "Though there's some that say Simus has more than his fair share of charm."

Joden grunted, but I could see a slight smile. I dug in the basket, and found a small bottle of orchid root which I handed to the other man, the one with the braids. "You are?"

"Prest."

"See if you can get him to take two swallows of this. No more. It will ease him for when we clean the wound."

Prest nodded.

"I will return when I am done with the others." I stood. "Roll up the tents sides." I called out. "Let's air the place as best we can." We had done this before, to add some light and fresh air to the tent. The guards were not happy, but they let me do this when I felt the need. As the walls were lifted, I could see the guards that ringed the tent on the outside. Xymund was taking no chances.

As the men started moving, I got up and visited my other patients, checking wounds, using my salves and potions where needed. At first, I'd been pushed away, treated rudely whenever I tried to help. It had taken time, but I was tolerated by most, and welcomed by a few. But now there was a difference. While the men treated me well, I could tell that their attention was on my newest patient. Some who had never spoken to me before even went so far as to try to ask me about the man.

Whoever he was, I suspected he was important.

The kettles for the hot water were brought, and the bathing began. I had smuggled some old soap out of the castle that had hardened, forgotten in a storeroom. It had the faint scent of flowers, but was mild and worked well. I never made mention of this part to anyone in the castle. One could imagine the response to the idea of a Daughter of the Blood in a tent with naked men. But for some reason, it hadn't occurred to anyone that a healer at some point had to deal with the actual body.

I'd gathered old tunics and trous, so that they had spare clothing. Each man washed out his own, and the guards had been bullied into setting out a drying line. It was when they stripped down for bathing that I'd first seen the tattoos that each man had on his arms. A different pattern on both arms and I could make no sense of them. I'd asked about them but been rudely rebuffed.

Before I returned to my new patient, I went to the guards by the entrance. The older one jerked his chin toward the back of the tent. "Is he bad, Lady?"

"Yes. I'm going to clean the wound. It won't be quiet."

He winced. "Aye, I would think not. I'll warn the others as to what you are about."

"Thank you." I cocked my head. "More water would not go amiss, either."

He sighed. "You know the King's commands . . ." His voice trailed off as I looked at him. "Aye. More water, then." He called through the tent flap as I turned to go back to my newest patient.

They had stripped the man and gotten him on a pallet. Prest was standing to one side, carefully folding the man's clothes in a neat pile. As I knelt, I could see that he looked better. The beads of sweat were gone, and his eyes were closed. His breathing seemed easier, too. Instead of tattoos on his dark skin, there seemed to be scars, but in a pattern as the others.

"Two swallows." Prest reported. I nodded, but my eye had already been caught and held by the wound. I waved the men out of my light, and leaned closer to get a better look.

The wound had been packed with the man's cloak. It was wadded up, and the blood had crusted to the cloth. I took fresh water, and soaked the material, easing it away from the scabs. Clearly, the wound had been tended in the field, but neglected since then. I glanced at Joden. "You did this?"

Joden grunted. "It was all I had time for, before we were taken."

I grimaced in understanding and worked in silence. Once the material came free, I let it drop at my side as I got my first good look at the leg.

It was bad. The gash started at the groin and got deeper as it went the length of the thigh. The edges were swollen, and white pus had gathered in its depths. There was grass and dirt and small stones embedded in the flesh. I reached out, touching the sides lightly, and felt the heat radiating off the flesh. I bit my lower lip.

"Will he lose the leg?" Joden was standing above me.

I looked up, noticing for the first time that Joden didn't seem to have a hurt on him. But my eyes were drawn back to the gaping wound. I worried my lip, then spoke. "I don't know."

The men around us murmured, but I had no time to fuss with them. "We'll start with the cleansing." I turned to my supplies, and dug out the bottles and cloths that I needed. "It is going to hurt. I've warned the guards. But I need your help to hold him down."

Joden sank to his knees next to me but made no move to help. "I wished for something to sing of, and the elements answered." His tone was one of sorrow. "It would have been better to have granted him mercy and be done."

The men around me recoiled. "You failed to give him mercy?" Rafe asked, hushed, his eyes wide.

I jerked my head up. Joden's face was haggard and looked gray in the light. There had been tales of this practice, of the Warlord's men killing their own on the field, but I had not believed. I rose on my knees, glared at them all, then jabbed Joden in the chest with my finger, drawing his attention. "You will not. To come this far, only to have you ki—." I could not finish that word. "No. I will not have it so."

He considered me, and seemed to laugh behind the pain in his eyes. "You think to save him? And the leg?"

"I think to try." I glared at him. "I think to hope."

He huffed again, looking at my small finger in the center of his broad chest, but nodded slowly. "We will try, healer." The unfamiliar word caught on his tongue. "We will hope."

I sat back on my heels. He gestured to some of the others. "It will take more than me to hold him, though. He is a strong one, make no mistake." Three other men approached. Each, with Rafe, Prest and Joden, settled down, and took a hold. I moved closer and grabbed up the bandages.

The men tensed. Joden frowned at me, then muttered something about chants under his breath.

Rafe snorted. "She uses no spells, Joden. No chants to the elements."

"No?" He sounded slightly disappointed.

I ignored the comments, and went to work. We were fine for about three breaths. I had even convinced myself that the orchid root would let him sleep through it. But as I spread the wound to scour deeply, he started to thrash under our hands.

"No! No!" His strong voice rang out, and he bucked up, trying to throw us off. Thanks to the Goddess I had large men to aid me this time. The apprentices would have been flung off in a heartbeat.

"More help here. Now." Joden's quiet command was obeyed and more men moved our way. Joden gave up his position to kneel by the man's head. He placed his large hands on the broad shoulders. "Simus, you're hurt. We're tending it. Lie still."

Simus did not see it that way. "Warriors! To me!"

I was glad that I had warned the guards, for the man had a voice like thunder. I worked as quickly as I could, fearing to cause more injury if I went too fast. It had to be cleaned, and better that I did it right the first time than to have to do it again.

"Joden!" Simus cried out as he writhed below us.

"I am here." Joden put his head down by the other's ear. "I am here. Hold on, my friend." He glared at me. "Hurry."

I ignored him.

Prest had both hands and his full body weight pressed on the man's forearm. "We could burn it."

"Shut up." I snarled.

Simus howled and arched his back. I sat back on my heels as they wrestled him flat. Out of the corner of my eye, I could see the others watching us with looks of horror.

"Why not burn it?" Joden asked. He had moved his hands along side Simus's head, and his thumbs were stroking his temples. The big man settled down and I doubled my efforts.

"Burning it will mean deep scarring." I tried to think of the right words. "He may not walk. May not be able to ride."

Joden grunted his understanding.

Finally the wound was cleansed. I bound the leg as tight as I dared, using fresh bandages, then pulled back, surveying my work. My audience looked as well.

Joden frowned. "You have not tied it."

"No." I glanced at him. "The wound must heal open. If I tie it, stitch it, it could . . ." I shook my head in frustration. "Sour. Go bad."

"Putrefy." Rafe had come up behind me.

Well that was extreme but I agreed with the translation.

Joden seemed to understand as he watched Simus. Now that we were finished, he had fallen into an uneasy sleep. I reached for fresh water to bathe his face, only to see my hands tremble in front of me.

"No." Joden had risen and was standing next to me. He lowered his hand and held it out. "We can look to him now."

I nodded, and grasped his hand, letting him pull me up. My legs were numb under me and I staggered a bit to the table where I had left my basket. The sun had fallen while we worked, and the tent was darker. The bathing had finished, and I could see that the men were feeling better as a result.

Certainly, it smelled better.

I found the jar of fever's foe and returned to kneel again by Joden. Simus seemed to be resting easier, his breathing a little slower and deeper.

Joden rumbled at me. "My thanks."

I smiled. "Do you need tending?"

His face seemed to close off. "No. I am not hurt."

Which was when the horn for the change of the guard sounded. I had overstayed my time.

"Joden, take this." I put the jar in his hand. Joden looked inside at the thick brown paste. "Cover your fingertip with the paste," I dipped my finger in to show him. "Then put your finger in his mouth. Do this every hour." I opened Simus's mouth and put my finger inside, spreading the medicine on the roof of his mouth. "It will fight the fever."

He listened and watched, absorbing the information. "Will you return?"

"Yes. Tomorrow." I stood again, and dusted off my trous. "Prest has the orchid root. Use it if he becomes restless. But only two swallows and only once more this night. You can dose him again after sunrise if he needs it."

Behind me, I could hear the guard changing. They were calling for the tent sides to be dropped, and I heard my name as well. It sounded like Arneath. I hoped not.

My patient sighed and seemed to relax a bit. Prest continued to bathe his face and arms. I reached down for the bloody cloak and the cloths I had used for the cleaning, and bundled them together. They could be boiled and used again. As I did so, I felt something cold and smooth under my hand. Through the fading light, I looked closer.

It was an onyx brooch, a large fierce cat poised in midspring, with yellow eyes that glared in defiance. It seemed to gleam with its own inner light. Especially the eyes. My own eyes widened as my poor tired brain took it in. I knew what the brooch meant. This man, my patient, was a general, a leader in the Warlord's army.

Goddess. Xymund would kill him.

My eyes darted to Joden's. His eyes filled with consternation at my knowledge, then narrowed. His hand clenched at his side, as if looking for the handle of a dagger. If a weapon had been at hand, I am not sure I would have left the tent alive. He opened his mouth to speak as the guards approached from behind.

2

I didn't think. I just took the brooch off the bloody cloth and slipped it into my hand.

"Lara." It was Arneath, Captain of the Palace Guard. There'd be no cozening him. "You must leave. Now."

"Yes, I know." Arneath would take great pleasure in preventing my visits to the prisoners. He'd made it clear long ago that I, a Daughter of the Blood, demeaned myself by learning a craft. I turned, placing the remaining jars in my basket, using my body to shield as I slipped the brooch inside. I stood, the handle tight in one hand, the bundle tucked under my arm. "I'm ready."

Arneath stood behind me, unconvinced. I think he had been expecting an argument. I looked at Joden and spoke in his language. "I'll return tomorrow. Do not let him try to walk or stand." I ignored Arneath as he shifted from one foot to another, looming behind me.

Joden's face and tone did not change. He remained kneeling at Simus's side. His dark eyes glittered in the remaining light. "Do not betray him, or I will break you over my knee."

I didn't reply. I just turned and brushed past Arneath. Rafe nodded to me as I left, staying well back and out of the way. He had learned early on that Arneath struck hard when he was not obeyed.

Arneath followed me out. "What did that last one say to you?" He looked suspicious.

"That no matter the healer, medicines always taste terrible."

One of the other guards guffawed at that. Even Arneath chuckled as he held open the tent flap for me. We emerged into the twilight. The cool night air felt good after the stuffiness of the tent. The stars above were peeking out. Once outside, I realized that Heath had already left. He was probably in the castle kitchens.

Arneath's mirth faded as he took up his position. "Don't see why you waste time on them. Nothing but animals." His gruff, oily tone followed me as I started off toward the castle. "Or maybe you're thinking that helping the dogs will make you friends in the enemy camp. In case things go bad."

I pulled up short, stopped in my tracks. There were chuckles from the guards, but they were uneasy ones, as if they believed that evil lie. I turned and managed to keep my voice even. "It is by the King's command, Arneath. Besides, I am a Master Healer. I treat any who are in need." I tilted my head and smiled. "Did the ointment you asked for clear up that crotch rot?"

Arneath flushed as the guards guffawed. Amidst the laughter and taunts now aimed at him, I turned and continued on my way, entering the overgrowth. Once out of sight, I let my shoulders sag a bit. I shouldn't have done that. Father would have shook his head in despair at my flash of temper, and my crudeness. Worse, Arneath was in a position to take his frustrations out on the prisoners. I scowled at the hapless path below my feet. Still, he'd deserved it. How dare he imply that I, a Daughter of the House of Xy would—

I remembered the brooch in my basket and flushed.

The shadows were deeper now. I narrowed my thoughts to staying on the path and shivered slightly in the night air. As I walked, I mentally started to inventory my supplies. I wanted to go to the market early on the morrow to get what I needed. Xymund had made it clear that none of his supplies were to be used on the prisoners. I rolled my eyes. As if he had ever gathered herbs for the still room.

At that, I started to worry my lower lip. It was easier to think about herbs than to think about the brooch in my basket. It marked the large black man as a leader of men, something I was sure no one had yet realized. If Father were still alive, I'd have no hesitation in telling him. He'd have used the situation to his advantage, but he'd not kill a man in cold blood. I could tell Heath, but he'd have no choice but to go to his superior, which was Arneath. My steps slowed as I thought about that option. Arneath would kill the man, of that I was certain. If Heath took the information to Xymund directly, it would place Heath square between us if it came to an argument, and I'd not do that to him. Same for Othur, the Seneschal. Now, Lord Marshall Warren, he I could trust. Father had appointed him to his office and had faith in him. He would stand against Xymund to the extent that anyone could. I took a deep breath. It would be some time before the man was conscious. I would tell Warren and let him decide what to do with the information.

I remembered the rose hips as I came to the briar and decided to try to gather enough for a potful of syrup. It was dusk, true, but I could see well enough and touch would tell me if they were ready. I set the basket and bundle down and reached into the bushes, feeling my way. The scent of the remaining roses surrounded me and filled my lungs. And my memories. The scent of roses by Xyron's bedside, as he lay dying.

Father had sickened slowly, gradually. Like the shades of gold that dust the trees at summer's end. The signs had been there, but I'd missed them along with everyone else. Once it was obvious, the illness had continued, regardless of the remedies that we'd tried. He'd wasted away slowly, growing weaker with every passing day. Nothing had helped.

Xymund had slowly taken up the reins of power, trying to ease the burden on our father, but that had not gone well. At first, Xyron had encouraged Xymund to take up his ceremonial duties, so that he could conserve his energies for the business of ruling. But as his energy waned Xymund had to try to fill the holes. I'd credit him that, for my half-brother never once moved forward unless he saw that Father was no longer able to perform a duty, or concentrate on a problem set before him. But Xymund had fumbled a few decisions while learning his role, and members of the Council and the Guilds had gone to Xyron directly, setting ailing father against fledgling king.

Serving my apprenticeship and performing my journeymen duties had pulled me out of active Court life. I'd been isolated even further when Father grew ill, for my attentions were all spent on him. Xyron was a warrior betrayed by a body that had served him long and well, and his temper grew worse as his body failed. He was quick to anger, and even quicker to blame, finding fault with everything. This made his relationship with Xymund harder. It made keeping servants to attend him almost impossible. So my role was healer, daughter, and peacemaker. I rarely left my father's side, and at the end, rarely left his chambers. We'd used flowers and rose oil to sweeten the air as he lay dying. I suspected the scent would always bring back those long hours.

I continued to pick, dropping the fruit into the basket, covering the bottle and jars. I had to move slowly to avoid the thorns. Best to get some before Anna the Cook descended on the briar to pluck and snip for her own uses. Her rose-hip jell was wonderful in the winter months, spread on toasted bread with honey. My arm stretched in further, getting several good scratches for my pains. Perhaps this had not been such a good idea after all.

I froze of a sudden. The hairs on my neck had risen and drew my attention to the unnatural stillness.

There was something out there.

I held my breath. All the normal sounds of the garden were gone. The tiny birds settling in for the night, the small sounds of rabbits and the like, all were missing, as if a large predator was in the area. I wondered for a moment if one of the hunting dogs had gotten loose. Though my brother rarely hunted, he still kept a few dogs for the use of the huntsmen. But those dogs were all tail and wiggles, eager for a touch on the head and a scratch behind the ear. They'd not stay still for a minute.

I pulled my arm back slowly, and took a step away from the briar. I drew in a deep breath and held it, straining to hear over the noise of my own body. Nothing moved, and I could hear no sounds. I remained quiet and unmoving for a minute or two, glancing about as if my eyes could pierce the night.

Then my stomach growled and reminded me that the morning meal had been some time ago, and that Kalisa's cheese only went so far. I laughed nervously. Overtired for certain. I dropped the last of the rose hips into my basket, then indulged in a good stretch. Which, in turn, caused my hair to fall out of its bun. Again. I cursed and fumbled with it, managing to get it pulled back. There was a tie in my pocket and I pulled it out to restrain the curly mass. The night was still silent when I picked up my basket and moved on.

Apparently I was the only large predator prowling the garden tonight.

The warm light spilled out of the castle windows as I moved through the kitchen garden and approached the back door. The High Court must be in fine fettle tonight. Considering that there was a war on, it seemed rather odd and inappropriate. But then, the lords and sycophants that made up the bulk of the Court would think nothing odd about it.

In our glory days, Xy had been a center for trade. The valley and the mountain passes were a gathering point for caravans, according to the history books. Xy had maintained a standing army, bolstered by the wealth of the merchants and the produce of the fertile soil. But in my great-grandfather's time, the trade routes had dried up. To make matters worse, in my grandfather's reign the Sweat had devastated the land. Grandfather had sealed the great trade gates, closing the mountain passes and isolating Xy even further. The standing army had been disbanded, leaving only the Palace and City Guard, and not many of them. The landed gentry that remained farmed the valley and Xy survived, small and alone, a shadow of what had been.

Xymund longed for the glorious days of old, and attempted to maintain a 'court', gathering the 'lords and ladies' and their children to fawn upon him. Since my father had added the craftmasters and the clergy to his council, there was quite a crowd willing to eat at Xymund's table, and play at the game of nobility.

Once the Warlord had started his march up the valley, many of the Lords had fled their farms and manor houses and sought the city, bringing the fighting men at their command. This left the hamlets and villages normally under the lord's protection to the mercies of the Warlord, and allowed the brute to advance swiftly, apparently to our very gates.

I slipped in through the old wood door, and tarried for a minute on the threshold. For all its size and huge hearths, the kitchen always seemed hot, overcrowded and cluttered. Here Anna the Cook reigned in all her glory. She was standing in the middle of the room, directing serving staff, cooks and footmen like the skilled general she was. A huge, fat woman, whose apron was covered in food stains, she tolerated nothing and no one. I noticed with envy that all her straight black hair stayed in its bun. Wielding her wooden spoon, she was a force to be reckoned with. Nothing escaped her scrutiny.

Including me.

She took one look and gave an exasperated snort, which set all of her chins wobbling at once. "Child, look at yourself." Her voice boomed across the kitchen. Some of the staff looked up and glanced at me with sympathy, but then continued on with their work. Anna made her way over, scowling, her keys to the spice cupboard rattling as she moved. "You look like a ragged pilgrim." She threatened me with her spoon. "You haven't eaten, have you." Her voice carried easily over the noise and confusion.

"Anna, you can read me like a book."

"As if I would waste time reading a book." She bellowed

something out and before I knew it, she and I were seated at a corner of the large, battered wooden table amidst the dishes, eating fresh hot bread with her special honey butter slathered all over it. My bundles had been added to the dirty rag pile, and my basket sat on the table. She kept a stern eye on the staff as we ate and occasionally erupted into admonitions when things weren't being done to her standards.

She sighed. "Have you been out working all this day?"

I stuffed my mouth with a bite of bread and waggled my eyebrows at her. Anna leaned back in her chair and let out a laugh that set her whole body to shaking. Anna, Goddess love her, knew how to laugh. She caught her breath, laid her fat arms on the table and looked at me shrewdly. "His Mightiness pulled the army back within the walls this day, against Warren's wishes. The Warlord's men are before the walls."

"I heard as much in the market. Is that true?" Not that I doubted her. Anna always seemed to be the first to know.

"Aye." She leaned forward and snagged the last of the bread. She turned her head and bellowed at someone over by the fire. Then she looked at me. "I hear tell that Warren was saying that His Mightiness panicked." She sniffed. "Blood tells."

"Anna." I scolded her. She hadn't liked the foreign queen and didn't like Xymund and never had. But Anna was an institution and Xymund loved his comfort and his meals. So there was a truce of sorts. He stayed away from her domain, and she let him run the kingdom with a full stomach.

She shook her head, setting the chins to wobbling. "Heard tell he's sent a messenger to ask for terms."

My eyes flew open at that. I thought that the battles had been going well, but perhaps Xymund's pride would not allow him to admit to anything less. For Xymund to even agree to talk to the man who had beaten him so soundly, so recently, was a sign that things were bad.

A plate appeared on the table, this time with slices of toasted bread and cheese, with roasted onion. I dug in, getting a piece before Anna could reach for one first. The cheese was still hot and bubbling on top, and I blew on it, eager for a taste.

Anna inhaled her piece, impervious to the heat. She reached out a fat finger and prodded my basket. "Does he know that you were out there again today?"

I shrugged, my mouth full.

"I suppose you charmed your way past that son of mine."

I shrugged.

She tapped her finger on the table, which caused ripples to move up her fleshy arm. "Watch yourself, child. Xymund is not Heath, to be wound around your finger. You are a thorn in his side, and you can only push so far."

"Look whose talking."

Anna focused a serious look on me, but said nothing more.

The doors to the main dining hall opened and in walked Othur, Anna's husband and the castle seneschal. A great barrel-chested man, he made his way through the servants toward us. He was sweating, his brown hair plastered to his skull. He looked very tired and very pleased at the same time.

"Anna, my love." He put his hand on her shoulder and gave her a hearty kiss. "You did a wonderful job as usual."

"Goddess spare me from High Courts." She grumbled, but I could see that his praise had pleased her.

Othur grabbed a chair and sank into it with a sigh. He snagged the last slice of bread and cheese. "And you, young lady." He bit into the bread and chewed. "He is looking for you. And getting worked up about it."

I didn't have to ask who "he" was. I sighed and started to wipe my mouth with the back of my hand. Anna smacked my head and bellowed something that resulted in a bowl of warm water and cloths being set in front of me. "Child, you are filthy. At least see to your face and hands. What is that on your jerkin?" Anna pushed away from the table. "No, I don't want to know. Let's see if we can clean you up." I did not resist. Since I had been a child, and after the death of my mother, Anna had the raising of me. While my smiles had no effect on her, she was always there with the warmth of her hearth and her love. I knew better then to try to avoid her fussing.

Othur wisely sat quietly, with a mug of ale, while I

washed. He was always a quiet one, but when he spoke, you needed to pay attention. Anna tsk'ed over the state of my tunic, and took a wet cloth to the worst of them. The activity of the kitchen seemed less frantic now that the meal was done, and the clean up started. After I passed Anna's inspection, and been given a quick hug, I swept up my basket and followed Othur out to the castle proper.

We kept to the back halls, passing the occasional servant. The cool quiet made for a relief from the busy kitchen. I worried my lower lip with my teeth. Perhaps I should tell Othur about the brooch after all. But all my reasons remained the same. I frowned as we walked. There was no one that I could really confide in, no one to turn to for advice. Maybe at least Othur could advise me as to how to . . .

"Lara." I looked up as he drew me to a stop.

"I need to see to some of the guests that are staying. You've heard about today's events?" He placed a hand on my shoulder. I nodded.

"He is in his study." Othur squeezed my shoulder. "Try not to anger him."

That was like asking fire not to burn.

I grimaced, but nodded. Othur gave me a doubtful look, then hurried on his way toward the guest tower. I continued on mine, up the spiral stairs to the King's tower, shaking my head as I walked.

It was soon after Xymund's mother died when the King married my mother and I was born. Xymund had been well in his majority and acknowledged as heir at that time, but I was sure that his resentment of me had started with the first coo from my father's lips, and intensified with every word of praise that followed.

I still had no understanding of it. He had been the rightful heir, and anointed King since our father's death these three years past. But the jealousy was still there, even when I had made it very clear that I would not train for high office, that I would follow the healer's path. I smiled, thinking back to Father's outraged reaction to my decision. But he had come to accept it and was grateful at the end for my skills, even though I could not defeat death's shadow for him.

But even when Xymund had been acknowledged King, anointed and crowned, the envy and ill feeling continued. I didn't understand. He had power, wealth, and women falling in his path eager to become the next queen. But some form of happiness eluded him, and I was fairly certain that I was to blame. It soon became apparent to everyone in Court that being a 'friend of Lara' did not advance one in the King's good grace.

Even so, I'd tried to step back into the Court life after Father's death, only to find that I could no longer tolerate the pomp and nonsense. The conversations were inane, the meals long and tedious. I had little in common with the ladies, and the lords all looked at me as they would a prize breeding mare.

Which gave me more time for my studies and exercising my skills.

Father had left me lands, which generated a modest income. Xymund held those in 'trust' saying that a healer knew little of managing lands. I had tried to leave the castle, tried to retire to an estate, where I could set up a house of healing and maybe a school. But when I raised the topic, Xymund would refuse, saying that my value as a potential wife in an alliance marriage outweighed the value of my school. Although there were limited candidates in the neighboring kingdoms, especially given my age, he had always refused any offer for my hand.

He seemed to take pleasure in denying my dream.

I shrugged and gave myself a shake. Anna, Othur, and I had talked this out and agreed that when Xymund wed and had his own heir, he would let me live my life as I chose. It seemed likely that he would wed within a year's time. There had been talk of at least two prospective alliances. Or at least it had seemed so before the Warlord's attack.

Which reminded me of that man in the tent. I stopped and chewed my lip.

Goddess forgive me, I was not going to betray a wounded

and sick man to Xymund just so that he could undo all my work. Others might think it a betrayal of my king, but to my mind it was extending the Goddess's mercy. Just in case, I ducked into one of the alcoves off the hall and put the brooch into the top of my boot. I pushed it down far enough to insure that it would not fall out. The boots were big enough. One would not be able to tell it was there. I'd wait and speak to Lord Warren tomorrow. He'd make sure that the right thing was done.

A moment more, and I was before the guards at the door to the King's study. I nodded to them and set my basket down against the wall. There was the sound of raised voices from within. The argument sounded heated. I glanced over at the guard, who shrugged. He knocked on the door. There was instant silence, then Xymund's voice granted entrance. The guard swung the door open. I kept my eyes down, advanced five steps and sank to my knee.

Xymund loved the pomp of his circumstances and required the formality. Father would have kicked him in the buttocks for it. Othur felt it showed Xymund's lack of self-confidence and I agreed.

The guard behind me cleared his throat. "Xylara, Daughter of the House of Xy." I turned my head and shot him a look out of the corner of my eye. He caught my meaning. "And Master Healer."

The argument hadn't stopped when I entered, they were too caught up in the dispute. I could have been a chair for all that they noticed. I risked a quick glance up at my half-brother. He was not a tall man, but looked impressive, still dressed in formal court garb, bedecked in a dark blue tunic and pants with silver trim. He wore a simple coronet, having discovered that the full crown had an annoying tendency to fall if he moved his head too quickly. His brown hair was graying at the temples, and his face bore lines of worry that had not been there a few months ago, although the lines were hard to see in the angry flush that covered his face. When he shifted in the chair behind Father's old desk, it creaked. He had gained weight in these last few months.

Another quick glance at Lord Marshall Warren, standing over by the fireplace. Spry and thin, he always seemed to me to be in motion. No flushed face there, instead his face was white, drawn and pale. "Please, Your Majesty. We can drive them back from the walls if you let—"

"Do you question my competence, Warren?"

The slight pause didn't help matters. Xymund tightened his lips, but Warren was quicker. "Majesty, none of us have had to deal with horse archers before this. We're not used to their tactics—"

"Damned horses." Xymund was snarling. "I hate those horses."

"Their horse archers are devastating against the foot, Majesty. But they have no siege equipment at hand, and the snows will come before they can build sufficient—"

"ENOUGH!" Xymund barked and Warren closed his mouth with a snap.

I looked down at the carpet, unwilling to rise from my knees and draw attention to myself. Xymund's breathing was audible, harsh and fast. It took long moments to slow.

"Rise, Xylara. You were not at dinner." Warren was standing at the fireplace, looking at the smoldering coals. Xymund continued. "You should make an effort to attend our Courts."

"Yes, Your Majesty." The word 'brother' had not seen use since Father died.

He looked me in the eye. "You went out there again, didn't you."

"Yes, Your Majesty."

His face hardened. "Why do you insist on aiding my enemy?"

So it was to be the same old argument. I started with my usual rebuttal. "Sire, I tend to our wounded before I go . . ."

He held his hand up, and I stopped obediently. I saved my defiance for when it really counted.

"Let's not start." He glanced off with a frustrated look. "It's not like you will obey me in this anyway." Xymund continued. "How many prisoners are in the tent?"

Surprised, I thought for a moment. "I have not taken an actual count, Sire. I would guess around twenty. I don't really know."

He looked unhappy. "Well, the exact number is not important." He fixed me with what he thought was an intimidating glare. "You are not using my supplies on those animals."

I shook my head no. "I am following your instructions, Sire."

"Are any of them likely to die in the next day or so?"

An odd question. "Not likely, Sire. I have one that is badly wounded, but other than that they are healing well."

"Very well. You are dismissed." He had the look of a man thinking about something else, and not happy in his thoughts.

I looked over at Lord Warren, but his gaze was fixed on Xymund. I sensed that now was not the right time to request an interview. Instead, I bowed to the King, and backed away. I managed to leave without banging into the door.

The sun on my face woke me the next morning. I rolled over, burrowing my head in the blankets and pillows, and sought the return of sleep. My muscles were warm and limp and the bed was so comfortable. I could feel myself starting to drift. But something niggled at me. I drowsed for a bit, trying to remember what was so urgent. Then I heard horns from outside.

I threw back the covers, darted to the window, and threw open the shutters. From my little window, I could see the city sprawled below, beyond the walls, and into the valley stretching far below. The Warlord's army lay there, the small white tents covering the fields beyond. It was an impressive sight. I stood for a moment, then scrambled about my small room, looking for the clothes I'd tossed aside last night.

I took a sniff, and decided that fresh ones would be a good idea.

I found a simple gray dress in my trunk and dressed quickly, shoving the brooch back into my boot before I finished. It was safer with me than not.

I would get a hurried look at the big man, check his wound, go to market and get the items I needed, do my rounds with

Eln, then back to the tent, spend a few hours brewing in the stillroom, and with luck, be back in bed before the next dawn. I dug my money pouch out from under a pile of notes, and stopped in dismay.

I hadn't realized how little was left. My only income was from the sale of some of my mixtures and lotions to ladies of the court. I usually had enough for my needs, since by living at court I had no real expenses. But I had been buying herbs and other supplies for a while now, and my coin had depleted quicker than I expected. I frowned, dug out what coins there were and glanced around my room. There was nothing here that had much value, and I had not the time to make any lotions. I reached for my belt pouch and the pile of notes that I had shifted fell to the floor to reveal a potential source of funds.

It was an old book, the first that I had purchased for myself. A listing of herbs and a discussion of their properties. I stared at its leather cover. I almost had the darn thing memorized, I'd had it so long.

I didn't think twice, because it would have hurt too much. I swept up the book, grabbed a satchel and crammed it in. I slung the whole thing over my shoulder and headed down to the garden.

The garden seemed its usual self this morning, bright in the sunlight. I had to stop when I entered the tent and give my eyes time to adjust. No one was stirring, so I made my way quietly to the big man's pallet. I managed not to step on anyone or anything as I made my way.

He looked good and seemed to be sleeping. I hesitated to rouse him, but curiosity won out. Carefully pulling back the blankets, I uncovered the leg and lifted the bandage, holding my breath at what I might see.

I let my breath out with a whoosh.

It looked great. The heat was down, the redness had eased. There was still pus, and it would need to be cleaned, but I could already see signs of healing. The skin had that healthy tone. It would scar, no aid for that. Although I had heard that a mixture of . . .

A soft sound drew my attention away from my musings.

Joden had awakened and was lying on a pallet on the other side of my patient. I looked into his eyes and smiled at him in delight. He looked at me for a moment and then slowly, a smile crept over his face as well. "Simus is well?" He said softly in his own language.

My face almost cracked, my smile was so wide. "He is very well. Very good, very well." I didn't have the word for fantastic or wonderful, but I was fairly sure that the glee in my voice made up for the lack. I carefully replaced the bandage and the blankets, and tucked him in tight. The big man never stirred. "Has he woken?"

"Yes. He knew me, but slept most of the time."

"Do you have any of that drug I gave you yesterday?" Joden nodded. "Good. Keep giving it to him. I will bring more tonight." I leaned back, rejoicing quietly. I'd not lose this one. I scrambled to my feet and threw a last smile at Joden. "Do you have everything that you need? Food?"

Joden sat up, rubbing the sleep off his face. He shrugged. "The food is food." He got a soft smile on his face. "This one will be like a wet ruffled bird because there is no kavage."

I cocked my head. "I do not understand 'kavage'."

Joden chuckled. "A drink. Very strong." He gestured at the sleeping man. "He will be . . ."

I lost the rest, unable to understand. "He needs the kavage? Like a drug?"

Joden looked at me, puzzled. It was clear that we weren't communicating well. I just shrugged and repeated the word, wanting to make sure that I had it right. Joden nodded. I grabbed my satchel and threaded through the tent. I lingered for a moment and smiled at the guard like a lunatic, feeling almost giddy with relief. He blinked at me a few times, then smiled back.

I barely noticed the walk back up to the castle, and through the gates. The big man was healing very well, something I had not been sure of when I had first seen the wound. Oh, there was still danger of fever and blood poisons, but I was optimistic. I wound my way through the city to the markets with a light step and lighter heart.

It was early enough the market was not crowded. Most merchants should have been setting out their wares. But there was an eerie quiet to the place, an unusual stillness. When I reached Remn's shop, the door was closed, the windows shuttered. I knocked, and he let me in with a worried expression. Shorter than even me, and twice again as round, he greeted me with a smile, but there was a sadness in his eyes. "Xylara. What are you doing out this morn?"

"Good morning and good trade to you, Master Remn." I slipped through the door, and watched him bolt it behind me.

"Trade." He heaved a sigh, and gestured at his shelves. "In war time, no one buys books, Lara. We are free to sit and drink and eat my wife's tarts in the echoing silence of my shop." He shook his head in despair.

I pulled the book from my bag. He smiled when he saw it. "Ah, I remember when you bought this. Your first, yes?" He turned it over and ran his large hand over it. "Does it need a repair?"

"No. I was wondering how much you would give for it."

He looked at me, dark eyes questioning. "Word in the market is that you are buying healing supplies for the prisoners."

I shrugged.

He thinned his lips and thought for a moment, tapping the book with one long finger. "Wait here." Abruptly, he went in the back, and returned with a small pouch. He handed it to me, and it clinked in my hand. "My brother's son was lost in battle. We have heard no word, but I do this in his name. I pray to the gods that there is one on that side with a heart such as yours."

I opened the pouch and looked in. "Remn, this is too much . . ."

He held up his hand. "I hold your book as surety, Lady. I know that you will repay me." He pointed his finger at me. "Mind you don't take too long about it."

I laughed and hugged him. He brushed aside my thanks and urged me to go home. I refused, gently.

He scowled at me. "Very well, then. Take one of my apprentices with you. You should have an escort, young lady."

"I've only to go to Estoval's. I'll be fine." He grumbled, but opened the door and I waved as I continued on.

I stopped briefly at Kalisa's cart. She was busy with actual customers, who looked close to buying all of her stock. So I tucked a bottle of my joint medicine into her gnarled hand and moved off. She called her thanks behind me.

Next to Estoval's. He was farther down the street, and now the early morning crowd was beginning to enter the market. But the merchants weren't opening their windows to display their wares, instead they were dealing from behind their doors and shutters. There was an air of desperation from those seeking to purchase goods. I hurried my feet and concentrated on trying to remember another mixture that was supposed to help scarring. I could remember goat's milk boiled thick, but the rest eluded me. Ah, well. Perhaps Estoval would know. Also, I needed plenty of lotion makings. I'd no wish to sell any more books.

As I moved through the crowd, a funny feeling began to creep up the back of my neck. As if someone was watching me. I stopped for a bit and rummaged through my bag as if looking for something. I glanced through my hair, trying to see if someone was following me, or watching me, but I saw no one. I shrugged. Guess the hours that I was keeping were getting to me.

"Xylara." Estoval greeted me cooly, surrounded by his pungent stock. "How may I help you?"

I rattled off my mental list, and he gestured for his apprentices to gather up the items. I moved about, picking up the items that looked best for some of my lotions. "Estoval, do you recall an unguent to prevent scarring? With goat's milk boiled thick?"

His tone was even cooler as he recited the recipe for me. I added those items to my growing pile. He stayed close, nervously sorting some of the stock near me. "I was wondering if you had heard anything, Lady? About the war?" His tone was fawning, but I heard the fear underneath.

I responded, keeping my tone calm and my information general. He nodded, listening carefully, and I was sure my words would be all over the market within minutes of my departure. I kept it simple, and positive, and made no mention of the truth. That was for Xymund to announce, not I.

Finally I had what I wanted and headed to the counter to where the apprentices had set out the other items. I gave them a sharp look, for they were clearly Estoval's older stock—wilted and withered and not at all suitable. I gave Estoval a sharper look when he named his price.

He avoided my eyes. "Prices go up when supplies are limited."

"Supplies aren't limited yet, Estoval. And I wouldn't feed some of this to a goat, much less use it in medicine."

He lifted his chin. "You're healing those barbarians. The better stock is reserved for Xyians, not those filthy—"

I cut him off. "By the Order of the King, Estoval." I drew myself up, and fixed him with my best High Court look. "As I am a Daughter of Xy, and as I execute the King's Command, you will sell me the best you have and at your normal prices. Or answer to Xymund and his Council."

Estoval shriveled up. With a quick gesture, his apprentices brought out fresh items, and I paid a fair price for it, exchanging herbs for coins in silence. I was grateful that he had relented for there would have been no support from Xymund. Of that I was certain.

As I was packing the last of my purchases, Estoval's normal civility to a customer took over. "Was there anything else you required, Xylara?"

"No, I think that I have everything for today, Estoval." I hesitated for a minute, thinking. "Have you ever heard of kavage?"

Estoval wrinkled up his nose. "Is it a herb?"

"No." I shook my head. "It is a drink of some kind. I have no idea what it is. I think one of my patients would enjoy some, but I doubt that there is any to be had."

"One of the prisoners?" Estoval sniffed, but his merchant's instincts won out. "You might try the tinker's cart three stores down, if he is there. I think he has snuck out of the city and is trading with the warlord's men. Mention my name, Daughter of Xy."

I nodded my regal thanks, and headed off in the direction he'd indicated.

I spotted the tinker's cart easily, decorated with pots and pans, and ribbons aflutter in the breeze. I paused for a bit, since he was dealing with a customer, a tall, broad-shouldered man in armor. I occupied myself by looking over his wares. There was all matter of trinkets and metalware that gleamed in the sunlight. After a bit, the tinker turned his attentions to me.

"How may I help you?" His eyes gleamed in anticipation.

I smiled. "I am in no hurry."

The tinker winked. "This fellow can't make up his mind. While he ponders, you and I will treat. What can I interest you in?"

"Estoval told me that you might be able to help me. I am looking for some kavage."

He wrinkled his nose. "Ugh. What would you be wanting with that foul stuff?"

"I am tending some of the prisoners. One mentioned that it is a drink that they enjoy." I wavered, thinking. "Is it some form of spirits?" I had visions of trying to explain a tent full of drunken prisoners. Xymund would kill me.

"No." A deep voice with a faint accent answered me. I turned to see the other customer looking at me. Short black hair and skin tanned dark by the sun caught my eye, but what startled me were his bright blue eyes. Tall, with broad shoulders, he seemed to tower over me and the tinker, almost blocking the sun. My guess was he was one of the mercenaries that had been hired by some of the wealthier lords to guard their lives.

The tinker laughed and agreed. "The land take me, no. It is truly foul tasting stuff that they make by dripping water through seeds." He started to rummage through his cart, head and shoulders stuffed into one of its compartments. His muffled voice floated back at me. "In truth, I traded for some a while back, but once I tasted it," He emerged with a good sized sack and some kind of strange metal implement. "I knew I could never sell this here. The citizens would cry themselves poisoned and the City Guard would be on my neck." His eyes gleamed. "I will sell it to you, fine lady, but give me no blame when it eats at your insides."

"Well then," I replied with a smile "must not be worth much."

The tinker tried for an offended look, but burst out in a laugh. "Ah, Lady, you have the advantage."

We dickered a bit, just to be polite, but were quick to come to terms. I paid him, well satisfied with my purchase. The tinker was kind enough to give me a sack to carry the beans and the pot in. As I toddled off with my burdens, I heard him call behind me. "Come again, lady, and buy some more of my wares." If my hands had not been full, I'd have waved farewell.

"They drink it with milk." The man with the bright blue eyes had moved up next to me, walking, matching my pace. He'd apparently lost interest in a purchase. "Would you like some help?"

The market was filling up. I would find it difficult to avoid the market-goers with my bulky bundles. I felt my face flush a little when he took the sack and satchel. His gaze was steady and very disconcerting. It was rare for anyone to pay attention to me like that. I told myself not to be foolish.

"I am Lara."

The man smiled. "I am Keir." We started back up the street. "The liquid is drunk with milk and honey." The phrasing was awkward, and that faint accent was there again. I couldn't place it.

I nodded, thinking. I had money remaining, and the cost of those items would be small. I smiled at Keir. "Then I must get some. It will be a treat for my patients." I looked at him. "You learned this in the fighting?"

He gave me an intent look. "One must always know the enemy." Keir shifted his burdens. "You are treating the prisoners, are you not?" I nodded. He continued. "Are you treating one named Simus?"

My feet slowed, wiser then my head. It took my head a minute longer to realize the implication. And before either could react, I was pushed into the alleyway off to the side, pressed up against the wall by a large body, and a large hand was covering my mouth. The packages lay at our feet, scattered.

I'd been warned, oh yes, Anna and Eln and Remn and the others. That if I wasn't careful I'd be assaulted in the market, alone and helpless. I'd never believed them. I'd always thought that I'd be able to scream or fight or get away from any foolish enough to try anything. But the body pressed against mine was strong and hard and held me effortlessly as I fought, trying to kick, struggling to get my hands free, anything to win my release.

"Be still. I will not hurt you." The voice rumbled, and his warm breath on my ear made me shiver. I forced myself to relax, glaring at the man, since it was all for naught anyway. I wasn't moving anywhere until he was ready to let me go.

Given the location of where we were and what he was doing, there was no reason to believe his words and every reason to believe that he would hurt me. And yet . . .

I believed him. I was not scared. In fact, I had never felt more alive. My whole body seemed newly aware of itself. It was like my skin had taken on a life of its own. He had pressed himself up against me, holding me to the wall, his mouth a scant inch from my ear. The power of his body warmed me even through my clothing. Was this what it was like to—

His voice cut through my shameful thoughts, his eyes focused intently on mine. "All I want is information. How is Simus?" He pulled his hand back slightly, enough for me to talk. I could still feel the warmth of his hand on my face.

"He is well." I darted a glance off to the sides, but there was no one near.

"When could he travel?"

I could see where this was headed. "Days. Even then, he would have to be carried."

He locked his eyes on mine for a moment, then seemed satisfied with the truth of my answer. "You will carry a message to him."

"No."

He looked at me sharply. "You heal the enemy . . ."

I cut him off. "No. I don't know who you are, or what you hope to do, but I will not help you."

His blue eyes gleamed. His hand moved down to my throat and rested lightly on it. "I could kill you now."

I swallowed hard and closed my eyes. "Who then would take the kavage to Simus?"

There was a huff of amusement. The hand left my throat, and I felt the heat of his body move away. I opened my eyes onto an empty alleyway.

I stood for a moment, just breathing, trying to let the feel of my body return to normal. But I could still feel the weight of him pressed against me, and the warmth of his breath on my cheek. Outside the alley, traffic ebbed and flowed, and the normal sounds helped me get myself under control. My packages lay at my feet, and I picked them all up, hoping that none of the bottles and jars had broken. There was still so much to do and time was wasting. I took a deep breath and started walking.

I was a fool. My cheeks flushed with embarrassment. An ignorant fool. I would talk to Lord Warren as soon as he was available.

Between the still room activities and helping Eln, it was late before I got to the prisoners' tent. I yawned as I took the final part of the path, heading for Heath's post. I stopped when I got to him, put down my satchel, sack and jugs, and stretched as high as I could, yawning with my mouth wide open. He smiled. "Tired?"

I grinned and nodded. "After this, I go to bed . . . no stops along the way."

Heath jerked his head toward the castle. "I heard the horns announce the arrival of the Warlord. Have you heard anything about the talks?"

I snorted. "Heath, I'd be the last person anyone would tell. I know that Warren is involved, but that's all I know." I sighed and picked up my bundles. I was tired, and the damn brooch was raising a blister on my ankle. I was frustrated as well, since I'd tried to speak to Lord Warren, but it hadn't been possible. "I hope they went well. It's nice not to have more wounded."

"Aye." Heath had that mischievous look in his eye. "You'll have more ladies of the court looking for lotions and potions." I rolled my eyes, and he chuckled as he lifted the tent flap.

I looked for Rafe when I went in and saw him near Simus's cot. As I moved through the tent, I could see that there were more men up and moving about. Although some were shaky and had others assisting them, they were moving.

"Rafe." I called a greeting. He, Joden, and the other man, ummm . . . Prest, were near to Simus's pallet. I set my parcels down and knelt to look at my patient.

"Has he woken?"

Joden shrugged. "He has been in and out all day."

Prest looked at me. "Will he be well?

"Let us look." Prest and Joden started the unwrapping process. I looked over at Rafe and grinned. "I found this in the marketplace. Maybe you have a use for it."

He looked puzzled, but took the sack and opened it. His eyes got very big and excited. "Kavage! It is kavage!" He looked at me as the others started to react. "Where did you . . . ?"

"There was a merchant in the market that had some. He could not sell it, everyone thinks it is a poison." The tent laughed, but Rafe paid me no attention as he and a few others started examining the contents and commenting on the seeds. They seemed sort of obsessed. I bit my lip and started to worry that I had done the wrong thing.

Joden caught my eye and smiled. "Have no fear, healer. It

is a drink like any other. But it is a taste of home, and it will divert them for a time while they figure out a way to grind the beans."

I smiled with relief and turned to the wound.

It was doing very well. I took a closer look than I had earlier and was still pleased with his progress. We cleaned and redressed it, smearing it this time with an unguent made of fever's foe and fairysfoot.

Satisfied, I left it to Joden and Prest to wrap up my patient. I started on my rounds, tired but pleased. Each man was well out of danger and healing well. As I worked, I could hear Rafe and his group talking excitedly as they apparently found different ways to grind the beans I had brought. I stopped to watch for a moment as one man tried to grind them against a piece of wood with his bootheel. "Will that not affect the taste?"

He nodded without looking up. "Aye. It will add flavor."

Eventually there was no noise at all, and I looked over to see the men in fierce contemplation of the metal pot the tinker had given me, hovering over one of the braziers of hot coals. I just shook my head and continued my work. Before long, an odd aroma filled the tent. Odd, but pleasant.

Finally, the last one was done. I went over to where Joden sat by Simus, and dropped down next to him. I dragged my satchel along, and started to re-pack everything in it. I was almost done when Joden nudged me, and I looked up to see Rafe standing before me, a mug of something steaming in his hand.

"We want you to have the first taste." Rafe looked proudly at me as he handed me the mug. The rest of the tent was watching me, all eyes bright. I took the mug in one hand.

"You would not try to poison an innocent young healer, would you?" I looked suspiciously at Rafe, who stared back as innocent as a lamb.

"No." Rafe looked very serious. "On my honor." Then his grin flashed. "I would not waste kavage that way."

Everyone in the tent started laughing, and a few pounded on Rafe's back for his jest.

Taking a deep breath, I put the mug to my lips and sipped. Once again the tent exploded in laughter as my face screwed up in disgust. I managed to swallow, but it was a near thing. The liquid was hot, thick and bitter.

Joden patted me on the back as the rest of the tent started to share in the pot and make plans for another one. "Most prefer it with some milk and honey to take away the bitter."

"Yes! That's right." I looked around for my other purchases. "Keir told me that. So I brought some with me."

The silence in the tent was immediate and thick. I froze under all those eyes drilling into me. And a voice, thin and weak, arose from the pallet that lay beside me.

"Keir? You spoke to Keir?" Simus struggled to sit up.

Joden and Prest reached out and pushed him down. I handed the milk and the honey to Rafe, who took it without comment. I turned back to Simus.

"I met a man in the market this morning who told me that the kavage was taken with milk or honey." I was suddenly very thankful that there were two guards inside the tent with me. Two guards that were looking very nervous. One caught my eye and I gave him a smile. They relaxed a little.

Joden made a gesture, and the rest of the tent started to break up, talking and drinking from their mugs. He helped Simus to sit up and Rafe came over to help. He brought with him a mug, and Simus's hand emerged from the blankets, weak and shaky, but latched onto the mug like a desperate man.

Joden looked at me. "A man with eyes like blue flames?" I nodded. "Did he send any message?"

I returned the gaze. "He wanted to. I refused."

Joden's eyes narrowed. Simus watched me over the brim of his mug as Rafe helped him drink from it.

I did not back down. "I am a healer of any in need of my services. But I am not a . . ." I could not think of the word for 'traitor'. "I am not an oath-breaker. I have an oath as a healer, but also to my king. Any rescue attempt this Keir tries will be without my aid."

The minute my mouth closed, I winced. Joden, Rafe, and Simus relaxed, I could feel the tension leave them when they heard my words. I had probably just delivered the very message Keir wanted them to have anyway. I flushed again.

Simus sighed. "This kavage is terrible. Who made it?"

Rafe coughed.

"I should have known." He looked up at Joden. "How long?"

"Two days." Joden replied. "You were brought in with a bad wound and fever." Simus raised an eyebrow at that, and gave Joden a long look. Joden looked away, as if ashamed, but continued on. "Lara here treated you, and the wound does well. I do not think you will lose the leg."

Even more tension left Simus's body at that news. He took another sip from his mug. "Any news?"

Joden shook his head. "I have had none."

Simus looked at me and raised both eyebrows. I saw no harm. "All I know is that the Warlord arrived about midday to talk peace."

Simus thought about that. "You are wrong, little healer. The Warlord is here to talk surrender."

3

As I walked back to the castle that night along the garden path, I felt strangely invigorated. The tiredness that I had felt before had dissipated as quickly as it had come. Before leaving the tents, I'd finished the mug of kavage, once I'd laced it with milk and honey. A strange herb. I wondered if it held healing properties.

Since there seemed little chance that I would sleep any time soon, I went to the castle stillroom off the kitchen area. I waved to Anna as I entered the kitchen, snagged a bowl of stew and some bread, and retreated into the dim recess to eat. I was starving, and couldn't remember if I'd eaten at midday or not.

Perched on my stool, I ate quickly. The room with its rows of shelves and worktables was cool and quiet. The candle lamp only lit the small area around me. I'd light the rest when I started working. The scent of the spicy stew filled my senses, canceling out the scent of medicines and mixtures. As I wolfed down the food, I looked about, making plans. I'd concentrate on the medicinal recipes. If the fighting started back up, I would need all that I had on hand, and more. The lotions and perfumes could wait awhile.

Hours later the braziers were hot and the mixtures brewing. Water and willow bark were in one kettle boiling down to make fever's foe. Another pot held the ingredients for the scar mixture, once I'd filched goats' milk from the larder. As I stirred some of the orchid root mixture, I heard horns blowing. I stopped, listening, but they did not repeat. The Warlord must be leaving out the main gates. If that was the case, they'd been at it a long time. I breathed a silent prayer to the Goddess that things had gone well. Xymund's pride had caused him to do foolish things in the past. But Lord Marshall Warren was a good man. I hoped he would see the wisdom to peace.

The bubbling pots and the homey smells relaxed me in a way that nothing else could. While I enjoy caring for people, this was a small pleasure of my trade, brewing elixirs that would ease pain and restore health. The closest I'd ever come to magic, that was certain. It gave me a true sense of being needed and a real feeling of accomplishment.

I was yawning madly by the time the orchid root was ready to be poured into the small bottles that I had prepared. Moving carefully, I filled each to the neck and stoppered them loosely. The corks could be tightened once the bottles were fully cooled. The last thing was the fever's foe. The paste had to be spooned into small jars and sealed with wax. I put the wax to melt, and started to work. It seemed to take forever, but eventually I was perched on my stool, pouring the sealing wax over the last of the jars.

A knock came at the door, and Othur entered. He looked tired as well, with bags under his eyes. I smiled at him as I set down the wax pot. He stood there, rubbed his face with both hands and sighed.

"Long night?" I blew out the flame and gathered up a few of the jars to move to the storage shelves behind me.

Othur nodded. "The King talked alone with the Warlord for hours and has been closeted with the Council ever since.

They've been at it, hammer and tongs, for some time. They've sent for you."

I put down the last jar, and turned. "Me?" I blinked at him owlishly, surprised. "Why?"

There was a bitterness in his eyes as he shrugged. "I don't know. But he wants to see you now." My father had allowed Othur in all the councils and his opinion had been asked for and taken seriously. Xymund had removed the privilege when he'd taken the throne. Yet another reason for Anna to dislike him so.

I quickly finished cleaning the work area, and blew out the rest of the lamps and candles. Othur stood to one side and held the door. I slipped past him, smoothing down the front of my jerkin as I went. There were wax droplets and other stains, not to mention the smell, but the council was just going to have to settle for my work clothes if they wanted a status report about the prisoners at this hour. My jaw cracked in a yawn as I followed Othur through the back halls.

We arrived at the doors only to hear a heated argument going on inside. Othur and I exchanged looks, but made no comment. It did seem to me that Xymund spent more time arguing with his advisors instead of listening.

The guard nodded and opened the door to let me in. The conversation stopped abruptly as the door swung open.

Once again I found myself kneeling before my brother. But when I was granted permission to rise, Xymund was standing looking out the window. He was in formal dress, standing stiff and straight in front of the huge window. His hands were clenched behind his back. I glanced around. It seemed that the entire council was crowded about the room. Lord Marshall Warren was there, along with Archbishop Drizen. Drizen was seated by the hearth and dressed in formal vestments, with Deacon Browdus beside him. Everyone looked tired and worn. Out of the corner of my eye, I caught side glances being exchanged. There was a tension, as if everyone was avoiding looking at me. Something was very, very wrong.

"Xylara, the Warlord has named his terms for peace." Xymund did not turn. He made his announcement as he stood looking out the window. His hands tightened around one another. I looked over at General Warren, who grimaced, and looked down at the floor.

"That is good to hear, Your Majesty." I swallowed, sensing a problem. "Are they acceptable?"

Xymund still did not turn. "I and my nobles are to swear fealty to him. The kingdom will remain under my control and the taxes and tithes that are to be paid are reasonable. All prisoners and wounded, if there are any, will be exchanged." There was a bitterness in his tone. Maybe because they had more of our men then we had of theirs. Xymund continued. "But he has claimed tribute." My brother's gaze remained fixed on the horizon.

My fears for a peace grew. If the Warlord claimed something of Xymund's, his pride would forbid acceptance of the terms.

"What does he claim?" I took a step toward Xymund. Still, he did not turn. I looked around, but no one would meet my eyes.

At last, General Warren drew a breath. "You," he cleared his throat. "He claims you as tribute."

"Me?" My voice squeaked and sounded like it came from a distance.

Xymund did not turn. "As a slave."

I stared at that broad back, certain that I had not heard that right. "Me? But . . ."

Warren nodded. He glanced at Xymund's stiff back, but when there was no response, continued on, "The Warlord has sworn for a true peace. No pillaging, no looting." Warren swallowed. "He offers a true peace in exchange for you, Daughter of Xy."

The Archbishop raged. "He takes a Daughter of the Blood as a whore. You cannot allow this, Majesty." He and the deacon both wore similar expressions of horror.

Protocol be damned. I sank into the nearest chair, body and

mind numb. "You have misunderstood. He can't want . . ."

Xymund's hands twisted around each other, as he shifted his weight from one foot to the other. The light caught the gold brocade of his tunic as he moved. Always the regal one, my brother. "He would take you as his possession, a slave to his desires. He would not explain what your ultimate fate would be. He just repeated that he claims you, that you must be promised to him." He moved his head slightly, but did not turn. "I offered him lands, cattle, or gold. He just shook his head no. 'For a true peace,' he said. 'I claim her.' "

I stared at him, blankly. From childhood, I had been drilled in my responsibility as a Daughter of the House of Xy. That a marriage of alliance would be expected of me. But as the years had passed, and I had gained my mastery, it had seemed a dim prospect. Yet here it was, the obligations of my birth and my house, in a form far different from any expectations. I licked my dry lips and tried to remember to breathe.

My legs managed to get me up out of the chair, and over to stand next to Xymund at the window. Father had chosen this room for its view of the length of the valley. The river, the lake, the farms and cottages. Now I saw what Xymund saw. Campfires. Hundreds of them outside the walls, scattered over the valley. The Warlord's men. I leaned my head against the cool stonework and looked out in despair.

Xymund shifted slightly and turned. For a brief instant I saw it in his eyes. Deep within, hidden from the men in this room, was his utter and complete glee. "You have already promised him his tribute," I whispered.

Xymund tilted his head to the side.

Rage filled me in an instant. I wanted to strike out hard and hurt him. Warren could rule better. *Othur* could rule better.

The rage drained away as quickly as it had surged, leaving me shaken. The glitter of those campfires reminded me of what faced us.

"Xylara." Warren was standing behind us. "No one can ask this of you." I turned to face him. He did not look at the King.

"We do not know this man's intent . . . there have been no assurances of your safety or . . ." He paused. "Or of your status. My men and I will fight—"

"And if you fight, Warren? What is the hope?" I asked.

Warren shook his head. "I cannot tell. We are ill prepared for a siege. Water is not a problem, but food . . ." His voice trailed off.

"There are the tunnels into the mountains." A large, older man spoke up. I couldn't place his name but knew he was one of the craftsmen on the council. "We can bring in supplies that way."

Warren shook his head. "The tunnels are old and rarely used. They are big enough for men to walk single file, but not for laden horses. We could not bring in enough food or supplies fast enough to feed a whole city." He took a deep breath. "The Warlord's men would need to build siege equipment. Winter comes on. There's a good chance that we could hold out til the weather drives him back to the plains."

I moved back to the chair and sank into it. There was an odd kind of numbness in my brain. Voices were raised, as they debated again, but I couldn't make out the words. I stared at Xymund's back, but he did not turn. He simply looked out over the valley.

I licked my dry lips again. "Warren?" My voice was little more then a whisper. It sounded strange to my ears.

The arguing continued in the background as he knelt by my chair. I looked into his eyes. I saw his fear.

His fear that I would not do this.

"Will it be a true peace?"

Warren nodded, his head close to mine. "Yes. The Warlord has kept his word to those he has taken. It is only where any have betrayed him that he has retaliated. When he is betrayed or defied, he is ruthless." The old man bent his head.

"I need . . ." I cleared my dry throat and looked down at my clasped hands. The knuckles were white. What I needed mattered no longer. I looked up and let my voice carry, cutting through the useless debate. "When is this to take place?"

Xymund turned. "Sunset. The ceremony will be at sunset

tomorrow." He gestured toward the window, where dawn could be seen on the horizon. "Today."

I nodded. It took every bit of strength, but I managed to get to my feet. "The House of Xy has always seen to the needs of its people." I took a deep breath. "I will be ready at sunset."

Everyone in the room but the King sank to their knees, removing helms and uncovering heads. I looked steadily at Xymund, who stared back at me, sullenly.

I turned and walked toward the door on legs gone numb. Once in the hall, I moved without really seeing anything. Next thing I knew, I was in my room. I stood for a moment, looking at my belongings scattered about, at the fire that burned so cheerfully, at my books, and papers, and . . .

I fell to my knees and managed to get to the chamber pot before retching up my supper.

I heaved and panted over the pot for what seemed an endless time. The spice of the stew burned my lips. It occurred to me that it would be a long time before I could stomach the taste of Anna's stew again. Then I realized that would not be a problem. My stomach cramped at the thought.

My eyes closed, I tried to concentrate on my breathing instead of the wretched cramping of my gut. A slave. The heaving began again, although there was nothing left to purge.

Sounds at my door, then hands pulled back my hair, and a cool cloth was on my neck. My breathing started to even out, and a cup of water was pressed to my lips. I took some water in, rinsed and spit. Supporting hands drew me up and away. It was Anna, who clutched me to her ample breast, making soft sounds, and rubbing my back with her hands. I buried my face in her neck and clung like a sick child. She smelled of bread, and grease, and home. Her big warm hands rubbed my back as she cradled me, both of us kneeling on the floor. My sobs eased as she hugged and rocked me. "You cannot do this thing," she whispered into my ear. ". . . you cannot."

Word travels fast.

"I must," I whispered back. "Xymund has already promised." I lifted my head and sniffled, wiping my eyes with my hands. Othur was seated on my bed, his eyes red-rimmed, his hands hanging between his legs.

Othur snorted. "He had no right." He took a deep breath, his lips thinning as he pressed them together.

"Bastard he is, bastard in blood and deed." Anna hissed. "Fine, then he can answer to the Warlord. We will get you away, hide you 'til this is done."

I dropped my head to her shoulder and allowed myself to be comforted for a moment.

"We have friends beyond the mountains, where you could go, Lara." Othur's voice was soft.

I lifted my head and looked into his worried eyes. "It wouldn't just be Xymund that answered to the Warlord, would it? It would be the city."

Othur dropped his gaze. He said nothing.

I pushed myself away from Anna and sat up. "Would it?"

Othur looked into the fire. "Rumor has it that the Warlord is ruthless when betrayed, or when a promise is not kept."

Anna spoke up. "Child, you are not responsible for . . ."

I looked at her, at her tear-streaked face. "What would Father have done?"

Othur sat up at that comment. "If your father were alive he would be horsewhipping your brother through the halls and down into the stables. He'd never have pledged you without consulting you first."

Anna nodded in agreement, her chins jiggling. She took up a damp cloth and wiped my face. "Child, please. There is no need for this."

"What is the alternative? I walk away from the city? From these people? From you? And leave you to what fate, Anna?"

I rose to my feet. Othur stood as well, and we both helped Anna get her bulk off the floor. Once she was on her feet, Othur swept me into a hug. "This isn't over, Lara. We need to talk about this before—"

The door slamming open brought him up short.

It was Xymund.

He stood in the doorway, a small chest under his arm.

Anna covered the chamber pot with the damp cloth, and picked it up. With a nod to Xymund, she left the room. For one brief moment, I held my breath, afraid that the contents of the pot would be flung in his face. But Anna went past him without a word. Othur bowed to Xymund, then followed his wife out. He cast a glance at me as he closed the door that told me that our discussion was not over yet.

Xymund placed the chest on the small table by the door.

"The Warlord's men brought this. His instructions are that you be bathed, oiled, and anointed with perfume. Your hair is to be down. Wear the garment that has been provided and nothing else. When summoned into the throne room, you will walk to the throne, kneel before the Warlord and extend your wrists for your chains."

I did not reply. I would not give him the satisfaction.

"I have something else to give you." He held out a small vial with a dark fluid in it. I took it, and looked at him with a question in my eyes. "It's monkshood."

One of the deadliest poisons known. Takes less then a few breaths. My voice barely emerged from my throat. "What am I to do with this?"

"The right thing." He put his hands behind his back. "I had no choice, Xylara. My generals tell me that we could not withstand him. By doing this I save the kingdom."

"And your throne." Suddenly I was very, very tired. I sat in a chair, and looked at the vial. So small. So deadly.

"I am giving you an escape. I will leave the timing of it to your discretion."

I let the bitterness escape. "My thanks, to be sure."

He stiffened. "The best time would be after the ceremony, but before he can . . ." His voice trailed off, and I closed my eyes. "I know that you will do what is best for our people." Bitterness and something even darker now lay in his tone. I looked at him and found it on the tip of my tongue to ask him why he hated me.

I doubted that I would get an honest answer.

He endured my look for a moment and then turned on his heel and left the room, closing the door behind him.

The brown liquid flowed back and forth as I turned the vial in my hand. I stared at it as I turned it over and over . . .

All I had ever wanted was to heal. To fix the hurts of others. A school of my own, a place to study and learn and teach, and heal. Now, I would be a. . . .

I swallowed as the bile rose in my throat again. I stood and started to pace in the confines of my small room. I kept going over the scene in Xymund's study, trying to find another way, an alternative to what he had promised our enemy. Xymund's words kept running through my head. 'I and my nobles are to swear fealty to him. The kingdom will remain under my control and the taxes and tithes that are to be paid are reasonable and proper. All prisoners and wounded, if there are any, will be exchanged. But he has claimed tribute.'

' . . . claimed tribute . . . '

' . . . claimed tribute . . . ' But there was something else, something . . .

'All prisoners and wounded, if there are any, will be exchanged'

Dearest Goddess. 'if there are any'!

I stood suddenly, dropping the vial onto the bed. Xymund had no intention of exchanging prisoners. He would obey the letter of the agreement but not the spirit. I swallowed hard, glancing out the window to the rising sun. It might already be too late.

I was up and moving without another thought. I flew out of the room, reaching the circular back stair, throwing myself down them as fast as my feet could go. I burst through the kitchen door, and bless the Goddess, Othur was still there with Anna. They looked up, staring at me as if I had taken leave of my senses.

I hurried over, talking as fast as my breath would let me.

"Slow down, Lara, slow down." He frowned. "Xymund wouldn't. He's too afraid of that demon to . . ."

Anna wiped her face, her expression grim. "He would, damn him. A sop to his pride. What can we do?"

"I think I can get them safe to the castle gates, but beyond?" I trembled at the thought of a slaughter, of its effect on the peace.

Othur rubbed his chin. "Let me worry about that. Go to the tents, Lara. Maybe we're wrong, but go anyway."

I nodded, ran to the still room, and grabbed up my satchel. Without further thought I exploded out of the kitchen and down the garden path, running for all I was worth, praying that I was wrong.

I stopped at the briar patch, just out of sight of the first sentry post, and tried to catch my breath. No point in giving myself away. I dropped the satchel, bent over, hands on knees, and concentrated on breathing.

Once I had it under control, I picked up the bag and started walking down the path at my normal pace. I had to be in time, had to be . . .

The first sentry appeared unconcerned, giving me a genial wave as I passed by. I returned it, and continued on. One slow step at a time. The next sentry came into view. I waved and kept my pace normal.

The guard was a familiar one, but I could not place the name. He nodded to me. "You're early this morn."

I nodded and smiled, not trusting my voice.

He lifted the flap. I took a breath and stepped inside.

Everything was as it had been. I let out my breath slowly and swayed with the relief that coursed over me. Most of the prisoners were still asleep and not yet stirring. Someone was about, though, for I could smell kavage, and some of the braziers were alight. Maybe I was wrong.

Maybe.

I looked over to where Simus and Joden were, and headed toward them. The shadows clung in that area of the tent, where the light of the fires did not reach.

Joden looked up first and seemed startled to see me. He rose from his knees and held out a hand, as if to ward me off. I moved past him and knelt by Simus, who exclaimed sharply as I reached over to pull back the blankets. I looked over, startled, then followed his gaze to the tent wall. There, where the darkness was deepest, I discovered something important.

There was a man hidden in the shadows.

I froze. Joden had moved behind me, blocking the guards view. Simus was struggling to sit up, and I assisted him almost unconsciously, my eyes never leaving the blue eyes that gleamed from the shadows above us.

Keir.

Joden was speaking softly and it took me a minute to remember his language. ". . . please. Don't betray him, Lara. I beg you."

"I won't." I answered, keeping my own voice low. I glared into those blue eyes, so bright in the darkness. "Is this some kind of foolhardy rescue plan?"

White teeth gleamed in the shadows.

I tore my gaze away and concentrated on Simus's leg. My hands trembled as I opened the bandage to inspect the wound. First Xymund threatens the peace and then this fool. My mouth tightened as a wave of anger passed over me. Was I the only one who cared?

Simus lay back down. "Something has happened." He looked back and forth between me and the silent man in the shadows.

"There is to be peace, and a prisoner exchange." I worked quickly, trying to see the wound in what light I had.

Simus stared at me. "Peace?" He shot a glance at Keir. "Under what terms?"

I didn't look at him. "Fealty, taxes, land. A prisoner exchange. Tribute." The shakiness in my voice surprised me.

Joden's voice came over my shoulder. "Tribute?"

I didn't know the word in their tongue, so I used my own. "A slave." I was digging through my satchel, hiding my face. "Me. I am to be given to him at sunset."

"Slave," Joden said, puzzled. "I do not know this word."

Keir's soft voice floated over us, barely a whisper. "You could flee."

"Yes," I nodded. "There are people who would hide me and help me get away." I faltered in my digging. "But if the Warlord is as ruthless as they say, what will he do to my people if I don't go through with the ceremony?" I closed my eyes, actually picturing it for the first time. "If the Warlord is true to his word and it is a true peace, then any sacrifice would be worth it to save my people." I jerked my head up and shot a glance at Simus. "Can I trust his word?"

Simus nodded. "Yes. If he has set the terms, he will not be the one to violate them."

I looked down into the satchel and watched the jar in my shaking hands. "My father," My voice trembled but I continued. "Father always said that the price of privilege is responsibility." Even as I said it, I knew it to be true. Xymund may not be honorable. I could not control him. But I could act with honor. I took another deep breath and turned back to my work. As I worked, I cast a look up at Keir, hidden there in the shadows. "Xymund gave me a vial of poison."

Keir's face tightened. Joden sputtered behind me. Simus levered himself up onto his elbows.

"The drug would give you release." Keir's voice was dark and heavy as it floated through the dark. "Your people would suffer the consequences. The Warlord would level this city, and destroy the people if you were to die."

I looked over at him in the darkness of the tent. His eyes glittered at me from the shadows. A hysterical giggle bubbled up inside my throat. "You have listened to too many ballads. He probably wants a healer to ease the ache of sore muscles or lance his boils. I. . . ."

Keir's head snapped up, and he looked at the tent entrance. I stopped, listened, and heard guards, many guards approaching outside.

Dearest Goddess. I had been right.

My mouth dried in an instant. Quickly, I pulled the blankets up and over Simus. I staggered up, pulling my satchel with me. Keir was silent, wrapped in a cloak. He looked over at me, his face intent. "What is this? The exchange is to take place at sunset."

I didn't answer. I fumbled in my satchel and pressed my small knife into Joden's hand. "Here. Hold this for me." I turned and strode toward the entrance. I got there just as the captain of the guard stepped through. From his look, he was surprised to see me. As he squinted at me, he opened his mouth to say something. I didn't give him the chance.

"Arneath. I am glad that they sent you to take charge of the exchange. I don't quite have them ready to go yet."

Arneath closed his mouth and shot me a look. "My men can assist them to prepare. Why don't you wait outside?"

Oh no. He was not getting me away from them. I prudently stayed out of arms' reach.

"Tis a joy for me to aid them, since it means the return of our men so much quicker." I smiled and shrugged. "They are eager to leave. It will not take long." I turned and called out in their tongue. "The trade of prisoners is to happen now. Everyone get ready."

Eager faces turned my way, and the men started to stir themselves. I felt Arneath moving behind me, and stepped away, toward where Joden stood. While I was fairly sure that the guards had no understanding of the language, I took no chance. "No one walks alone. Everyone must aid their fellows."

I started to make my way back to Joden, ignoring Arneath's protest from behind me. "Some of you take up the cots of those who cannot walk."

I reached Joden.

"Simus must go on a litter. Keir, you and Prest can carry him."

Joden started to reach for Simus, but I got in the way. "No, Joden. Stay next to me." He looked at me, puzzled. I leaned forward and whispered in his ear, "You may need a hostage to get through this." His eyes widened, then hardened.

As the men gathered themselves, I waited for Arneath to order me taken from the tent. His men had the weapons. But I was gambling that his instructions were to be quiet and discrete. Hard to do that in front of the woman who was being given into slavery before the entire Court in a few hours.

We started out, surrounded by the guards. I walked beside Joden, sticking close. Arneath said nothing, but watched me carefully. If he were going to do anything, it would be in the depths of the garden, out of sight of the castle, where bodies

could be buried. The path was narrow, and the men were
strung out. If Arneath was to act, it would have to be there.
The briar loomed before us. I breathed in the scent of the
roses, and prayed to the Goddess. These men moved so
slowly, even helping one another. We reached the briar and
crawled passed. I bit my lip, desperate to look behind, and yet
not quite daring to do so. Finally, I couldn't help it. I looked
back.

The last prisoner staggered past the briar, followed by the
last of Arneath's men. I breathed a little easier. Keir was at
the foot of Simus' litter. He blended into the group well, as if
he had always been there. The only difference was the
glances he darted in my direction from time to time.

When we reached the castle gates one of the gate guards
approached me. "Xylara, the King has instructed that you are
not to leave the castle grounds."

Ah, Xymund. Brave enough to order the deaths of un-
armed men, but afraid to face the Warlord without his little
gift under his control.

Arneath looked like he had lost the battle but won the war.
There were alleys, and dark places in the city. He could still
carry out his mission.

There wasn't much more I could do. I nodded to Arneath,
as the gates began to open and turned to the group of men.

Joden squeezed my shoulder and moved to take the burden
off Keir. Keir stepped back, never letting his eyes leave my
face. I avoided his gaze, stepped up to the litter and put my
hand on Simus's shoulder. He covered it with his own. "My
thanks. Be well, little healer." I nodded, and stepped back.

The gates swung open. Arneath stepped forward to lead
the way.

Only to be blocked by a large group of townspeople.

Remn, the bookseller, stepped forward, along with the
Head Priest from the Temple of the Goddess. "We have come
to offer our help to these men. As we would hope that their
people help our men at this time."

I smiled and watched as the two groups merged into one
and headed down the street. Anna and Othur had gotten the

word out. Arneath looked like he had swallowed something bitter. He would be hard pressed to carry out his orders now.

I stood as the gates swung silently closed. In the few moments before they came together, I thought I saw a flash of blue eyes as Keir looked back at me.

It was wishful thinking. Nothing more.

I spent the rest of the day in the still room with Anna. We reviewed the supplies, and I went over the various recipes, updating the records and recording my notes. Eln would send apprentices, and eventually a master would take my place. It felt as if I was in a dream, with a kind of blanket around my head, muffling my thoughts. I concentrated on the work at hand and thought of nothing else. At some point, Anna placed food before me, but I couldn't eat it. My thoughts were muddled, but my stomach was perfectly aware and it rolled at the suggestion of food. At the last, I gathered up my precious books and journals, and tied them together with twine. Eln would see that they went to the right people and that the knowledge was not lost. I looked at the little bundle sitting in the center of the cleaned and cleared table. It looked somehow forlorn and lost. Of all my things, these were the hardest to let go.

Anna's hand grasped my shoulders and moved me to the kitchen, pressing me down onto the bench. A large mug of tea was placed before me, and I watched as she added honey to it. She placed the mug in front of me carefully. "Drink. I will get some bread and cold meat."

"No, Anna. I'm not hungry." My stomach was barely willing to take the tea.

The kitchen was quiet and there were only the two of us seated there. Anna sipped her tea. I stared at mine. We sat in uncomfortable silence. In another few hours.

"Lara. Child." I lifted my head to see Anna staring deep into her cup and turning the brightest shade of red I had ever seen. Her rough voice dropped to a whisper. "If your blessed mother were here, she would want you to know what to expect."

"Anna." I reached for her reddened hand on the dry boards of the table, trying not to laugh. "Anna, I may not know the specifics, but I know the general way that things go. It will be all right."

Anna looked up, tears streaming down her face. "As you say, child."

Neither of us believed it.

I looked away, then rose. "I best go and get ready."

Anna wiped her face with her apron. "I'll have hot water sent up to your room. I'll be up shortly to help you."

"Anna, you don't have to—"

A fierce look from her cut off my words. "I'll be up. Go on." She looked away as fresh tears welled up in her eyes.

I made my way to my room, and stood at its center looking around at my personal items. I sorted out my clothing for the maids, Anna would see to it that they were given to the right people. I had little jewelry, but a few rings and a necklace that had been my mother's. No fine jewels here, just a simple gold locket on a chain. That was for Anna. The few remaining coins, I'd donate to the Goddess. I had some perfumes and soaps that I'd made for myself; I set those aside for Kalisa the cheesemaker. She'd cackle, and use them lavishly. The ones I liked the best were scented with vanilla oil. They were very expensive and I'd used them sparingly, saving them for a special occasion or an indulgence. As I looked at them, I wished I'd used them every day.

There were sounds outside, and I quickly dried my eyes as the servants started to haul in the tub and water, along with towels. Ordinarily, bathing in my room by the fire was a treat, one not to be indulged in too often, what with the servants having to haul hot water up the stairs. I bit my lip and got myself under control as they sloshed bucket after bucket of hot water into the tub. Once they were gone, I stripped, throwing my clothes in the corner. I sank into the tub and started washing, using my vanilla soap unsparingly.

Anna showed up in time to help me rinse my hair. Wrapped in towels, I sat by the fire, and rubbed the water from my hair. Anna sat on a stool next to me, looking through the small chest that had been brought to the castle by the Warlord's men. There was a small vial in the box, along with a garment of some kind. Anna uncorked it and we both jerked our heads back in dismay as the overwhelming scent of flowers filled the air. We could not get the cork back in fast enough. We looked at each other and burst out laughing like sick fools.

Next, Anna held up the garment and we both just looked at each other.

"Isn't there anything else in there?" I asked as I looked in the chest.

"No." Anna frowned. "You are going to catch your death."

Anna picked up the combs and gestured for me to sit with my back to her. She started to work the tangles out of my hair. I reached for one of my bottles and handed it to her. She looked at me. "The instructions said . . ."

"I'd rather smell of vanilla."

She sighed, but opened the bottle and began to rub the expensive oil into my hair. I started with the scented creams on my body. The vanilla's gentle scent surrounded us, but wasn't overpowering. Once I was done, I sat quietly, staring at the fire as Anna brushed my hair dry.

When she was done, as a further small act of defiance, I wound my hair up on top of my head as I was wont to wear it and placed more of the scented oil on my neck. Anna clucked like a hen, but I felt better for it.

Until I put on the garment. It was little more than a sleeveless shift of fine, shiny white cloth. It fell to below my knees, and clung in ways that brought a blush to my cheeks. Thankfully, the neckline was high, showing only my collarbone, since it was cut straight across. Anna stepped back, and we both looked at each other. It was fairly clear that the Warlord wanted to be able to inspect the merchandise before claiming it.

With a deep breath, I moved closer to the fire, and looked around the room. Anna picked up my slippers, but I shook my head. "I am to wear only what was in the chest."

Anna looked at me, and let the slippers fall back to the

floor. I moved about, telling her what I wanted done with my possessions. I pressed my mother's necklace into her hand, and hugged her hard as her silent sobs racked her body. "You'll see to this?"

She managed to nod, unable to speak.

The horns announced the arrival of the Warlord's party. Our heads jerked up together and we both stared out the window. Sunset had arrived. I looked over at Anna. She stood there, frozen, her misery reflected in her face.

I took one last look around my room, at my notes, my books. Xymund had said that I was forbidden to take anything with me. Slaves do not own property. They are themselves owned.

I stood in the center, closed my eyes, and took another deep breath. It did no good. My heart started racing, pounding out of my chest. I could not do this. I could not submit to this. I opened my eyes, and saw the vial where it sat on the mantel. One quick swallow . . .

Anna had already moved to the door. After she opened it, she knelt down slowly, wincing as her knees pressed against the stone. Gathering my wits, I walked to the door and paused to gently place my hand on her head. She reached up, took my hand and pressed it to her lips. She looked up, eyes brimming. "Thank you, Daughter of Xy."

I nodded and managed a smile before I stepped into the hall. And brought myself up short.

The corridor was lined with people. They stood on either side, pressed into corners and against the walls. I stood for a minute, looking. The nearest ones went down on their knees. I heard their quiet "Thank you, Daughter of Xy." I took a few steps forward, and more sank down.

As I walked down the halls toward the ceremony they each knelt and murmured "Thank you, Daughter of Xy." Through the main halls, down the stairs. There were servants, townspeople, healers that I knew, some of the wounded I had tended. The people who would not be in the throne room.

The ones I was doing this for.

They were with me, all the way to the door of the antechamber. Their thanks and their faces would be with me forever.

I could do this.

At the antechamber of the throne room, the guards on both sides opened the door, and I stepped inside.

My eyes clouded, and I stood for a moment, trying to blink them clear. One of the pages approached, knelt and held up a cloth. I took it, wiped my eyes, and returned it to him. Othur was standing there. "Daughter of Xy," he said. "The fealty ceremony has begun. The court herald will announce you when it is time."

I nodded and stepped into his arms, getting a quick hug. He whispered, "Thank you, beloved Daughter of Xy," in my ear, and quickly left the room.

I moved to the fireplace and felt the warm hearth stone under my feet. The fire crackled cheerfully, but I felt cold. I tried to rub the chill bumps from my arms.

I stiffened when the herald's voice rang out. "Xylara, Daughter of Xy, you are summoned to the Court." The guards opened the doors, and I walked forward.

I lost my breath in the next instant.

The white marble of the throne room gleamed in the light of the sunset. The lords of the Court stood against the walls, as did an even larger number of the Warlord's men. I could not make out the figure on the throne, but I knew that it was the Warlord. He would have been seated there for the ceremony. Xymund was off to the side, standing with the Council members.

The room was silent as I stepped within. The cold marble pulled the warmth from my feet as I lowered my eyes to the floor and advanced toward the throne. The quiet was unnerving. It took forever to cross the floor, one slow step at a time. I kept my eyes on the gleaming marble, and hoped that I was headed in the right direction.

There seemed to be no noise, no coughing, no shuffling in the crowd. Just the sound of my heart beating against my ribs, and the cold that had settled in my chest. After what seemed like years, I could see the step that lead up to the throne. A blue cushion had been placed before the throne, one I had never seen before. I was grateful to whoever had thought of it. I halted before the throne, and slowly sank onto the cushion. On either side, I could see two black boots broadly planted, and legs encased in black fabric. I was careful to keep my eyes down.

I took a deep breath, slowly lifted my hands, palms up, and silently submitted myself to what was to come.

The room seemed to stop breathing. I felt fingers at the base of my neck, gently unraveling my hair. Strong fingers ran through it, releasing and letting it fall free. I shivered, both at the touch and the implication that disobedience would not be tolerated.

Cold metal encircled my wrists. I heard a click as they locked into place. Surprisingly, they were heavy silver bracelets, with no chains. Weren't there supposed to be chains?

A deep male voice boomed above my head, in my language. "Thus do I claim the warprize."

It was a voice I knew.

My eyes flew up as the room shook with the response of the Warlord's men as they stomped their feet and cheered.

The blue-eyed warrior from the marketplace looked down at me, a very self-satisfied smile on his face.

Keir was the Warlord? How had he done this, or even learned of my true identity?

Before I could think, or say a word, he took my hands and stood, drawing me up with him. From behind him, he swept up a black cloak from the throne and twirled it around me, concealing me from all eyes, enclosing me in darkness. The fabric seemed warm and floated around me like night. It smelled of chain mail and oil and some kind of spice.

I was swept up and over his shoulder. The move made me squawk, but I doubted that the noise could be heard above the noise of the crowd. He started to move. Through the soft cloth, I could hear his men chanting his name. I squirmed, but the cloak had me pinned, unable to move my arms or see anything.

Then I squirmed for another reason. His hand was on my

buttocks, its warmth burning through the cloak. There was a caress, and then a soft swat . . . a warning to keep still.

I stopped squirming.

The hand stayed where it was.

4

My captor wasted no time. His boots clicked on the marble as he left the throne room, and the jostling told me that he had started down the stairs to the main doors. I could feel his breathing as he moved, and heard the jingle of his armor. The cold air cut through the warmth of the cloak as we moved out through the great doors. There were sounds of men moving about in the great courtyard, and the ring of the horses' hooves on the cobblestones.

We stopped, and I was swung down to lay like a babe in arms. The Warlord's voice rang out, but he spoke so quickly I couldn't understand what was being said. Instead of being placed on my feet, I was handed off to someone else. I struggled, not liking this change, trying to bring my arms up and get free of the dark material.

A whisper came to me through the cloth. "It's Joden, Lara. It is all right." I stopped moving, relieved at the familiar voice, and anxious for information. Before I could reply, I was lifted up onto the back of a horse. Arms encircled me again. Joden's voice rang out. "I return your warprize, Warlord."

The chest behind me rumbled. "My thanks, Joden." The horse under us shifted, and my stomach lurched. The black cloth pressed against my face, trapping my breath. It felt tight and close, like I couldn't get enough air. The Warlord shouted something, and a great roar went up all around us. We were moving then, and at a gallop. I could hear others around us, moving as well, yelling war cries and shouting praise for the Warlord. The thundering of the horses as they left the courtyard and ran over the wooden bridge to the city was frightening. I swallowed hard, my breath coming faster, and fought down the wave of nausea. I still couldn't move my arms. The fear of tumbling from my perch remained, so I tucked into the body that held me and stayed still. The sound of men's voices had faded, but they were all around us as we plunged on, the pounding of horses' hooves and the jangling of harness the only noise. Moving through the town, down the main road, and out through the main gate.

The cloak offered some protection, but outside the city walls, the wind was sharp. I shivered. In what seemed like moments, we were splashing through the river that lay between the city and the Warlord's camp, and moving up the slope that it occupied. There was no hail, no greeting, but the horse slowed. I wanted to ask what was going on, but held my tongue. I did not know if slaves were allowed to talk, much less ask questions. Instead, I clenched my fists in the fabric, and tried to get my breath.

The horse stopped. This time, the Warlord shifted in the saddle and slid down to the ground. My stomach lurched as we fell. I must have cried out somehow, for the arms held me close. "One more ceremony, then we're done." The whisper came from beside my ear. The sounds changed, and his boots strode on wood. I was placed on my feet, the cloak still enveloping me. His arms gave me a minute to steady myself as my bare feet felt the cold, rough wood underfoot. I swayed slightly, but regained my balance, and his hands withdrew.

"My warriors!" The Warlord shouted, and there was a note of pride in his voice. "Behold the warprize." With that, the cloak was whipped away.

I was standing on a platform, in a pool of light from the torches that surrounded me. The cold air cut through the cloth of my shift. Out in the darkness beyond, I could just make out people standing and staring at me, the Warlord's army, a full ten thousand strong, or so I had heard tell. I could well believe it when they roared out their approval to the night sky.

Startled, I stepped back, colliding with the Warlord, who stood behind me. He wrapped his arm around my waist, and I raised my hand to cover his. The heat of his arm seeped through the shift to my stomach. He held up his fist in the air, and the men renewed their cheers. Drums and voices seemed to explode into the night, more noise than music.

It was too much. My vision went gray, and my hand slipped from his arm. Next thing I knew, I was once again cradled in strong arms and moving. The cheers and music continued, but they were somehow muted and indistinct. There was an impression of many people that parted as I floated by. I lost track of things for a while, but then I was in a tent, and laying on something soft. Someone was speaking as a hand brushed my hair off my face with a gentle touch.

"Warprize. Did you eat or drink anything at the castle? Before the ceremony?" The sound was muffled, as if from a distance. It was the Warlord's voice, urgent, demanding an answer. Another voice, older and harsher, murmured in the background. The Warlord replied, but all I heard were fragments. Bastard. Poison. A soft blanket covered me. Hands reached under the blanket and felt my hands and feet. "She's cold, very cold." Odd. He sounded worried. Gentle hands were moving me, and suddenly there was warmth at my feet. Then by my hands. The warmth seeped into me, slowly, and I felt my body relaxing, sinking into the softness, heavy as a stone.

Someone lifted me up, putting a bowl to my lips, urging me to drink, but the voice was far away and distant. I swallowed, and warmth flooded my throat and belly. There was an odd taste, strong and pungent. Once the bowl was empty, I was lowered, and covered once again with blankets. The voices continued to talk quietly, as all that heat seeped into my bones.

The voices were gone. I lay still, eyes closed. The bed shifted, the blanket rose, and I froze, hardly daring to breathe.

Something soft brushed my lips.

A stab of fear went through me. It had come, and as much as I thought I could handle it, I was frightened. I fought to open my eyes, trying to gather my wits, and found myself staring into startled blue eyes. I must keep my part of the agreement.

The Warlord had other ideas, for he shook his head. "No, Warprize. Have no fear." A hand cradled my head. I closed my eyes and felt a soft touch on each lid. I did not have the strength to open them again. A hand moved to rest over my heart. Its warmth was a comforting feeling. He pressed down gently, as if he was claiming the organ that beat within. I relaxed back into the bed, letting the warmth and the comfort take me.

"Sleep, now." His voice soft and low. I managed to get my eyes open enough to see him lay down next to me, on his side, on top of the blankets and lay his head on his arms. He wore trous, but was naked from the waist up, and I could just make out the tattoos on his arm. In the dim light of the tent, I looked at him, puzzled. His eyes were closed, and his breathing regular, but I didn't believe that he slept. I turned my head slightly and stared at the tent above me. It seemed, well, a bit disappointing, somehow.

I puzzled over that idea until I fell asleep.

Something touched my hair.

I stirred, half waking from the movement of the bed.

"Go back to sleep."

I gasped at the sound, my body jerking awake. My eyes flew open, and I looked about, taking in my surroundings. The tent was in shadows, the only light from braziers that held a sullen glow. There was a strong smell of horse, and something sharp and clean that I didn't recognize. The tent was large, with what appeared to be stools and a table, with trunks and benches lining the sides. Outside, I could hear men and horses milling about.

Someone stood with their back to me, dressing quickly, sorting through gear that was laid on a bench. A half-dressed man, whose back muscles rippled in the dim light.

I so rarely see healthy men.

There were scars there, old scars. The light played over the skin, dancing with the shadows over the hollows and rises as he moved. Then Keir turned, and a gleam of an eye looked my way. I stared openly as he moved closer. There were tattoos on both arms and scars on the front too, harder to see because of the chest hair, but there all the same. They told tales of battles fought. So many scars.

He stood for a bit, looking down as I looked up, frowning at me. He dropped his gear on the end of the bed, and pulled a tunic over his head. I watched from where I lay, wary of what was to come. He hurriedly strapped on sword, dagger, and a small pouch, and secured them to his belt. Keir looked me in the eye, leaning down with his free hand out, as if to touch me.

I flinched back.

He froze, then pulled back, looking grim. A voice was raised outside, announcing that his horse was ready. Keir clenched his jaw, turned and left through the flap. Within moments, the men and horses were gone. An odd silence descended, only to be broken by the cough from one of the remaining guards.

It took time for my body to relax, but eventually it did. The warmth of the tent, and the blankets pressed me down into the bed and my body seemed to sink deeper and deeper with each breath. My heavy eyelids closed, and I drifted off on a lake of warmth and darkness.

The next I knew, I was on my side, looking at the tent wall. I lay for a while, thinking about nothing really. Or perhaps, trying hard to think of nothing. After a bit, my stomach gave out a rumble. Then other parts of my body started demanding attention. So I stirred, and sat up.

Only to realize that I was stark naked under the blankets and furs.

I clutched the coverings to me, and remembered where I was. What I was.

The tent was a big one, and seemed to be made of hides. The floor was covered with all sorts of woven mats in blacks and browns. There was a table made of tree trunks and rough-hewn planks, with fat, short stumps around it as seats. Three braziers gave off heat. The bed where I lay was huge, with many pillows, and a large dark fur that covered the entire expanse. There was no sign of the shift. Or of any other clothing. Maybe slaves were kept naked? I shivered at the thought.

Part of the tent wall twitched, and I could see someone peering inside through the flap. A very short man, bald as an egg, popped in. I stared openly. His right eye glared at me. The left eye was gone, and the entire side of his face was horribly scarred. The flesh was mottled, with no hair. The ear was gone, and the left corner of his mouth seemed stiff and unmoving. Belatedly I remembered my manners. I focused my gaze on his one good eye, and fumbled for a greeting in his language. "Good morning."

He glared at me. "I am Marcus, Token-bearer and Aide to the Warlord." There was obvious pride in his voice. He stepped back, then re-entered the tent with a bundle in his arms. "Hisself left instructions to feed you when you woke. Hisself gave me an idea of your size." Marcus frowned and eyed me critically. "We'll see how close he came to the mark." He placed the bundle on the end of the bed and moved off to the tent wall on the other side.

I clutched my blanket closer and cleared my throat. "Where did the Warlord go?"

Marcus moved another flap to reveal a smaller chamber beyond. Apparently, this tent was larger than I thought. As Marcus moved, I could see that the scarring also covered his left arm. The skin had an odd texture to it, with no hair that I could see. It was hard not to stare. "Hisself is dealing with attacks on the herds." He turned. "You'll be washing first, then food." His lopsided mouth seemed grim.

I ran my hand through my hair. "Wash?"

"Aye." He nodded toward the smaller room. "I'll fetch water."

He left. I scrambled out of the bed, dragging the blanket with me. I grabbed the bundle and went into what appeared to be a privy area. Here, the floor was of hides, except for a small wooden platform in the center. Rough-hewn benches lined the walls, and there were tree trunks scattered about, and rough-hewn boards formed a table of sorts. There were what I assumed to be chamber pots under the benches.

Marcus bustled in with a steaming bucket, dropped it with a grunt, then left. I washed my face and hands quickly, and pulled on the clothes. There were trous of brown cotton, and a tunic of a red-brown cloth, like the shift, but heavier. It all fit well. Some thick socks and a pair of brown shoes that were a bit too big. As I dressed, I could hear men moving about outside, apparently guards. The sounds made me nervous, and I hurried to get into my clothes.

When I emerged, cleaner and more awake, food was laid out on the table. Marcus stood next to the table, a small pitcher and bowl in his hands. He gestured and I sat on one of the stumps and eyed the groaning board. "Are you eating with me?"

"No." Marcus frowned at me. "Hold out your hands."

Puzzled, I held them out. He placed the bowl beneath them, and poured water over them, muttering some words I couldn't hear. He nodded to a cloth on the table, and I dried my hands. Marcus seemed satisfied. "Hisself says you need to eat. Tuck in to this, now."

Nothing looked familiar. The meat had been chopped up into small pieces. The bread was flat, but soft. There was no knife, or fork. I picked up a piece of the flat bread, and dipped it into the meat. I took a bite, and was pleasantly surprised to find that it tasted good. Marcus nodded, as I took a second bite. There were grains as well, and I found that more of the food made its way into me then I had thought possible.

Marcus poured a mug of kavage for me, setting down a small bowl of white pellets as well. "We've no sweetening for this just now." I took the mug anyway, and dared a sip. It was better then what Rafe and the others had made. I eyed the white pellets, and reached out for one. It felt slightly soft, like a piece of dried whey. I popped it in my mouth, and bit down.

A horrible, bitter taste flooded my mouth.

Marcus had drifted away, moving around the tent as I ate, straightening as he went. Not that it was necessary, the sleeping area was very neat and plain in its furnishings. Too neat. There was no place to spit the stuff out. I screwed up my face and swallowed, followed by a long drink of kavage. Whatever that stuff was, it was awful.

Finally, I reached a point where I could eat no more. Marcus grunted and started to clear away the dishes. "Now, Hisself says, rest and sleep. He will be back for the night meal."

I nodded but really had no mind to go back to bed. "Marcus, do you know a Simus? He was one of the wounded—"

I did not have to finish. Marcus was nodding his head as he balanced the dishes in his arms. "Oh yes, that one is a snarling bear. Unhappy at everyone and everything." He frowned. "How do you know Simus?"

"I treated him in the city."

"Treated?" Marcus's one eye glared. "You treated his wound?"

I nodded.

He sniffed. "A warrior-priest, you think you are?"

I stiffened. "I am a healer. I would like to see him."

"Healer, eh?" He rolled his one eye. "Well . . ." he shrugged. "Gets you out from underfoot." His eye focused fiercely. "You understand that you are to take nothing except from the Warlord's hands? Nothing at all?" At my hesitant nod, he placed the dishes back on the table. "Come."

Marcus took me outside. It was only then that I realized how big the tent was. It was divided up inside, to make the sleeping area and other rooms. This flap led to a bigger area that seemed like a large meeting room. Here too, wooden blocks and sections of trees were about, with pillows and a raised platform at the end of the room.

Marcus led me past that, and held open the tent flap for me

to exit into the open. There were two guards standing at the entrance, and they acknowledged Marcus with a nod of their heads. I stepped out and got my first glimpse of the camp. Marcus didn't follow.

We were on a slight rise, down in the valley below Water's Fall. I swallowed when I saw its walls rising in the distance. From here, the camp spread out before us. There were tents everywhere, varying in size and placement, broken up with fire pits. There were horses everywhere, in clusters picketed near the shelters, and a herd that roamed the open expanse in the fields around the camp. Given its size, I could easily believe that the camp housed ten thousand men. It was huge, and seemed to stretch out all around us. It also seemed very quiet. "Where is everyone?"

Marcus grunted from inside the tent, and the two guards exchanged grins. "Sleeping off the celebration last night." He pointed some ways off. "That is the tent of Simus." He fixed me with that eye again, and I found myself taking a step back. "You go straight there, understand?"

I gulped, and nodded. He grunted again and folded his arms over his chest, making it clear that he intended to watch.

I moved off, walking on what appeared to be a beaten roadway. I had been a bit surprised when he said I could go, but now that I had seen the size of the camp, I understood. There would be no escape, even if that had been my intention.

The wide path between the tents had been beaten down by the passage of many horses. The shoes I had been given clomped through the bent grass. The sun was in and out of the clouds. Pennants snapped on the poles in front of various tents, of such bright colors that I had to stop and admire them. How did they get such bright colors? I wondered if they were decorative, or had other meanings. The pole in front of Simus's shelter had quite a few, in a wide variety of colors and shapes. One look over my shoulder told me that Marcus was still watching me. I stopped before the closed flap, suddenly uncertain. Simus might welcome a healer, but what welcome would there be for a slave?

Before I had time to make a decision, the flap opened and

Joden's face appeared. It lit up when he recognized me. "I thought I heard someone out here. Come in, come in. No guards with you?" He stepped back, holding the flap open. "Simus, here's someone new to listen to your grousing." I ducked in and stood there blinking.

This tent was smaller than the one I had just left. There was a back area, but the front was kind of a sitting room with wooden blocks and pillows and a large brazier in the center that gave off a low heat. Simus was on a platform, propped up on pillows and covered with blankets. He glared at me as I came through the opening, but his face cleared when he recognized me. "Little healer!" He laughed, his white teeth flashing against his dark skin. "Welcome!"

I relaxed, and returned his smile. "Greetings, Simus. How are you?"

Simus gestured at Joden. "I am fine, but for this ox telling me that I cannot get out of this bed." He glared at Joden, who returned the look. "Come, take a look, and tell me what you think."

I knelt as Joden uncovered the wound and removed the bandage. I looked at the wound with a great deal of satisfaction. It was coming together nicely, and there was no sign of problems. "It looks well." I started to put the bandage back in place, but Joden stopped me.

"Let me get clean ones, Warprize." He moved to the back of the tent and disappeared behind the flap.

There was a cough outside the tent flap. "Come!" Simus called.

A large, blond man with a scraggy beard entered the tent. "Greetings, Simus."

"Greetings, Iften." Simus's words were welcoming, but his face was reserved. I stayed where I was, daring a glance up at the big man. Not so tall as Simus, he was broad and strong, with big, rough hands. He glared down at me, then flicked his eyes to Simus's leg. "A bad wound, Simus. Will you walk again?"

"If he is careful," I answered. "And follows my advice."

Iften stiffened, but did not respond. I could feel his eyes on the back of my neck, and they weren't friendly. I didn't move, staying still and silent for fear that slaves weren't supposed to talk. I kept my eyes on Simus's leg. Iften continued, ignoring me. "I wish words, Simus. This peace is madness."

"Madness? Keir has won his victory, and achieved more than any had hoped." Simus gestured toward me with his left hand. His right was buried in the blankets, and seemed curiously stiff. "You swore oaths to Keir, knowing his plans. Are you breaking them? Or perhaps you envy him his warprize, eh?"

Iften growled behind me. "She's not—"

"Have a care, Iften. You hold no token." I darted a glance to see that Simus's face held a deadly look, which eased as he leaned back against his pillows. "The skies were with me. The warprize saved my life and leg." Simus stressed the word.

Iften snorted. "Your life was saved by—" He cut off his words when Joden stepped back in, fresh cloths in his hand. Joden's face closed off when he saw Iften. Without a word, he handed me the fresh bandages, then stepped back. I took them without comment, and started to work, aware of a curious tension between the men.

Iften cleared his throat, reached in a pouch at his belt and pulled out a strip of small bells. "I would have words, Simus. Alone."

Simus kept his smile, but the look in his eyes changed. "I am speaking with the warprize, Iften. If you wish to wait . . ."

Iften snarled. "I will return." He stomped past Joden, stuffing the bells away and left quickly.

Joden let out a breath I had not realized he was holding. "Simus . . ."

Simus pulled his right hand out from under the blanket, turning his head to give Joden a hard look. "Pah, you worry too much. Iften is all piss and wind."

Joden busied himself with a container of kavage, answering in a quiet, worried voice. "He was a candidate for Warlord, and holds influence with many."

"And lost the challenge for both Warlord and Token-bearer." Simus snapped back. "Iften's a fool, but an honorable one. He'll not challenge out of season." Joden didn't respond, but a curtain fell over his face. "Work in the shadows, yes. Challenge? No. Leave it to me, old friend." Simus softened his voice. "You've material for a hundred songs now, eh? With more to come." Joden scowled, but Simus held up a hand. "Yes, there are problems. We will deal with them. Together." Simus smirked. "With me at your side, and Keir's support, who can stand against us?"

Joden relaxed, and rolled his eyes. "You've conceit enough for all three of us."

Simus laughed. "It's well that I do!" He grinned at me as I finished my task and sat back on my heels. "What say you, little healer?"

"Is there any of the fever's foe left?"

Simus barked out a laugh. "Your warriors took it before we were released."

Joden chuckled. "One tried to get the kavage pot from Rafe, but when he smelled the contents he dropped it to the ground and kicked it. Rafe scrambled after it and has it still."

I frowned, not liking this. There was always a danger of fever, even at this stage. "Maybe there is a healer here in camp that would have more."

Simus growled. "No. Our warrior-priest was killed in one of the skirmishes a few days before my capture." He sighed. "I wish no man death, but he caused more trouble than it was worth to have him along. He opposed Keir at every turn."

"Besides," Joden added. "I have never seen anything like that stuff you gave us."

I perched among the pillows. Joden reached out toward me with a full mug of kavage, and then hesitated, as if not sure I'd accept. I took it, and smiled my thanks. He smiled in return, a big wide smile, and Simus's smile echoed his as Joden served them both. Joden also produced a bowl of the little white pellets and held it out. "Gurt?"

I managed not to wrinkle my nose in disgust. "No, thank you."

Mug in hand, Simus growled and pinned me with a glare. "When can I get up and out of this tent?"

Ah, the familiar cries of a healing warrior. This I could deal with. I took a sip of kavage first, and the bitterness of the liquid burned in the back of my throat. "Not for at least five days . . . maybe more. If you stress the wound it could split open." I smiled, trying to soften the effect of my words. "You would spoil my hard work."

Simus looked away, scowling. "It's fine."

I knew that look. He was going to get up and move, regardless. No different from any Xyian warrior. I glanced over at Joden and caught his worried frown. Well, there's more than one way to treat a wound. I leaned back on the cushions. "I am sure that you are right." I let a frown cross my face. "Of course that is what Lanis told me after I bound up his foot when it had been sliced up in a stag hunt." I shook my head, looking into my mug. "Lanis was a great bear of a man. Told me that it was a scratch and nothing more. Then he went off to drill his men and marched right along side them." I looked over at Joden. "The next time I saw him was when they brought him to me. The wound had split open and putrefied. I did what I could, but the wound would not come clean." I casually looked over at Simus. I had his complete attention. "He wept like a child when I had to cut off his foot." I took a swig of kavage.

"How did he fare then?" Joden asked quietly.

"Oh well, the foot came off, but the blood poisoning had spread up into his leg." I played with one of the tassels on the pillow. "It started to turn black and swelled to twice its size." I took another drink. "The puss just oozed out. It was a shame, but we had no choice. A few days later I took his leg off at the knee." I stared at the coals in the brazier. "I really thought I had gotten all the bad flesh out and that Lanis would make it."

Simus coughed. I looked up and smiled at him. "The stump looked great. I was really proud of the work I had done."

Simus cleared his throat. "How did he fare after . . ."

My face fell. "The blood poisoning got into his brain. We dosed him heavily with our best herbs, but he died screaming in agony." I let the silence go on for a bit. "Could I have some more kavage, please?" I held out my mug to Joden, who filled it woodenly. "Oh, but that was nothing compared to . . ."

After the second cup of kavage, Simus was grey, Joden looked faint and I felt wide awake and full of energy.

I wondered what was in that stuff.

I didn't stay much past the second mug. Once his color came back, Simus looked tired. I knew that he should rest. So I stood, said my farewells, and left the tent. Joden followed me out, saying that he needed more wood for the fire. Once outside, he put his hand on my shoulder. "My thanks. Simus will listen to you."

I looked up. "I hope so. I didn't make those stories up."

Joden shuddered.

"Joden, where are the tents of the healers?" I frowned. "I am sure that they must have more fever's foe, or something like it."

"The warrior-priests do not share their knowledge," Joden pointed off behind the tent and further down the rise to a group of tents clustered together. "His tent was there." He hesitated. "My thanks again, Warprize. For the life of my friend."

I studied him for a moment. "You used my name before, Joden."

He smiled ruefully. "You are the warprize now."

I grimaced, and turned to leave as he returned to the tent. I moved but a few steps toward Keir's tent when I heard it. The sound of a whip being applied to someone's flesh. I hesitated, and turned toward the sound, taking a few steps between the tents. A quick glance told me that the guards weren't paying that much attention, so I moved a bit farther and looked toward the sound.

Behind the tents a man was tied to a post, stripped to the waist, his back bloody. Two men were standing there, one lashing at him with a whip. I knew military discipline was harsh, Father had talked about it. But it was one thing to talk of something, another to see. The lash fell with a regular rhythm, the man making harsh grunts as they landed. I froze in fear, horrified, as they stopped, untied him and watched as he dropped soundlessly to the ground. The other men picked him up by the arms, dragged him to the warrior-priest tent, and dropped him just inside the flap. They walked off, as if he was no longer their concern.

I expected some kind of outburst, some kind of response from inside the tent, but nothing happened. There were bedrolls, of warriors sleeping around open fires, but none stirred. I could still see the man's foot in the tent entrance. No one was helping him.

The camp around us was stirring a bit more. I could see men moving about with weapons and horses, bent on various tasks. He'd be found eventually. But if he roused, and rolled over into the dirt . . . I took a tentative step forward, then another. There was no outcry, no calls of 'escaping slave'. I hurried forward to help. The man's foot never twitched as I carefully raised the flap of the main entrance and went inside.

I was hit with a terrible stench first thing. Gasping, I covered my nose with my shirt and looked around. What in the Goddess's name . . .

It was a large tent, with fewer cots then had been up at the castle. Men lay in them, some moaning. The stench came from the overflowing slop pots under each cot. The man at my feet was unconscious, but breathing. From the look of it, none of these men had been tended, or bathed recently. There was no one about that looked to be caring for the men at all.

I staggered back out into the light and air, wiping my streaming eyes. I looked around, furious at this lack of care. There appeared to be some dozen warriors, sleeping around a fire pit at the side of the tent. The large cauldrons nearby told me that it was probably used for laundry. I stomped over, braiding up my hair as I went. Sure enough, these men looked healthy and sleeping off a drunk.

I hauled off and kicked the nearest one in the shins.

He yelled, coming out of the blanket. I had already moved on, kicking each body in quick succession. Their curses filled the air. I was unimpressed.

"Are you tending the men in that tent?" Spittle flew from

my lips as I shouted, I was that angry. "How dare you sleep while men are suffering?" The one I was yelling at rubbed his face, looking at me owl-eyed. A hand came from behind me, gripped my upper arm and spun me around.

"What business is it of yours, dog? Eh?" A big blonde woman towered over me, clearly a veteran of long battles and hard living. The wonder of a woman warrior escaped me at the time, since she gave me a hard shake, her fingers digging into the muscle. I tried to pull away, but had no luck. I glared up at her.

"Those men in the tent need help while you laze by the fire."

She shook me harder, and my hair came tumbling down. I braced my feet, trying to yank my arm free. That made her madder. I watched her other hand swing up to strike me.

The men grabbed her upraised hand, and voices raised, urging her to stop. One leaned over, whispering frantically. The veteran paled, dropped my arm like it was poisonous, and backed away. I rubbed my arm and followed her, step for step. "How can you leave men like that, while you take your comfort?" I stopped and took a deep breath, trying to calm down. They started to offer excuses and explanations, but I was in no mood to hear them. I spit on the ground before them. "That for your stories." I gestured to the cauldrons. "Get the fires going and heat water, since that seems to be all you are good for." With that I stomped back to the tent. I turned before I entered. "But don't one of you set foot in this tent with these men. Do you understand me?" I did not wait for a response.

With water and much coaxing, I got the whipped man onto a cot, where he passed out again. I struggled to get the sides of the tents rolled up to air out the place. It was not a job for one person, but I'd be thrice damned before I'd ask for any help from the uninjured warriors outside the tent. Once that was accomplished, I moved through the tent and checked each one quickly. The majority were recovering from wounds although a few were clearly feverous. One had a bad cough that worried me greatly. They all had warm blankets, although it was clear that none of those had been changed in some time.

I stomped back outside and hollered at those lazy dolts. "Get some kavage and food for these men." I stomped back in. I didn't wait to see if I was obeyed. They'd feel my wrath if I wasn't.

There were clean blankets and bedding in an area at the back. A table was spread out with some jars, knives and other tools. Most of the jars held nothing I recognized, but one had a thick, gooey substance. I held it to my nose, and knew it immediately. Boiled skunk cabbage. I tried some on my inner wrist, and felt the tingle. There was soap as well. I made a quick round, assessing them, trying to decide who to aid first. There were five, and it quickly became clear these men were not mistreated, but had been neglected. The bloody back was in need of aid first, then I'd see to the others.

Hot water was waiting by the tent entrance, and I bathed the poor man's back, wishing for my basket of medicines. Thankfully, the man didn't rouse as I used the skunk cabbage to clean the wounds. I moved on to the others, bathing sweating faces and chests, easing their misery, checking wounds. I noted the ones that would need more treatment in the way of medicines and herbs as we moved along. Goddess knew where I'd get the medicines, but that was a problem for later.

A young boy appeared soon after I started, a gangly child with red hair and brown eyes. He was loaded down with kavage, warm biscuits and gurt. He seemed startled to see me, but cheerfully agreed to help. He had a tendency to talk, mouth running like a mountain brook as he gave each man some food and kavage. But his piping voice was a contrast to the rough tones of warriors and put smiles on all our faces.

Food and care roused the men, and with help, most could manage to get themselves clean. That bunch outside at least managed to keep a supply of hot water coming. I had started a pile of dirty linens outside the tent. When the blonde suggested that they aid me, I didn't say a word. I just pointed at the pile of linens. They took the hint.

The red-haired lad popped up next to me as I was cleaning

a gashed forearm. "I's done, warrior. I's saved ya some bis-cuits and kavage, though they be cold now."

"I'm not a warrior." I replied absently. "I'm a healer."

His eyes got large suddenly. "You're the warprize."

I reddened but kept working. My patient however, jerked up his head, and stared at the boy. "Warprize?"

"Lie still." I snapped at the man. He did just that, and made no further complaint.

The lad leaned over my shoulder and craned his long neck. "What ya doing?"

"Cleaning out this wound. It's soured." This was the worst of the injuries, and I was concerned about this man's condition.

He didn't pull back. "How can ya tell?"

"Smell."

He drew in a breath through his nose, which wrinkled in disgust. "That's the smell?"

I nodded as I tied off the bandage.

He seemed to think for a minute. "I's need get back, they'll be looking for me. I's be back later, with some soup and bread." He took a step away, then turned back. His brown eyes focused on me thoughtfully. "You're not like a warrior-priest, is ya?"

"I am a healer."

He looked confused, but smiled anyway. "I's can ask ya questions? You don't mind?"

"Of course I'll answer your questions." I looked up into his eager face and had to smile. "What's your name?"

"I's Gils." He grinned, "I's be back with the supper." Off he went, whistling down the path.

At last, we were done. Each man was warm, clean, treated, and fed. Time to start the last chore. I started at the far end of the tent and worked my way toward the entrance, carefully taking each slop pot and emptying it into a large bucket that looked to be for that purpose. I then took the bucket by the handle and walked it out of the entrance of the tent, passed the slackers, who were by the large fires trying to look busy. And innocent. On my first trip, one had approached me to help, but I had glared him off. Now they just sat and watched. Each time I walked past, they seemed to sink lower in their seats by the fires.

I emerged from the tent with the last bucketful to a sky faintly tinged with pinks and yellows. I didn't even glance to the sides, but set my weary eyes on the latrine. A slight noise distracted me, and I looked off to the side to see the slackers standing there at attention, looking rather pale. From behind me I heard a cough, and I turned quickly. Too quickly, as the bucket slopped over on to my trous.

There sat Keir on his warhorse, all black leather and armor, leaning forward, arms crossed on the saddle before him, looking angry and grim.

I blinked.

He raised an eyebrow, and spoke in a calm and even tone. "Would someone care to explain why the warprize is cleaning slop pots?"

I drew myself up, being careful with the bucket this time. "Because these *bragnect* are not worthy of the task." There were gasps from behind me. I ignored them. I turned and headed to the latrine to finish my task.

I'd have to remember to ask Joden what that word meant.

When I had finished my job and rinsed the empty bucket, I turned and walked back up the rise. The Warlord was still there by the tent. The warriors that had been standing there were gone. Keir dismounted, secured his horse, and followed me into the tent without a word.

I stood there for a moment surveying my handiwork. The tent smelled clean and fresh, and the men were resting in comfort. Keir moved past me, and started talking to his men, moving through the tent with ease. I went over to a stool near where they stored what medicines they had, and started sorting them. At least, that was what I pretended to do. Instead, I watched my master. I really hadn't had a chance to see him clearly. Well, other than this morning. My face warmed at the thought. He moved among them with no ceremony, no formality. Even knelt to speak to the whipped warrior.

While the movements of other warriors were controlled

and powerful, he was different. There was a flow, a grace that I had not seen before. The way he grasped one man's hand, how he would tilt his head and listen to another. And one breathtaking moment when he smiled at a comment and his face relaxed into a thing of beauty.

Which made my role as sex slave even more wildly absurd. Especially with women like the blonde around, tall and strong and . . . ample. With women warriors like that wandering the camp, how did one brown-haired, short and . . . well . . . less than ample warprize compare?

He finished, stood and looked around. I looked back down at the various bottles and jars and really had no idea what was in them at all. As he walked over to me, it suddenly occurred to me that I had not done as Marcus had bidden me. I stood when he approached, but kept my head down.

"There will be men coming with the evening meal who will tend these men."

I looked up quickly, scowling.

"Different men, not the ones that were here earlier." Keir looked around. "Our supper is waiting for us." He held open the flap and waited for me to go first. I paused and looked up at him. He just stared back, noncommital. No anger that I could see. I stepped through and waited for him to retrieve his horse. I thought he would mount, but he grabbed up the reins and started walking. I followed behind, but he waited for me to move up beside him. Then he wrinkled his nose. The horse snorted, and shook its head. Keir moved to the upwind side and we proceeded on.

I cleared my throat. "I checked on Simus. He is doing very well."

No response. I continued. "He wants to be up and moving, but I think I convinced him to stay off the leg for another day or so."

Still no response. I sighed and decided to shut up. The sun was almost gone now, the colors of the night sky fading into black over our heads. We were getting closer to his tent, and I was getting nervous. Finally, I blurted out, "Are you going to punish me?"

Silence.

"One of the warriors had been beaten, and just dumped inside the tent." Nervously, I blithered on, afraid of the silence. "I couldn't just leave him lying there. Those men needed aid, they had no one to help them, no one to care for . . ." My voice trailed off and died at the expression on Keir's face.

"Marcus became concerned when you did not return. He sent for me, and I have been searching for you. It looks bad to lose one's warprize on the very first day." The voice was quiet, his face unreadable.

"Are you going to punish me?" My voice cracked slightly.

"No." Keir handed his reins to one of the guards who came up. He turned with an odd expression on his face. "I won't need to."

Just then, the tent flap pulled back. I turned, startled, to find one very angry Marcus standing there. His scarred face transformed into a snarl of rage.

I gulped, and stepped back a pace, bumping into Keir.

"Where have the likes of you been?" His voice cut through the night. "Had to send Hisself out to find you, that I did." He moved back to allow me to step into the tent. "How hard is it to find the tent of Simus? Eh? Then return here?" he glared at me, his hands on his hips. "Where have you been?" He frowned, then drew in a deep breath. His eye widened and his face screwed up in disgust. Keir had followed me into the tent, and I heard a soft chuckle from behind me. Marcus's glare deepened as he raked his eye over my clothes. I looked down. For the first time I noticed the stains and wrinkles. I swallowed hard and looked over my shoulder for help.

None was forthcoming. Keir arched an eyebrow at me. "I'll return after awhile." I could have sworn he grinned as he turned away and left the tent.

"No sense, no sky-blessed brains." Marcus grabbed me by the shoulder and pushed me into the back sleeping area. "Been rolling in the muck pits, eh?" He vanished for a moment and returned with a sheet. "Strip and wrap up in this."

"Marcus, I . . ."

That one eye glared at me fiercely. I grabbed the sheet and held it to me as I slid out of my shirt.

"Hisself says 'take care of warprize, look after warprize.'" Marcus stomped off with the shirt. I took the opportunity to shed the rest and get the sheet wrapped around me. His voice floated out of the other room. "Doesn't tell Marcus that the warprize doesn't have the brains that the elements gave a gosling." He stomped back in and gathered up my stuff, holding it at arms length. He fixed me with another glare. "Standing there? When there is hot water going cold?" He gestured into the privy area.

I moved rapidly, but with some dignity into that room, closing the flap behind me. Marcus followed me in. "Stand there." He pointed to the wooden platform in the center. "Water drains out below. You understand? Or do I need to wash you myself?" His one eye cut into me as I shook my head and clutched my sheet tighter around me.

Exasperated, he flung up his hands. "Warprize you may be, but nothing there I've not seen before." With that he stomped out, but his voice pierced the canvas as he left. "Gosling? Did I say gosling?" He growled out the words. "More like the brains of an ox."

I cringed back from the door, and stood for a moment, getting my heart and breath under control. Really, Marcus was no different from Anna, right? I kept trying to convince myself of that as I turned and found four buckets of water steaming there, and soap and scrub rags waiting on a small table. Marcus was still talking, his voice fading in and out as he moved about. Thankfully, I couldn't make out the details.

There were stones under the platform and I realized that it had some sort of drain underneath it. I dropped the blanket, stood on the platform, and carefully poured some of the first bucket over my head and body. The warm water felt wonderful. I grabbed the soap and rags and started to lather, working over every inch of my body and up into my hair. I missed the great pools of the castle bath house, where you could soak in the warm water up to your neck. But this must pass for luxury in an army camp. I relished the feel of the mild soap on my body. I closed my eyes at the feel of the grime of the day washing away.

"Need help with the water?" Marcus growled, calling from the outer room. "Not be making a mess in there that this one has to clean?"

I froze in the act of stepping off the platform to reach the next bucket of water. I looked at the floor of the tent and decided that modesty was not worth more of his anger. "Yes, please." I called, as I returned to scrubbing my hair, trying to keep the suds from flying about.

Suddenly, there was a small amount of water trickling down over me, rinsing the suds from my hair and body. Grateful for the help, I quickly finished the scrubbing, and used my hands to rinse the soap from my body. The water continued to come down in a steady small stream. It felt wonderful.

"Thank you, Marcus. I feel much better." I reached blindly for the towel that had been laid out on the table. One was placed in my grasping hand.

"Good."

That was not Marcus.

My hands jerked convulsively to cover myself when I opened my eyes to stinging soap, and up into blue eyes, but I stilled them. I was his property after all. I dropped my gaze and clutched the towel. Keir took it from my hands and wrapped it around me. He took another one and wrapped up my dripping hair.

Without a word, he scooped me up, walked into the bedroom and sat me on the edge of the bed. He stepped back, then sat on one of the tree trunks. I used the towel to work the remaining water out of my hair, keeping my eyes downcast. Fingers through my hair would have to suffice, since I had yet to see a comb. There was a bundle of clothing on the edge of the bed next to me.

"What scent did you have on your hair last night?"

"Vanilla." I shivered as his eyes roamed over me. He stood, and started to remove his armor and weapons, placing them on the bench by the bed. I gathered up the clothes that had been put on the edge of the bed, and very casually moved back toward the bathing area.

Just as I was about to dart within, he spoke. "I liked it."

I froze, but he said nothing else, merely continued to work at the straps on his breastplate. I took a step, dropped the flap, then dried and changed with all the speed I could. Once clothed, I felt much better. The same kind of tunic and trous this time, although black in color. I folded up the drying cloths, and stepped back into the sleeping area.

Keir was on a bench, removing his boots. Dishes were rattling off somewhere. Marcus must be making our meal.

Keir glanced up.

I risked a smile. "I think that Marcus is calming down."

"Really?" His expression did not change, but there was a hint of laughter in his voice. "Marcus?" he called out. "The warprize did not eat at noon."

The rattling dishes stilled and I heard an enraged cry. I hunched down as Marcus stomped into the room. "What? You think you live on air and light?" He glared at me, with both hands on his hips. "City dwellers." He said it with disgust, and switched his glare to the larger man.

"I had kavage with Joden and Simus." I voiced a small protest.

Marcus focused on me again. It was amazing how much anger one eye could hold. "You were told to take nothing except from the hand of the Warlord."

I cringed and looked over at Keir, who gazed at us both with a straight face. This time I was sure I saw a glimmer of laughter in those eyes.

"Marcus is right." Keir's eyes grew serious. "While Simus and Joden have my trust, you are not to take anything from anyone else." He rose from the bed and went to take his turn in the privy room. Marcus let loose a stream of words under his breath, and stomped out, using words and phrases that I did not understand. I sat there quietly as he stomped back in with two buckets of water for Keir. He was still muttering under his breath when he emerged, radiating anger with every step. I opened my mouth to say that I couldn't have eaten if I couldn't take food from another's hand, but closed it quickly. Silence seemed wiser.

Marcus returned with a heavy tray and started the dishes to rattling as he placed them on the table. "No food." He transferred dishes at a rate that made me fear for my life. "Didn't rest." He stepped back, surveying his handiwork. "Rolled in muck pits, that she did." That one eye was focused on me again. "Sit." He pointed to the chair.

I sat.

"Hands."

I held them out, and Marcus poured the water over them, muttering something that did not sound like a prayer.

"Eat." He crossed his arms.

"Shouldn't I wait for . . ." My stomach chose that moment to express its interest in the food. At the sound, Marcus' sole eye tapered its focus and drilled into me.

"Eat."

I ate.

As soon as my mouth was full, Marcus started to explain, in detail, the meaning of the words 'food' and 'rest'. I decided that the wisest choice was to keep nodding and eating.

Finally, Keir emerged from the privy room. "Marcus."

Marcus stopped and looked over.

"Enough."

Marcus clamped his mouth tight, poured the water over Keir's hands, then stomped off, muttering.

The food in my mouth turned to straw. I managed to swallow, but it was a struggle. I'd no idea what to say, how to act, suddenly very aware of the bed behind me. I worried my lip, kept my face down, and focused on the table.

The Warlord was in no hurry. He helped himself to the food and started eating. After a bit, I decided that it looked odd, to sit without eating or talking, so I started back up as well, careful to take small bites.

"It was my fault."

I stopped chewing when he spoke. With a mouthful of food, I simply raised my eyebrows.

"The tents. I knew that our warrior-priest had been killed

in one of the battles. I meant to assign someone else to the wounded, but Simus went missing and in my rush, I forgot." He looked down and toyed with his food. "I apologized to the men."

I swallowed hard at the last and stared at him in disbelief.

Marcus chose that moment to come back into the tent, a wineskin and two goblets in hand. As he poured, he eyed us both. "Much good the food does, sitting on the table. Eat." He set the goblets down on the table, slung the wineskin on the back of Keir's chair, and cuffed Keir lightly on the head. "You as well, oh mighty one." Then he stomped off, still muttering to himself. I held my breath at his nerve. Keir smiled a wry smile, and reached for the meat.

Uneasy, I kept eating. Thankfully, Keir seemed more focused on his food than on me. I took another bite, determined to stay quiet, but something was bothering me. After a sip of kavage, I risked a question. "What of the other healers?" I asked. "Why didn't they just do what needed to be done?"

Keir shrugged. "There are no others."

"What?" I dropped my bread. "An army of this size, and you have no other healers? No assistants or apprentices?"

Keir pulled some bread from the loaf. "Every man in this army is a warrior. There are no healers. The men pick up some basic knowledge on campaign. Men assigned to the wounded are on punishment detail." He shrugged. "So it has always been."

"That's insane! With an army this size? What about wounds like Simus's?"

"Men die from them." His face was shadowed. "Either the wound kills them, or they are granted mercy."

I stopped, appalled to see his face full of pain. Someone this man had cared for had died that way.

Keir turned his head. "Marcus is coming."

I started shoveling food into my face. Marcus walked in and surveyed the table with a frown. He grunted, apparently satisfied and walked back out. As soon as I figured it was safe, I spoke. "That ends now." I glared at him. "That is what I do, part of what I am, and I am good at it."

He looked at me. "You would do this? Would ask to do this?"

I faltered and dropped my eyes. A little late to be remembering my place, but I'd be damned before I let those men be neglected. "I would." I risked a glance up, trying to read that expression, with no success. But hope grew when he nodded slowly. "You'll let me?"

He gave me a long look. "Yes. It would strengthen the peace, after the deaths."

"Deaths?" I asked, then remembered. "The horses?"

"Slain with bolts from crossbows. A weapon only Xyians use."

"You must get word to Xymund. He will find the—"

His look was dark. "What if he has ordered these attacks?"

"Xymund would not do that. He has given his oath, he has given—" I stopped, not wanting to think about that aspect. "He would not do that." Yet deep within I remembered the hatred in his voice when he talked to Warren about the horses of the Firelanders.

Keir seemed skeptical, and turned his attention to his plate. He seemed lost in thought for a moment. We ate in silence, and I wondered how far I could push. Finally, I took a drink of wine. "I will need supplies for the tent."

"Supplies?" He pushed his plate back with his thumb and just looked at me. I looked down at my plate and found it empty, as were the other dishes. Guess I was fairly hungry after all.

Marcus bustled in and cleared the dishes, leaving the skin and the goblets. He stood with a tray in hand and looked at me.

"Warprize."

I looked up, surprised.

He stared at me, no trace of his former anger, his voice calm. "I have heard of your actions this afternoon. That was well done." Then he scowled. "But next time I will truly give you the sharp edge of my tongue, you don't follow my direction. Yes?" He gave Keir a nod and bid us both good night.

I looked at Keir. He was leaning back in his chair, contemplating his goblet. I took another sip of mine. It was rich and fruity on my tongue.

Keir stirred. "Supplies? What do you need?"

"Herbs and the like. I need medicines, especially willow bark."

"Willow? What is that?" he asked, puzzled.

I opened my mouth, shifting on my seat. The rough wood of the stump caught at my trous, and I gasped, realizing what I was sitting on. I stood up, threatening to over turn the table, and knelt by my stool. Crowing in delight, I started to peel the bark off the wood. They'd cut the blocks from willow.

"Warprize?" Keir leaned forward to see what I was doing.

I laughed, and tore at the wood, stripping the drying bark off the block. I turned and held it up. "Willow bark!"

He frowned, not understanding.

"I can brew a medicine from this. It's called fever's foe." I shook my head. "I've been sitting on it all this time and . . ." I piled the bark on the table.

Keir laughed. I looked over and met his steady appraisal. "You are passionate about your trade." He cocked his head. "Your profession?"

I nodded.

He stood and stretched, taking his time. It was a treat to my eyes. Then he leaned over me, and I was caught by bright blue eyes.

"Let's explore what other passions you may have." With that he swept me up and over onto the bed.

5

I closed my eyes and clutched for a handhold as I was lowered to the furs. It had finally come, I wasn't ready, and yet . . .

I'd known my duty since I was a girl. I'd thought perhaps, at some point, that I'd lie with a man, one chosen for me by my father, a man bound to me by sacred oaths in a ceremony performed in the throne room of the castle. I'd thought my husband would honor and respect me, and maybe even come to care for me in time. But those dreams had faded over the years, since Xymund had been in no hurry to give me in marriage.

Now the hands on my body were the hands of a master, and there were no promises or bonds between us. No ceremony, no oaths, no idea of what my future held. I'd been given at the command of my king and I had obeyed, but my heart cried out for all the lost possibilities. Respect. Honor.

Love.

Just like the night before, Keir's hand pressed against my chest, over my heart. Its warmth blazed through my shirt, and drove all rational thought from my mind. The bed shifted as he lay down next to me, on his side, slightly pressing against my body. I drew in a deep breath, but when nothing else happened, I cracked open my eyes.

He'd moved forward, his face close to mine. Startled, I turned my face away ever so slightly, embarrassed by the intimacy. He leaned in and nuzzled my ear. As skin touched skin, I gasped at the contact. Undaunted, he placed a gentle kiss at the edge of my jaw. His warm breath tickled my cheek. He leaned in farther, and this time licked the same spot on my jaw, a light flicker of the tongue. I squirmed. His hand pressed me down slightly, as if to command my stillness. I managed to stop moving, but my breath was coming faster than normal. There were feelings as well, a kind of ache. A kind of longing.

I wanted to say something at that point, but he moved like a large cat, looming over me. His elbows were on either side, his legs pinning mine. I barely had time to note the look in his eyes before he captured my mouth with his.

I was swept away, by lips that tantalized and teased and took exactly what they wanted. He didn't just press lips together, he was using it all, mouth, tongue, and teeth. After a bit, he backed off to allow me to breathe. He didn't retreat, just pressed soft, small kisses at the corners of my lips as I desperately pulled air in.

His face held a satisfied look. One hand reached up to stroke my face gently. Keir moved his hand, running his fingers through my hair, spreading it out over the fur. His eyes flared with blue light.

"Want to know the best part of being a warlord?" came a hoarse whisper.

I bit my lip, puzzled by the question.

Keir's mouth curled up slowly into a smile. "I always get what I want."

His lips came down on mine, demanding, coaxing, then taking. Again and again, over and over, he brought me to the brink of something till I was unsure of where he ended and I began. At some point, I would be overwhelmed by it all, and a trace of fear would touch me. Each time, he would back off, calm me down with soft sounds and touches. Letting me take in air.

Then he would proceed to do it all over again.

I wanted more. My arms had been pinned down, and now I struggled to bring them up to enclose him, touch him. He chuckled, then moved slightly to give me room. My upper arm came in contact with Keir's hand, and I hissed slightly at the touch.

Keir froze, and moved back. "What's wrong?" He frowned. "I hurt you?"

I shook my head, confused by the comment. It was hard to think, since my body seemed to have other concerns. Keir was not convinced. He reached for my shirt and eased it open and down my arm.

"Who has done this?" Keir's voice was a growl.

I was startled. The man staring at me was one I had not seen before, his eyes cold, his face hard. I looked down, horrified to see bruises on my upper arm. Clearly, the fingerprints of a large hand, probably the woman warrior who had grabbed me.

"I will kill the one who has hurt you." Keir jumped from the bed and strode to the tent entrance. "Marcus." His voice whipped out. He started pacing in the space available.

"I—" I sat up and struggled to cover myself with the shirt. "It's nothing . . ."

Keir turned, his eyes like blue ice, and I froze. Dearest Goddess, he was serious. His eyes were filled with rage.

Marcus ran in, looking as if he had been roused from sleep. He took one look at Keir and was on his knee, head down. I struggled to cover myself, fumbling with the shirt.

Keir barely gave Marcus a glance. "Someone has injured the warprize." He stomped over and towered over me. His hands gently turned me so that the bruises were visible. "Look."

Marcus looked up. His eye widened at the sight. He dropped his eye again almost immediately. Keir pulled the shirt back up to cover my breast and shoulder. "Who did this?" he said, in a very calm, very deadly voice.

I took the example Marcus had set, sank down on one knee, and bent my head as well to let my hair conceal my face.

Keir resumed his pacing, moving like a caged animal. "I am waiting for an answer."

I swallowed. "Warlord, it was an accident. I was at the tents of healing, tending to those in need." My mouth was so dry I could barely get the words out.

"You've been hurt. No one touches what is mine." Keir was almost roaring, his anger white hot. I trembled at the force of his voice, but did not move or look up.

"Warlord, I was treating a wound." I swallowed hard, trying to get some moisture in my mouth. "The warrior was startled. The fault was mine."

"Are you trying to get yourself killed? Destroy the peace?" There was an odd note of anguish in his voice.

"No! I wouldn't betray—"

"You will tell me who it was. He will answer to me."

"No." I closed my eyes and held my breath.

Keir came to stand next to me. I could feel his hot glare, hear his heavy breathing.

Yet, somehow I knew that he would not hurt me. Slowly, I raised my head and looked up. His anger had not abated, it was merely held in check. Carefully, I reached out and placed my hand on his arm. The muscles underneath quivered with tension. "Warlord, I am unhurt. The bruises will fade."

He was unappeased. "You're under my protection. Whoever did this will pay for his actions."

"When the action was unintended?" I rose up slowly and moved my hand to his shoulder. I moved carefully, staying as close as I dared. I could just make out Marcus, still kneeling by the entrance. "A warrior taken unaware?"

"As Simus was in the garden?"

I nodded.

He seemed to understand, but had a grim expression on his face. "You are defying me." His voice rumbled, but it was softer then before.

"Only in defense of one who does not deserve your

wrath." I looked up into angry blue eyes. "Don't you take the occasional bruise when you practice with your weapons?"

"No." He snorted, but I could feel some tension leave his arm. "I am better than that."

"Well, I'm not." I shivered. "Forgive me."

"Marcus. Leave us." Marcus was out of the tent as fast as he had entered.

In no time, I was covered in the furs, warming up nicely. Keir lay beside me, on his side, head propped up with his hand. I yawned, trying to fight sleep, unsure of his expectations.

"You have no skill with weapons." It was more statement then a question.

"You mean, like a warrior?" It seemed an odd question.

"You can not defend yourself." His voice sounded odd.

I yawned again. "I can always run."

He snorted. There was a pause as my eyelids got heavier.

"You are untouched." His voice rumbled in my ear.

"I got bruised." I argued.

"No," he paused again. "I mean you are untouched. You have no children."

I sucked in a breath, suddenly wide-awake. "I am an unmarried Daughter of the House of Xy." I stared at the ceiling, and worried my lower lip. "I am . . ." I rolled my eyes and considered the absurdity of this conversation. It was hard to continue, but he waited patiently. I could feel his eyes on my face. "I was a candidate for a marriage of alliance. As such, I was . . . am . . ." The rest froze on my tongue.

"Untouched." He looked at me through half-closed eyes, studying me like prey. "Ignorant."

I blushed, then frowned. "I am a healer. A Master Healer. I am not ignorant. I have the knowledge. I just lack . . ."

"Experience." He raised an arm and brushed a curl off my forehead.

I moved my head away from his hand, but a huge yawn overcame me again. "That's right. Knowledge, but no experience."

"Yet you heal. You see . . ."

I could feel the heat on my cheeks. "Yes, I know what men

and women look like and I know what they do. I just haven't . . ."

"This is your peoples' way?"

"Yes."

He sighed and rolled over onto his back. As I watched, he closed his eyes and sighed again. Without opening his eyes, he spoke. "Sleep, Warprize."

I closed my eyes, wondering if I would ever hear my own name again.

I woke when something rumbled next to my ear.

There were voices, speaking softly. Keir was talking to someone. I wasn't really interested in opening my eyes. It was so warm and I felt so boneless under the furs. It felt so good to just lie there.

The voices stopped and footsteps faded off. Keir spoke softly. "I must be up. Sleep awhile longer." With that, he slid out, letting in cooler air, ignoring my mumbled protests. I crawled over into the warmth, trying very hard not to wake up. The splashing noises, and the scent of breakfast made that impossible.

Whatever was cooking smelled spicy. When my stomach made its opinion known, I sat up and let the furs pool around my waist as I adjusted my tunic, which had twisted in the night. I reached my arms up, twining them around each other and stretched, arching my back. When the bones in my back had realigned themselves I lowered my arms.

Keir was standing there, watching me.

He was naked from the waist up. Water still glistened on his face and neck.

He had the oddest look on his face.

I flushed and looked away. Once out from under the covers, I darted into the privy area. There was plenty of warm water left, and someone had left a change of clothes for me on one of the benches. I splashed through a wash as quick as I could.

When I emerged, Keir was already eating and Marcus was

standing there, his arms crossed. He pointed to the other chair, and I sat quickly. Marcus fixed me with his eye and didn't stop staring at me until I started eating. He gave me a last look and left the room.

Keir leaned back, a cup of kavage in his hands. "You wish to return to the healing tent?"

I nodded, my mouth full of some kind of porridge. He drank his kavage hot and bitter. I noticed that he did not add anything to it. "And check Simus, if I may."

"I am calling senel at the nooning. I want you to be there."

I nodded and wondered what a senel was.

Keir continued. "I am assigning two guards to be with you at all times."

I choked on my food.

Marcus had come in with more bread. "Good," he muttered, and left the room.

Keir held up a hand as I tried to clear my throat. "No arguments. I would have you protected, something you can not do for yourself."

I sputtered. "I am not helpless."

His eyes strayed to my upper arm. I flushed at the implication and opened my mouth to argue. He cut me off with a gesture. "If it is not acceptable, you may stay here, nap and let Marcus feed you." I heard an exclamation from the other room.

I glowered at Keir.

He was impervious. "I have sent for the guards. They will be here shortly." He finished his kavage and stood. I grabbed some bread and tore at it, trying not to watch as he strapped on his weapons.

Marcus came in and started to clear dishes. "It's for the best, Warprize." I glowered at my mug of kavage. "And yourself?"

"Simus and I need to talk," Keir responded.

"The attacks on the horses." Marcus's tone was grim, and he muttered something under his breath.

"Aye." Keir caught my questioning look. "Someone is shooting at the herds, killing horses. We believe they are your people."

I opened my mouth to deny it, but closed it with a snap. Keir was watching me carefully, but he said nothing further. I finished my food in silence, as Keir armed himself, and Marcus fussed.

Sounds at the outer entrance let me know that my guards were coming, and I quickly started to peel the bark off the stump I was sitting on. Marcus demanded to know what I was doing, as Keir moved to greet the guards. I looked up to see Prest and Rafe standing there, grinning like fools. I smiled when I saw them. Maybe this wouldn't be so bad after all.

Keir led the way, with Rafe and Prest flanking me. Marcus voice called out behind us. "Mind now, be here for the senel. With time to get cleaned up!"

Simus was not in the best of moods. "About time." He grumped as we entered his tent. Rafe and Prest took up positions outside. "What about these attacks? Any sign it's the damned city—"

Keir cleared his throat as I entered.

"Good morning, Warprize." Joden greeted me with a twinkle in his eye. "Be warned that Simus has not yet had enough kavage to be human."

Simus growled, and I almost laughed out loud. Who'd think a patient in a foul mood could be such a comfort? "I could come back later." I offered.

"No!" Simus struggled up on his elbows, furious, then drew a deep breath when he realized I was teasing. A small smile crept over his face. "Good Morning, Warlord. Warprize."

"Good morning, Simus of the Hawk." Keir sat on one of the stumps off to the side. "Can't say that I blame you for being in a foul mood." He gestured toward the leg. "I'd not have the patience to endure."

Simus glared at him. "Made all the harder when I get no word of what is happening—"

Keir held up a hand. "Let the warprize look at your leg."

"You talk while she works." Simus was pushing aside his

blankets and furs, exposing his leg. Joden moved to help him, and I knelt along side.

"There were no attacks last night. Bolts were found in the horses that were slain. We will discuss our actions at the senel that I called for this nooning."

Simus grunted. "Which of us uses crossbows? Even if we did, none of us would do such a thing."

"I've decided to send Iften to the Xyian King, to inform him of the attacks and to get answers."

"Iften?" Simus's full attention was on Keir now. "Why Iften? Why not go yourself?"

I looked over my shoulder, curious as to what Keir's response would be, only to find him giving me a veiled look. "I'll not leave camp."

"Ah, well. Maybe 'tis best. Let him show his true—"

Keir cut him off. "Let the warprize finish her work and be on her way. You and I have much to discuss. Including Joden."

I glanced at Joden, but his face was impassive. Simus was not so silent. "There's nothing to talk about."

"No?"

"No." Simus looked at Joden, then gave Keir a sly look. "Joden's not the first to deny mercy to a friend." When Keir didn't react, Simus grinned. "Joden and I will be at the senel."

"Simus . . ." Joden was standing there frowning.

Simus glowered at his friend. "We will both be there." He raised a hand to prevent Joden from saying anything further. I looked at both men's faces. Joden was clearly unhappy, and Simus looked angry. I didn't understand that at all, but Joden was uncomfortable. I cleared my throat and drew Simus's attention. He shifted his gaze, focusing his dark eyes on me. "Well?"

"It looks well enough. But only a few steps."

"Hah!" Simus brought his hand down into his fist. "You watch, little healer. I will dance out of this tent."

I rolled my eyes. "I am sure. But just in case, let Prest and Rafe support you for the first few steps." Simus grimaced, but was willing to put up with anything just to get a chance to walk, calling in my guards impatiently. Rafe and Prest supported him on each side as he rose from his bed and managed a few steps. Very quickly, he was grey and shaky from the effort. We got him back onto his pallet and Joden helped him get comfortable. Once that was taken care of I knelt and began to strip the bark of the stumps in his tent.

Simus coughed. "Warprize, what are you—"

I ignored him. "It's a medicine." I kept peeling. "I'll use it to brew fever's foe."

He rolled his eyes. "Oh, great joy. I must confess, little one, that muck tastes terrible."

Prest and Rafe left the tent, hands filled with bark. I moved to follow, with both hands full.

"I will see you at senel, little healer." Simus called after me.

I turned, and brandished my bundle as if to admonish him. He raised his arms to ward off a blow. "I know, I know. They will carry me to the tent." I smiled at him. I turned to find Keir in front of me.

He stepped in close, lifted my chin. "Be on time for senel." Then he kissed me, hard and fast. I just looked up at him when he pulled back. With a smug look, he nudged me on my way.

As we moved away from the tent I looked over at Rafe. "What is a 'senel'?"

He puzzled for a bit. "A gathering, a taking of advice from others, a . . ." He looked to Prest for help, but Prest just shrugged. Rafe rolled his eyes.

"Who will be there?"

"The leaders, Keir's . . ." He screwed his face up. "Secondaries? We call them warleaders." The morning sun caught the glint of metal off to the side. I turned my head to see a group of warriors in a large practice field. A tall woman was standing in the field, as a large horse raced toward her.

I stopped in my tracks. "What?"

Rafe chuckled. "Watch, Warprize."

Prest was giving her a sharp eye, and grunted. I turned

back to watch as the horse charged the woman. At the last moment, the horse brushed past her, and suddenly she seemed to leap into the saddle. There were shouts from the group watching as she swung the horse back toward them. She seemed pleased with her performance.

"How did she do that?" I asked.

"Practice," said Prest.

Rafe nodded his agreement. I gave him a doubtful look as we continued walking. "No, its true, Warprize. We all practice our riding skills in the same fashion. Each is required to be able to mount a galloping horse."

I sighed. "Rafe, you used my name in the city."

Rafe nodded. "True. But you are now the warprize."

Prest nodded in agreement.

At the healing tent all was well. It took almost no time to check the wounded, and take care of their needs. The worst was the one who'd been whipped, but he was still asleep, so I waited to check him. Instead, I started a pot of water boiling on one of the braziers and corralled one of the wounded into watching it. I was careful to explain that he had to add water as it boiled away. As I moved among the cots, the only problem was that I kept bumping into Prest and Rafe as they hovered over me. Finally, I turned to Prest.

"This is foolish. Go sit in a corner of the tent and watch me." Rafe frowned and opened his mouth to protest. I snarled. "Take your big feet, and go over there out of my way."

Prest laughed and pulled Rafe with him. They settled down off to the side. Soon, Rafe was working his sword with a whetstone. Prest appeared to be carving something from some wood. Some of the mobile wounded joined them, and they were laughing and talking quietly as I worked. But I noticed that one of them always had an eye on me.

I gathered up the boiled skunk cabbage and some clean cloths, and went to where the warrior lay sleeping on the cot. His back looked good under the bandage; the lash marks hadn't been as deep as I feared, and there was very little redness or swelling. The warrior stirred as I started to work more of the ointment into his wounds. "I know it hurts, but it will aid with healing. Lay as still as you can."

The warrior turned his head and looked at me with bleary eyes. "You a warrior-priest?"

Prest had moved up behind me with Rafe, who shook his head in disgust. "Sleeping on watch, Tant? When will you learn?" He crossed his arms over his chest. "When are you due back on?"

Tant blinked. "Nooning." He glanced at me again. "Where'd the warrior-priest come from?"

"She's the warprize," Prest responded.

Tant jerked, his eyes wide.

"Fool." Rafe turned. "Finish your work, Warprize. I'll get kavage so we can get him on his feet. If he doesn't report, its another lashing."

"The warprize?" Tant's voice was a squeak.

Finally, I had time to sit down and look at the supplies that were available to me. I sorted through the tables and baskets. It was pitiful. There were few herbs and none of the traditional remedies that I knew. One bottle smelled so vile that I asked one of the wounded what it was for. Turned out it was a well known remedy for coughs that was rubbed on the chest. It was made from goose grease and horse dung.

He offered to help me gather the makings. I declined, emptied the bottle and set it to soak.

A scream in the distance caught all of us by surprise. Rafe and Prest stood and moved to the tent entrance. I followed, emerging to find them gazing out at the practice field. I could just make out a crowd around a downed figure. There was all kinds of general ruckus, but no further screams.

Prest was sucking on his lower lip. Rafe looked gray. "I'll wager it's broken."

Prest nodded his head. Both men looked grim. I looked, but could see no one moving to render aid. "Will they bring them here?"

Rafe turned in surprise, his eyebrows raised. "Why? Most

like they'll just grant mercy where they lay." I looked at him, offended, and started off immediately toward the crowd. Prest and Rafe scrambled after me. "Warprize, where are you going?"

I ignored Rafe, and kept moving onto the practice ground and right up to the milling group. They were certainly upset, so much so that I had to push my way forward to get through.

I dropped down next to the wailing figure. It was a woman, the blonde who had leaped to her horse. She lay on the ground, her hands over her face, moaning. I cast a quick look at the leg, but could tell nothing through the leather trous. "Rafe, lend me your knife."

Silence cut through the crowd. The blonde gasped in horror and moved her hands. Even though her face was red and swollen, I recognized her. It was the woman who had grabbed my arm. Her eyes filled with fear, she covered her face again and started to wail.

Rafe slowly handed me his knife. "You'll take the leg, Warprize?"

At the question, the blonde threw her hands forward, as if to ward me off. Her face was filled with horror. "No, Skies, NO!" she shrieked. "I am cursed!" She keened in an ear-piercing tone.

I winced at the sound as I cut away her trous. It was clear that it was broken, but the skin was whole. It looked to be a clean break. The woman shrieked again as I touched her knee.

"Stop that! Are you such a coward?" The blonde looked at me, frozen but thankfully silent.

I gestured to Rafe. "We need a blanket to carry her to the tent."

"No, no, no." The blonde sobbed. "I cry mercy, rather than lose my leg. Mercy!"

I looked at her. "Silence!"

That got everyone's attention.

"Have I said that you will lose it? Love of the Goddess!" I cursed in my own language. "You'd rather die then let me heal this?"

Prest was standing behind me. "Heal?" The blonde's brown eyes stared at me from her tear-stained face.

I turned my head and looked up at him. "Yes, of course." From the expressions of those around us, I realized that there was no 'of course' about this for them. "A blanket. Now."

Prest nodded and one of the men ran off.

I placed a hand on her shoulder. "Lay back. Try to relax. I know it hurts, but I need you to stay still."

She grabbed at my arm, her sweaty palms trembling. "I won't lose it?"

"Not if you do what I say." I looked up again and focused on the closest man. "I need rawhide. One large piece and then strips. Can you get that?"

He nodded and ran off. I raised my voice to be heard. "I need rocks as well. Good sized, about the size of two fists." Two other men ran towards the river. "At least four," I called after them.

The first man returned with a large blanket in his arms. We managed to get it under her and hefted her up without jostling the leg too much. I urged them to go slow and careful as we carried her to the healing tent. Once there, I directed them to put her on an empty cot and started to strip her trous off. Looking up, I realized that the entire group was in the tent, all of them, watching me work. "Out."

"But . . ." Rafe objected.

"Rafe, you and Prest stay. The others leave."

"They want to watch, Warprize. Please."

I frowned. "Then roll up the sides of the tent, but have them stay out of the way." I continued to remove the trous. The blonde bit at her lip as I worked.

"What is your name?" I asked, trying to get her to focus on something else.

"Atira. Warprize, I am cursed, I know it. I am cursed. The elements . . ." She sobbed. "Because I hurt you."

"Hush, Atira. It's a broken leg, not a curse. An accident."

The other men entered, with about twenty more rocks then I really needed and lengths of rawhide. Gils popped up out of nowhere, and I had him cutting strips and wrapping the rocks so that I could use them as weights. I put Rafe and Prest at Atira's head and went to the end of the cot. I called over a tall, husky type and had him stand next to me. Atira was big, and I would need help setting the leg. I explained what we were going to do. The silence in the tent was absolute. I ignored the looks and the whispers, but it was unnerving. Everyone was fascinated by what I was doing. For a moment doubt crept in. What if I couldn't heal it? It was a clean break, but there were no promises with legs, and if the patient didn't obey me, it could end up healing crooked or . . .

Eln would have boiled me over a hot fire. I pulled myself back and focused on my work. The future belongs only to the Goddess, I'd have to leave it in her hands.

Once I was sure that everyone understood, we got ready. The two men braced Atira's shoulders, and she grabbed them, wrapping her arms around their hips. The other man took her foot gently in his hand and waited. I reached over and handed her a piece of willow bark to put between her teeth. "All right, Atira. Ten deep breaths, then we begin."

She nodded, closed her eyes, and took a deep breath. Then another. On her third breath, I grabbed her ankle with my helper and we pulled hard on her leg.

She exploded off the cot, her cries muffled by the bark. The men held her in place. My helper maintained the pull as I ran my hands over her leg. They kept the tension steady, increasing the pull until I felt the bone go together under my finger tips, and heard the familiar grating noise. Once it was in position, I secured the splints, and tied it off. I tried to move swiftly.

When the splints were in place I nodded, and they eased off the pressure. I concentrated on feeling the bone under the muscle. It felt right. They kept the foot elevated, as I wrapped the limb with a layer of soft bandages and then placed the wet rawhide over it. That was well secured with straps of leather, and we finally lay the leg back down on the cot. Atira was pale by now, and I deeply wished for a sleeping draught to give her. I tied the rocks and strips of rawhide to her ankle, hanging them over the edge of the cot. The pull would aid in keeping the leg straight.

I finally sat back on my haunches and wiped the sweat off my forehead. Atira looked at me, wide-eyed. "You lied!"

I looked at her in surprise. "I did?"

"You said 'ten breaths'." She glared at me.

I maintained my expression for as long as I could, then grinned at her. She was starting to relax and was fighting sleep. "My leg, Warprize?"

"Atira, it is a simple break. We will be careful, and go slow, but all should be well." I smiled at her doubting face.

"How long, Warprize?"

"It will take forty days to heal completely, Atira."

"Forty days?" Gils looked at me with horror in his eyes. "Forty days in this cot?"

"No, not forty days in the cot. Forty days to heal completely. She'll be able to use a crutch but that will be at least half of that. You can't risk putting weight on it before then."

"I will keep it." Atira's voice held awe. The men standing around remained silent, exchanging glances.

"You must lay still, as still as possible. It will mend. It will take time, bone is slow to grow. You must be patient."

One of the men let out a nervous laugh. "That will be hard for her. She is not the most patient of women!"

The resulting laugh released some of the tension in the tent. But everyone, the men, the wounded, Prest and Rafe, all had the oddest look on their faces. Her friends handed Atira her weapons, and to my horror, she placed them on and under the bedding well within reach.

"You'll get hurt!" I didn't like the idea of sharp blades so near her skin.

Atira shook her head. "Couldn't sleep without them." She arranged things to her satisfaction, then settled back. I knew she'd sleep. I gestured to everyone to clear out, and they moved quietly, talking amongst themselves.

Gils lingered by the table with my meager supplies. "Warprize?"

I smiled, trying to encourage him. He sat on one of the other stumps, his knees almost up to his chin. "It's forty days?"

"Yes, for the bone to heal. Then she will need to exercise the leg to regain its strength."

He leaned forward, intent on my answers. "You won't cast spells to make the healing go faster?"

"No." I smiled. "I can't force the body to heal any faster. I merely make sure that the leg stays straight as it grows back together. There are some salves that I can make to heal the bruising, keep the skin supple and ease some of the pain, but that is all I can do. Time takes care of the rest."

Gils looked at me. "You can heal everything?"

I shook my head, ruefully, remembering the blood that had welled up through my fingers just days ago. "No, Gils. There are some things I can't heal."

Gils watched me closely. "How did you learn this, Warprize?"

"My name is Lara."

He looked at me as if I was out of my mind.

I sighed. "I was apprenticed to a healer who agreed to teach me for my services." I smiled as I remembered the fuss that had caused. Eln had been nonplused by a Daughter of the Blood wanting to be a healer. Father had been incensed. I looked away for a moment, blinking hard. Three years, and I still missed him.

"What's 'apprentice'?"

I gave Gils a stern look. "Won't you be missed in the kitchens?"

He grinned. "I's say you needed help. And I's did help." He looked at me defensively.

"True." I chuckled. "Well then—" I spoke softly as I explained how the process worked. Gils was filled with all kinds of questions that spilled out of him like beans from a jar. He was older than the healing apprentices that I had worked with, but his curiosity was just as strong. We were deep in conversation when Rafe clapped his hand to his forehead. "The senel!"

With that, I was hustled back to the tent. Marcus was waiting, and rushed me past Keir and into the privy area. There was warm water waiting. Marcus fussed about my tunic and trous, but satisfied himself with brushing me off. I ignored him and washed quickly. I could hear Rafe talking to Keir as I piled my hair up in a knot on my head.

Keir was waiting when I re-entered the sleeping area. I could hear the main area of the tent filling with people. He gestured me to his side. "I understand that you have a new patient in your tent."

I nodded. "One of the warriors broke her leg. It was a clean break."

He had a very slight smile on his face. "You healed it?"

I shook my head. "I set the bone. Bone healing takes time."

"It will heal? She will use the leg again?"

"Yes."

Marcus had moved to stand by the tent flap. Keir looked at him. "This should prove to be an interesting senel."

Marcus's lips twisted. "Aye to that. Ready?"

Keir nodded.

Marcus stepped to the table and picked up something that was decorated with feathers and beads and a small string of copper bells. He moved through the tent flap first, and called everyone to attention. "Rise and hail Keir, Warlord of the Tribes and the warprize." Keir went first, and I followed.

The meeting area was filled with men and women, all standing about the room. There was a path down the middle to the raised platform, where two stumps sat slightly off center. Keir moved forward to stand before the stump closest to the center and faced the room. He gestured for me to be seated to his right.

Marcus had followed us and moved to place the thing in his hands on an empty stump in the center of the room. I got the impression that the stump had been placed there for that purpose.

"Where is Simus?" Keir asked.

As if at his command, the flaps of the main entrance opened, and there was a commotion as Simus was borne aloft on a cot by four men, like the roast pig at the mid-winter festival. I had to smile, and saw that others in the crowd were not immune to the humor of the image.

"Make way!" Simus boomed out, his voice filled with laughter. "Make way!" He grinned like a fool, white teeth gleaming in his dark face, carried aloft over everyone's head, propped up with brightly colored pillows. But his joy changed to a yell of panic when one of his bearers stumbled slightly. This caused an outbreak of laughter in the crowd, as Simus berated his bearers for their clumsiness.

Finally, Simus was settled next to Keir on his left. Once that was done, Keir looked at me, and I sat down. Keir sat, and the crowd followed after.

Keir spoke as they settled down. "I have called senel, to speak of events, to hear your views, and to make my decisions. Let us eat as we talk."

Marcus and three others started to pass through the crowd with pitchers and wooden bowls. I noticed that one was Gils, who carried his pitcher with extra care. Each person held out their hands and washed in turn as water was poured over their hands. Each uttered soft words that I couldn't hear.

Marcus served Simus and then moved to stand before me. It surprised me, since I had washed moments ago. He glared when I did not hold out my hands. Feeling awkward I leaned forward slightly and whispered to him. "Marcus, I don't know what to say."

"Say?" Marcus darted a glance at Keir, who was talking to Simus, and then focused back on me. "You give thanks, Warprize. You say what you wish." He kept his voice down, and drew no attention to us.

With relief, I held out my hands and thanked the Goddess as the water was poured. Keir was the last to wash, and as soon as he was done, food and drink were served.

There weren't as many people as I'd first thought. I counted heads and came up with ten people seated before us, spread out so that each could rest his plate and cup on a nearby stool. An equal number of men and women, all veterans by the look of them.

As soon as everyone had food in hand, Keir started asking questions concerning the status of the army, the camp, and the herds. The talk was casual, with each individual joining in with no regard to status or degree. It was clear that they felt free to talk, expressing opinions, and not hesitating to discuss the bad as well as the good.

I listened, interested in the discussion, comparing it to what I knew of my father's councils. The talk here seemed free, easy. Unlike the Court, where every statement seemed to hold hidden meanings.

A cough interrupted my thoughts. Marcus was standing next to me. His eye caught mine, flashed down to look at my untouched plate, then back up to my face.

I started eating.

A tall, thin woman with short, curly brown hair was speaking. "We've three injured horses and five dead, Warlord. Crossbow bolts, shot from cover." She scowled.

"They attacked in the darkness and fled before the herders could react."

"What do you need, Aret?" Keir asked.

"More watchers spread about the herds," she responded quickly. "Since the attacks come from cover, maybe a squad to patrol the tree line."

"Doubt they'll use the same move twice," Simus offered.

"Not the first time an enemy's made mistakes," a man with darker brown hair and a crooked nose replied. "Let me take some archers into the trees. We'll set them up high and let them wait out the night. With starlight, we'll spot them first and that will end it."

Aret nodded. "I like that, Yers. But you may have a long night of waiting."

"Me? Not so." Yers grinned. "I'll send the young ones, full of enthusiasm and energy. It'll teach them patience." That drew chuckles.

"This morning I sent Iften to speak to the Xyian King about these attacks. Iften, tell us what you learned."

It was the blond I'd encountered in Simus's tent. He rose from his seat near the center of the room, a smug look on his face. "I went into the city with an escort and demanded speech with the defeated king."

Simus guffawed. "That attitude made your welcome sure."

Iften didn't look at Simus. "I gave him the courtesy that the Warlord bade me. Not that he deserved it."

Keir frowned, and Iften continued hurriedly. "I told him of the attacks, and he denied knowledge of them, and also denied that his people would do such a thing." Iften turned slightly, as if addressing the room, rather than reporting to Keir. Behind me, Marcus muttered something under his breath. "I told this city-dweller that to murder a horse is to murder a child, and that swift and deadly punishment would fall on any who so dared. The defeated king said that he would investigate the matter." Iften's disdain was clear.

"What was his manner?" Keir's voice was soft.

"As one who brushes aside a fly," Iften snarled. "I told him to report to you and he said that would be done."

Keir sat quiet as the room stirred about us. I half expected an explosion of temper from him, but none came. "Aret, set the extra watchers. Yers, your idea is a good one, but I want patrols as well. You and Aret decide the placement and timing."

Aret seemed well satisfied, as did Yers. Iften, as if realizing Keir was done with him, moved to sit down with a disgruntled look.

"Iften." Keir's voice carried over the heads of everyone present.

"Warlord?" Iften stopped and rose to his full height.

"Have a care, Iften, for Xymund is my defeated king, and you will offer him respect or answer to me."

Everyone fell silent, and seemed to study their kavage closely. Iften gave Keir a nod, then settled back on to his stool. I noticed that the disgruntled look had become more pronounced.

"Sal?" Keir turned to an older, grey-haired woman. "Supplies?"

They launched into a discussion of food and gear, and I was stunned to learn that the Warlord's army was paying for supplies. While the conversation had moved on, clearly Iften remained unhappy. But I had other concerns. There was such a need for medicines and the like, but I didn't know my place at this meeting. I felt more prize than participant. The Warlord had a temper, that much was clear, one that flared fast and hot. I shuddered inside, remembering his fury at the sight of a few bruises. How angry would he be if I spoke out now?

Keir finally sat back, and handed his empty plate to Marcus. "We've covered the concerns I had. Before I speak as to my plans, is there anything else?" The other servers were passing though the room with fresh kavage. Marcus was leaning over to get my plate when he stiffened. I looked around him to see a man step forward, and pick up the bundle from the stool in the center of the room.

"Wesren?" Keir's voice held a questioning tone.

He was a short, stocky man with thick black hair and beard. "I hold your token, Warlord. I give voice to one truth."

Marcus moved back beside me, handing off the plates to another server. His eye was firmly fixed on the speaking man.

"You've said there's to be no releases from regular duties, or leave of camp." Wesren drew a quick breath. "Been some time since that's been granted, and that's passing hard, Warlord." He shifted, uneasy under Keir's stare.

Keir paused for a long drink of kavage, looking at the man over the rim of his cup. "Any further truths to voice?"

Wesren stood, holding the token. "No, Warlord."

"You felt the need to hold my token for this?"

Wesren stiffened. His movement jangling the bells of the token. "Ways are changing under your hand, Warlord. Felt the need to be careful." Keir's gaze never wavered and Wesren shifted his weight again, his eyes darting about the room as if looking for support.

Keir put him out of his misery. "I will speak to your truths."

Wesren nodded, placed the token back on its stool, and returned to his seat.

"Although it appears that we have won, still I have doubts about this peace."

I jerked, alarmed at his words. If he noticed, Keir did not

react. "This peace calls for their king to acknowledge me as Warlord of this land. His oath has been given, yet out horses are attacked in the night. Until I am satisfied of his obedience and our safety, we will remain on alert and on guard, as if in enemy lands." Keir held up a hand to control reactions, since the decision was not popular. "Besides, I remind you that their ways are not our ways. Before our peoples intermingle, we need to make sure that there is understanding. For example, Xyian women do not lay with men until they are bonded." That set them all aback, and every eye focused on me. The expressions ran the gauntlet from pity to amazement to mirth. I flushed at the attention, and focused on my shoes.

"To prevent problems, everyone remains in camp." Keir emphasized his order.

"What of a pattern dance, Warlord?" Simus flashed his grin. "That would work off excess energy."

That was met with laughter and smiles. Keir laughed as well. "Good idea. What say you, Wesren?"

"We'd all enjoy a good pattern, Warlord."

"Announce it then, for two days hence. Plenty of time to weave new patterns." Keir stood and stretched. "If there are no further—"

"I hold your token, Warlord."

Conversation stopped. Iften was standing with the bundle in his hand. I caught Keir and Simus exchanging a glance as Keir sat back down. Iften lifted the item in his hand and shook it slightly so the bells chimed.

"I give voice to two truths. Joden remains unpunished for his violation of our ways."

There was a stir at this statement.

"The other truth?" Keir's voice was very non-committal.

"That your attempts to rescue Simus by going into the city alone were reckless, and showed disregard for this army and your responsibilities."

My mouth dropped open. A statement like that would have Xymund calling for executioners. Keir merely sat up a bit straighter on his stool. "Any further truths to voice?"

Iften stood, holding the token. "No."

"I will speak to your truths." Iften nodded, placed the token back on its stool, and returned to his seat. "Before I speak to these truths, I would tell you that a rider fell in practice this morning, breaking her leg."

The overall reaction was one of dismay. One voice rose from the back. "Her name?"

Keir responded. "I do not know. We will ask it of the warprize, who saw the incident, had the warrior taken to the healing tent, and healed the leg."

All eyes focused on me. I swallowed my food. "Her name is Atira." There was a general murmuring at that. I darted a quick glance at Keir. "But the leg is not yet healed.

Bone healing takes time."

One woman leaned forward on her stool. "You have done this before? Healed a broken limb?"

I looked at her. "Yes."

Talk swelled, but Keir spoke over it. "I acknowledge the truth that Joden's actions were not of our tradition. I leave it to Simus as to what punishment there should be for the man who failed to grant him mercy in the face of capture. However, I voice the truth that had he followed our tradition, there would be no warprize." He looked at me, a pleased expression on his face. "I think you all begin to see what I see."

I shifted on the stool, uneasy as the object of attention.

Keir focused back on the group. "I answer to the other truth that has been raised." He grinned ruefully. "I acknowledge the recklessness of my action. When have I not acted so?" Laughter met that statement. "I'll consider the truth that I had no regard for my men and my responsibilities." I could see Iften scowling, less than satisfied. But Keir was not finished. "But do not think to turn me into a fat king that directs his men from a tower." There was another burst of laughter at that, and from the sly looks in my direction, I had a feeling they were talking about Xymund.

Keir gestured, holding his hands up, palms flat. "Who can say what caused Joden to stay his hand. I can not. I have spoken to these truths, and I thank Iften for his truths."

Simus raised his hand. "Warlord, I would speak to this truth. I would speak as to Joden's punishment."

Keir turned a bit, so he could see Simus. "Speak, Simus."

Simus's voice carried far, yet he seemed to make no special effort. "The Warlord has left to me to determine the punishment for Joden, who has violated our tradition. I say, how is one to punish the man who saved his life?" Simus shifted a bit on his pillows. "But tradition has been broken and punishment there must be. Summon Joden to stand before me."

Joden stepped in to the tent, as if he had been waiting just outside. He looked anxious, but his step was firm, and he stood with an easy confidence. "I am here."

Simus's teeth gleamed as he smiled. "As I have done privately, so I now do publicly. I thank you, Joden, for the gift of my life."

Joden smiled back, his round face made rounder so.

"Now, as to punishment. As you all know, Joden is a singer. Not yet a Singer of the Tribes, but singer none the less. So, hear now the punishment I would impose. Joden must sing of his decision on the field of battle."

There was a stirring at this, but I couldn't tell what their reaction was. Simus waited for a bit, then continued, "Now, the words of a singer can not be forced or dictated. That too is tradition. So I say to Joden, do you accept this punishment? Will you sing of this for all the Plains to hear?" More murmurs, more reaction. I was getting the idea that the offense and the punishment were so unusual that no one was sure how to react.

Joden nodded. "I accept the punishment. I will sing of this."

"So be it." Simus leaned back on his pillows and waved his cup in the air. "Bring me and Joden kavage, Marcus. This is punishing work." There were groans at that, and Simus laughed as Joden took a stool. "I have spoken to this truth. I thank you, Warlord."

Keir lifted a mug. "The sky favors the bold." Other mugs were lifted in response. As they were lowered, Keir caught Iften's eye. "I thank you for your truths, Iften."

Marcus moved to offer more kavage to him and Simus as the rest of the room talked among themselves as if nothing had happened. Under its cover, Simus leaned over. "That one grows brazen."

Keir made some response, but I did not hear it. My eyes were drawn to the bundle, the token, there on its stool. Maybe I could use its protections to ask for medicines and supplies. Without further thought I slipped off my stool, and moved toward the token. It was almost in my grasp when my wrist was caught and jerked back. I gasped, and shrank back from Keir, his face contorted in rage.

6

Keir's grip on my wrist tightened as he pulled me back to the platform. Ice cold sweat formed down my spine as a vision of the man tied to the whipping post filled my eyes.

I was pulled back to reality when Keir released my wrist and pushed me back down on my stump. "What would you say, Warprize?" The words ground out between his teeth as he towered over me. Wanting nothing more than to sink into the earth, I dropped my eyes and caught a glimpse of Iften behind Keir, smirking in delight.

"Well?"

I glanced over at Simus, who nodded as if encouraging me to speak. Lifting my chin, as well as my courage, I met Keir's eyes. "I have two truths."

"What?" Keir snapped at me, and I got a clear glimpse of his teeth.

"Supplies for the healing tent." I swallowed hard. "I can do more with medicines, herbs and equipment."

There was a murmur of reaction to that, but Keir's eyes continued to bore into mine. "More?" The anger that had flared seemed to smolder beneath the surface. "You would aid any who came to you?"

"Yes." My wrist throbbed, but I sat still and straight.

One of the men snorted from the back. "Our warriors will become soft as city-dwellers if we let them complain of every ache and pain."

"Oh, and they fight so much better when they have a rash under their arms, or flux dribbling out of their ass," I snapped back, letting my temper flare.

The room exploded in laughter.

Simus threw back his head and roared. "Ah," he gasped, wiping his eyes. "This one'll not let slackers lay idle. She'll have them empty slop pots!"

More laughter. Keir's posture didn't relax, but there was a hint of a smile on that stern face. I carefully kept my eyes on his, not daring to look away. After a moment he returned to his stump and gestured for more kavage. "And your second truth, Warprize?"

I shifted so that I looked directly at him, but he stared ahead, so all I had was his profile. "You need to understand that I am a healer, not a—" I bit my lip, at a loss for the right word. "Not a worker of wonders. I can't wave my hand and fix Atira's leg so that she can jump up as if nothing happened." I drew a breath. "I have set her leg, but bone healing takes time." I dropped my eyes to the rough planks of the platform. "I can't heal all illness. Would to the Goddess that I could."

There was silence in the tent. Keir's voice was low, but it carried. "You'd try to help any who came to you?"

I looked up, surprised he even had to ask. "Of course."

Keir looked around the room, and I could see that some of the warriors were nodding their heads, although Iften and a few others were scowling. Keir opened his mouth to speak, but at that moment Marcus approached and bowed to Keir. "Warlord, there is a man of the city outside. He says that he has business with you, as you owe him a debt. He will talk to no one but you."

"Let him approach."

The tent flaps parted and Remn entered, moving with quiet dignity toward the high seat. I sat up and smiled. His eyes caught mine, and a look of relief flashed over his face for just a moment. He made no sound. Instead, he focused his eyes on Keir and continued to advance. A servant followed him with a small bundle. About five steps from Keir, he stopped, and bowed low.

"Greetings, Warlord. I am Remn, a humble bookseller. I thank you for this audience. I apologize that I do not speak your language. Is there one who can interpret my words?"

Keir nodded. "I speak your language. I am told that you have come to collect a debt from me, bookseller. I owe no debt to you that I am aware of."

"Noble Warlord, the debt is owed by one of your house."

Keir raised an eyebrow. "How so?"

Remn folded his hands in front of his chest. "Noble Warlord, one of your household came to me seeking a loan. She sought the money for the purchase of herbs and medicines for your men held captive at the time. In return, she pledged a book to me as a surety of the repayment of the debt. The book has not yet been redeemed."

Keir glanced at me, then back at Remn. "And the name of this person?"

Remn bowed low and left his head down. "Forgive me, Noble Warlord, but by the orders of my King I am forbidden to speak her name."

Keir frowned. The room stilled somewhat, sensing his displeasure. "It is not wise to offer insult to the warprize."

Remn raised his head to look Keir in the eye. "Forgive me, Mighty Warlord. It is not I who offers the insult."

I sat there, stunned.

Keir rose. The room started to rise as well, but he gestured them down. "Be at ease. I will return when I have concluded this business." He looked at me. "Warprize."

We moved toward the sleeping area. Remn took the package from his servant and followed.

Once in the privacy of the room, I turned, unsure of my welcome. Keir seated himself on the end of the bed. Remn ignored him, opened his arms and embraced me. Tears filled my eyes as I buried my head in his shoulder. He smelled of old books, dust, and home.

"Dearest Lara." Remn whispered in my ear as he held me tight. "We feared you dead or worse." He stepped back with tears in his eyes. "All we knew was that after you disappeared into the camp it erupted into lights and noise and celebration. Anna feared you sacrificed. She has not eaten since you left. I swear that she has actually lost weight in these last few days." He laughed shakily and wiped his eyes. "I hear tell that the food in the castle has all the taste of straw of late." He darted a glance out of the corner of his eye at the brooding figure of the Warlord. "Othur came to me and asked if I would try to find out how you were. So here I am."

I wiped the moisture from my eyes and smiled. "I am well, Remn. Truly."

Keir, looking stern, interrupted. "What do you mean that you cannot speak her name?"

Remn sighed. "The King has ordered that no one speak of her, or make inquiry as to her health or well being."

Keir frowned.

I placed a hand on Remn's shoulder. "Please tell Anna that I am fine and well treated. She mustn't worry. Tell her to eat or she will get sick."

Keir snorted at that, as if he understood the jest.

Remn smiled and hugged me again. "I will. And here . . . here is the book that you pledged. I cannot keep it and would not sell it." He opened the package and pulled out my old friend. The leather had been cleaned and it smelled of saddle soap.

I laughed, delighted, and without thinking, turned to show the book to Keir. He looked at me oddly. Turning toward a chest, he opened one and pulled out a small pouch. "My thanks, bookseller. Here is the money that was borrowed, and a little for your troubles in collecting it."

Remn stood straight. "Warlord, that is not necessary. I do this for friendship's sake."

Keir gave him a serious look. "Then let me do it in the name of the men who were aided."

Remn bowed, then straightened. He looked up into Keir's eyes with a stern expression. "You were given a treasure, Warlord. The King may not see it that way, but my people do. See that it is cherished."

"Remn." I admonished him, a blush rising in my face.

Keir merely nodded, as if in agreement. "I must return to my men. Warprize, return to the meal in your own time."

With that he left the room.

Remn clutched my arm. "Lara, Othur sends you a message. Xymund was the one to clear your room of the last of your things after the ceremony. He was in the room for a long time. And emerged in a towering rage. From the way he talks, it seems that he has somehow convinced himself that you betrayed him to the Warlord. Even when he spoke to the Warlord's man alone, his rage seems centered on you. Be careful, Lara. He hates you."

"Remn, I have obeyed Xymund. He has no reason to hate me." I clutched the book to my chest. "Can you stay?"

Remn shook his head. "I must get back and get word to Anna before the poor woman loses another ounce." He smiled and hugged me. I held on hard, until at last he slipped from my arms, his face wet with tears. "Be well, my child." Marcus escorted him out as I wiped my face. I placed the book under my pillow, took a few deep breaths, and returned to the meeting area.

Keir was speaking when I entered. ". . . so plans must change as well. Provided the peace holds, we will make new division of our forces. I now have no choice but to return to the Heart of the Plains with the warprize. Simus, I would leave you here in my stead."

"Ah, my suffering in your service knows no boundaries," Simus replied in mocking tones. I stepped to my seat amidst the chuckles with a pit in my stomach that had not been there before. While my head knew that I was the Warlord's possession, my heart had denied the possibility of leaving my home. Just talking to Remn made me long for Anna and the kitchen. How could I bear never to see them again?

Keir continued to speak. "I've called for a ceremony honoring the dead, both Xyian and of the Plains, to be held at the castle tomorrow night. Discuss among yourselves who should attend. He stood and looked about. "If there is nothing further . . ." From his tone, there had better not be.

"I's hold your token, Warlord."

My eyes widened. Gils had somehow managed to get into the tent and now held the token in his hand. His young voice quavered, but he stood tall before the crowd, fresh scrubbed from the look of him. His tunic had no sleeves, and the tattoos on both arms were displayed clearly.

Keir sat back down, his face serious but there was warmth in his voice. "What truth would you voice, warrior? At a senel that you were asked to serve, not join?"

Gils swallowed hard, but did not back down. "I's Gils. I's give voice to one truth. I's wish to a-pren-tice," he spoke the word slowly and carefully, "to the warprize and forsake the way of a warrior for the path of healing." The feathers on the token were moving, and I realized his hands were shaking.

There were cries of outrage as warriors leaped to their feet. Gils's eyes widened and his hands clutched the token tighter, making the bells ring. He didn't turn to see the men behind him. Instead, he kept his eyes focused on Keir.

Keir held up both hands, bringing silence with a gesture. "He holds my token."

The others sat back down.

"I will speak to your truth." Keir stood at the edge and looked down at Gils, who nodded. The youngster returned the token to its place, but remained standing next to it.

"What you speak of is not our way, Gils. This truth would change your life forever, especially in the eyes of our people." Gils opened his mouth, but Keir raised a hand. "I will consider your truth. This is not a decision made lightly, nor should your truth be answered while we are in the field. Continue in your regular duties."

Gils's shoulders slumped. Keir studied him for a moment. "What are your secondary duties, Gils?"

Yers spoke up. "Kitchen helper, Warlord." The man shook his head. "He's talked of nothing but the healing tent since he started taking meals there."

"If I remember, kitchen duty is much sought after, if only for the treats one can sneak." There was general laughter to that comment. Keir continued, "Gils, is it your truth that you would rather empty slop pots than work in the kitchen?"

Gils looked up and nodded. Even I could see the hope in his eyes.

Keir looked up and shrugged his shoulders. "Well, it is your truth, lad, strange though it may be. So hear then, as I speak to part of your truth. Your secondary duties are now to the healing tent, as helper." Gils opened his mouth, but Keir again held up a warning hand. "As to the rest of your truth, I will consider that upon our return home. You are not released from your duties as a warrior." Keir looked out over the crowd. "I suspect a few months of slop pots may change your mind." Laughter swelled at that.

Gils beamed. "My thanks, Warlord." He turned and left the tent, avoiding a glaring Marcus on the way out.

"No." Keir watched him go. "My thanks for your truth, warrior." Keir raised his head to look out over the crowd. "If there are no other truths, then the senel is closed."

The warriors were all talking, some standing and milling about. Keir moved to stand by Simus. The black man looked grim. "Iften is planning something." He spoke so quietly that I had to strain to hear him.

Keir nodded, looking out over the heads of his men. "I agree. If you feel well enough, I'd like to talk, Simus."

Simus laughed. "I wouldn't miss it, Warlord. Let us retreat to my tent for kavage and discourse." He turned his head. "Joden! Where are you?"

Joden appeared on the platform with the four bearers. "Offering bribes of kavage and meat to these men to heave your fat carcass back to your tent."

"Fat! I'm not fat." Simus tried to look offended, but no one was fooled. The young warriors got into position with much groaning and moaning and sarcastic comments from Simus.

"Come and see me tomorrow, little healer!" Simus laughed. "I wish to hear all the details of your newest escapade." He shook his head with a great smile. "Healed a broken leg. The warrior-priests will curse the skies!" With a grunt, the men lifted his cot and started moving away, staggering under the weight. "Have a care!" Simus growled, then laughed. "Have a care!" Guards held the main flaps open as they left.

Keir turned and gestured for me to precede him into the sleeping area. His growl came from behind me even before the tent flap fell closed. "You're not to use the token."

I turned and faced him, clasping my trembling hands in front of me. "There was a need—"

"There was no need." Keir growled, his jaw clenched. "This is hard enough to accomplish without you—"

"I cannot heal without—"

"Damn the supplies! This is about the peace." Keir bellowed. I blinked.

Keir ran his hand through his hair. "A peace you seem determined to threaten."

"I!" My back stiffened at that. "I've kept my part of this bargain, Warlord. Nor has Xymund violated its terms."

"The attacks on the horses—"

"There may be a few malcontents, as there are in this camp." I raised my voice to match his, and glared just as hard. How dare he imply—

"My people hold to their word, Warprize. Explain why your brother offers such insult?"

I dropped my eyes and stepped back a pace. How to explain what I didn't understand myself? Lowering my voice, I fell back to my strongest argument. "He will not risk his people by violating this peace."

"His head, you mean." Keir stalked about, as if needing to pace.

My temper flared back. "His head, then. He has no reason to jeopardize his life or throne."

"His actions will speak for him." Keir snapped. "If he's behind these attacks on the herds, he'll answer for it." He turned on his heel to go.

Marcus popped in front of him, arms crossed over his chest. "Done with your snapping?"

Keir raised his eyes to the ceiling. "What?"

"You are taking her to a mourning ceremony? Tomorrow?"

"Yes." Keir cast a glance back at me. "It would not be a bad thing for her to be seen in the city. Rumor has her treated badly."

Marcus tightened his lips. "What's she to wear? Trous is fine for camp, but city women wear dresses more often than not. I've managed to keep her clothed so far, but she needs other things."

I pressed my lips together and looked away.

Keir's voice was thoughtful. "I had not thought of that."

Marcus snorted. "Seems to be happening a lot of late."

I looked over at that, to see Keir arch an eyebrow and tilt his head. "So, the clothing of one woman is a task beyond your skills, old man?" He moved past us, to the main flap. "Who'd have thought it?"

"Where are you off to?" Marcus demanded.

"To Simus's tent."

"And me?" I demanded.

"As you like." Was the comment tossed over his shoulder. With that Keir disappeared.

Marcus glared at me.

I glared right back. "This is not my fault. I wasn't permitted to bring anything with me!"

Marcus nodded. "As it should be. The Warlord has claimed you. You take nothing except from his hands." He frowned. "I will think on this, Warprize."

"Lara!"

He sniffed and moved away to finish cleaning.

I stomped out, half a mind to stomp all the way back to the

castle and home. How dare he imply that Xymund or I would risk breaking the agreement. Admittedly Xymund was motivated more out of self-interest than anything else, but motivated he was. Still, the hatred in his voice had been so strong. The idea that Xymund would take such a risk made me furious and sick, all at the same time. There's been other times in the past that he'd taken actions that benefitted himself more than the country. The fact that Warren and Othur cared deeply for the kingdom gave me some measure of comfort. They would stop him, if they knew what he was doing. Xymund had a slyness that I did not trust.

Rafe and Prest were waiting for me when I emerged from the tent, and thoughts of flight went out of my head. But other thoughts whirled about, skittering around like colts on ice. I turned toward the healing tent, guards in tow.

How had Keir's opinion of me come to be so important so quickly? My fears came up in my throat, and for a moment I could barely breathe. I'd been well treated so far, better than I'd hoped. The demands on me . . . my face flushed at the thought . . . had not been uncomfortable. Truth be told, they had been . . . interesting.

I wondered how many warprizes Keir had. I knew he had taken other cities, there might have been more. Was it one warprize per kingdom? Where were they?

Were they happy?

I frowned at the ground beneath my feet. At least I was being allowed to practice my craft. Whatever the future held, I had that at the very least.

Of course, who knew what would happen when the army returned to its homeland. I took a deep breath and focused on my feet again, watching myself take one step after another. I had been promised. I had fulfilled the promise, and would continue to do so. I was sure that Keir would not harm me physically.

But there are other kinds of pain.

* * *

The healing tent was in an uproar when I arrived.

There were people everywhere, spilling out of the tent and milling around like bees on honey. The sides of the tent had been rolled up, and people were gathered on all sides. I lengthened my stride, leaving Rafe and Prest behind, and pushed my way through the crowd.

At the center lay Atira, surrounded by admirers. There was a piece of wood laying on her chest, with stones on top in some kind of pattern. Atira was craning her neck to see, as the people who crowded around her cot reached down and moved the stones around. There was lots of talk and laughter, and Atira's face was flushed.

"Word travels on the wind." Rafe commented. Prest nodded his agreement.

"What in the name of the Goddess is going on!" I stood there with my hands on my hips.

Everyone turned in consternation, took one look at my face, and took to their heels. The few that remained tried to offer explanations, and there were mentions of a dance and the pattern, and their plan. Atira was trying to hide the board with both hands, and I realized that she was trying desperately not to laugh.

"Out of my tent!" I shooed at them with my hands. "Out! Out!"

Atira lost her fight as hardened warriors fled before me. Rafe was laughing, leaning on Prest, who was roaring as well. "Silly fools," I grumbled. "This is no way to treat an injured warrior." I gestured to the sides. "Help me lower the sides." I grumbled as we worked, and Rafe and Prest were hard pressed to keep their faces straight.

"Warprize, we were planning the pattern." Atira was wiping her eyes with her hands. "They meant no harm."

"What is a pattern?" I asked as I moved up next to her.

"For the dance!" She hastily covered the board. "Don't look, Warprize! It's bad luck."

"Very bad luck." Joden walked into the tent. I smiled to see him. "I heard the noise, and came to see if you needed aid."

He looked around the tent. "I see that you have routed the enemy without my help."

"Atira's needs rest." I started to check the leather and the straps.

"May I speak with her for a moment?"

Atira's eyes grew round. I looked over at Joden, but his face was calm and serene. "Of course, Joden. But not for too long. Do you need privacy?"

"No, Warprize." Joden moved to a seat by Atira's cot. "Warrior."

"Singer." Atira's tone was respectful and questioning at the same time.

Joden shook his head. "No. I am not a Singer yet. But that is why I have come to see you."

"Really?" Atira propped herself on her elbows.

Joden nodded. "I am working on a song. I would sing of your injury."

Prest sucked in a breath. Rafe stood up straight. I could barely hear Atira's response. "For all the sky to hear?"

Joden nodded. "I need to hear your thoughts and words. Would you think on this, then speak to me of what happened?"

"Yes." Atira looked solemn. "I will."

Joden stood. "We will talk tomorrow." He smiled at the rest of us, and walked out.

Atira fell back onto the cot and let out a gust of breath. I laid a hand on her shoulder. "Are you all right?"

She smiled up at me, her eyes filled. "Oh yes, Warprize."

I smiled back. "Well then, do you feel up to bathing?"

She looked delighted. "I can?" She glanced at her leg.

I smiled as I checked the bindings, pleased that the swelling was minor. "It will be awkward, but we can do it. Is there any pain?" She denied it, but I could see tension in her eyes. "Well, with bathing and all, you'll start to feel it. I'll give you something for it before we are done." I stood. "We can rig a blanket curtain—"

She looked at me oddly. "It's not necessary, Warprize."

It wasn't easy. I helped as much as I could, but Atira did

most of the work herself. My job was to ensure that the leg stayed as straight as possible.

Atira moved slowly and carefully, and showed no embarrassment in bathing where all could see. It made sense that a woman warrior would have no qualms about that, but I found it unsettling. It took longer, since she was unable to move, and I had the tent walls lowered to keep the heat in. No sense her taking chill on top of it all.

By the time we were done, everything near and around Atira was wet, and the rocks that pulled at the leg needed to be retied, but she was cleaner and thankful for it. It was short work to clean the mess and change the linens of the cot. Once dry bedding was in place, and her weapons restored to her side, Atira lay back and heaved a sigh of relief.

"I'll get a clean tunic for you."

"Thanks, Warprize, but no. More comfortable naked." She sank back and pulled the blanket up.

I fixed an eye on her. "I can give you something for the pain now."

She wrinkled her nose. "Warprize, I'd prefer not. I'm not in pain as such, just achy."

I opened my mouth to argue, but saw that this was a matter of pride. So I merely nodded. Looking about, I could see that my other patients were tending to their own needs. I leaned a bit closer to Atira, picking up soap and cloths. "Atira, could I ask you a question?"

"Of course."

"You might be offended."

"Offended, Warprize?"

I flushed slightly. "Well, the Warlord uses a token . . ." My voice trailed off as she frowned.

"No one explained?"

I shook my head.

It was her turn to shake hers. "The Warlord's token, or anyone's token is for truths or questions that they may not want to hear." Atira answered softly. "Those who lead have elaborate tokens and bearers, which bespeak their status." She shifted slightly to get more comfortable. "We are a warrior people and weapons are always at hand when tempers flare. Without tokens, there'd be little truth telling for fear of killing ourselves off!" She grinned at me. "For one such as I, a token can be a stone, a tool, a shoe even, if that's what's at hand."

"A dagger?" I asked, nodding toward her weapons.

Atira wrinkled her nose. "That's not done, Warprize. It can be done, but its insulting in its own way. Now, with leaders, warlords and the like, they set the token out where it can be seen. An invitation to use it. With me, you must ask." She fumbled for one of the pattern stones. "Now, ask for my token."

"Atira, may I have your token?"

She handed me the stone. "You hold my token, Warprize. What truths would you voice?"

I clutched the stone in my sweaty hand. "I have a question."

She inclined her head. "I will answer."

I pointed to the tattoos on her arm. "What do these mean?"

She chuckled. "You need no token to ask that!"

"But how do I know?"

The despair must have been in my voice, for her smile faded as she looked at me. "Healer you may be, but you're a horse in a strange herd, aren't you?"

I nodded, not trusting my voice. My homesickness lay in my stomach like a rock.

"It's best, if you are not certain, to use the token." She spoke carefully, as if to a child. "But as warprize, any who would lift a weapon to you would answer to the Warlord. You need not be concerned." She looked down, and picked at a nit on the blanket. "Truth is, if the Warlord knew that I had grabbed you that day, I'd like be dead at his hand."

"He found out." Atira went white, her eyes wide. I shook my head. "He saw the bruises. I refused to tell him who had done it."

Atira's color slowly leached back into her face. "You refused?"

"You didn't mean any harm, and I lost my temper." I flushed, embarrassed.

"It appears that I owe you for both life and limb, Warprize."

"No, Atira, please. No debts between us."

She tilted her head. "So, at this point I reply 'I will answer to your truth'. Then you return my token. Or, if you fear my anger, you may hold the token, until I answer."

I handed her the stone, and her smile grew wider. "As to your question. This tattoo?" She pointed to her right arm. "It bespeaks my tribes back four generations." There were two columns of four lines each, black ink against her tanned skin. None of the designs repeated. "So you can see what tribes mix within my blood. Each tribe has its own pattern. The right column is the women, the left are the men."

I nodded, not completely sure I understood.

"Now this," displaying her left arm, "this is my required births." This was a row of five lines, each line a separate design. "I took the tribe design of the man for each child." She had a look of satisfaction on her face.

My buttocks hit the ground with a thump. "Five children?"

Atira looked up, puzzled by my reaction. "Aye, Warprize. Before any can enter military service, they must first bear or breed five children for the theas."

"Of course." I answered faintly. There was a roaring in my ears. Keir had similar tattoos. Five children? Different mothers?

Atira reached for my hand, concern in her eyes. "Warprize?"

"Do you raise your children?"

"Skies blessing, no!" Atira laughed. "What would I know of tending babes? Theas do that, in the safety of the Plains. Three months of milk is more than enough for me."

"Were you . . . did you . . . marry the fathers?" I had to use the Xyian word.

Atira frowned. "Marry?" I explained as best I could, and she chortled, shaking her head. "No, Warprize. Bonding is for later, if I meet the right person. Those matings were for the tribes, to flourish the tribes. You understand?"

Dazed, I think I nodded my head.

Atira settled back, satisfied. "Now I say 'I thank you for your truth', and the ritual is complete." She yawned.

Concern for my patient cut through my confusion. "Sleep, Atira."

She nodded, and I moved away to check the others, my hands steady, but my thoughts tumbled. Sure enough, each one had similar tattoos on their arms. I worked about the tent as my patients dozed, thinking hard about not thinking about Keir's five children. Or the five women that had borne him five children. Or the fact that I might be required to bear five children.

Thankfully Gils interrupted my musings, showing up with dinner for my patients. There was another man with him, who walked up to me with a wry grin. "Greetings, Warprize."

"You're Yers. From the senel."

"Aye. Gils is one of my group." He shook his head. "Knocked me off my horse, making his request that way." He lowered his voice as Gils moved about with the food. "Solved a problem, to be honest. Gils gives his best, mind, but he's not a natural fighter."

"He's so young."

Yers nodded. "Younger than most. Triplets twice, if you can believe."

I blinked. "Triplets." Sure enough, a quick glance showed me the six tattoos on his left arm.

Yers raised his voice. "He'll do well enough for you, Warprize, but I'll not let him slack his duties. Here, now," he called to Gils. "Done?"

Gils nodded.

"Then we're off." Yers gave me a wink. "You'll have him again in the morning."

I wasn't hungry, so I made sure that everyone had what they needed and returned to my small table, more to think then to accomplish anything. The differences between us seemed so vast. I almost laughed out loud to think of the Archbishop's reaction. Five children, with no blessing of the Goddess. But then I stopped. Did that mean they were free to lay with each other at any time? If so, what need was there for a warprize?

A cough interrupted me. I turned to find a stocky woman standing there, skin brown and weathered, her short hair a pale white. "Warprize. The Warlord has directed me to find out what your supply needs are. I am Sal, supply master."

I stood. "Sal, I am glad to see you. I had hoped to have a list ready, but . . ."

Sal snorted, then sat. "What good would that do? Tell me what you need."

"Well, if you know what the former healer used, I can work off those items."

Sal looked at me, her hands on her knees. "Warprize, the Warrior-priest would not have deigned to speak to me, let alone tell me his needs."

"But how did he heal so many with such limited supplies?"

Sal gave me a grim look. "He didn't. Now, what do you need?"

So I started telling her about fever's foe and orchid root and all the other things that would supply me with the basics. She kept her eyes on mine, only occasionally stopping me to ask a question as to what something was, or to make sure that she knew how much I required. Hesitantly, I also asked about braziers and bowls to mix my medicines. She grunted at that.

Finally, I ran out of ideas. She nodded once and settled back on her stool. "So. Let me make sure I have it right." She took a breath, and started reciting.

I was impressed. She had remembered every item, the quantity and its description. I listened carefully as she recited, nodding as she went along. I didn't have to correct her once. When she was done, I nodded and smiled. She relaxed a bit, but there was no smile on her dour face. "All right?"

"Perfect."

"Only the sky is perfect." She stood and stretched, and moved to where Gils had left a pitcher of kavage. She brought it over with two mugs. "Not the hottest, but wet." She poured two mugs and handed me one. "Now, I have questions for you." Seated back on the stool she leaned forward, an odd look on her face. "What do you know of the city merchants?" Her eyes were alight with a strange kind of glow.

"Well, I know a number of them."

She leaned forward. "Have you bought from them?"

"Yes."

"Tell me," she said "tell me about them." There was a scowl as she drank her kavage. "I must needs deal with them for supplies. These ways are new to me. Tell me how they deal and what they are like."

I chuckled. I knew that look now. It was the same look that Remn got in his eye when he was haggling over the price of a book.

We talked for a long time. Sal had questions about sellers of livestock, produce, cloth, and everything an army could want. She already knew all the types of coins used in the kingdom of Xy, and their relative values. She was not so interested in the butchers and bakers, and I couldn't answer her questions about the dealers in swords and armor. She seemed well satisfied, and stood and stretched, looking out the entrance of the tent. "I've kept you late, Warprize. My thanks." With that, Sal left as quickly as she had come.

I looked after her in surprise. "Is she always that abrupt?"

Rafe and Prest chuckled at my expression. "Unless you're haggling, Warprize," said Rafe.

"Let me check Atira one more time."

Atira blinked at me as I checked the leg, and smiled drowsily. "Warprize."

"Atira. How do you feel?"

"Good, Warprize."

I sighed. "Lara. My name is Lara."

She yawned. "Yes, Warprize."

I sighed. Apparently I was wasting my time.

On the walk back to the Warlord's tent, we paused to look at the stars that hung in the sky, and the moon riding low. Rafe was explaining the significance of the fact that Joden wanted to talk to Atira. "It's an honor, to be in a song."

Prest nodded. "A great honor."

"To be honored for a broken leg?" I asked, skeptical.

Rafe chuckled. "Well, it would be better if it were a battle deed, but it is rare indeed to be in a song. Unless you're particularly brave or cunning—"

"Or dead." Prest added.

"Or dead." Rafe agreed. "Joden must also be planning on singing about you, Warprize."

"Me?" I stopped outside the tent.

Rafe laughed. "Why sing about the injury unless you sing about the healing?" He clapped his hand on Prest's back, and they walked off, leaving me standing there with a foolish look on my face.

Marcus greeted me when I entered the tent. "Can I get you anything, Warprize?"

I put my hands on my hips. "Lara."

He turned his one eye up to study the tent. "Kavage, perhaps? Some hot water?"

I snorted, but was too tired to fight him. "No, thank you. I think I will go to sleep."

Marcus nodded. "I will add some fuel to the braziers. The Warlord is still with Simus, and I think they will talk the stars away." He bustled about, as I sank down onto the bed, and bade me good rest when he left. I yawned, my face almost splitting with its strength. The bed felt wonderful when I crawled under the blankets and furs.

Later, much later, I woke to find Keir had crawled into the bed at some point. He lay off to one side, on his back, sleeping peacefully. There on his bare arm were those tattoos. I stared at him in the soft glow of the coals, then went back to sleep.

The dress was bright red. Bright, bright red.

Marcus smiled at me. "There, now. That will do us proud."

I tried to smile back at him.

The morning had started well enough. When I awoke, I found the bed empty and Keir already gone. After breakfast and kavage, I returned to the healing tent, to find Gils there feeding everyone and asking as many questions as he could with one breath. After some negotiation, I allowed some of Atira's friends into the tent, so they could make their plans. Whenever I wandered in their direction, they would cover up the board, and wave me off. The only times I pushed the issue was when I needed to check the leg, other than that I left them to their schemes. The morning passed quickly, and I soon found myself hustled back to Marcus and food and the dress.

As dresses went, it was quite comfortable. A high neckline and long sleeves, with a flared split skirt. I especially liked the skirt, given the chance of a side-saddle in this army camp was nonexistent. The fabric slid between my legs like water glides over skin. It was nothing I'd ever seen or felt. Somehow Marcus had even gotten slippers that matched the dress.

I soothed the dress, running my hands over the fabric with mixed emotions. I certainly didn't fill the bodice, the cut being made for more generous curves. The skirt fit fine over my more than ample hips, and the cloth flowed down my legs. Ordinarily I'd be pleased to own such a dress.

But not a scarlet dress.

In Water's Fall, red was the color worn by women whose profession I was not supposed to know about. At times, some of the bolder women of the court would dare to have a scarf, or some trim of that color, but not a whole dress. What made it that much worse was that I had never seen a red like this before, so bright and vivid. It was the bright red of new blood, brighter even than the roses in the briar of the palace garden. It put all the Xyian colors to shame, making them look drab and dowdy. A dress like this, as bright as it was, all but screamed my position in no uncertain terms.

I bowed my head, hiding my face with a curtain of hair. If I said something, Marcus might not understand, but he might not make me wear the dress. Trous would raise eyebrows, certainly, but this dress would have the lord and ladies of the Court collapsing with seizures. I didn't want to offend him, but I couldn't wear this. In the back of my head I heard Great Aunt Xydella's quavery voice. 'Speak up, child.' She'd say. 'I can't read minds.' Of course Great Aunt Xydella would have worn the dress and loved every outrageous minute of it.

I bit my lip, then opened my mouth. "Marcus—"

Keir walked into the tent and stopped short. His eyes widened, and his face lit up. "Fire's blessing." He stood, looking at me with approval.

I swallowed what I had been about to say.

Keir made a gesture, and I turned slowly, allowing him to see it. "Marcus, where did you find such a dress?"

Marcus drew himself up and arched his eyebrow. "The clothing of one woman is a task well within my skills, Warlord."

Keir smiled and acknowledged Marcus with a slight bow. "I stand corrected, old man." He straightened. He was outfitted in full chain that held a high gloss, with a black cape edged in fur. The hilts of his swords peeked over his shoulders. He moved to stand before me, a look of pride on his face. He held out his hands, and there were the bracelets that I had worn at the surrender ceremony.

I stiffened and looked away. They lay open in his hands, heavy silver symbols of my status. I didn't look up, for fear that I would betray my feelings. I simply extended my wrists and kept my head down as he snapped them into place. They felt heavy, like the bindings they were, and I let the weight pull my arms down to my sides.

There was a slight pause. Then Keir asked, "Is there a cloak, as well?"

There was, thankfully as black as Keir's own. I took it from Marcus, who looked at me with a puzzled expression. I put on the cloak as I followed Keir out into the evening air.

The dress was even brighter in the sun. If that were possible.

Our escort awaited us. There were ten mounted men, besides Rafe and Prest. Rafe was holding the horses. Rafe and Prest were also in their best armor, and they gleamed in the afternoon sun. Rafe's face lit up when he saw me. Prest turned, and a smile spread over his face. Rafe handed me the reins of one of the horses. "Warprize, you look—"

Keir coughed.

Rafe didn't miss a beat. "Well. Very well." He mounted his horse, as did Keir and Prest.

I had some difficulty, trying to get the skirt in the correct position, but managed to get up and into the saddle. I gathered the reins and turned, only to find everyone looking at me in varying degrees of dismay.

"What?" I asked, puzzled.

Prest just shook his head. Rafe sucked in a breath. "The way you sit—"

Keir looked at me sternly. "You should have told me you can't ride."

I frowned. "I can ride."

They looked at me, scanning me from head to toe. I sat up a little straighter, but all three shook their heads. The others in our escort all seemed to be very busy adjusting their tunics and weapons. Almost as if they were embarrassed for me.

Prest frowned. "Maybe a pregnant mare?"

Rafe looked toward the city. "We could walk the horses—"

Keir shook his head. "It would take too long. She can ride double with me."

"This is ridiculous." I gathered the reins, clicked my tongue, and urged the horse on.

Nothing happened.

Now the guards by the tent were looking at me, shaking their heads. Prest grabbed for my reins, as if afraid the horse would run away with me. Keir moved his horse along side mine, planning to snatch me from the saddle, but I was having none of that. Whore I may look, Warprize I may be, but I'd be damned before I was taken to the ceremony like a helpless child.

Rafe pulled his horse to the side, and I saw what he was doing. He used his toes under the horse's front legs, instead of his heels, and seemed to shift his weight forward. I did the same, and the horse obliged with a few steps forward. I fended off Prest and Keir and urged the beast on.

Keir's voice came from behind me. "It's not safe. You will ride with me."

I shifted forward again, and the horse broke into a trot.

There were calls from behind me, but I was not going to stop. I could ride. I headed down the path through the tents, toward the road to the city. It didn't take long for Keir and the others to catch up and form up around me. Rafe was still muttering about my skill, and Prest had a frown on his face, but I noticed that Keir had that look of pride again as he passed me to take the lead.

There were workers in the fields that we passed, and I gave them no notice at first. But the closer we came to the city walls, the more my awareness grew. They weren't harvesting or preparing the ground for the spring. They were still gathering the dead. It had been days since the fighting had stopped, yet still they moved about in their work.

Were there so many dead?

I had to focus on the road before me, couldn't look at the men with the carts any longer. I clenched my jaw. The peace had to hold, I had to do my part. Or there'd be more bodies, more lives wasted. If that meant I never heard my name again, so be it. Such a small price to pay.

Our appearance at the main gates of the city caused quite a stir. The ceremony was still some hours away, and from the reaction of the guard, we were not expected so soon. The gates were normally kept open for the merchant traffic. They had been closed due to the war, and apparently were being kept closed. The Warlord drew up to the gates and stopped.

The head guard stepped forward. "Hail, Warlord. Do you wish an escort or crier through the city?"

"My thanks, but no. The warprize knows the way."

The guard glanced at me, and his eyes bulged out. I looked away. We sat in silence for a moment as he stared.

"The gate," Keir growled.

The guard started, then gave a shout for the gate to be opened and the portcullis raised. As soon as the way was clear, we headed into the city. The only crowds were the normal crowds of a market day. Keir brought his horse up short and looked over his shoulder at me with a question in his eyes. I moved my horse up next to his. "Is there something you wish to tell me?"

"Tell you?" I flushed slightly.

He narrowed his eyes, and studied me. Finally he turned away. "Would there be time to see more of the city? I have only seen the main road."

I nodded and pointed off to our left. "That will take us along the west wall, and eventually to the palace."

Keir gave me a sly smile. "Where is the shop that sells the vanilla?"

"Close to where the tinker's cart was."

He nodded, looking around. "We will head that way. What is a 'crier'?"

I smiled. "Someone who walks in front of your horse, crying out your name and title. Usually used by someone who thinks he is of great importance and is afraid no one knows it."

Keir looked offended. He moved off in that direction, and I fell in behind, with our escort riding around us. That went against road custom in the city, to ride so far abreast. But I doubted any of the City Guard would fine us. Out of the corner of my eye, I spotted a guardsman running for the palace. I suspected that word would spread fairly quickly that we were in the city.

The townspeople's reactions were almost predictable. First there was outrage at the violation of road custom, then recognition of the Warlord. At that point, their faces were not welcoming. Then they'd spot me as the procession continued. My cloak was open, the dress visible, and it was causing quite a stir. Thank the Goddess that Keir had headed for the shops. The pleasure streets were on the other side of the city; I could only imagine how the denizens would have reacted.

Our escort stayed close, and Rafe and Prest stayed right by my side, scanning the crowds. Some of the townspeople tried to approach me, but Keir's glare and the presence of the guards discouraged them. I settled for a nod and a smile to any that I recognized. Most were content to wave and call out to me as we passed by.

The streets were crowded with marketgoers scurrying

about, their arms filled with baskets and bundles. One man went by with three chickens in his arms, squawking and flapping their wings. My horse shied a bit, which brought me dire looks from the men around me, but I brought it under control. I could tell that they hadn't spent time in cities before, or at least cities the size of Water's Fall. They were on alert, and on their guard, eyes taking in the crowds, the buildings crammed together, some leaning out over the streets. They were doing their best not to be overawed, but I could tell that they were impressed. Once in a while, one would wrinkle his nose at the smells, or start at a strange noise, but no one made a comment. We continued on without incident, moving past the army barracks by the Great South Gate. By now, word of our coming had spread, and there were folk lining the streets to see us. For the most part they were quiet, merely speaking among themselves as we passed. Needless to say, the dress drew its fair share of attention.

Finally, we arrived at the market. I pointed out Estoval's shop. Keir dismounted, and gestured for me to follow. The others took up positions, clearing an area in front of the shop. Keir opened the door, and I followed, curious.

Thankfully, the fragrant shop was empty of customers. Estoval turned to greet us and his mouth fell open.

I felt the heat rise in my face. Keir stared at the man, then looked at me for a long moment, eyes narrow. He opened his mouth, and took a breath to speak.

He grimaced then sneezed. Explosively.

That snapped Estoval out of his trance. "Warlord! How may I serve you?"

"Merchant, do you sell vanilla?" He pronounced the word slowly and carefully.

"Yes, Warlord, in many forms, although it is quite expensive. Did you want ground, whole beans, the oil?"

"Yes." Keir looked at me. "See to it." He sneezed, then caught my eye with a flash of a grin that took my breath away. "Buy lots. Buy it all. And whatever else you need." With a gasping wheeze, he headed for the door, his nose scrunched up against another sneeze. As he passed me, he slipped a purse into my hand. Then he ducked out of the shop, leaving me flushed and embarrassed.

Once Keir was out the door, Estoval relaxed a little, but I noticed that he kept an eye on the door. "Warprize, you honor my shop."

"Estoval, please. My name is Lara."

His eyes darted to the door. "Not anymore, Daughter of Xy." He gestured to his displays. "I have plenty of vanilla, even some scented soap, for no one is buying extravagances. But my stocks of other items are low. The Warlords supply master was here earlier, and bargained hard." He shook his head. "Bargained hard and meanly."

I suppressed a smile. Estoval started to gather up every kind of vanilla that he had on hand. I stopped, thinking for a moment, considering Keir's words. He had said..

"Estoval, I need an apprentice to run an errand. Are any available?"

"Of course." He raised his voice calling for a lad.

"And paper and pen, if I may?" He inclined his head. I wrote a quick note and in a moment a lad stood before me.

"Take these coins and run to the shop of Remn. You know it?"

"Of course, Lady."

"Tell Remn I want two books. Used, mind, cheap as possible. *The Epic of Xyson,* and a reading primer. Give him this note. Be quick, and I'll have a coin for you."

The lad grinned and was off out the back of the shop. I turned back to Estoval, and we continued our business. I was well satisfied. Remn would have both books, especially the Epic. A hoary old saga of my ancestor's heroic deeds. It was long, filled with battles, duels and the discussions of the virtues of various styles of weapons and armor. It was the bane of every child who learned their letters in Water's Fall. Atira would love it. I could read it to her, or use it as incentive to learn to read my language.

The lad was as quick as I could ask. He returned with a bundle and the two books. I gave him a coin and asked Estoval if I could use his back room for a moment. Once in that small area, I broke open the bundle.

Proper undergarments.

Bless Remn's wife. She was about my size and had included two of each kind. I could trust their discretion in this. Goddess forgive me, but I was too embarrassed to talk to Keir or Marcus about these items of clothing. I dressed quickly, feeling better able to face whatever was to come. When I emerged, I thanked Estoval, who handed me a small parcel, bowed me out and locked the door behind me. I had been awhile, and oddly enough the street was almost completely clear. Which made sense to a degree. Those that could not attend the Court for the ceremony would observe in their own homes, as part of the evening meal.

Keir and Prest were already mounted. Rafe stood, holding my mount and his. "Are you finished?" Keir asked, trying to hide his impatience and failing miserably. "I have sent the others before us."

"Yes." I tucked my two packages into my saddlebag and moved to mount my horse. As I swung my leg up, the horse shied and moved away from me, causing me to lose my balance. I dropped back to the ground.

So the lance passed over my head, instead of hitting my chest.

7

"Lara, DOWN!"

I barely had time to register what had happened before Keir somehow swept me back. His hands forced me down, against the wall of the shop. I fell to my knees as the horses danced about in confusion. The air filled with shouts, cries of frustration, and the clatter of hooves on cobblestones.

"Stay down." Keir hissed, as he turned and pulled his swords. I looked up to see the horses flee and Keir, Rafe, and Prest use those precious seconds to take positions, sheltering me in their half-circle. The attackers came charging from the shadows, a hodgepodge of ruffians, shields at the ready, weapons high.

"Death to the—" The lead man never finished his cry. Keir smashed through his defenses and plunged into the man's chest in one quick stabbing motion. I could hear the sound of steel on bone as he pulled the blade free. With fierce quickness, he struck at another, who barely deflected the blow with his blade.

Prest held his shield up tight, absorbing blows from his

two sword-wielding attackers. He waited, patient, then darted
in with his sword to take quick strikes when they left themselves open.

Rafe was barely holding his own against his opponent. A
big man, armed with an enormous club, was battering at his
shield, striking it with heavy, powerful blows. Rafe took the
blows, but each time, his shield went lower. Finally the giant
struck with such force that Rafe's shield came down, hitting
Rafe's forehead. Sensing this weakness, Keir feinted a rush-
ing attack on his remaining opponent. As the man stepped
back, Keir turned and drove one blade deep into Rafe's opponent. The man gave a grunt as it slid in easily. Keir's attention
focused back on his own enemy before the body fell from the
blade.

There was a cry, a clatter, and another man emerged from
the shadows, pulling a mace from his belt. He launched himself at Rafe.

I pressed against the wall, trying to stay small and out of the
way. The Watch should have come running by now, but the
street remained empty, with no sound of a hue and cry. The
only sounds were those of clashing weapons, heavy breathing,
and boots looking for purchase on the surface of the street.

With two down, the remaining attackers shifted their focus. Prest now had one opponent. Two pressed Keir. Rafe
faced one as well.

It proved to be a mistake. Prest bashed at his opponent
with his shield, driving the man back, ramming him hard
enough to get him off-balance. With a step forward, Prest
snaked his sword out around the edge of his shield and
plunged it into his opponent's ribs. As his man went down, I
assumed Prest would aid Keir. But he stayed in position,
scanning the street, keeping his place.

Keir needed no aid. He seemed to know his opponents'
moves before they were made, and blocked them with ease.
His attackers were breathing heavily as fatigue set in. When
one made the mistake of stepping back when his fellow
shifted forward, Keir did not hesitate. In a moment, another
man lay bleeding in the street, and two were left.

They broke and ran.

Rafe made to follow, but Keir barked a command. Rafe froze and kept position. Keir turned his head slightly. "Are you hurt?"

"No." My voice sounded so shaky, it embarrassed me. I tried to rise, sliding a hand against the wall for support. The wood felt warm and rough against my trembling hand.

"Stay down." Keir still scanned the street and rooftops, weapons at the ready.

It had happened so fast, my heart still raced in my chest. I concentrated on my breathing, trying to slow it down. For tense minutes, we stood there waiting to see if they would try again. After a lifetime, Keir relaxed. "It's clear. Anyone hurt?" Prest and Rafe responded in the negative, as they both moved to check the fallen.

I pushed away from the wall. "Rafe, you're cut."

"Scraped myself on my shield rim." Rafe turned his man over. "This one's dead."

I took a step forward, toward the other downed men.

"No." Keir stopped me.

"Please, let me . . ." I pushed against him, trying to move past. I might as well have pushed the wall.

Rafe spoke up. "Doesn't matter, Warprize. They're all dead." He was kneeling by one of the bodies, cleaning his sword. "Strange that they have no armor."

"An ambush planned in haste." Keir stood grim, scanning the market area, which remained strangely empty for the time of day. There was no sign of the Watch. "Warprize, do you recognize them?" Keir moved with me as I stepped forward to look at their faces.

They lay in their own blood, the smell of feces and death in the air. None of them looked familiar as Rafe rolled them onto their backs, and they wore nothing to identify themselves with any noble family. Even as I shook my head, Rafe pulled a belt pouch off one, and it spilled bright gold coins onto the cobblestones. More gold than a mere soldier might see in a lifetime.

Keir growled low in his throat. "Assassins. Xyian, all of them."

"This isn't."

We turned to see Prest standing at the wall, holding the lance in his hands, the tip broken. Black shards lay on the ground at his feet. "Full-tipped when thrown." Prest's eyes gleamed as he displayed the feathering on the lance.

Rafe sucked in a breath with a hiss.

Keir's lips tightened, then he glanced at Rafe. "Gather the horses." The animals hadn't wandered far and Rafe moved toward them, making soothing sounds. Keir turned back to Prest. "Wrap that and put it in my quiver. We're returning to camp."

"Camp?" I stepped back from the bodies, wrapping my cloak around my body. "But the ceremony . . ." I let my voice trail off as Keir ignored me, cleaning his swords on one of the dead. Prest was next to me, wrapping the lance in a cloth he'd pulled from his saddlebags. Hadn't Atira said something about featherings? Their patterns?

It was my turn to suck in a breath. "Who made that lance?"

Prest looked at me, then flicked his eyes to Keir. Rafe came up with the beasts and Keir took the reins. With a nod, he had Rafe stripping the corpses of gold and weapons. With an equally quick movement he motioned for me to mount. "Up, Warprize."

"You know who made it."

Keir's eyes rested on mine for a moment, softening slightly. He spoke, but not to answer my question. "Mount. We ride for camp."

I just stood there, trying to think past the rapid beating of my heart. "The ceremony . . ."

Keir drilled me with a glare. "Ceremony be damned."

I went to the horse, and clung to the saddle, trying to will strength into my legs. Trembling, I mounted. "What does it say if the Warlord runs to camp and hides when attacked by six men?"

Rafe chimed in. "Six men who weren't very good."

Prest snorted, but kept his eyes on the street.

Keir didn't glance at Rafe. "So speaks the man who will be practicing his shield work for the next week."

Rafe shut his mouth.

Keir grabbed his own horse and swung into the saddle. "It says that the Warlord is no fool." Prest and Rafe mounted up as well.

"We are not hurt." I swallowed hard, and fought down my fear. "There are many people gathered for the ceremony. What will they say when the Warlord does not appear?" I moved my horse in the direction of the castle.

Keir grabbed my reins as I passed, bringing my horse to a halt. "Then I will go alone. Prest and Rafe will escort you to camp."

I shook my head. "That leaves you alone and a target. If we all go, then we will have the escort of all the men who are attending on the way back." I caught his eye. "Besides, my people are expecting me. What rumors will start when I do not appear?"

Keir stared at me, his jaw working. I could see a small vein pulsing on his neck, but I didn't drop my gaze. Finally, he took in a deep breath and let it out very, very slowly. He released the reins, and turned his horse in the direction of the castle.

"What about them?" Rafe jerked his head back at the pile of dead.

"Leave them to rot."

The streets remained empty as we rode to the castle. Buildings that had once been friendly and familiar now held deep shadows where danger lurked. My reins grew damp from my sweaty hands, my shoulders tight with every step. Fear gripped me hard.

Rafe rode beside me, with bow and arrow in hand. His horse responded to knees and feet alone, the reins lay knotted in front of Rafe's saddle. Prest rode in the same manner, but slightly behind us. They both scanned the surroundings constantly, focused on catching the slightest hint of an attack.

Keir rode in front, his swords sheathed, looking outwardly

relaxed, but with his head moving from side to side, watching the buildings around us as we passed.

I cleared my throat to ask about the lance again, but Keir gestured for silence without even looking back at me. I bit my lip as my throat went even drier, and fought the urge to hunch in my saddle.

The horses sensed our tension and shifted restlessly under us. But Keir held our pace to a walk. It was only when the castle gates appeared in the distance, ablaze with lights and people, that he urged his horse to a trot. We sped up to follow him the final distance into the main courtyard.

People, both Xyian and Firelander, were clustered about, and palace guards moved forward for our horses. The sun still filled the area with light, causing my dress to glow like a bright flame. I tried to look confident and relaxed, but my stomach cramped as the Xyians around me reacted to the dress.

Keir, Prest and Rafe were still on guard, keeping an eye on the crowd. Keir swung down first, and gave me a concerned look as he helped me dismount, as if he sensed the strain. Rafe and Prest joined us, and they surrounded me as we entered the castle proper.

Othur appeared before us. "Warlord." He bowed. When his head came up, his eyes sought mine, filled with concern. I risked a small smile. His eyes crinkled at the edges as he continued. "Allow me to show you to the antechamber." He guided us into the same chamber where I had waited for the submission ceremony. It had only been days ago, but it felt like a lifetime. As we entered, my shoulders relaxed, now that we were out from under prying eyes.

Othur stood in the doorway behind us, and bowed again. "I will inform the King of your arrival. He will join you shortly."

Keir held up his hand. "We will delay for a few moments. I will send for Xymund when I am ready."

Keir moved further into the room, threw his cloak over one of the chairs, and started to pace. The light of the fire and the lamps played over his face, making his blue eyes dark and forbidding.

"Who were they?" he asked.

"Not one of us." Prest answered firmly.

"How do you know that?" I asked.

Prest shrugged. "They missed."

"He's right." Keir continued his prowl. "Had one of my people thrown the lance, you would have been hit."

"The fletching was Iften's." Rafe's voice was soft.

"Iften's?" I stared at Keir.

"Full-tipped." Prest added.

"What does that mean?" I asked, frustrated by the cryptic comments.

Keir sighed. "The tip was whole when the lance was thrown. Lance tips are meant to break when they hit. A scavenged lance wouldn't be whole."

"It's possible that one wouldn't break." My argument sounded weak, even in my ears.

"Unlikely," Prest observed.

"Horses get captured with quivers full." He shrugged. "But the fletching is Iften's and he's not lost a horse that I know of." Rafe paused, not looking at anyone in particular. "And Iften has been in the city."

I put my hand over my mouth. "Remn said that Iften met with Xymund alone." Or had he? I tried to remember what he'd said, but it slipped away from me.

Keir interrupted my thoughts, and I focused on him. "Yet those scum were paid well. That speaks of Xyians."

"My people would not risk the peace." I responded firmly. "One of your people could have hired them just as easily."

Keir shook his head. "My people are just learning about coinage and money. More like it was a Xyian." He hesitated. "Or a Xyian King."

I glared at him. "Xymund has sworn. He will not risk his crown or break his word."

"Risk to his head, I believe," Keir retorted. "I'm not so certain of his oath." Keir moved closer to me. "Not certain that he understands that if you die there is no peace."

"And if you die, Warlord?" I asked softly. "Would the peace hold? You were attacked as well, they even doubled up on you." The memory flashed before my eyes, and suddenly my stomach dropped. I had a flash of vision, of a wounded and dying Keir. Dearest Goddess. I closed my eyes and swallowed hard.

A warm hand on my shoulder pressed me into one of the chairs by the fireplace. I opened my eyes to find Keir kneeling in front of me. "I am sorry," I said.

"Don't be. You did well." Then that little-boy-mischievous look sparkled in his eyes. "For a healer."

Prest and Rafe snorted, a kind of nervous chuckle. I sat up straighter and tried to appear offended. "If you think that Xymund is behind this, confront him. Ask him—"

"No." Keir grew serious. "His actions tell me more than words. Say nothing about the attack to anyone. Let our enemy speculate as to what occurred." Prest and Rafe nodded. I did as well, all too willing to drop the subject. Keir stood, and gestured Rafe to the door.

When the door to the antechamber opened Xymund entered, followed by Lord Marshall Warren and the members of the Council. I moved to stand, but Keir's hand on my shoulder pressed me down. I looked up, puzzled, but Keir's gaze fixed on Xymund.

Xymund bowed his head to Keir. "Warlord."

"Xymund." Keir's voice sounded cold to my ears.

There wasn't time for more, for Othur had moved to the large double-doors. "Honored Lords, the Herald is ready to commence the ceremony. Please take your places." Keir moved to the doors as well, and everyone in the room started to adjust their position for the entrance into the throne room. I rose from the chair unsure of where to stand. As I did, my cloak fell open, and there were harsh intakes of breath around the room. Xymund, standing behind Keir, turned his head. His eyes widened as he took in the scarlet on both the dress and my cheeks. While his face remained impassive, his eyes danced.

Determined to retain some dignity, I spotted Prest and Rafe toward the back and moved in their direction.

"Warprize." Keir's voice cut through the sounds in the room.

I turned. "Warlord?"

His eyes flickered over to Xymund standing behind him. "Your place is here, beside me."

I gaped at him. The rest of the room quieted, recognizing a power struggle when they saw one. That blue-eyed gaze stayed calm and confident. My eyes darted to Xymund, who was clearly struggling with his temper.

"Here." Keir spoke again, indicating the place beside him.

I moved, to Keir's side. "Yes, Warlord." He looked down at me, scrutinizing me closely. I could feel Xymund's eyes like daggers on my back.

Othur had been watching the action, and had maintained a neutral face. Keir gestured for him to open the double doors. He did so and stepped out into the throne room. The Herald, standing there in full uniform, pounded the floor with his staff three times. "Lord and Ladies, all hail Keir, Warlord of the Firelanders—"

"No." Keir's voice rang out over that of the Herald's, causing a stir in the throne room.

The poor man's eyes bugged out of his head. "Warlord?"

"That is your word, not ours. We are of the Plains."

The Herald blinked madly for a moment, then cleared his throat. "Lord and Ladies, all hail Keir, Warlord of the Plains, Overlord of Xy." He looked at Keir, who gave him a nod. The Herald seemed to relax, until he spotted me, but years of training kept his voice steady. Without hesitation he continued, ". . . and Xylara, Warprize."

Keir advanced into the room, every step strong and confident. I walked at his side and one step behind. The throne room overflowed, with people crammed into every nook and cranny. There were as many of Keir's men as there were nobles. All bowed as we crossed and rose as we passed. The murmurs started at once, reacting to the presence of the Warlord, and his slave walking right behind him. I stared straight ahead. A second, smaller chair had been placed to the right side of the throne. Keir stepped to the throne, turned and faced the room. I made a move to the left, to stand at his side. Keir gave me a quick glance, then gestured to the smaller chair. My eyes widened, but I obeyed. Behind me, I heard the Herald announce Xymund.

Who now had no place to sit.

The crowd reacted when I turned to face them, displaying the dress in all its crimson glory. I ignored it, because as he walked across the room, I saw the exact moment Xymund realized what had happened. I dropped my eyes, unwilling to see the look in his as he drew closer. Keir must have made a gesture of some kind, because Xymund went to stand to the left of the throne. I heard the Herald announcing Lord Marshall Warren and the members of the Council, who followed him in and went to stand along the left side, ranging out from Xymund.

Once all were in position, Keir sat. I waited a pause, then sat as well. Everyone else remained standing.

Archbishop Drizen, followed by two acolytes appeared before us, bowed before the Warlord, and began the ceremony. The ancient chants flowed over me, a somber and bittersweet prayer for the dead. The incense smoked from the censers held by the two priests who swung them in slow arcs. Frankly, they could have paraded naked and rubbed dung on their bodies for all the attention I gave it. Instead, my thoughts lingered on Xymund and the insult Keir had just given him. Xymund was not dumb, he would not jeopardize the peace. I hoped. But to place a slave in precedence above the King . . .

I risked a glance at the Warlord, who sat on the throne with a confidence that I had never seen in Xymund. I tore my eyes away from that profile and tried to concentrate on the priests. I could not see Xymund from where I sat, but I could just imagine his expression.

I suspected that he would not be inviting us for a drink after the ceremony.

The Archbishop had concluded the prayer and bowed before Keir. The lords and ladies seemed to think this the end of the ceremony, but Keir motioned with his hand, and Joden emerged from the crowd. His round face held a somber look, and he was dressed in his finest armor and weapons. He approached the throne and bowed. Keir nodded in return. "Joden, you grace our ceremony." He glanced about the room. "Our tradition is to lament the dead with song. Joden has agreed to sing for us."

Joden raised his right palm to the sky. He spoke in his language. "May the skies hear my voice. May the people remember."

The response rose from those who understood him. "We will remember."

Joden lowered his hand, took a deep breath, and began to sing.

His voice sounded richer and far deeper than I expected. It filled the room and brought the small rustles and murmurs to a halt. Somehow, the sound of his voice pulled us all in, let us share his pain, and for a brief moment, be as one within it. Language didn't seem to be a barrier. For those who understood, the words spoke of a loved one that would never see the sky again, nor share the sweetness of a glass of wine. Or the joy of a laugh. It spoke of an emptiness at the table, at the fireside, and in the heart. My eyes filled as I thought of my father, and the warrior who had died giving me his blessing. I lowered my head and tried not to give in to my grief.

Others were moved as well. A glance showed me Keir's hand clenched on his knee, knuckles white.

The song changed then. Joden's voice rang with the hope of reuniting, riding again under endless skies, sharing wines not yet tasted. I managed to lift my head at that and looked at Joden as the last notes hovered in the air. As I wiped at my eyes and snuffled my nose, I noticed others doing the same.

The last notes faded. Joden lifted his palm again. "May the people remember."

Again, the response came. "We will remember."

Keir echoed the words, then continued, "My thanks, Joden. You honor us."

Joden bowed, and moved back into the crowd.

The Archbishop came forward, prepared to give the traditional blessing of the monarch. With an uneasy glance in Xymund's direction, he stood before Keir, bowed, and recited the blessing. Keir nodded deeply to him at the conclusion.

Without further thought, the Archbishop turned toward me, and I saw his eyes widen when he realized what he had done. Tradition required a blessing for the Queen as well, hardly appropriate for a warprize. The poor man seemed quite flustered for a moment, then elected to nod his head in my direction. I returned the nod. I doubt he even realized the sigh of relief that he gave as he turned to render the benediction to the crowd.

Even before he stopped speaking, Keir stood. I waited but he extended a hand to help me rise, so I joined him at his side. We walked toward the antechamber in silence.

The crowd, a mixture of Xyian and Firclander, had filled in the space before the door, and they parted to allow us though. The Xyians were unsure as to the courtesies to extend, whether to bow or curtsey and to whom. The Firelanders had no such problem. They remained tall and upright, with solemn looks. As we moved closer to the door, I saw many familiar faces, including Lord Durst. Scowling, he stepped back as if to avoid touching me, his lip curled in a snarl. He craned his head forward, having caught my eye. "Whore."

Durst spoke forcefully, his voice low, but it carried. I flushed and looked away, mortified. I barely registered that Keir dropped my hand. There was a sound of drawn steel and a flash of movement. I looked back to see Keir's sword buried deep in Durst's chest.

In endless time, the man's eyes bulged and he sank slowly to the floor. Keir pulled the weapon out of Durst's body and flicked it, sending blood onto the clothes of those nearby. Durst made an odd huffing noise as his hands clutched at the wound. People stepped back to allow Durst to fall at their feet, then the screaming began as they jostled both to escape and to get a better view.

"Silence." Keir's command rang out, even as he pulled out a cloth to wipe the blade clean. The room watched in horrified silence as he dropped the bloody cloth and sheathed his sword in a ring that hung from his belt. The sound of metal on metal almost did more to grab everyone's attention than his voice. "The insult is avenged." The quiet grew even deeper, but to my horror, Xyian nobles started to place their hands on their swords, eyeing the Firelanders around us.

"Warprize."

My eyes snapped up to see Keir standing there, his hand held out for mine, the hand that had slain Lord Durst in an instant. The same hand that had saved my life in the market.

Everyone was frozen, focused on that hand, and I knew that the peace, in that instant, was balanced on the edge of a sword. Reject that hand, kneel to aid Durst, and there'd be those who'd use it as an excuse to draw their swords.

Mindful of my status, mindful of my obligation, and mindful of the dead still being buried beyond these walls, I placed my hand in Keir's and allowed myself to be led from the throne room.

Xymund followed, along with Lord Warren. The voices rose behind us, only to be cut off as the door to the antechamber shut.

We stood in silence for a moment, then Keir moved to the fireplace. "The ceremony went well." His voice was as calm as if nothing had happened. As if a man had not died in the throne room. As if I had not left him lying in a pool of his own blood.

Xymund did not respond. Warren cleared his throat. "Thoughtful of you to include our priests. It is appreciated." He too was ignoring what had happened.

Keir tilted his head. "We honor the dead of both sides." He gave Warren an appraising eye. "We haven't spoken outside the confines of negotiations or parley. I would welcome an opportunity to talk with you about your strategies, especially your use of the river."

Warren's mouth curled in a wry smile. "I would welcome that."

"Tomorrow? At the nooning. Bring your officers and we will dine."

Numb, I watched as they talked of nothing, as if all were

well and fine, as if Keir hadn't just killed a man for a simple insult. My heart drummed in my chest and the air in the room seemed close and over-warm.

Keir pulled his cloak off the chair where he'd thrown it before the ceremony. "I wish to see the castle."

Xymund's voice grated. "Othur will show you the building."

"No," Keir interrupted. "I wish to see it through the eyes of the warprize."

Xymund's jaw clenched. Never had I seen him so angry and so afraid. His right eye seemed to twitch very slightly, his hands clenched in fists. I held my breath, waiting to see which emotion would win out.

Xymund's hands relaxed. His head jerked as if to nod, and he went to the door. With a resigned look, Warren made to follow.

"I will need to know the extent of that lord's holdings." Keir's voice came as a low purr. Xymund stopped dead in the doorway. Keir continued, "I will need to appoint a new lord as soon as possible."

Warren half-turned toward Keir. "Warlord, our tradition is that a man's son inherits his father's holdings. Durst's son, Degnan, is his heir."

"Is this Degnan capable?"

Warren shrugged, clearly at a loss. He looked to Xymund for support, but none came. Finally, he looked back at Keir. "He is the heir, Warlord."

"I will consider this." Keir lifted an eyebrow. "You are excused."

Goddess, was he deliberately provoking Xymund?

Xymund said nothing and left. Warren followed.

I released the breath I had been holding. Didn't he understand, didn't they know what a horrible thing had happened? To slay a man without warning, for a slur? Bad enough to insult Xymund's pride, to humiliate him before the Court. The Warlord had made very clear that his token was not for me to use, I had no protections from the consequences of my words, but if the peace were to last past the dawn someone had to voice this truth.

"Rafe, I want company for our tour. Ask Joden, Yers, Oxna, Senbar and Uzania to join us. I saw Epor and Isdra in the crowd, ask them as well. Tell the rest to return to camp. In a group, no stops. Tell them to be alert."

"Your sword, Warlord?" Rafe paused by the door. "Do you wish me to see to it?"

"It's well enough. I will see to it myself."

Rafe nodded and slipped out.

Keir watched the fire. I moved closer, licked my lips and drew in a breath. He glanced my way. "You wish to point out my mistake."

I closed my mouth. His blue eyes glittered in the light of the fire and I waited for that temper to flare. Instead he gave me a rueful smile. "So much for my talk of change, eh?"

I didn't understand, and would have asked, but a knock at the door brought Rafe into the room with the others, talking quietly among themselves.

The moment was lost. I might risk the truth in private, but not in front of others. As Keir stepped away, I looked for a friendly face and found it in Joden. "You have a wonderful voice, Joden."

His smile was wide and a relief to see. "My thanks, Warprize."

"Come," Keir gestured us to the door. "Show us this stone tent of yours."

I took them to the highest point, in the tallest turret, to start. The young guard at the top almost dropped his spear, startled to find himself hosting the Warlord when normally his only company were the bees that buzzed in and out of the skeps that Anna kept on the heights. The sun was down, but in the fading twilight, we could still see.

The battlements fascinated Keir. The views from this height allowed one to look clear into the valley below, and even beyond their camp. Keir, Rafe, and the others pressed themselves against the outer wall, trying to look down as far as they could. The breeze that always blew at this height whistled past, catching at our hair and clothing. Prest, on the other hand, pressed himself against the opposite wall by the door, his eyes wide, the whites showing, his dark complexion turning ashen. He seemed quite grateful when I pulled them away from the views and we headed back down.

They asked question after question about the building, about how I could stand to be surrounded by walls all the time. Some of the narrow corridors made them nervous, and I'd see them all looking up, as if searching for the sky. Some of their questions I knew the answer to, some I didn't. They admired the thick walls, wrinkled their noses at the privies with their small holes, and mock fought on the circular staircases. I showed them the places where old kings had started building, and young kings had built on. Impressed as they were with its age and fortifications, I gathered that Keir did not care for the length of time it had taken for the castle to rise to its current heights.

The halls and corridors were strangely quiet as we proceeded, empty of the normal traffic of servants and nobles. It made me uneasy even as I led them into the castle chapel.

The room was lit with hundreds of candles, and behind the altar, the white marble statute of the Goddess gleamed brightly. She was lovely, her arms holding a basket of herbs and flowers, her face serene and peaceful. I paused in the center aisle and smiled.

"So it's true. You worship people." Surprised, I turned to see Joden standing behind me, looking around in amazement.

"This chapel is dedicated to the worship of the Goddess, The Lady of the Moon and Stars." I fumbled around for the right words. "She is more than a 'person.'"

"He means no offense," Keir spoke softly as the others gathered around us, gaping and gawking. There was a general sense of disapproval. "It's odd to see, that's all." Keir waved his hand to encompass the room. "Another difference between us."

"A big difference," Yers muttered, his crooked nose twitching.

On that note, I turned and lead them out, before one of the

Priestesses should appear. Tensions were high enough without a religious debate.

"Your Goddess, she is a healer?" Keir moved up beside me.

"Yes," I decided to show them my old room and headed in that direction. "She is the Goddess of Healing and Mercy." I looked over my shoulder. "Not the kind of mercy granted on a battlefield."

Keir grunted.

"There is a temple in the city to the God of the Sun, who is the God of Purity and Strength."

"You worship the sun as a man?" Joden asked, his disbelief apparent in his voice.

"How did you come to be a healer?" Keir changed the topic so smoothly I had to smile.

"I was playing with one of my friends in the castle gardens, chasing him down the paths. We were very young and the kitchen maids lost track of us. We were running and laughing, and suddenly down he went, tripping over a huge . . . porcupine?" I wasn't sure if they knew what the creature was, but a few people winced in sympathy.

"Needle-rat," Rafe clarified, and now everyone understood.

"His face and arms were filled with quills and he started screaming and crying, and the kitchen maids came running, Anna came running, everyone was screaming and crying, so I started screaming and crying too."

"A man appeared, a tall man who looked like a gray lake bird, tall and quiet. With a few words he calmed everyone down, and had my friend giggling as he dealt with the quills. Like a miracle, peace was restored." The memory was a good one and I smiled at Keir. "He restored my world with his quiet voice and gentle skill."

"As you wish to do."

I nodded as I opened the door to my old room.

The room had been stripped down to its simple furnishings. Keir looked around and frowned. "This was your bedroom?" Prest and Rafe crowded in with us, the others watched from the door. Keir continued. "Seems small for a Daughter of Xy."

I shrugged. "I didn't need a lot of room. Besides, I had other rooms to play in. I will show you."

Keir looked at me and slowly smiled in response.

Rafe stood by the fireplace. "Guess they are using it to burn trash now."

I turned. There in the fireplace were the ashes of books and papers. The pile looked familiar.

It was.

I could still make out the cord I had used before I had left. The fire must have been huge. A wonder that it had not caught the chimney on fire. I knelt and reached out, but the ash collapsed at the touch of my fingers. A lump rose in my throat.

"Something important?" Keir asked.

I stood. "No. Nothing important." I wiped my hands together as I moved woodenly toward the door. "We should move on. There is much more to see."

Othur was standing in the hall when I emerged. The lump in my throat grew tighter when he saw my pain. "He burned my books," I whispered.

Othur reached out a hand, his eyes crinkled in sympathy, but let it drop when Keir appeared in the doorway. "Seneschal, your presence is not required. The warprize is guide enough."

Othur bowed his head. "Warlord, forgive me. I was told that you had no need of me, but I have served two kings in this castle, as my father did before me. Excuse an old man his pride."

Keir paused. "Did you 'inherit' your place?"

"No, Warlord. Xyron selected me for my skills, and Xymund chose to retain me as Seneschal."

"And your son?"

"My son has no interest in serving in this capacity, Warlord. He prefers the way of a warrior." Othur smiled. "I would be honored it you would permit me to show you the castle defenses."

"Lead on."

Othur did, and was soon explaining about battlements and

murder holes. I fell back, not really paying attention to what was being said. Why had he done that? For certain, Xymund burned my notes and books. I couldn't imagine it. I'd done as he commanded. Why was he so angry? So furious that he couldn't even greet me, or note my presence in a room.

Othur led us to the rooms above the castle's main entrance, and everyone was enthralled with murder holes and the winches for the portcullis. I drifted to the back, and Othur managed to slip to my side. "Durst?" I whispered.

"He lives, but barely. Eln is with him." Relief surged over me as Othur continued, keeping his voice low. "Warren's clearing the castle and the courtyard of hot-tempered fools. He's got things under control for now. I had Degnan locked in his rooms, under guard. Can't decide if he's angrier over the attack or the loss of his inheritance."

"Xymund?" I breathed, fearing the answer.

"In his chambers, refusing to see anyone." Othur passed a hand over his damp forehead and dried it on his trous. "I fear a bloodletting if Durst dies."

Keir and the others were still focused on the defenses. "Othur, there is a ceremony, a ritual. You ask for the person's token." I spoke quickly. "It protects you when you tell a Firelander something insulting or that would upset them. I'm not allowed—" I cut my words off as Keir approached.

"A wondrous tent of stone, Othur." Keir looked about the room. "I wonder at your ability to keep it repaired and supplied."

Othur smiled. "No more that I wonder at the skills required to keep an army on the march, Warlord." He cleared his throat. "I have a question, Warlord, but I would not offer offense."

Keir looked rueful, and glanced at me. "Ask, Seneschal."

"Would you be willing to explain the use of tokens by your people?" Othur's voice was reasonable, but he tensed, waiting for Keir's reaction.

"I would." The tone of Keir's voice surprised me, for I heard a sense of shame behind his words.

"Perhaps over food and drink? My Lady Wife is the Castle

Cook and would welcome you in her kingdom." Othur placed a hand on my shoulder. "She's very fond of the warprize."

"That would be Anna?" Keir asked. At Othur's nod, he nodded. "It's not wise to offend a cook," Keir smiled. "Lead the way."

The kitchen was empty, save for Anna and one of the serving lads. Anna looked drawn and tired, dressed in a clean gown and fresh apron, her spice keys on her belt. Her face lit up like the sun when she saw me. Either she hadn't noticed the dress, or someone had seen fit to warn her of its color. We paused in awkward uncertainty for a moment as she debated how to greet me, but I took matters into my own hands. "Warlord, allow me to present Anna, who rules this kitchen and all our hearts."

Anna gave out a nervous laugh, and after a quick glance at the Warlord, stepped forward to sweep me up in a hug. As the others came in she turned slightly, and indicated the table, set with sweets and goodies. "Please sit and refresh yourselves, my lords." The serving lad started forward to hand out mugs of ale and Keir and Othur settled at the table, deep in conversation, Anna kept one arm around my shoulders and pulled me over to the great hearth. She clung to me fiercely as she whispered in my ear, "Are you all right?"

"I am fine and well," I said, smiling at her.

She pulled back a bit, and gave the scarlet dress an evil look. "No." She shook her head so hard all her chins bounced. "Are you all right?" She searched my face anxiously.

I flushed and pulled her back into the hug. "Yes," I whispered. "Yes, I am all right."

She pulled away, wiping her eyes, her face full of doubt. "Remn said as much, but what does he know?" She frowned, more to keep back her tears than in anger. "You must be starved."

Now my eyes filled with tears, for that was Anna's response to any problem or pain. She pulled a mug for me and pushed one of her confections into my hand.

"Warprize."

I turned to find Keir gesturing me over. With an apologetic

look at Anna, I moved to sit by his side. Keir shifted on the bench to make room, and as he did I felt his breath in my ear. "Do not eat or drink."

Everyone else was laughing and eating, trying the various treats that Anna had prepared. I kept my head near Keir's, and my voice down. "Excuse me?"

Keir stared into his cup, still filled with ale. "Prest will tell us when it is safe."

I stared at him, the reason for his behavior dawning on me slowly. I opened my mouth to say something sharp, when Prest leaned across the table. "Warlord, you must try these!" In his hand was one of Anna's special treats, a small tart with nuts and honey.

Keir reached out for the one in Prest's hand, and bit into it. His face melted into a look of pure pleasure. "Anna!" She spun around. "Anna, what's in these wonderful things?"

She glanced at Othur, who reassured her with a smile. Cautiously, she replied, "Warlord, they are just flour, sugar, eggs, and vanilla, with nuts and honey from the castle bees."

Keir looked at me, with that boyish smile. "Vanilla. That's why I like them so much." He took another bite. "Could you teach my cook to make these?"

She looked at him through narrowed eyes, and I knew that she found it hard to see the wild-eyed killer in the eager, boyish face before her. "Aye, Warlord, if your cook has any skill at all." She seemed to relax slightly.

Othur leaned forward. "About the tokens, Warlord."

As they talked, Anna bustled about, making sure that the others had enough to eat and drink. I stayed by Keir's side, and listened as Keir explained the use of the tokens much as Atira had.

"So, if I have your token, and I use that to insult you, what then?" Othur asked.

"I'd reply that the truth you voice is a false, and would issue challenge." Keir looked grim. "Your choice is to withdraw your words or fight me."

"So insults are only made under the protection of a token?"

"No, but when insult is given without a token, it's expected that you have a weapon ready, for the insult will be answered immediately."

"Ah," Othur responded. "We give insult, but expect to be challenged before a sword is drawn."

"I know that now." Keir placed his mug on the table. "We must return to camp."

As the others stood, I placed a hand on Keir's arm. "Let me show you something." I led the way to the still room door. "I spent a lot of time here over the years, distilling medicines and herbs in this room." I swung the door wide. "This was my kingdom."

The door opened on an empty room.

I stared. Not a table, not a jar, nothing remained. Only the faint lingering scent of herbs in the air betrayed the fact that it had been a stillroom.

Othur came up behind us. "I should have warned you, Lara. The King had it cleaned out the night you . . ." He paused almost imperceptibly. "Left."

I rounded on him. "Othur, there were valuable supplies here, not to mention my . . . the equipment. What did he do with it?" Othur studied the floor. I grabbed his arm. "Please tell me he sent it all to the Temple of Healing."

Othur did not look at me. "He may have. But I don't know."

I spent most of the ride back to camp lost in my own thoughts. Keir had allowed no long farewells. One hug from Anna and we were mounted and gone, traveling quickly through the night, weapons at the ready. Keir hadn't bothered with the niceties of farewells to Xymund either, and I was convinced that it was calculated.

The night covered the fields, so I was spared another glimpse of the graves. The stars gleamed bright in the night sky, and I heard the Firelanders muttering something that sounded like prayers. I sighed softly. I shouldn't use that term anymore, since it wasn't what they called themselves. I wondered for a moment why Xyians called them 'Firelanders'.

Of course, I wasn't really Xyian anymore, was I? I wasn't really anything, was I? I closed my eyes, and lost myself in my pain.

Only when Rafe coughed did I realize that he held my horse's head and that we were in front of Keir's tent. I slid out of the saddle and rubbed my forehead to ease its ache. Marcus stood just inside the tent, the lamps bright behind him. "Warprize? Are you all right?"

Keir came up behind me as our horses were led away. His hands were on my shoulders, and he directed me toward the sleeping area. I stumbled along, guided by his warm hands, over to the bed, where he made me sit down. I could hear murmurs, Keir and Marcus talking. "I'll get kavage," Marcus said quietly. "Maybe some bread." I had to smile. Apparently Anna was not the only one to ease pain with food.

"No," Keir responded. He knelt down in front of me and pulled off one of the bright red slippers with a gentle touch. "We need sleep, Marcus. Go to bed."

Marcus gave him a doubtful look, but he left. Keir removed the other slipper as well, but I didn't look up. "Why would he do it? Why would he burn them?" I asked.

Keir paused and glanced at me.

"They were just my notes, my observations. Scribbles really." I stopped as the pain welled up inside my chest.

Keir snorted. I looked at him in surprise. "You are attacked in the market, insulted by the court and your brother, and what troubles you the most is the loss of some papers." He stood rather abruptly.

Anger surged up inside me. "They may have just been papers, but they were important to me."

Keir lifted an eyebrow. "That's why they were burned."

I sagged, exhaustion flowing over me like a wave.

Keir sat next to me on the bed and removed his boots. He started in on his armor, carefully removing each piece and setting it on the benches. I gathered strength, stood and went into the bathing area to remove the dress carefully. I tried to fold it, but the material slipped and slid, the dress ending up on the floor every time. Tired, frustrated and upset, I finally gave up and left it lay on one of the benches. A tunic and trous were set out for me, and I climbed into them for sleeping. After washing out my undergarments, I washed up quickly. My hair was windblown from the tower and the ride, so I gathered up a comb and returned to the other room to try to deal with the tangled mess.

Keir slipped into the room as I came out, and I heard him splash about as I tried to draw the comb through my hair. It hurt, but not as much as the idea of all that work burned, or all those herbs and mixtures destroyed. It made no sense, to ruin the stillroom. Why do it? Why think that Anna would poison me? The idea was laughable. Nor would Xymund hire mercenaries to destroy the peace. My head hurt with thinking about it, and I yanked my hair into a handful and started working at the tangles with a vengeance.

The bed sagged, and the comb was tugged out of my hand. Keir moved behind me, and wrapped me in his arms, and held me tight. I lowered my head, embarrassed at how good it felt to be held. It was strange to be held so, embraced so intimately. Yet how quickly his touch had become familiar and welcome. We stayed that way for a long moment, then with one hand, Keir swept the hair from the back of my neck, and nuzzled my nape. His warm breath stirred the smaller hairs, and I shifted slightly, uncomfortable with the touch and yet stirred by it. Keir moved his hands to my shoulders and stroked down my arms until he reached my hands.

He cradled my right hand in both of his and started caressing it, tracing each finger slowly, and moving his fingertips over my palm. I could feel his sword calluses against my skin. His lips were at my ear as he spoke. "I was taught that we are of the elements. Flesh, breath, soul, and blood." His voice was a mere whisper as he kneaded the ball of my thumb. "Sometimes, the elements within us become unbalanced, and it takes the touch of another to bring us back, to center us." His hands continued to work on mine, rubbing the nails and working my knuckles. I felt a warm tingle building in the center of my palm.

I sighed, leaning back against his chest, and Keir switched

to my left hand, moving slowly and carefully. "The soul is made of fire, and sits within the left hand." He repeated his actions, I absorbed it all in silence. "The breath is made of air, and sits within the right hand." He continued until that hand tingled as well. I felt my heart slow and my breathing fall into harmony with his. The warmth of his body seeped into me through the fabric of my tunic.

"The peace will work, Lara." His hands took mine and wove our fingers together to form a fist. "Together, our peoples will be stronger. A united whole, under one ruler."

"Under your rule." I whispered.

Keir pulled me back slowly to lay against the pillows, then moved to the end of the bed. He took my left foot in his hands and started rubbing gently. "The blood is made of water, and sits within the left foot." His words seemed like a ritual of some kind and his touch was pure pleasure. I lay quiet, in a daze of warmth and bliss.

"Xymund has sworn fealty to me as Warlord." Keir's touch was still gentle, but his voice had an edge to it. "He will obey." He flexed my foot in his hands, pulling at my toes and working his fingers into the muscles.

It took me a bit to gather my thoughts. "Yet you deliberately provoked him this evening."

"Yes." Keir released my foot and moved to the other one. "I did. His actions will speak louder than his oaths." He worked this foot as he had the other. "The flesh is made of earth and sits within the right foot."

I focused on him and smiled, feeling safe and lethargic. Keir's eyes glittered, and he released my foot and crawled up the bed to lay by my side. He hovered there, looking down, his eyes glittering. I looked up, expecting, waiting . . .

He sighed softly, and eased back to the foot of the bed. It seemed somehow that I had failed him in some way, but I wasn't certain what made me think that. I stared at his back as he sat there. I had to say something to break the silence. "And Durst?"

Keir's head came up with a jerk. He sighed and shook his head, turning slightly to look at me. "A mistake. I knew it

even as I pulled my sword free." He got off the bed. Marcus
had stoked the braziers before he had left, and they radiated
warm heat into the room. Keir moved over and threw a handful of leaves into the closest one. It flared up, but the flames
died quickly. The room gently filled with a soft spicy scent
that hung in the warm air. Amazing how much warmer a tent
was than a stone castle.

Keir settled on one of the benches, pulling bottles and
cloths from a small chest below. His sword was there, and he
took it up, looking at it ruefully. He started wiping it with one
of the cloths. I curled on my side to watch him as he wiped
the sword with careful attention. There was a long silence between us before he spoke. "I ask my warriors to change their
ways, and yet in the heat of anger I strike according to our
tradition."

I didn't have an answer to that.

He set aside the cloth, and started to work the edge with a
stone, making a soft 'shushing' sound. One of the bottles was
open, and I got a faint whiff of clove oil. I yawned, watching
him in the faint light.

"Go to sleep, Warprize. I will sit for a while, and think on
my errors and how to learn from them."

I had melted down into the bedding, and hadn't the
strength to get under the blankets. Even with blurry eyes, I
saw the lines on Keir's face. "He didn't die."

Keir's hand stopped moving. "He lived?"

"Othur said he was still alive before we went to the
kitchens." I closed my eyes, and started floating off.

The 'shushing' sound started back up. "So. Tomorrow will
tell the tale. I'll send for word, or go myself. Sleep now."

I tried to resist, but the darkness won out.

*I swing my leg up and out, the horse shies and moves away. I
lose my balance and drop back to the ground abruptly.*

The lance passes by my head.

*"Death to the . . ." The lead man never finishes his cry.
Keir smashes through his defenses and plunges into the man's*

chest in one quick stabbing motion. With his fierce quickness, he moves to strike at another.

I press against the wall, trying to stay small and out of the way. The only sounds are those of clashing blades, heavy breathing, and boots looking for purchase on the surface of the street.

"Wake up. Open your eyes."

The four remaining attackers shift their focus without a word. Prest has one opponent. Two now press Keir. Rafe faces one as well.

Prest bashes his opponent with his shield and rams him hard enough to get him off-balance and a sword between his ribs. I assume that Prest will aid Keir. But he stays where he is, scanning the street, weapon at the ready.

Keir is in no need of aid. He knows his opponents' moves and blocks them with ease. His attackers breathe heavily, and move slowly. When one makes the mistake of stepping back when his fellow shifts forward, Keir does not hesitate. But it is a move his opponents are waiting for and in an instant Keir is down on the street, bleeding from his chest.

"Wake up, Warprize."

I cry out and kneel at his side. My hands reach out, but they cannot stop the blood as it gushes forth.

"I'm fine. All's well. Wake up."

Keir turns his head, but his eyes are wide and unseeing. I scream, cry out, but there is no help, no aid, all is sorrow, all is death . . .

8

I awoke screaming, sitting up in the bed and covered in sweat. My heart thundered in my chest.

Keir's arms gathered me close. As my vision cleared, I could make out the tent, with Marcus standing not far from the edge of the bed, holding a small lamp. The flame flickered, weak and feeble, and the shadows danced with it. I turned, fumbling at Keir's chest, checking the wound. I had to stop the bleeding, *Goddess please*, I had to stop the . . .

Keir kept his arms around me, but gave me the room I needed as my hands fumbled over his chest, the skin supple, the scars old and healed. Frantically, I checked, then raised my eyes to his. "There was blood, so much blood. I couldn't stop it."

"A night horror. Just a night horror." His strong arms enfolded me, and I allowed myself to be pulled into his embrace. I felt Keir gesture for Marcus to return to his bed, and then tensed as the light receded. "Marcus," Keir called softly. "Leave the lamp."

The light remained, even as Marcus left. We stayed that

way, as my breathing and heart slowed. Finally, I pushed back a little, pulling my hair off my sweaty forehead with shaky hands, and croaked out a weak laugh. "I'm sorry. I am acting the fool."

Keir pulled me down under the furs, refusing to release his hold. "It's not a foolish thing. Night horrors are very real."

I rested my head on his shoulder, feeling heavy and tired. "When I was very small, Anna would hold me when I had one. She would hug me, kiss my forehead, and stay with me til I slept."

Keir chuckled softly. "Go back to sleep." He brushed his lips against my forehead.

Comforted, I closed my eyes.

At some point I found myself awake, lying in the dark. There was enough light to see Keir lying next to me, on his back, close enough to touch. I closed my eyes and listened to his regular breaths and reveled in the sheer comfort that it brought. The nightmare had been so real, so terrible. I wanted to believe that my fears in the dream had been for the peace between our people, but concern for the man had been there as well.

Keir murmured and shifted his weight slightly. I opened my eyes, studying his face, trying to gauge his age. He was no youngster, but it was hard to tell. Older than Xymund. Not so old as Warren. I yawned, letting my eyes drift closed. Caring for broken and ill bodies doesn't teach the joy of shared warmth under covers. So far, that seemed the only use for a warprize.

"WHERE'S HIS TOKEN!"

I jolted up, clutching the blankets, to find Keir half out of bed, sword in hand. There were sounds of many men outside and grunts, as if they were carrying a heavy load. "MAR-CUS!" The voice bellowed again. "WHERE IS THAT FOOL

OF A WARLORD?" The very walls of the tent seemed to tremble.

Keir collapsed back on the bed, still clutching his sword, his face twisted in a grimace. "Simus must have talked to Joden."

"SILENCE!" I jumped again as Marcus called out, his voice loud enough to rival Simus's. "I'd no sleep last night and none this morn, thanks to your bellowing!"

I flushed, and looked at Keir. "I'm sorry about last night."

He turned his head and gave me that impish smile. "I'm not. Since it means that you were in my arms most of the night."

More heat flooded my face.

"Get me in this tent, and bring me his damned-by-the-snows token," Simus bellowed again. "I've a few choice truths to tell."

Keir stood, and shouted back. "You've not bothered to use my token in years, why start now?" Keir grabbed up a tunic and belted on his sword.

"Easy! Be careful, I'm a wounded man, not a dead deer!"

A man backed in through the flap, carrying Simus on a cot. Simus was sprawled on his stomach, holding on to the sides. There were four men carrying him, but they only seemed to be getting in each other's way. "Here," Simus directed. "Put me down here." The cot was dropped, and before Simus could complain, the men were gone. Simus growled, since he was half in, half out, with the flap laying on the small of his back. He fixed his glare on Keir. "What, your brain was in your sword last night?"

Marcus appeared from the other entrance and thumped a pitcher of kavage on the table, along with mugs. "I suppose you'll be wanting food, now that you've frightened the herds with your cries?"

"I'll need it to keep up my strength so that I can beat sense into this one's head." Simus adopted an air of injured dignity. I clutched at the blankets, and ran my hand through my hair, trying not to give into hysterical laughter.

Marcus snarled and clucked like an old chicken as he

turned to go. "Body can't get any rest, what with the screaming and the crying out all night." He stomped out of the tent.

Keir poured kavage, handing a mug to Simus. "I had good
reason—"

"To gut one of them? In their own throne room?" Simus
rolled his eyes. "Let me guess, you insulted their poor excuse
of a king as well?" When I frowned, Simus glared at me.
"I'm voicing truths here, Warprize, and you'll pardon me if I
don't fear your blade."

"How's your leg, Simus?" Keir asked pointedly, as he
handed me a full mug.

Simus ignored him. "And your reasons, oh great Warlord
of the Plains? For throwing rocks at rutting ehats?"

I frowned. What was an 'ehat'?

"The man gave insult to the warprize," Keir responded.
"He called her a whore." He used the Xyian word.

"Eh?" Marcus was bringing in food. "What's that?"

I took a long drink of kavage as Keir explained. How did
they not have a word for that? What did that mean about these
people? That any were free to lay with all? That seemed so
barbaric.

"They sell it?" Marcus looked slightly ill, then moved
away, muttering something about water for bathing.

Simus said nothing, merely drinking from his kavage.

Keir sighed, and sat down on the corner of the bed nearest
Simus. "I knew I'd made a mistake even as he slid off my
blade."

Simus remained quiet.

"How can I ask my warriors to change their ways when I
couldn't change mine in that instant?" Keir ran a hand
through his hair.

"Change is easy to talk of, hard to do." Simus's voice
dropped, his eyes serious. "You tell them the truth, of
course."

Marcus came in with two buckets, and disappeared into
the privy area.

"You tell them that you regret his death, but that all must
take heed from this incident."

"He's not dead," I spoke up. "The last we heard, he still lived."

"He did?" Simus asked, then let his eyes slide over to Keir. "Losing your touch?"

A cry of outrage filled the tent. I grabbed at the blanket, as Keir stood, sword in hand. Simus had two daggers that appeared from nowhere. I looked at the privy entrance, to see Marcus standing there, waving my underthings in his fist and shaking them in the air. "Where did the likes of these come from?"

I jumped up and grabbed for them, but that scarred little man dodged me. "Those are mine!" I made another attempt, darting around the bed. Simus roared out his laughter and Keir got out of the way.

Marcus danced away again. "The Warprize accepts nothing, except at the hand of the Warlord!" His face was bright red, the scarring a dull white against it.

"Give me those!" I went after him again and this time managed to wrestle the cloth from his hand. Flushed and breathless, I shoved them behind my back and faced down Marcus, toe to toe. "You have no business—"

"Nothing, except at the hand of the Warlord!" Marcus roared out, spittle flying from his mouth.

"You bragnect! I bought them with his coin!"

Marcus blinked. Apparently it was an effective curse in their language, since it seemed to leave him speechless. His recovery was quick. "Could have asked Hisself or I."

I rolled my eyes, just imagining that conversation.

"No more than she could tell us about the dress, apparently."

My turn to lose my tongue. Keir's tone was mild, but his look sharp. Simus was watchful, his two daggers gone, and the kavage back in his hand. "Tell us, Warprize. Tell us what you did not tell us yesterday."

Marcus scowled, eye darting between the two of us. "Dress? What was wrong with the dress?"

"We don't have cloth like yours, with the colors so strong, so bright." I ran my free hand through my hair, pulling it back.

Marcus snorted. "City folk all dress like drab, dull geese, waddling about, squawking at—"

Keir had seated himself at the table and was filling his plate. "They acted as if I had branded you, marked you somehow." He tilted his head. "Did I?"

Marcus snorted, turning to Keir. I took the opportunity to tuck my underthings under one of the pillows on the bed. "It's a fine dress, the color of flame, it honored her. How is that a problem?"

"For us, it is an honor." He pinned me with his eyes. "For you?"

I sighed. "In Water's Fall, only a whore wears red."

Marcus's eyebrow shot up, and he glanced at Keir before he looked at me. "A whore? That insult?" I nodded. Marcus turned to face Keir, placing both hands on his hips. "Do you hear this? We do not have such a word, thanks to the skies." He threw his hands up in the air. "This will never work. Bringing together their ways and ours, it cannot hope to—"

Keir slapped the table with his open palm, rattling the dishes. Marcus and I both jumped. "It will work." Keir stood there, grim and determined. "I will weave a new pattern between these ways." He glanced at Simus. "I will use my mistake as an example for my people." His eyes flashed at Marcus, who stood, radiating disapproval. "We will learn of our differences, ask questions when needed." His glare centered on me now. "Offer information freely, with no fear." I flushed and looked away. "Am I understood?"

Simus and Marcus both bowed their heads. "Yes, Warlord."

I did the same, biting my lip.

Keir settled at the table and reached for bread. "Simus, have your men return you to your tent. Marcus, the kavage needs warming." Marcus retreated. Keir didn't look at me. "If you wish to bathe before eating, you may."

I fled to the privy.

Keir and Simus were gone when I emerged. Marcus wasn't there either, but I could hear him rattling dishes beyond the tent walls. I rummaged in the saddlebags, and put a touch of vanilla oil on the back of my neck. I closed my eyes and took a deep breath of the warm fragrance. Just for a moment, I was back in Anna's kitchen as a child, hearing her laughter and the jingle of her keys, surrounded by those I loved. The tightness in my shoulders eased. I took a few deep breaths before sitting at the table.

Marcus entered, placing a heaping plate down before me. "Warlord's gone to send a messenger to the castle." He poured kavage in my mug, hesitating before setting it down. "I meant no offense, Warprize." I looked at him, puzzled. "The dress. I meant no insult."

I stared at my plate. "I should have said something, Marcus. You were just so proud for having found it, I just couldn't—"

He shook his head and grimaced. "Not the first time my pride got in the way, won't be the last."

"Marcus—" I pushed the food around on my plate. "Marcus, do you support Keir in this peace? Does the army?"

"We're a people who've known nothing but battle and raiding. Conquering and holding land, the blending of our ways with yours is a new idea. And one Hisself is bent on." Marcus's eye was lost in the distance, and his fingers drummed on the pitcher. "All knew of his plans for this place, and followed in that understanding, but there's miles between knowing and doing." He wrinkled his nose as he focused on me. "Hisself holds the reins, but there's always someone that frets at the traces. Iften would gladly see Hisself fall off this horse."

Marcus sat on one of the stumps, slumping. "Then there's you."

"Me?"

"Aye. A warprize must be taken to the Heart of the Plains. That's a month of travel at the start of the snows. You, who's never lived beyond stone walls for all her days." Marcus shook his head. "Hisself is a good man to follow, to trust with your life, but the risks on this path are far greater than the one's he's taken in battle. As I've followed him in war, who am I to refuse to follow him in this?"

"But you don't think it will work." I breathed, my heart sinking.

He stood quickly, scowling at me. "You should see to Atira. Eat now, Rafe and Prest will be here soon, and the food does no good to the plate."

Try as I might, I could get no more from him.

With Gils's help, the morning flew swiftly, what with washing, bandaging and the like. I was amazed how quickly Gils learned. He would recite things back that I had told him, word for word, but even with his memory, hands on learning was necessary. It's one thing to be able to recite how to clean a wound. It's another to have a living patient who wiggles and complains as you do it. Halfway through the process, I heard noises coming from outside the tent, as of men working. I looked over but Rafe and Prest showed no signs of concern, so I ignored it.

My patients were progressing well, and there were only two left, including Atira. She was also coming along nicely, although she was uncomfortable when I adjusted the tension on her leg. The ache seemed to ease once she was settled again, with her weapons arranged in proper order. Privately, I conceded that having one's patients naked under the blankets was a time-saver, but not one that I'd be able to introduce to my Xyian patients.

That thought brought me up short. I'd lost myself in the comforting routine of caring for people, forgetting that I'd never have Xyian patients again. A wave of homesickness came over me, and I had to bite my lip to prevent tears. I felt lost and alone and—

I wrenched my thoughts back to the moment, and concentrated on the tasks at hand.

I desperately wanted to ask Atira questions, about the Heart of the Plains and her life there, and what she thought of the Warlord's plans, but she had her planning board out, and was moving stones around. Besides, there were listening ears all about us. I was afraid that Marcus was right, that Keir's plans to unite our peoples and learn each others ways was doomed from the start. What would happen to Keir if he failed? What would happen to me? I flushed, feeling sheepish. Later, I'd ask, when Gils was gone and everyone was drowsy. I'd ask for Atira's token.

Once all were settled, I pulled out *The Epic of Xyson*. I'd managed to hide it from Marcus and smuggle it down to the healing tent with no one the wiser. "I have a surprise for you all." I smiled as I opened the book. "I thought I would read this to you. It's a story of one of my ancestors—"

There was a crash. Startled, I looked up. Gils had dropped the pitcher. Everyone was staring at me. Atira, propped up on her elbows, was pale and wide-eyed. "Warprize, you keep your songs on paper?"

I nodded and turned the book so they could see the writing.

Gils looked at it carefully. The other patient came over, straining to see. Even Rafe and Prest left their positions by the door for a closer look.

"I have heard of this, but the sky as my witness, I thought it a fable told to children." Rafe frowned. "How can the marks hold your songs?"

"Listen." Returning the book to my lap, I read out loud, "Hear now the tale of Xyson, Warrior King, and his defeat of the barbarians of the southern lands. Xyson, tall and strong as the mountain had led his people well for ten years before the barbarians fell upon the villages and raided his people." I paused, suddenly unsure. It occurred to me that the barbarians the book talked about were Keir's own people.

Prest snorted. "How old?" he asked, nodding at the book.

"The story is almost four hundred years old. Xyson is my father's father's father back some nine generations."

Prest looked impressed. Atira lay back against her blankets. "A song so old. You do us honor, Warprize."

"Don't be so quick to say that." I smiled at her and the others settling around us. "You haven't heard it yet."

I read for about a half hour. My audience hung on every word, even though the tale talked about numbers of troops, supplies, and the appointing of a Warden for the kingdom.

Dull as the story was, it forced me to learn new words as I translated. Rafe and Prest took their positions back at the entrance, but when I saw them straining to hear, I raised my voice slightly. There was silence when I finally stopped and closed the book. Atira cleared her throat. "I'm not sure what your custom is, Warprize. Normally we would give thanks to the singer."

"Thanks is good." I stood and stretched. "I'm glad to share it with you. But now I am hungry. Is the nooning close?"

Gils jumped up. "I's be checking." He darted out the door and ran into someone coming in. "Sorry, Warlord!"

"Watch where you're going, boy," came the gruff response. Rafe and Prest stood as Keir entered the tent. His face was clear of the anger he had shown this morning. "How goes it with—" He stopped abruptly when he saw the book in my hands.

It was time to confess. "I bought this with your coin yesterday." I smoothed one hand over its cover nervously. "It's an old story called *The Epic of Xyson*. I thought it would distract—"

"You're reading to my people?" The surprise in his voice was clear.

I nodded. "I also bought a primer. A teaching tool. So that I could teach Gils to read my book on herbs." I chanced a glance at his face.

Keir looked very satisfied. "You would teach him?" He moved over to gaze down at Atira. "Could she learn as well?"

"Yes." I nodded. "If she is willing."

Atira's eyes got even bigger. "Warlord, at your command, I'll try."

Keir narrowed his eyes, nodding. "That is all I ask, Warrior. This is no easy horse to master, but it would please me for you to learn."

She nodded her acceptance of the charge.

Keir arched an eyebrow. "I've announced a pattern dance for tomorrow night."

Atira brightened, but her face fell quickly. "I'll miss the

dancing, but it's my pattern they'll be weaving." There was pride mixed with the disappointment.

Keir smiled. "If Simus can be carried to the senel, why not you?"

I frowned, considering. Keir watched me, focused on my face. "Explain to her, Warrior. Tell her why it is important to you."

"Warprize, it's an honor to be asked to design the pattern." Atira pleaded with voice and eyes. "To not see my first pattern woven, it's like a dagger thrust here." She put her hand over her heart.

"The leather has dried and hardened. If we are careful, and if you swear that you will not move, and let yourself be carried . . ."

"All that, all that, I swear, Warprize."

Atira was so serious, so earnest, that I had to smile.

"Well then, if all is well here, I have something to show you." Keir tugged on my sleeve and pulled me toward the entrance. Prest and Rafe were also standing there, grinning like fools.

I gave them a narrow look. "What's going on?"

"Nothing." The reply was in unison. My skepticism must have been obvious, because they all laughed.

The day had turned overcast, and held the promise of rain. Keir took me by the shoulders and turned me to walk around the corner of the tent. Prest and Rafe were slightly ahead of us.

There was a second, smaller tent there, that had been put up recently. I looked at Keir, who smiled. Prest and Rafe stood next to the tent flap. "Look!" said Rafe as he pulled the flap aside. Keir gave me a light push and I entered the tent. They followed.

I stood there, stunned.

There were all the supplies that I had requested, crates of them, everything that I had asked for, and . . .

Stillroom equipment. I moved forward, eyes open in wonder. There were flasks, and bowls, and mortar and pestle, and small braziers, and jars and bottles. They covered the three tables in the tent. I turned and stared at Keir. He was smiling, looking back at me. Prest and Rafe were laughing.

"When did you do this?"

Keir grinned. "Last night and this morning. When you told me of a 'stillroom' and what it contained, I sent Sal to your friend Remn. They gathered what I wanted and what was needed. Now, you have a 'stilltent', yes?" His smile faded as he looked around. "I had not thought . . . these items are fragile. We will need a way to carry it when we move." He moved around the small tent as he thought. "I will talk to Sal and see what she thinks."

I stood there, a tangle of emotions. Joy at the gift. Fear at the idea of leaving. I laid a shaking hand on Keir's arm. "Thank you."

He smiled down at me. "I would help, but Warren is coming for the nooning with some of his men. He has sent a messenger to confirm that he will come, and to tell me that Durst still clings to life with the aid of Eln the Healer."

I caught my breath. "Eln is very skilled. I apprenticed to him."

Keir cocked his head. "Skilled with porcupine quills?"

I smiled. "Yes, that too."

Keir lifted his chin, a gleam of humor in his eyes. "We will review battles and tell lies about our bravery. Do you wish to attend?"

I looked around the tent. "There's so much to do here. Do you mind?"

"No." His lips twitched. "Although you are missing Simus at his best, full of food and drink and tales of his prowess." Keir shook his head. "Prest and Rafe have asked to be there. I will send someone to relieve them."

I shrugged and smiled. "I'll be fine."

Keir frowned. "No. They will be relieved. I'll have food brought to you as well." He reached up, cradled my head in his hand, and kissed me. His lips lingered on my mouth. "I will be thinking about you." He lowered his voice. "And about this morning." He leaned forward and whispered in my ear. "And about tonight." He stood and smiled at my blush.

"Maybe there will be night horrors again tonight?" He chuckled as he left the tent.

I threw myself into the work, rather then try to think about anything else. Prest and Rafe helped me arrange the tables, with the crates below. It took a while to sort through everything and to get the heavy crates maneuvered into position.

At last, we were down to one unopened crate. Prest had found something to pry off the top. He and Rafe were wrestling with it when their relief arrived, hailing from outside the tent. With one last heave, Prest pried the lid off. They both scrambled to their feet, eager to go.

Rafe pulled the new guards inside. "Warprize, this is Epor and Isdra. They will guard while we are gone." Prest and Rafe turned and left with my thanks floating behind them.

I smiled at the older man and woman, the same that were with us in the castle. I remembered him for his bright gold hair and beard that shown like the sun. He had a warm, easy smile, and was big, like the paintings of the sun god in the temple. The crinkles at the corners of his eyes and the slight silver at his temples told me that he was older than most Firelanders that I had met. He was different too, in that he had a long club strapped to his back, the top jutting up like the hilts of Keir's swords.

Epor smiled back and nodded. "I am Epor, Warprize. This is Isdra. Let us know if you need help. We'll be outside if you need us, if Isdra can stop gaping."

The woman, who was almost his height but thinner, had a long braid of silver hair that hung down her back. Her skin had a yellow tint to it, and her eyes were oddly slanted. She wore a shield on her back, and a sword and dagger at her side. She'd been busy looking around at all the things in the tent. She seemed a bit more reserved to me but at Epor's words, she whipped her head around, flinging the braid and glared at Epor with her grey eyes flashing. Epor just laughed, and pulled at her braid as they left the tent. I noticed that they each had some kind of metal wire laced along the outer rim of their left ears. It glittered in the light as Isdra turned her head. I'd have to ask Atira what it meant.

I watched as Epor and Isdra took up stations outside the flap. It still seemed so strange to me, to see women dressed in armor, with weapons she clearly knew how to use. All of the women that I'd seen were so strong, confident of her abilities and secure in her position. I envied them to a degree, having so freely what I had to fight to achieve.

I turned back to my work and lifted the lid of the last crate.

I sat down. Hard. And stared.

It was filled with paper. Ink. Blank journals.

In one wonderful, horrible moment I knew that I was lost. Keir, Warlord, had taken me, claimed me, made me his warprize. But somewhere, somehow, he had managed to find a way into my heart as well.

How had this happened? I'd given myself to a barbarian, a ravaging, crazed warlord, expecting little more than abuse and dishonor at his hands. But this man had offered nothing but kindness and respect to me, his property. I knew this gift was by his hand, I'd not spoken to Sal about paper or ink, and she'd not understand its importance.

Could he care so much that he paid attention to this tiny detail?

Did he want me to be happy?

I clutched one of the journals to my chest as my emotions overwhelmed me. Joy and confusion warred with one another. My mouth went dry, and I closed my eyes. What would happen when we returned to his home? Such a warrior as Keir had other . . . conquests. At least five. Of that I was certain. The image of him in another's arms came to me and I felt sick. I closed my eyes and let the nausea pass through me.

Keir moved his hand, running his fingers through my hair, spreading it out over the fur. His eyes flared blue light. "Want to know the best part of being a warlord?" I just looked up and nodded. Keir grinned. "I always get what I want."

I put my head down. The pain threatened to overwhelm me. Please Goddess, let him want me. Let him want me forever.

Enough. I sat up and scrubbed at my face with my sleeve. I had work to do.

I returned to the tent to check on my patients. The man was well; drowsy after eating. Atira was awake, though, and gestured me over when she saw me. I waved Gils off, since I knew he had other duties, and moved to sit by her side.

"Warprize." Atira looked deeply concerned. "Warprize, may I have your token?" She looked anxious and worried.

I reached for one of her stones and handed it to her. "You hold my token, Atira. What truths would you voice?"

She hesitated, looking at me closely. "I have heard a rumor in the camp about you, and I would ask you if it is true, and voice a truth if it is indeed true."

I had to think for a minute. "A rumor? About me?"

"About your people." She nodded "And you." She rubbed the stone between her fingers. "Is it true that you are untouched? That your people do not mate until they bond?"

I reared back, physically. Consciously or not, Atira did so as well, keeping a tight grip on the token and holding it up between us. It took me a minute to gather my wits. "Atira, who told you—"

"Skies above, it's true," she whispered, staring at me in utter horror. "You bind when young and sleep only with your bonded?"

I managed a nod, my face so hot it hurt.

"Who teaches you then? Who instructs . . . ?" Her voice trailed off as she looked at my eyes. "No one? You are both left to fumble about?" She collapsed back on the cot in silence.

I closed my eyes and pressed my fingers to my cheeks to try to cool them.

"None told me, Warprize. I listened to the stories of your people, and the Warlord's intent to follow your ways, and made a guess. But I must say this. *Stupid.* That is so *stupid,* Warprize."

I looked at her, puzzled. "What is that word? Stupid?"

"Dull-witted. Foolish. Ignorant." Her angry face glowered at me. "We have initiators. Teachers. Joden is one. He would be an excellent choice. You should request him." She sounded like a parent recommending a Master to study under.

I choked up, laughter and tears both in my throat, trying to find the words. "Atira, we believe that two people should come to the bonding . . . untouched . . . and learn together."

She shook her head, and held up the token. "The Warlord said to learn and respect different ways. But that is barbaric and stupid." She held the stone out to me, frowning as she did so.

I took the stone. "I thank you for your truth, Atira. As you say, our ways are very different."

"All I ask is that you think on my words, Warprize. Keir is experienced, but he is not an initiator. You have no thea to advise you in your choice, but come to me after you have thought on this and we will talk. I will mention this to no one."

I fled to the stilltent to throw myself into a frenzy of the familiar.

As I had so often in the past, I lost myself in my work. Soon, I had various pots simmering and bubbling on the tables. A double batch of fever's foe was cooling in some jars on the far table. I had a jug of my rose hip tea steeping in the corner. There were papers set out on every available surface as I tried to reconstruct my recipes for the various salves and lotions that I had made over the years. I had no marvelous memory to rely on and I found it hard going. It would be easier when I started mixing, since my nose would remember the smells as I worked. At least, that was my hope.

I also hoped that the warmth that lingered on my cheeks was from the effort, and not from the discussion. Dearest Goddess, initiators? Would I be called on to bear five children? And what if Keir couldn't father five children on me? Would I be required to 'use' someone else?

There was a noise at the entrance, and I looked up to see Marcus wrapped in a cloak, carrying a large basket. He fixed me with that one eye. "As Hisself thought. Past the nooning, and you with no food in or near you." He tsk'ed at the look on my face. "Aye, lost in your work, as I expected. Well then that one of us has the common sense the elements gave all creatures." He looked around. "Already? No space for food or drink?" I laughed and we pulled out some crates to sit on. He pulled out some dishes and a flask from his basket. I dug in, suddenly starved. Marcus was wandering around and sniffing my concoctions.

"Is Warren still here?" I asked around a mouthful of food.

"Aye." Marcus sniffed the fever's foe. "They're swilling kavage and telling old war tales." He rolled his eye. "From the sound, one would think that they were fighting all the battles over again."

"Marcus?"

"Aye?" He replied, still poking around.

I cleared my throat. "What happened to you?"

He turned swiftly and stared at me. I thought I might have offended him, but he snorted. "Healers." He laughed quietly, "I figured you'd ask eventually." He pulled up a crate and sat down. "All right then, 'tis simple enough. Ever hear of fiery pitch?" He gestured for me to keep eating, so I just shook my head.

"Thought not." He sighed. "Nasty stuff. It's flung against an enemy. It's a substance that burns when fired and sticks to whatever it touches." He studied his feet. "I was in such a battle, and was stupid enough to have my head up when a shot landed nearby. I caught just the edge of it, but t'was enough." He sighed. "It coated me and burned and burned. I'd thought better to die, but a young warrior, barely dry behind the ears, would not listen to my plea for mercy." He looked up, serious. "Hisself would not do it. He would not let me go. Through the pain and fear of the days that followed, he would not let me go."

Marcus stood. "When it was done, and I was healed, well . . . my days of battle were over. I would not last on the field for long with a blind side." His hands flexed at his sides, and he rubbed his face and head with them. "The sorrow of that loss hurt worse then the burns." His hands lowered and his one eye looked off in the distance. "Hisself cursed me for a fool, and made me his bearer." Marcus shrugged. "I have served him ever since."

"So he did the same thing Joden did." I thought for a moment. "Was he punished?"

Marcus had to laugh at that. "No, Warprize, not in the sense that you mean. I was a simple warrior, no second-in-command. Keir's refusal was not treated well, and caused many a comment, but you've seen him fight. There's none that would challenge. Many took his token and criticized him for the violation of tradition, but he answered to their truths every time."

He stood and wrapped the cloak about him, covering himself completely. "Nay, Joden's action was different. His failure to give mercy resulted in Simus being captured and there's the point, Warprize. While Keir supports him and Simus has thanked him, there will be larger problems with the Council of Elders. Aye, and maybe with the Singers, too.

"How did the healers . . ."

Marcus grimaced. "I have no idea who did what, or how, and no wish to remember the details. It was long ago, Warprize." He glared at me and pointed at the plate of food. "Eat. I must return to the tent and see if Hisself requires anything." He smirked and raised an eyebrow. "Simus is telling his tall tales, and those city-dwellers are believing every word. I needs get back and poke holes in the bucket he carries his conceit in."

I chuckled as he left the tent.

I worked as I ate, jotting down notes as I recalled the recipes. When they were done, I set the pots to cooling. I had time to distill a cough remedy that I remembered, if I could find the ingredients in the crates. I looked to see if I had remembered to get honey. Added, it would sweeten the brew.

Suddenly, there were noises outside, of men and horses. The flap opened, and Isdra stepped in. "Warprize, there are wounded."

"Wounded?" I jumped up, removed my last pot from the brazier, tied back my hair, and hurried out.

The healing tent was filled with milling men as the wounded were brought in. The captain of the scouts saw me and hurried over.

"Warprize. There are six wounded men. The worst is a gut wound, we have placed him at the back of the tent. The rest are fairly minor, although there are a number of deep slashes and cuts." He took a deep breath. "I've sent a message to the Warlord."

I nodded, thinking quickly. The gut wound was my first concern. With Gils at my side, I gathered up water and cloths. I got him started helping the more mobile patients. Atira was awake, but only moved so far as to prop herself up on pillows. I headed toward the back, fearing what I would find.

Two men stood over the man writhing on the cot. The one looked familiar under his helmet, but my eyes were drawn to the wounded man. His bloody hands clutched at the hilt of a dagger that had been driven into his groin. Blood seeped between his fingers. I swallowed hard. Ah, Goddess, it was a bad one.

I knelt by the cot, putting the water and cloths beside me. "I am a healer, let me help you." I reached over, trying to move his hands from the weapon and get a better look. "Gently, gently." I pried back the man's hands and checked with my own.

There was no wound. There was blood, but no injury. The dagger was flat against his belly, up under the armor. Puzzled, I looked up and into eyes I recognized. "Arneath?"

I staggered back. Those eyes held no pain, rather they held a fury I had never seen before. Before I could react, he was off the cot, lunging at me. He had one hand around my throat, the other clutched the dagger. He bore me to the ground, and we fell back. My breath huffed out, his weight falling full on my stomach. The hand at my throat squeezed, cutting off my breath.

Arneath's companions reacted as well. I caught a brief glimpse as they drew their weapons, yelled and charged the wounded. There were screams and sounds of fighting all around us.

Arneath swung his hand up, dagger flashing. It plunged down just as swiftly. I managed to get my hands up to grab his wrist. But Arneath had his full strength behind it, and the dagger continued toward my heart slowly but surely. Arneath squeezed my throat again, cutting off air and sound. His eyes gleamed with a mad brightness. "Die, traitorous bitch."

With what strength I had, I fought to deflect the blade. The weapon plunged down, the pain flared up, and the darkness embraced me.

"Open your eyes, little healer." The whisper was soft, but insistent. Simus's voice seeped through the blackness and the pain, soft and quiet, with an underlying urgency to the sound.

"Little healer, open your eyes. Wake for me."

I moved my head toward the sound, but stopped when pain flared up. The air that I pulled in was tainted with the scent of blood and death.

"Thank the skies." Simus's voice took on a new urgency, even as he whispered. "Don't move, little one. Just open your eyes and speak. Keir needs you."

Keir needed me? I dragged my lids up.

Keir was standing over me, swords in hand. He was splattered with blood, poised as if for battle, on guard against an opponent.

"At last." Simus's voice was coming from the side, still soft and low. I turned my head slowly, to see his black face on the ground, pushed under the back wall of the tent. His features were tight, but he flashed a smile at me. "Warprize, Keir is raging. Try to call him back."

I couldn't really see, couldn't tell what had happened. I licked my lips and panted against the pain. "Keir?" My voice was little more than a whisper itself, my throat in agony.

Keir's eyes flickered down, then back up, as if watching for the enemy. His swords were coated with blood.

"Keep trying, little one," Simus whispered. "He doesn't

know us and won't let us in the tent. Battle rage, eh? You understand?"

I'd heard of it. Hadn't someone in the *Epic* suffered the affliction? I blinked a bit, confused.

Simus spoke again, urgently. "Stay with me, little one. Stay awake."

"Keir." I tried to clear my throat and my voice strengthened slightly. "Let them help. They're friends." His eyes settled on mine, wary, suspicious, then flicked back to the tent walls. I shifted a bit, trying to get a better look, but that proved a mistake. A cry escaped me as the pain ran over me in a wave. I couldn't move my shoulder.

"Warprize?" Simus's worried tone cut through the grey that swamped my vision.

Keir snarled, one sword pointed toward Simus, the other at the entrance. There were others outside, I could hear their voices. The tent walls vibrated when they moved.

I swallowed back my fear and panic. "Simus, get everyone quiet and away from the tent."

Simus's face disappeared and there were murmurs outside. Keir tensed, his swords held at the ready, blood running down the tang. I flicked my eyes away from that, and tried to slow my breathing. The quiet seemed to help, for it seemed that Keir's stance changed slightly.

"Keir." My voice grew stronger. "Warlord."

His eyes met mine again, but this time they seemed more puzzled than wary. I smiled at him weakly. "Let Simus come in." I closed my eyes and took a breath against the pain, afraid that I'd lose consciousness again.

"Simus?" Keir's voice was rough, almost a growl.

"Friends. Be easy, Keir. They will help us. Simus," I called. "Take off your weapons, and come in."

I heard a rustling and movement outside. Simus or someone was slowly cutting the back wall of the tent, making an entrance. Keir spun, placing himself between me and the widening gap.

Simus crawled through, on hands and knees, dragging his

wounded leg behind him. Keir tracked his every move with the tips of his swords. Simus stopped just out of reach and lowered himself to lay on the floor. "My Warlord, the enemy is slain and all is secure. What is your command?"

Keir stared at him for a bit, then lowered his swords slowly. "Simus?" His voice was rough and puzzled. "What . . . ?"

Simus did not raise his head. "Battle rage, Warlord."

Keir was already looking around, turning this way and that. His eyes fell on me. "Skies." Through a haze, I saw him drop his swords and kneel by my side. Simus reached over and pulled the weapons to his side. "Get in here and help her!" Keir roared.

I would have laughed, but it hurt too damn much.

Gils appeared beside me, muscling his way in. Joden appeared from nowhere and grabbed at Keir's shoulders, pulling him back. "Let the boy work."

"Warprize, can you hear me?" My vision was graying, but I could make out a shock of red hair and anxious eyes. Gils turned away, then suddenly there was a movement under my nose. A deep breath and suddenly everything was bright and sharp. The scent from the crushed leaves in Gils's hand cleared my confusion.

"Warprize." Gils swallowed hard, and continued with a shaky voice. "The dagger went through your upper arm to the hilt. It holds you pinned to the tent floor." He swallowed a sob. "There's be a lot of blood."

Well, that certainly explained a few things. I trembled for a moment, but not from the cold. Images returned, memories of what had happened. "What of the others?" I forced the words out past the pain. "Atira?"

Keir grunted. Gils spoke quickly. "You're the worst."

Simus nodded. "Tell us what to do."

"Roll me over so that the dagger comes clear. Clean it well, then pull it from my arm." I took another deep breath. The scent of the leaves was still there. "Gils, you will need to clean and dress the wound. Use boiled skunk cabbage, there is some in the tent." Another tremble went though my body. It seemed that I was teaching a class from some distance away.

"Get me warm and watch for signs of fever." The haze was back, the leaves could not stave it off any longer. I could just make out Gils's nod and worried look. "You'll do fine," I whispered. "Simus."

"Warprize." Simus was still with Keir.

"Once it's clean, I want you to pull out the dagger." Keir started to object, but I didn't let him continue. "Warlord." I managed to lift my other hand. Keir knelt and took it. "Let them do what they must." I caught his eyes with mine. "I will be fine."

Simus knelt by my side. Gils knelt next to him, poised with supplies. They shifted me slightly, and I gasped at the sensation. I tried to focus on Keir's eyes through the haze. They were so blue, so frightened.

Frightened?

Puzzled, I opened my mouth to ask why at the same moment that Simus pulled the dagger out. The pain cut through the haze nicely, revealing the blackness beyond.

9

I didn't want to wake up; the darkness where I floated was warm and comfortable. But my ears ached from the sound of an angry voice that pulled at me. I cracked my eyes open, only to squeeze them shut as the bright light burned them. The voice continued, ranting in its fury. I eased my eyelids up again, squinting to let them adjust.

I was in Keir's bed. The tent seemed to glow it was so bright.

"Ah. There's my girl." A whisper caught my attention.

"Eln?" I turned my head slowly, my neck achy and stiff. Eln was sitting on the bed next to me, holding a small bowl. I stared at him, puzzled.

"It's me, child." He kept his voice low. "How do you feel?"

"Feel?" I didn't understand, but even more confusing was the angry voice that had not stopped or cooled. I turned my head slowly back to discover that the tent wall had been rolled up. Keir was pacing back and forth where the wall normally hung between bedroom and meeting area. Still dressed in black leathers, the silver wrist bands catching the light and glittering as he moved like a large cat. A large, angry cat. I could just see the tops of heads beyond him, filling the meeting area. Something wasn't right. I sat up.

Rather, I tried to sit up. The arm I asked to support me objected mightily, and I gasped at the pain. In that instant it all came back, details of the attack flooding into my head.

Keir was by the bed in an instant. He half climbed into the center, and placed a hand on my chest to keep me flat. "You're awake. Warprize, are you all right?" He was speaking my tongue.

I eased back onto the pillows. "I think my arm is going to fall off." My voice was a croak.

Keir sucked in a breath.

"It's *not* going to fall off." Eln responded firmly. He frowned at me and gave a sharp jerk of his head, telling me in a not-so-subtle manner to watch my tongue. "I'm sure it hurts, but the wound is clean and well bandaged. There is bruising on your neck, but no real damage. You will recover fully." Gils hovered behind Eln, his face tight with worry. Eln continued, "Your student did well, Lara."

Keir snarled. "One of the few who did well." He returned to his feet. "Tend to her," he snapped as he resumed his pacing. None of the others had stirred.

I lay back on the bed as Eln leaned forward and placed his hand on my forehead. Gils stood next to him, nervously watching us.

"Eln, how—"

"Kidnaped from my home by mounted warriors and slung over a saddle like a sack of meal." Eln snorted as he checked my heartbeat. "It took a while before someone who spoke our language explained what had happened."

"How long have I been out?" I asked, still sounding rough. Gils flicked a look from my face to Eln's and back.

Eln grunted. "I don't know. You were unconscious when I arrived, and I have been here for a quarter of an hour."

I repeated my question to Gils in his language.

"Warprize, you were unconscious for about an hour. I's did the best I could, but I told the Warlord to send for a real healer from the city, and I knew your teacher's name." His face was pale under his red hair. "I's told him that I's your apprentice."

Eln raised his eyebrows when he heard a familiar word. "Your 'apprentice' did a fine job of cleaning and binding the wound. I have checked it, and it would seem that stitches are not required." Eln inclined his head toward the lad. "You might tell him that for me."

I did, and Gils collapsed next to the bed, his body seeming to fold under the weight of his fears. "I's so scared, Warprize. That I's be hurting you, that the Warlord be hurting me . . ." Keir's angry voice was raised again. Gils swallowed hard. "I's think most of the blood we saw be your attackers, not yours."

Eln produced a cup. "I want you to drink this, then sleep."

I smelled the contents. "Lotus? No, Eln. I want my wits about me."

"More fever's foe then, and water." Eln didn't fuss at my refusal.

I looked into the main tent, at the heads that remained lowered, as Keir moved back and forth. "What is going on?" I asked.

Eln looked over his shoulder. "From the tone, I believe the Warlord is going to start ordering executions."

I struggled up, heedless of my arm. Gils moved to support me, kneeling behind me on the bed.

Keir's voice was razor sharp. "I am looking for answers as to how the warprize came to be attacked inside my own camp, while she was under the protection of my warriors." His head swung angrily toward the kneeling warriors, and I could hear the snarl of an infuriated cat in his voice.

Dearest Goddess, he was angry. The tent contained Epor and Isdra, the captain of the patrol, his men, Simus, Prest, and Rafe. Many of them had bandages as well. General Warren and his men were also on their knees, heads bowed. I thought I saw Iften's blond head, way in the back. Everyone was on their knees, with the only exception being Simus, who was sitting on a stump near Keir.

Keir continued, pacing all the while. "This much I know. My patrol came across six men of the city watch, who

claimed to have been hurt in some type of attack." His voice
was cold and hard as he glared at the hapless captain of the
patrol. "They rendered assistance by escorting them to the
warprize." His tone was of one who had been offended.

"Which was what your warprize had requested." I kept my
voice calm and moderate.

Keir swivelled his head to look at me. He gave me a hard
look and turned away.

"Once they were in the tent, they attacked as soon as the
warprize was vulnerable." He resumed his pacing.

"Once in the tent, I tended the most severely injured. That
is my job as Master Healer."

Keir turned back and glared at me. "There was no injury. It
was a trap, an assassin's trick aimed at your death." He
swung back to the men. "The so-called wounded attacked
you and everyone else in the tent."

Goddess. "Was anyone else hurt?" I whispered to Gils, as I
scanned the crowd.

He lowered his head to my ear. "No, Warprize. We'd just
enough warning to get out of the way and let the patrol and
your guards handle them." He paused, and a look of awe
came over his face. "Atira killed her assailant and didn't disturb her leg at all." He was clearly impressed by her actions.
"And when the Warlord burst into the tent . . ." He shuddered
and continued quietly. "We're never gonna figure out which
head goes with which body."

Keir was still ranting. "When I learn who was behind it, I
will . . ."

I leaned against Gils, feeling very tired. "Arneath." It took
almost all my energy to speak his name.

General Warren's head came up and he stared at me.

I nodded. "It was Arneath, a member of the Palace Guard."
I closed my eyes. "I think one of them was Degnan. I didn't
recognize the others."

"Degnan? Son of Durst?" Keir sounded outraged. I heard a
low growl, and opened my eyes again. Keir was towering
over General Warren, his sword in his hand. Warren was
smart enough to jerk his head back down and keep it bent.

"This was a trick, your presence, the watch . . ." Keir's voice was low and keen and deadly.

Warren didn't move. "No. The day my king swore fealty to you, you became my liege. I am a soldier and a man of honor. I would never allow a hand to be raised against a Daughter of Xy." He lifted his head and looked Keir squarely in the eye. Keir stood there, and I held my breath, thinking to see the man strike as he had in the throne room. Instead, Keir sheathed his sword.

Warren spoke. "Let me return to the castle and make inquiry. I'll return with the information, and if my people planned this, you may have my life. Do not let the actions of a few destroy the peace."

"I believe him." I added my voice, hoarse as it was.

Keir did not respond, but resumed his pacing. I could see that every muscle was tense. His jaw was tight, and the muscles at the back of his jaw seemed to pulse with anger. I felt uncomfortable, disheveled and laying in the bed, when everyone was in the room. My arm ached, throbbed. I shifted it slightly, and stifled a cry when the pain flared sharper.

Keir was at my side in an instant. "You must rest." He fixed Gils with a glare. Gils moved with all due haste to get me back down on the bed. Keir turned.

"Warren. Take the dead and return to the castle. Inform me of what you find." He gestured with his hand, switching to his own tongue. "Leave us. All of you."

Men rose and left quickly. Simus had two men to help him walk out. Eln quirked his mouth. "I take it we are being dismissed." He rose from the bed. "I will check your patients before I go. With your 'apprentice'."

"Healer." Keir held out a bag of coins. "For your trouble." He tossed it to Eln.

Eln stood tall and regal, and watched the bag as it arched toward him and fell to the floor with a plinking sound. He looked straight into Keir's eyes, his eyebrows arched in quiet anger. "Long before she was your warprize, she was my friend and student." He looked down at me and warmth returned to his face. "Be well, Lara. If it is permitted, I'll check on you again."

He left with that slow stride of his, with Gils in tow.

Epor and Isdra had remained on their knees, and their presence drew Keir's attention. "Leave."

Epor raised his head. "Warlord, we failed you." Isdra nodded her agreement.

Keir scooped up the bag of coins and stood looking at it for a moment, the small muscle in his jaw throbbing.

Marcus cleared his throat. "Body guarding is far different from warrior's work. Who knew wounded would rise to the attack?"

Keir glared at Marcus, who returned the look, unimpressed.

"Warlord, we feel the shame of this, Epor and I." Isdra spoke. "We ask the chance to wipe this disgrace away."

I felt the need to speak. "It wasn't their fault."

Keir's glare scorched my skin. "It was. They were to protect you." He tossed the small bag of coins onto one of the chests. I opened my mouth to respond, but a quick gesture from Marcus kept me silent. After long moments, Keir spoke. "Return to your duties. But never let this happen again."

"Never again." Epor confirmed.

"Our lives for hers." Isdra pledged.

At a gesture from Keir they were up and out of the tent. Marcus silently lowered the tent wall. Keir moved to the braziers and started to add coal. "Keir," I said quietly. He did not turn.

Marcus came up beside me and fussed with the furs. "Some broth? Some wine, or kavage?"

I nodded. "Yes, Marcus, please. Broth and kavage."

He shot a glance at Keir's back, then left on his errand. Keir was standing, staring into the sullen coals. "Keir, please. I need your help." He turned, looking at me with haunted eyes. I started to struggle to sit up. He was there in an instant, helping me. "Privy," I said, smiling at him. He swept me up, and carried me to the room. No smile. No response. After the business was done, he carried me back, placed me gently on the bed, and pulled the covers up tight. He sat there, staring at me, stroking my hair. I put my hand to his face. "Keir, what . . ."

Marcus walked in, carrying a tray. Keir got up and resumed pacing. Marcus helped me sit up. "Soup I had simmering," he murmured. "Drink it all." His one eye glared at me as he set the bowl in my hands. I sipped obediently, enjoying the warmth. It tasted good. Rich, salty, with a bit of spice I didn't recognize. The salt clung to my lips and stung slightly. I took a few more sips, relishing the flavor before I identified the aftertaste. "Marcus, you drugged this!"

"Aye." Marcus stood, unrepentant. "Gils and the tall one gave it to me. Will do you good. Finish the bowl." Marcus picked up the wine jug and poured some into a cup.

"And this for you." He thrust the cup at Keir.

"No." Keir turned away.

Marcus frowned, but turned back to me and eyed the bowl in my hands. I gave up, knowing that Eln had been right, but unwilling to take my own medicine. Besides, my neck and arm ached. I finished the bowl and handed it to Marcus.

"Leave us," Keir growled.

Marcus picked up the dishes, caught my eye and nodded in Keir's direction. I nodded back, pleased that he trusted me to take care of Keir. The tension in his face eased with understanding, and he left the room.

Keir was still moving about, still wound up. I settled into the furs and pillows, already feeling the effects of the lotus. Keir knelt by the bed. "Are you well?"

I smiled. "Fine. Marcus is right, sleep will help." I yawned and shifted around, trying to get comfortable.

He looked at me intensely. "You could have been killed. If I hadn't heard the noise and headed over, he would have killed you." Something in his face closed off. "If you had died, the peace would have broken."

Alarmed, I tried to force my eyes open. "The peace is more important than any one person."

Keir took a few of the pillows, and moved them to support my arm. "Don't fight it. Close your eyes."

I looked up through half lidded eyes, unable to resist the pull of the drug. He seemed so tired, so worn. He kissed me softly. "Sleep."

"If you will."

He shook his head. "No." But he eased onto the bed, setting his sword close at hand and gathering me in with the other. "Sleep."

Exhaustion pulled at me, but I resisted a moment more. "Keir. Don't do anything . . ." I couldn't think of the word.

"Rash?" Keir asked softly.

"Stupid." I yawned, and heard his chuckle as I floated off.

I awoke to the dark tent and the sound of rhythmic steps. It took a moment to orient myself. Everything seemed slightly fuzzy, which was one of the effects of lotus. It was tempting to drift back into the warmth and the darkness, but the sound of the pacing drew me out of the covers.

Keir was pacing back and forth. I yawned and watched him move in those black leathers. I frowned when I realized that he hadn't gotten any sleep. "Keir? What are you doing?"

"Keeping watch. You are under my protection. You have been hurt. It will never happen again."

My eyes widened at that and the fuzziness receded slightly. I managed to get up on my good arm and stare at him. "Keir, there is an entire army out there. They can . . ."

"It wasn't good enough, was it." He paused and looked at me. "It will be tonight. I put the entire army on alert, with double watches."

I groaned, closed my eyes and let my head sink back on the pillows. No one was getting any sleep tonight.

Keir came to my side. "Are you well? Should I call Gils?" I studied him, and the lines of worry on his face.

"Keir," I spoke very firmly. "Take them off the alert."

His frown deepened. "You must be . . ."

Enough. I interrupted. "I'm safe. I'm here with you." I curled myself down into the bed. Keir hesitated, then moved to the flap and went out. I lay in a kind of stupor, imagining an entire army of warriors muttering about having to protect the Warlord's prize. With double watches, yet. I yawned, closed my eyes and drifted.

At some point Keir came in and stood by me. I reached out from under the covers, taking his hand. It was cold, and I could feel the tension in his muscles. I yawned and tugged. He looked at me oddly, but allowed himself to be pulled under the covers. I moved over, letting him have the warm spot. Through the haze, I could feel his body was easing a bit. I moved closer, putting my head on his chest. The black leather warmed slowly under my cheek.

We lay there for a moment, warming each other. I yawned again, and my jaw cracked. He chuckled and stroked my hair. "You should go back to sleep."

I raised my head and tried to focus, but it was a losing battle.

Keir's chest rumbled with another laugh. "I think you will be sleeping late tomorrow, Warprize."

Tomorrow. I dropped my head back down. "What is a pattern dance?"

"Eh?"

I raised my all too heavy head. "What is a pattern dance?"

"A group dance. Many men and women dancing in a pattern that they weave with their bodies." I felt Keir shrug. "It's hard to explain. You have to see it to understand."

"See it tomorrow." For some reason I felt happy about the prospect.

Keir's hand stilled. "I canceled the dance."

I tried to lift my head again, but only succeeded in rolling off Keir's chest to lay by his side. I managed to focus on his eyes. "They'll hate me."

He turned onto his side to face me. "They won't blame you."

I lost the focus, and his face blurred. The next yawn made my eyes water, and my jaw cracked again. I said something, but it came out all fuzzy. Like my vision.

Keir sighed, and shifted, moving out from under the covers. He tucked me in, letting none of the cooler air touch me. "I'll take care of it. Sleep."

I drifted off, wondering what I had said.

* * *

The evil taste in my mouth woke me first. Another of the effects of lotus. The irony of suffering the same effects that my own patients complained about was not lost on me. I would have to remember that the next time I dosed someone with it. It wouldn't stop me from giving it to them, but I'd try to be more sympathetic.

The bed was empty, and I could tell that it was fairly late in the day. My stomach was reminding me that I had missed at least two meals. I stretched under the blanket, being careful not to include the arm. The worst of it was my neck, stiff and sore. The arm hurt as well, and I really didn't want to move.

The tent flap from the main room opened, and Keir stuck his head in. "You're awake."

I nodded as I moved to sit on the edge of the bed, feeling heavy and dull. I still had my trous on, but my shirt had been removed. My breast band had dried blood on it, and I made a face.

Keir pressed his lips together as he studied my throat. I grimaced, imagining that the bruising was at its worst now. "I'll get Marcus for hot food, and kavage. We'll send for Gils."

"I want a bath."

Keir cocked his head. I repeated my request. He frowned. "Marcus can bring warm . . ."

"No." I gripped his arm with my good hand and tried to pull myself up. Keir helped me without even thinking about it. "I want a bath now. I stink. I don't care what the water is like."

Keir blinked. I stood there for a moment, getting my balance and waited to see if I would be dizzy or nauseous. Yet another effect of the drug.

Keir frowned. "Gils needs to check—"

"Gils can check it after I have bathed."

"Gils said—"

"Who is the healer here?" I took a step.

His lips quirked. "Master Healer, if I remember right."

I smiled. "The Master wants a bath."

He smiled. "Then Master, you shall have one." He wrapped his arm around my waist as we walked together to the privy. Thank the Goddess for his people's attitude toward cleanliness. I was grateful that he didn't question my need to be clean any further.

Once inside, Keir placed one of the wooden blocks on the washing platform, and I sat to strip off my trous and breast band. They were both soiled, but not harmed. As long as I moved slowly, the pain was no more than a dull ache. Keir put water within my reach, then handed me soap and a cloth. I got a whiff of the soap and held it to my nose. It smelled like vanilla. I looked at him, but he wore an innocent expression on his face.

Marcus called from the other room, and Keir moved about, taking a bucket of hot coals for the brazier, and more water. I washed out my breast band as the room warmed. I lathered up the soap and started on my face and neck, enjoying the scent of home. The arm wasn't a problem, as long as I didn't try to raise it, or use that hand over much. I hummed quietly to myself as I washed. The tepid water felt wonderful on my skin, and I was careful to keep the wound dry as I worked.

Keir came back in and settled in the corner, where the shadows were deepest. I glanced over quickly, but could only make out his eyes, gleaming in the darkness. I blushed slightly, bit my lip, but kept going. It felt uncomfortable to be watched so, but it was also somehow satisfying, to know that I was the object of his interest. My feelings confused me, so I concentrated on getting clean. When I reached my groin, I sensed a slight movement in the corner, but I moved on quickly to legs and feet and toes.

Keir did move forward at that point, bringing another bucket of water over to me. It had been closer to the brazier, which meant the water was slightly warmer. I used a bowl to rinse with, for fear of getting the wound wet. Once done, I wrapped up in the towels that he gave me. I decided against washing my hair. I was tired and felt a trembling that indicated I needed to eat. Instead, I grabbed a comb and tried to stand.

Keir swept me up, and carried me into the bedroom, placing me on one of the stumps close to a brazier.

"I can walk, you know." I started to comb my hair. "Your turn."

Keir made a negative gesture.

I lifted my head, sniffed the air, and raised an eyebrow.

He took the hint. He went out and brought in two more buckets of water, and fed the brazier again. Then he returned, stood in the center of the room, and looked at me.

I rested my eyes on him. He was glorious in that black leather, which fit him like a glove yet let him move like a cat. He lifted a hand to his collar and started to loosen the lacings of his jerkin.

I couldn't look away. He pulled the lacings out ever so slowly, pulling them out to their full length, then starting on the next one. When he finished, he lifted the ends of his shirt, and ever so slowly pulled the leather up and over his head.

I stopped combing.

The man was certainly healthy. I swallowed hard. The faint light of the brazier shone over his muscles as he carefully placed his leather jerkin on one of the benches. He sat to remove his boots, and the thick socks underneath. He sat for a minute and wiggled his toes. He stood and nonchalantly started to unlace his trous. Slowly.

I turned my back to him. I'd cared for many a naked man in my time, but the sight of Keir's body was different somehow. It affected me. Made me want to reach out and touch him—to feel those muscles move under his skin. To experience more of his touch, and maybe a few of his kisses. The idea made me shiver.

I could feel his amusement on the back of my neck. There were sounds behind me, as he removed the trous. I bit my lip again, finding that the imagining might be even more embarrassing then the actual seeing. My fingers continued to run the comb through my hair, but my mind was elsewhere. The sounds stopped.

He drew my hair off to the side, and kissed my neck.

I jerked as lightning coursed through my body. Tingles ran

from my neck right to the soles of my feet. I turned my head quickly, but all I saw was a brief glimpse of the tent flap falling into place behind him. I sat for a minute, waiting for the tingling sensation to pass. My hand kept combing my hair, but it took a long time for the sensation of his lips to leave my skin.

By the time Keir emerged, Marcus was loading the table with too much food, and Gils had crept quietly into the tent to change my bandage.

For something that felt like an enormous hole in my arm, the wound was small. It looked good, with no signs of angered flesh or swelling. Gils changed the bandage with meticulous and agonizing slowness. I complimented him on his work, and then meekly accepted a dose of fever's foe. He'd brought some of the liniment, and he applied it carefully to my neck, all the while casting glances at the privy entrance as if Keir was going to leap out at any moment, battle-raged, and swords in hand.

Finally, Gils sat back on his heels, looking satisfied. "I's checked Atira, Warprize, and she's well. And Simus let me look at his leg."

"How is it?" I asked.

We were both startled when Simus replied. "It's well, little healer." Simus entered the tent, grinning at me. "If it can take me running to the healing tent and crawling on the ground, then I think I can walk on it well enough."

"Simus . . ." I chided.

His teeth gleamed in a smile. "It's not like I'm going to join in the dancing today." His face turned serious. "How's the arm?"

"I'm fine." I smiled at him. "Gils is seeing to me."

Gils stood, gathering his supplies. "I's see you at the dance, Warprize. I's chores to do before then."

Simus sat on the bed, next to me. "Marcus! I need kavage!"

I looked at them both. "I thought the dance was canceled."

Gils stood. "Oh no, Warprize, the Warlord announced it

late last night." A slight noise from the privy and he was out and gone.

Marcus brought kavage for both of us, and grimaced at Simus. "I suppose you've not eaten yet?"

Simus laughed.

Marcus scowled. "I've bare enough for these two, much less fill your belly."

Keir emerged, dried and dressed. "Simus, join us."

Simus smiled broadly.

Marcus huffed and left. Keir, Simus, and I pulled up stumps and dug into the food. For many minutes, there was only the sound of chewing and dishes being passed. The bowl of gurt was offered to me a number of times, but I politely declined. Simus leaned back first. "Never could figure out how Marcus manages such good food in camp."

"Years of practice," Marcus said as he returned with more kavage and served us all. "There's not much time before the dance starts."

Keir nodded. "Any word from Warren or Xymund?"

Simus shook his head. "No."

Keir scowled, but said nothing as we rose to leave. He merely wrapped his cloak around me, and made as if to sweep me up in his arms. "I can walk." I fought him off as I also tangled with the smothering cloth as best I could, trying to pull it up so that I wouldn't trip.

Simus stifled a laugh. I looked up to see that his eyes were dancing with mirth. "You look like a child playing with her thea's cloak." I laughed, curious as to the meaning of the word, but Simus held out his arm for me. "Warprize."

Keir growled, and swept me up into his arms, stomping out of the tent. I looked behind to see Simus rolling his eyes and following behind with Marcus.

The sky was clear when we emerged and headed for the gathering area. The entire camp seemed to be headed in that direction, everyone armed. It didn't look as if they were going to a dance. I wrapped my arms around Keir's neck. "Will everyone be at the dance?"

"No." Keir slowed his walk to allow Simus to catch up with us. "The watches will rotate." His voice lowered. "I believe you would call that a 'compromise'."

The flat area in front of the wooden platform had been cleared and the area was ringed with a circle of unlit torches. We made our way onto the platform, and sat close to the front. There was no formality. We took our seats even as bodies milled in the space in front of the platform. Simus remained standing, looking off into the crowd. He laughed, then pointed. "Here they come."

Looking out, I could see that someone was being carried on a cot, much like Simus had been carried to the senel. It was Atira, laying flat on the cot as some of her friends carried her through the crowd. The stones had been removed, but her leg was still in a cast.

"Bring her up here." Keir called out, and the cot started to head toward the platform.

"Warprize!" Atira called out when they drew nearer. "Are you well?"

"Very well. How's your leg?" I asked, curious to see how the leather was holding up.

"It itches." She complained as they brought her cot up and placed it next to me, so that she had a good view of the grounds. "That grey one came and looked at it, and seemed pleased. Gils has been watching it too." She smiled at me as she propped herself up. "I'm glad to see that you are well. Scared me to the snows, let me tell you, you being attacked." She looked around. Keir was kneeling at the edge of the platform, talking to a few of the warriors. She dropped her voice and continued. "I managed to throw a knife and take one out, but got knocked to the ground before I could do more. It was the Warlord's raging that saved our hides."

"Were you there when he . . ." I let my voice trail off, unsure how to ask the question.

"When he was standing over you?" She rolled her eyes. "Aye, half under my cot and fearing to breathe. I've heard tell of battle rage, but never saw it before. Knew enough to lay still and quiet. Good thing you talked him out, Warprize. Not something they can always do." She flashed me a grin. "But never mind that, there's a pattern dance to watch!"

Keir had risen to stand at the very edge. "Would you see a pattern?"

"AYE!" Every voice seemed to shout, and cheering began.

Keir held up a small wooden bowl. "Iften, call the dancers forth."

Marcus was behind us, wrapped deep in a cloak. He muttered something that I didn't hear, but that Iften picked up as he approached. There was anger on his face as Iften took the bowl from Keir's hands. But he moved off into the center of the field without a word. Iften held the bowl before him with both hands. "Hear me!"

The crowd grew quiet.

"Heyla!" Iften called out.

"Heyla!" The crowd responded.

"Who would dance a pattern for us?"

From all around the circle, nine running figures emerged from the crowd, dashing up to Iften and placing some sort of token in the bowl that he held. As they dropped in their tokens, they continued on, disappearing back into the crowd. The last one jumped up just before he reached the bowl and dropped the token in with a flare, prompting laughter from the crowd. After a pause, Iften raised the bowl over his head. "Let the sky hear our voices."

I was startled when a sound like a crack of thunder was heard, until I saw the drummers in the crowd, with large drums at their feet. Each had struck their drums once, and the vibration filled my ears.

"Let the earth feel our feet." Iften made a quarter turn to face another part of the crowd. Again the drums sounded. "Let the wind sense our strength." He paused as the drums sounded in response. "Let the flames see our patterns." He shouted, as he made another turn. This time, in addition to the drums, the torches were lit. The crowd roared out with the drums at the last call, crying a tremendous 'heyla'!

Iften reached in and pulled a token from the bowl. "Red, dance your pattern." He called, then moved off the field.

Again, runners emerged from the crowd. It was a group of ten men and women. They were dressed in tunics and trous, with red headbands, and red streamers flowing behind them as they ran. They ran to the center of the field, and stood in a circle. There was a pause, then the drums began to beat a fast, steady measure.

The dancers took one step forward, linked their arms, and began to dance. It didn't take me long to see what they were doing. I'd been taught court dances when I was a child, and seen the romps and rills that the servants danced when they celebrated the harvest. But I had never seen anything like this before. They wove a pattern with their bodies, stepping in then out of the circle then around each other to form the circle again. Just when I was sure they were coming to an end, from nowhere they produced wooden sticks, like axe handles, and started to beat out a counter rhythm to the drums. On each other's sticks.

I watched, amazed, waiting for someone to hit a hand or arm instead of the sticks. But the dancers never seemed to miss a beat as they wove and pounded on each other. The crowd was yelling now, some calling out encouragement and others yelling insults. The group formed two interlocking circles and wove their patterns together. As each passed the place where the circles joined, they had to beat out the rhythms on the other sticks. I laughed with joy to see them move with no errors, in a perfect pattern. "How do they do that?"

Simus laughed. Keir shot me an amused glance and responded. "Practice. Lots of practice."

The dancers were smiling, but I could see the concentration on their faces. I didn't know whether to watch their feet, or their hands, and ended up trying to watch it all at once. Finally, just when I was convinced that fatigue would start to set in, the dancers all cried out at once, spun in place to wind their streamers around their bodies, and stood frozen, spaced evenly in a circle, facing inwards.

The crowd erupted with cries of 'heyla' and praise. I

clapped my hands together, which drew some odd looks from Atira and Simus. "That was amazing!"

Atira sniffed. "I've seen better."

Marcus was handing me some kavage. "They were slightly off, Warprize. But not by much."

I took the drink eagerly. "When is the next one?"

But Iften had already moved into the center of the field and was pulling the next token. He waited for the crowd to settle, before calling out 'Yellow'.

This was a larger group, some twenty people with yellow streamers came running into the field. Keir leaned over to me. "This group is trying for a very large pattern. Not so intricate but harder with so many." The drums began again, and I tried to pay more attention to the dancers individually. Sure enough, after just a few minutes, there was a groan from the crowd, and the dancers broke apart and ran off the field.

Simus grunted when he saw my disappointment. "They stop when the pattern is broken, Warprize. The dance can't continue if an error is made."

The next group summoned down to the field was brown. Their pattern was intricate, but started very slowly. As the drums speeded up, so did their steps, and the blows to their sticks. I watched in anticipation, trying to see the dancers the way Keir did, but all I saw was a wonderful explosion of movement, rhythm and color. Just as it seemed to reach its peak, the drums began to slow, and the dancers slowed at the same time, until they stood in their original positions. As the last drum beat faded, the crowd erupted into cheers. The dancers ran off, and the crowd started stirring.

Keir stood and stretched. "The watches are changing." He looked at me. "Warm enough?"

I nodded, as Marcus held a plate before me. There were small buns there, and I took one in one hand. "What are these?"

Atira grinned and reached for the plate as Marcus offered her one as well. "Warprize, take a bite."

I looked doubtfully at her, but she bit hers with relish, so I did the same. There was an explosion of spice in my mouth and I opened my eyes wide. Atira laughed.

The spice was strong, but it didn't burn. There was a sweetness to it that seemed strange at first. "What is this?"

"Bread tarts." Atira took another bite and talked around her mouthful. "Rare to get them in camp."

Keir and Simus were eating theirs, obviously pleased. Marcus had a proud look on his face, and even quirked his mouth in a grin when I took another bite. We were all enjoying the treat when a warrior came up to the platform. "Warlord, a messenger has come from the city."

"From Warren?" Keir asked.

"From their king, Warlord."

"Bring him here."

The crowd was starting to settle, and Iften seemed to be looking at Keir for the signal to start. Keir gestured for him to continue, and the opening ritual was repeated. This time the dancers were wearing bells on their hands and feet, and carrying sticks. As they danced, Marcus frowned in disapproval. Apparently the bells were a distraction from the pattern, and Marcus was quick to express his opinion. Keir leaned over at one point and spoke softly, "Marcus danced patterns well before he was injured. But his eye gives him no vision on that side, and he no longer dances." I nodded, but I liked the chiming of the bells, and was quick to call out 'heyla' at the end.

"Warlord."

We turned to see the warrior standing behind us, with Heath at his side, grinning like a fool.

"Heath!" I jumped to my feet, leaving the cloak behind me. The cooler air hit me, giving me goose bumps, but I paid no mind as I ran over to greet him.

Heath was stiff, but he relaxed and brought his arms up to give me a quick hug, before pushing me back slightly. He brought his hand up to cup my neck, then let his hand fall as he stepped back. He dropped to one knee. "Warlord."

I turned, to see Keir standing there, a dark expression on his face. I caught my breath, suddenly understanding that I'd made a mistake. Heat flooded my face. Keir pointed at the stool where I had been seated, and I returned to it. Marcus draped the cloak back over me, and made sure that it covered me completely.

"Your message?" Keir's voice was cold, as behind us Iften called the next dance.

"Warlord, King Xymund sends word that Lord Durst still lives. Eln the Healer believes that he will recover." Heath lifted his head. "Lord Marshall Warren and the King continue to question and investigate the attack on the warprize and will send further word tomorrow."

Keir grunted, but I saw a brief flash of relief in his eyes.

Heath continued, "Warlord, I also beg your forgiveness on behalf of myself and your warprize. We are childhood friends, who played in the kitchens together when we were small." He swallowed hard. "I had heard that she was hurt, and asked to carry the King's words in order to see for myself and report back to my mother."

Keir narrowed his eyes. "Your mother is Anna the Cook?"

Heath nodded. "She who rules the kitchens, and will beat me with a spoon if I do not report back on Lar—the warprize's condition."

Simus chuckled. "Never anger a good cook, Keir."

Keir still looked grim, but his voice was polite. "Stay then, and talk with the warprize. Would you see a dance?"

Heath smiled, stood and moved to sit on the platform, leaning back against the side of Atira's cot. He looked at her leg, and grimaced. "Broken?" I nodded. He smiled at Atira, and pointed at her leg and then at his. "I remember what that is like. Tell her she has my sympathy."

I translated for Atira, and she nodded her thanks, eyeing Heath's leg and its apparent health.

Keir and Simus settled back down as the next dance was called. Atira propped herself a little higher when Iften called the color. "These are my dancers!"

I quickly explained things to Heath as the dancers ran out on the field. Their ribbons were blue, and they formed a square in the center of the field. But instead of sticks, they carried what looked like rocks. We watched as the drums pounded and the dance began. The dancers wove a pattern for some time before they raised their rocks and cracked them together. The sound it made was far different from the sticks, and the crowd cried out in astonishment as sparks flew from the dancers's hands.

Keir and Simus stood, and Marcus moved to the front of the platform to get a better look. I stayed where I was, not wanting to block Atira's view. The dancers beat out the pattern with their feet, the drums seemed to build in intensity, and every so often the sparks flew as the rocks were struck. The crowd started to stomp their feet in time with the drums, and seemed to be chanting 'heyla' over and over to their beat. The sound was infectious and I clapped to the rhythm. Atira was grinning, and Heath seemed spellbound by the sight.

At last the dancers came to the end, and the crowd cried out their approval. Atira collapsed back onto her cot, letting out a large nervous laugh.

Marcus put a hand on her shoulder. "Well done, pattern weaver."

She smiled at him with tears in her eyes. "Thank you."

"It was your pattern?" Simus asked, visibly impressed.

"My first." Atira grinned. Heath was looking puzzled, so I translated for him. By this time, the dancers had run to the platform and formed a group in front of Keir. The tallest one stepped forward. "Warlord, may we take Atira? We wish to praise our weaver to the skies."

Keir gestured to the cot, and the breathless men and women swarmed the platform to lift her high. "Have a care of that leg!" I called.

One stopped and bowed toward me. "We'll take her to the healer tent, Warprize and celebrate there. We'd not risk that she'd not dance again." With that, they disappeared into the crowd.

Heath stood and moved next to me. "I should go as well, for Anna is dying for news."

I smiled, but refrained from hugging him. "I'm fine, Heath."

He smiled back, and cupped my cheek again before turning

to make his respects to the Warlord. Keir signaled for someone to escort him, and he too disappeared into the crowd.

I knew I had a broad grin on my face, but I didn't care. I loved the dancing, like nothing ever seen in the Kingdom of Xy before. I looked about to see if the next dance was about to be called, but the crowd was still moving around. I noticed that Keir was watching me intently, his expression stern. I ignored him, not wishing anything to steal the pleasure of the next three dances from me.

The crowd settled, and once again Iften moved to the center of the field. This time, he had no bowl in his hand, but stood with naked sword in one hand, shield in the other. "Warlord!" His cry echoed over the field. Keir and Simus both stiffened. "I cry challenge on you."

All was quiet and movement ceased.

"The time of challenge is in the spring, Iften." Simus rose and moved to the edge of the platform. He limped slightly and I suspected he'd pushed the leg too far. His strong voice carried easily over the crowd. "Your challenge is improper."

Iften stayed where he was. "I cry challenge on you, Keir of the Cat, named Warlord of the Northwestern Range for this Season of War. I cry challenge for all the elements to see and witness."

Keir spoke. "There is no challenge on campaign, Iften. You've sworn oaths to follow me until you are released from my service."

"That woman beside you is no true warprize and of a people who use assassination and treachery as their weapons. Are these the ways you wish us to learn?" Iften beat his sword against his shield, and I jumped, startled by the sound. "I swear I will kill you and the woman and lead this army to take what is ours by right. Come and fight me, Keir! Fight and die!"

10

In an instant Rafe and Prest stood beside me, weapons drawn. Marcus shifted as well, standing at Keir's side. I sat frozen, not understanding how everything could change in an instant.

Simus spoke softly, turned slightly to look at Keir. "Do you think he's behind—"

Keir responded in the same tone. "I don't know." He stayed seated, raising a voice that held a clear disdain for the man before him. "I've made no secret of my intent, Iften. I will bind these lands together, weave new patterns from our ways and theirs." His voice carried with no difficulty. The watching warriors had their eyes on him, and few stirred. There was only the soft breeze and the fires of the torches that moved and crackled. Keir continued. "We will be stronger for it. Take back your flawed challenge. You swore an oath for all the elements to see that you would follow me. I hold you to your oath."

"Their ways are foul and tainted. I cry challenge now, before you destroy us all."

Marcus snorted. "His wits have been scattered by the winds." Keir grunted but didn't turn his head.

"Where is the singer?" Iften shouted out. "Where is Joden?"

Joden emerged from the press of bodies off to the side, his broad face unhappy. "I'm here, Iften."

Iften raised his sword and shield, almost as if he were offering them. "What says our singer to my challenge?"

Joden took two steps out and stood with his arms crossed over his chest. "I have not heard your protests in senel, Iften. I have not heard you raise these truths with Keir's token in your hand. I hear only your challenge, out of season, and against your oaths. I'm not yet a Singer." Joden continued, his voice resonant and firm. "But were I the Singer of singers and standing at the Heart of the Plains, still I would call you Oathbreaker."

The crowd responded to those words with a buzz. To my eyes it seemed that Iften shrank a little when he heard Joden's words. Still, he remained standing at the center of the field.

Keir stood. The crowd grew silent. "A new pattern is hard to dance, and we are all in need of practice. There have been mistakes made, and I acknowledge that. This is also a mistake, Iften. Withdraw your challenge. These matters can be discussed in senel, and if your concerns cannot be satisfied, I will release your oath in the spring." Keir shifted his stance slightly, taking a more threatening posture. "Or repeat your challenge without my token and die."

Iften seemed to freeze, as if he couldn't make a decision.

"Hell of a way to ruin a dance." Simus grumbled, just loud enough to be heard by those closest to us. Laughter started and continued, as his words were passed on. The tension released, like water pouring out of a bowl.

Iften stood for another moment, but he had lost and he knew it. "I withdraw the challenge." With a sullen look, he sheathed his sword and slung his shield on his back. A young man raced out and handed him the wooden bowl, and he started the ritual to begin the dance. Keir and Simus returned to their stumps. Rafe and Prest faded back to their original positions.

Marcus held a mug of kavage in front of me. "Drink this, Warprize. You are as white as snow."

I took the mug and sipped. Keir turned, and looked at me with concern. "Are you well, Warprize?"

"He threatened to kill you."

Simus snorted, accepting kavage from Marcus. "Iften always speaks before he thinks."

"Still," Keir watched the dancers as if he had no other concerns. "He did speak. There may be others that agree with him."

Simus rumbled in agreement. "And where did he get that courage, I wonder?"

Keir shrugged, and both focused on the dance.

I watched as well, although I couldn't remember the colors that danced or their patterns. I waited for my heart to stop racing in my chest. Everyone acted as if nothing had happened, as if having someone challenge a warlord to fight to the death were something that happened every day. I sat, trying to understand it all as the last dance ended and Iften performed some ceremony to bring things to a close. Keir was next to me before I could even stand. With a simple gesture, Rafe and Prest were called to my side.

"Take her to my tent, and guard her well." Keir spoke in low tones. "Stay with her until I return. I'm going to walk the camp. Simus?"

Simus stood, and I noticed his hesitation. "He can't. He's been on that leg far too long."

I stood, pulling up the cloak. "I'd better look at it."

Simus wrinkled his nose, but nodded. "She's right."

"Take them to Simus's tent. When she's finished, escort her to mine. Marcus can send Gils to her." Keir glared at them. "Don't leave her for an instant."

"Will you call a senel?" Simus asked, as we moved off the platform.

"We'll talk after I've tasted the mood of the warriors." He strode off into the growing darkness.

*   *   *

Simus's tent glowed with warmth when we arrived. He eased down onto his bed with Marcus's assistance. Once his trous and the bandages were off, I could see that the wound was healing well. "You've just pushed it too hard, Simus."

"Perhaps, little healer." He sank back "But how could I miss a dance?" His smile grew wide, and his eyes gleamed. "And such a dance!"

Joden entered the tent in time to hear his words. "Aye, Iften is a fool."

Simus laughed. "Iften is a good warrior, but he fears change. Keir makes sweeping changes. You're surprised that they clash?"

"Shall I fetch Gils?" Marcus asked me quietly.

I dug through the supplies by the bed. "No, I have what I need here."

Joden sat on a stool out of the way. "A surprise that he would call challenge."

"That's a truth voiced." Simus stared up at the ceiling of the tent. "Where did he find the nerve?"

"I don't understand what he thought he was doing." I worked as I spoke. "He threatened Keir with death. According to our laws, that would make him an outlaw."

Simus grimaced slightly at my touch. "We only give positions of power to those who've earned them. Challenge is a part of determining who will lead."

I blinked at him. "Xymund rules by right of blood, as confirmed by the gods."

"It's not because of his skill as a warrior." Marcus commented.

"That's why he has men such as Warren," I snapped, stung more by the criticism of my people than in defense of my half-brother. I looked at Simus. "So Xymund, as King, would have to face challenges to stay on the throne."

Joden chuckled. "It's not that easy, Warprize. One must qualify to give challenge. Iften has the right to challenge Keir, but no one may challenge on campaign."

The silence that descended was a thoughtful one. I concentrated on re-bandaging the wound, and dosing Simus with fever's foe. I offered lotus as well, to help him sleep, but he declined. As soon as I finished, Marcus hustled me out.

Once outside, I resisted. "I want to check Atira's leg."

"None of that." Marcus barred my path. "Hisself said 'to the tent' and off to the tent we go."

Rafe coughed to draw my attention and spoke once he had my eye. "It's the Warlord's command."

I would've argued, but my arm was throbbing. We returned to Keir's tent, only to engage in a heated discussion of just how Rafe and Prest were going to guard me. They interpreted their instructions literally, and intended to sit and watch me sleep. After some heated discussion, Rafe and Prest took up positions outside, and Marcus and I went in alone.

I folded up the cloak and laid it on one of the benches, careful not to use my arm too much. "Marcus, do challenges happen often?"

"Of course, Warprize. Before the armies are gathered, the challenges are fought to determine ranks. But that is for the early spring. No one issues challenge on campaign."

"Iften did."

"Iften is a fool." Marcus chuckled softly. "Hisself took care of him without raising a sword."

"Could someone challenge Simus? While he is hurt?"

"That's not done, Warprize. Another would take his place while he healed. Iften in fact, since he stands third in rank." Marcus fussed with the brazier. "Although few heal from such a wound." He frowned into the coals, then turned, regarding me. "It's off to bed with you. Hisself won't be in until late, if I know him."

I lay awake for quite some time, wondering about a world where a warrior held his rank and title by merit instead of class or birth. My dreams were filled with the images of Xymund fighting Warren for the crown when I slipped into sleep.

I awoke to a warm embrace, a frowning countenance, and Keir's voice in my ear.

"You are not to leave this bed today."

The day deteriorated from there.

Marcus was cranky from lack of sleep. Keir was wound tighter then he had been the night before, if that were possible. I was upset because my arm ached, Marcus was cranky, and Keir was impossible.

He ordered me to stay in bed.

I refused.

He ordered me to stay in the tent.

I refused.

He ordered me to accept an escort of my guards, Rafe and ten more men to the tents, have my assistants check my arm, and return to his tent.

I refused. I asked to go into the city with him to see Warren. He refused.

During our discussion, we bathed, dressed, and ate. And discussed the matter at the top of our lungs.

Finally, Marcus emerged from his area and roared "Enough!" We both stopped talking, and turned to glare at him.

Marcus glared right back. "You." He said, pointing at Keir. "Go to the city with some men and find out what Warren has learned." He turned and pointed at me. "You. Go to the tents with your guards." He glared at both of us. "Damned fools." He stomped off. "And don't come back 'til after my nap!" he yelled from the back.

Keir grabbed up his cloak and sword, and stomped out. I glared at the tent wall as I finished my kavage, then grabbed up my cloak and stomped out. Epor and Isdra were waiting outside, and they eyed me with trepidation as I walked past them. They fell into step behind me, and were smart enough to stay quiet as we walked.

I strode to Simus's tent, wanting to check his wound, but Joden was emerging as I walked up. "He's sleeping, Warprize. He and Keir were up late, talking."

"I'll let him sleep."

"I'll walk with you, if I may. I wish to talk to Atira." Joden fell in step next to me. Epor and Isdra followed.

"For your song?"

Joden nodded. "I wish to see what happened through her eyes."

"Will you sing of what happened last night? Iften's challenge?"

Joden snorted. "No, Warprize. The songs I create now must be great songs of great events, songs that will aid me in earning the title of Singer. I will not sing of fools."

Gils awaited us at the healing tent, smiling next to a pile of bandages and a pot of fever's foe. Atira was the only patient, propped up on her cot; they both looked up eagerly when we walked in. Epor and Isdra arranged themselves by the tent flap, sitting on stumps. Isdra flipped her long braid back and pulled out some leather work. Epor had some oil that he seemed to be rubbing into the wooden handle of his war club.

"You must tell me what happened!" Atira threw up her hands in disgust. "They brought me back here last night, and I only heard this morning. Is it true? Did Iften challenge?"

Joden snorted. Gils guided me to a cot close to Atira and started to help me pull off my tunic. Joden pulled up a stool next to Atira's cot. "He did challenge. Would you hear my words?"

Atira's eyes widened. "Please, Joden."

Joden started speaking in his warm voice as Gils unwrapped my arm. He spoke plainly, with no embellishments, but his tone of voice left no doubt as to his opinion. Gils worked as Joden spoke, although he seemed flustered by the fact that I kept the tunic on and kept myself covered as best I could. Keir's people may be casual with their bodies, but I was more comfortable with my own ways. I looked around, but everything had been cleaned up and set right. You couldn't tell that there'd been an attack in this tent at all, other than the new exit at the rear of the tent where Simus had cut his way in. It had been finished off and was now tied shut.

Gils sat back, examining the exposed wounds. They looked good, but I stared at them and scowled. It would scar, I was sure of it. Two puckered parallel lines on my upper arm. Gils rewrapped and tied off the bandage, as Joden concluded his tale.

Atira exclaimed, and I focused back on their conversation. "It's only field discipline that saved his life."

Joden nodded. "Aye, he'd be dead otherwise."

"Field discipline?" I asked, struggling back into my tunic.

"All's well?" Joden asked, looking at my arm.

"On campaign, we are under a different rule than on the plains," Atira explained. "The Warlord was generous. Maybe overly so."

"The elements will judge." Joden eyed Atira, and she subsided, but I had the distinct impression that she had her own opinion in the matter. Which reminded me of something I'd meant to ask.

"Marcus said something to me last night. Something about offending the skies." I bent to check the leather on Atira's leg, so it took a moment for me to realize that there had been no response. I looked up into puzzled faces.

"He'd offend the skies, Warprize, to show his disfigurement," Joden responded. Gils and Atira nodded.

"But—" I suddenly understood why Marcus stayed in the tent almost all the time. "Those are honorable scars—"

I stopped when Atira shook her head. "No. There is a difference between an honorable scar and being no longer whole."

"So everyone who is crippled or severely injured goes cloaked?"

Joden's face was grim. "No. They ask for mercy."

There was no answer to that. I checked Atira's leg. The swelling had gone down, and the leather was loose. With all of them watching closely I checked the placement of the leg, but it was still set and straight. I sat back on my heels, and considered. "New leather, I think. It needs to be tighter, to allow the stones to work."

Gils shifted his weight nervously. "I's want to help, Warprize but I's due at weapons practice."

"Go." I stood up and arranged Atira's bedding. "We'll do it after the nooning, when you can return."

"So Joden and I can talk now?" Atira asked.

"When one talks to a Singer, it's usual to be private," Joden explained. "So that the singer can focus on your words alone, and no one can influence your words."

"That's fine." I smiled. "I've work to do in the other tent."

Epor and Isdra rose and followed as Gils walked out with me. "Warprize, I's be upset when I looked for things to tend you with. The stilltent isn't as neat as you left it." The red of his cheeks matched his red hair.

I glared at him. "How bad is it?"

He gulped. "I's be happy to stay and help."

"And miss practice and get us both in trouble? I think not." I waved him off.

"You'll be careful of the arm?"

I rolled my eyes, and he laughed as he sprinted off toward the practice grounds.

Standing in the center of the stilltent, it was easy to assess the damages. It wasn't that bad, really, just some mess from where Gils had rifled through stuff, looking for supplies. While I got things back where I liked them, I organized my head for what I wanted to accomplish. A few jugs of liniment might be helpful. I liked having a few bottles of that available, and it would aid the bruising on my own neck. I also had the ingredients for a potion that worked well with the flux. Have one case of flux, and there'd be ten cases of flux. I lit the braziers, and started to ready ingredients. Epor and Isdra were kind enough to help me with any lifting, and soon the tent was filled with the smells of brewing elixirs and steeping ointments.

I wrote with pleasure, enjoying the scratch of the pen on the page. The work was soothing. Once again, I spread out my papers and books so I could make notes on everything I did, so that I could recall what worked and what didn't. It was all so familiar, so much like home that I lost myself in it. Until the tent wall slapped in the breeze and brought me back. One thing I made sure to do was brew a tea from willow bark. Not as strong as the fever's foe, still it helped with my aching arm. I sipped some as I worked.

The tea helped a little, but the truth was that a pall had been cast over the day. It all seemed so strange and disturbing. These people were so different, saw the world through different eyes, had such dissimilar standards. Yet, they bled, hurt, and healed the same way we did. Yet they were so harsh. Offend the skies? Was that any reason for a warrior, injured in service, to kill themselves? Yet an honorable scar brought admiration and praise.

Keir wanted to bind the lands together, but I didn't see how. Xymund surely had not known of Keir's plans. I wondered if he knew now? What he and the Council must think of that idea. Of course, no one had thought of a Daughter of Xy as a tribute, and yet here I was.

But what exactly was I? Keir seemed interested in me physically, but talked of honoring our traditions. Certainly, I seemed to have no real slave duties, other than to sleep in the same tent. Which was just as well. While I brewed an excellent elixir, Anna had despaired of ever teaching me to cook a meal. Marcus had mentioned that I had to be taken to the Heart of the Plains, but had not explained further. My imagination ran riot with ideas and images, none of them good.

I sat and stirred the flux potion, staring at the tent wall.

The sound of thunder drew me out of my trance, and I moved the pot off the fire to go outside. Epor and Isdra stood as a large group of horsemen rode up, Keir in the lead. They milled around as Keir swung down from his horse, and stalked over to me. He wore armor, helm and his black cape, and looked damned impressive, gleaming in the sun as he walked toward me. I lost myself in his blue eyes as he came to stand very close to me.

"I couldn't leave without . . ." he paused. "This morning, I . . ." He looked away, then looked back at me.

I nodded. "I feel the same. It spoiled the day, didn't it?"

The skin at the corner of his eyes crinkled. "Yes. It did." He leaned in and gently kissed me. Just a touching of lips. "I'm looking for Joden."

Joden emerged from the healing tent. "Warlord?"

"We're going to the castle, to learn firsthand what is known of the attack. I want you with us."

Joden headed for the spare horse that Simus was leading. I frowned to see Simus mounted. "Is your leg well enough for this?" I asked Simus, as Keir mounted his horse.

Simus shrugged. "It will have to be, little healer." He flashed a smile. "Someone has to make sure that Keir doesn't rage through the city, slaughtering everyone in his path."

Keir glared at Simus, as the rest of the group chuckled. I smiled, even though I could sense that to some degree Simus was serious. Keir pulled his horse around, and they headed out, the horses' hooves churning up the dirt. I took two steps around the tent, standing where I could see Water's Fall in the distance, and the road that led to the main gates. Epor shifted with me, watching my back.

The city walls and the castle gleamed in the sun. The scattered greenery on the mountain held the first faint traces of yellow. Soon the first snows would come, the water falls would freeze, and for the first time in my life, I wouldn't be here to see it. The thought was both terrifying and exhilarating at the same time.

The wind caught my hair, whipping it into my eyes. With a last look, I returned to my work.

"I have given up expecting you to remember the nooning." I looked up as Marcus entered the tent with food and drink.

"I'm sorry, Marcus. I lost track of time."

"Sorry, sorry, that doesn't fill a body." He shed his cloak and fussed, clearing space for his load. "And what is that awful smell?"

"A potion for the—" I frowned, not knowing the right words. "For an illness of the bowels."

He wrinkled his nose in disgust. "Eat. If you can."

I dug in and smiled at him. His face remained stern, but his eye twinkled. "You are in a better mood, eh?"

"So are you."

He mock-glared at me. "I managed a nice nap, thank you kindly."

"Has Keir returned?"

Marcus shook his head. "Hisself is probably making them miserable up there, poking and prodding for answers. Don't be worried for him." He moved off toward the tent entrance. "See that you bring the dishes back with you this evening."

I kept working, cooling the potion and storing it away. The liniment took more mixing then anything, and I made up multiple bottles, including one for myself. I rubbed it on my throat, feeling the warmth as it worked into the tender flesh.

I contented myself with smaller tasks until Gils returned. Atira was more than ready for a bath, and we made quite a mess between getting her clean and soaking the leather. Gils and I were tired when all was done, and I sent him to fetch some kavage for us from the cook tent. Horsemen came thundering by as he returned.

"The Warlord's be back," Gils reported as he served. "Looking awful mad."

Someone had brought Atira a bunch of daggers to sharpen to keep her busy. She and Gils both worked on them as I read to them from the Epic, translating as I went. Atira and Gils were fascinated, by both the story and by the oddity of the written word. The poem was entering the planning part of the expedition, and while I was bored to death with the number of bales and pack mules, my audience was absorbed in the telling. I'd reached the part where Xyson was expelling the evil creatures from Xy when the sound of an approaching horseman interrupted us. Someone had come up to the tent and was speaking to the guards.

I closed the book. "Enough for one day."

Atira nodded. "Maybe tomorrow we can start reading?" She used the Xyian word.

I nodded, stood, and stretched. Joden stuck his head in. "Warprize, may I talk to you?"

Gils objected. "The bandage's be needing changed, Warprize."

I sat back down. "I'm at the mercy of my healer, Joden." He smiled, his face unreadable. I gestured toward one of the stumps, as Gils helped me with the tunic.

But Joden shook his head. "I'll wait for you in the other tent."

I stared after him, wondering, as Gils bandaged my arm.

"Is there any news?" I asked as I entered the stilltent.

Joden sighed. "Durst does well. Xymund denies any knowledge of Arneath's actions. He claims that there is a faction of the city that is unhappy about the peace. Warren hasn't found any hint of a conspiracy. Keir questioned many people, but we could find no trace of . . ." he paused, an unhappy look on his face.

"No trace of Xymund's involvement." I finished calmly.

Joden nodded, sitting heavily on a stool. "Simus has taken him to the practice grounds to work out his frustrations." Joden held up a hand to stave me off. "Simus said to tell you that he will only sit on the sidelines and yell insults." He heaved a sigh. "It will do them both good."

I moved to one of the tables and started rearranging the items there. "Joden, as far as I know, everyone wants peace between your people and mine." I shrugged. "There may have been members of the Guard that were upset by it." I gave him a wry glance. "There may be members of this army that are upset, since Keir had them on alert the other night, for no good reason."

Joden looked at me, puzzled. "That is not so, Warprize. You are treasured."

Treasured. I tightened the cork on a bottle, then made a decision. Whatever the answer, whatever my status, I needed to know.

"Joden." I kept my eyes on the bottle, turning it in my hands. "Has Keir ever sold a warprize?"

I heard a slight choking sound behind me, but I lacked the courage to turn around. "I mean, I think I could learn to share him with the other warprizes." I gulped against the lump in my throat. "But to never see him again, I don't think I could do that. I mean, I know that I am his slave, but I . . ." I shut my mouth before I babbled any more. The silence from behind me seemed to confirm all my fears. My shoulders slumped, the weight of my pain pulling them down. Goddess.

"Lara?"

I caught my breath, hearing my name spoken like that. As if I were a person, not a slave, or a thing, or a warlord's prize. Joden was using my name as if I was a person he valued. Someone who mattered. I hadn't realized how important that was to me until I'd heard it again, spoken in a caring voice. Tears flooded into my eyes as I turned, to see Joden pat the crate next to him. I stumbled over and sat, wiping my eyes. I couldn't quite bring myself to meet his gaze.

"Let us just be Lara and Joden for this moment, alone, in this tent." His voice was sympathetic. "You used a word . . . 'slave' . . . what does that mean?" I flushed, embarrassed. Joden put his hand on my shoulder. "Please, favor me. Tell me what it means."

"It means a person who is owned as one would own a horse or a knife. A slave is absolutely subject to the will of his or her master."

Joden leaned toward me, and I knew that he listened intently to my words. "A slave has no rights?" he asked. "No status?"

I nodded, keeping my eyes down.

He sat back, and took a deep breath. "No voice in his or her life?"

I nodded again, trying to control my tears.

"Lara, you believe yourself to be Keir's slave, yes? Who told you this?"

I looked up at that. His face held only care and concern. "Xymund. Before the ceremony."

Joden nodded again, frowning a little. "I would like to think the error unintentional, but I have doubts." He shook his head. "And I think we are partly to blame, maybe because you seemed to learn our language so fast and so well." He looked over my head, as if thinking, and came to some decision. "Lara, please listen to me carefully. And if I use a word you do not understand, ask me to explain it. Do not assume you know the meaning. Yes?" I nodded, and he leaned back a little, his hands on his knees.

"Among our people, warlords are warriors with experience in battle, enough so that they inspire men to follow them. A warlord does not get his army from his father, nor pass it to his child. It is earned by his own deeds. A warlord uses his or her skill to challenge for the right to gather men into armies, and use their armies to raid and pillage for the gain of all. So it is and so it has always been."

I made as if to speak, but Joden held up a hand. "Now, our traditions tell us that there is yet another treasure that a warlord can obtain in battle. That is a warprize. A warprize must be discovered during the course of a battle, or on or near a battlefield. A warprize must render aid to the warlord or his men." Joden lifted a finger. "Most important, a warprize must be attractive to a warlord, must spark feelings of desire." He grinned slyly. "It is said that the attraction between warlord and warprize is as the heat of the sun that shines in the height of summer."

I sat, my eyes wide, and listened.

"Now, once a warlord recognizes a potential warprize, he stops the fighting and enters into talks with the leaders of the land. He must negotiate for the warprize, making the best deal that he can." Joden leaned back a little and chuckled. "Keir did well there." He sobered and looked at me. "Having done that, a warprize must submit willingly to the warlord, before witnesses of both their peoples. Then a warprize is displayed to the warlord's army. Upon their return to our lands, the confirmation ceremony is held before the Council of Elders."

Joden reached for a flask of kavage that Marcus had brought and two cups, and poured for both of us. "But even these ceremonies do not create a true warprize."

Joden took a sip from his mug. "Lara, a true warprize is a rare thing. We value them, for our people have found that the warprize brings a new way of thinking, of doing things. It makes us better, stronger, when we are exposed to new ways and new ideas. You cannot fake a true warprize, nor pick one, nor force one. They happen maybe once in five generations, and we see it as a benediction from the elements themselves, even for the upheaval that they bring."

I sat there, trying to make sense of his words.

"Our people started as tribes, tribes based on our totem animals. Keir is of the Cat, Simus is of the Hawk, as am I. There was a time when the tribes fought among themselves. It was the first warprize, long ago, that created that change, that united the tribes." Joden rubbed his hand on his knees. "Why did you submit to Keir, if you thought you would be a slave?"

I had to swallow before I could answer, my mouth was so dry. "To save my people."

Joden smiled slightly. "Lara, there are no other warprizes. When you submitted to Keir, you were submitting to give him a chance to court you, a chance to show you what you could and do mean to him." He frowned again. "And this was explained to your king, probably privately, during the talks."

He tilted his head, looking at me as if I was a child at my lessons. "Do you understand? You are not a 'slave'. You are a mate, a consort. You are second only to Keir in this camp. If you demand your freedom and leave this camp no one, including Keir," he emphasized, "would lift a finger to stop you. By our laws and by our ways, you cannot be held here. Your presence in our camp is a gift to your people and our people and we acknowledge that gift."

I blinked. "The bracelets . . ."

Joden smiled. "Keir had the bracelets crafted in hope. They are not a symbol of your . . ." He stumbled on the word. ". . . slavery. They are symbols of your potential bond."

I still didn't believe. "The token. Keir said that the token was not for me to use."

Joden quirked his mouth. "How does it look if the woman you are courting feels she needs its protections?"

I just stared at him.

He met my eyes calmly. "You are not property. If you choose to leave, no one will stop you."

I stood.

He stayed seated and watched me walk out of the tent.

Isdra looked up. "Need help with a pot, Warprize?"

I looked at her oddly, hearing 'Warprize' as a title, not a label or a thing.

My silence attracted Epor's attention. He took up his war club and stood. "Warprize?"

Joden's horse was outside, cropping at the sparse grass. I moved forward and grabbed the reins. Epor moved as if to follow me. "No. Stay here."

Epor stopped dead. Isdra came to stand next to him. "Warprize," she spoke quickly. "We are commanded to guard you—"

"I wish to leave camp." I gave them a narrow glance.

Epor sucked in a breath. "If that is the case, we cannot stop you. But Warprize, please, let us get horses and escort you back to your people. Let us at least assure your safety."

"No."

Epor swallowed hard. Isdra went as white as her hair. Joden had followed me out of the tent and stood there looking at me. Isdra appealed to him. "Singer, please tell her that it's for her own safety. The attempts on her life . . ."

I waited.

"She is the warprize, yes? And to be obeyed?" Joden asked.

Epor and Isdra both nodded. I swung myself up into the saddle.

Joden's face did not change its expression as he looked up at me. "You are free, Lara. The only restraints on you are those of your own choosing."

I turned the horse, jammed my toes into its belly, and it sprang down the road toward the camp's main gate.

Through the camp we plunged, the horse's mane and my hair streaming in the wind. The horse was willing, and I could feel its muscles move under me as its hooves pounded into the earth. I leaned forward, wanting to laugh and cry at the same time.

There was no outcry behind us, no one tried to stop me.

Some saw me and waved a hand in acknowledgment, but showed no surprise nor consternation. I plunged headlong between the tents, urging the horse on and on, a rising feeling of excitement in my chest. We pounded through the main gate and out into the field beyond. The guards there seemed only mildly interested, if slightly disapproving of my riding style.

Out the gate and up the rise where the beaten road met the main road that led from the castle gates down into the valley. I pulled the horse to a stop, but it fought me, wanting to run. It danced beneath me, and I wheeled its head about, until at last it was quiet beneath me.

We stood there, the horse blowing and my heart pounding against my ribs.

No one was following, no one was reacting, there was no hue and cry, no chase. I was free. Truly, truly free.

11

I laughed, delighted at my freedom, at the sun on my face, at the wind in my hair. The horse danced under me, eager to go. I wheeled it to face the city and the castle.

I could go home.

The wind blew my hair into my face, and I used one hand to clear it away. I could go home, back to my old life, as if nothing had happened. Run to the kitchens and Anna's loving arms and Othur's grin and pick up the tatters of my life. Rebuild the stillroom, make Xymund see reason, and . . .

What if Keir was right? What if Xymund had tried to have me killed?

If I returned to the castle, I'd be under his authority. Anna and Othur may love me dearly, but they couldn't stand between us.

Even more, if I returned to the castle, I returned to the known. The commonplace, daily routine of my life. Yet I'd been ripped up by the roots and the pot had been broken, and I wasn't sure that I'd fit there ever again. Much less grow.

I hesitated, and wheeled the horse again. It puffed out its

breath and stamped at the grass. This time we faced the road that led to the valley. I had skills, and there'd be those that would help me. I could go to the lands that my father left me, and start that school, living out my days teaching and healing. I could even leave for some foreign land. With some supplies and a few coins I could make my way anywhere in this world. Leave Keir and Xymund to weave their pattern and get myself out of this tangle that they called a 'peace'.

The horse shook its head, jingling its tack, and stamped its feet, as if in disapproval.

If I tried to make my own way, I'd break a promise that my Blood had sworn to the people when Xy had first taken the throne. I might be free of my slavery to the Warlord, but my oaths and my duty still held me to my people. For it seemed to me that for the peace to have any chance, I must be at Keir's side.

I wheeled it again and turned to look at the camp. I could hear Joden's voice. *"You are free, Lara. The only restraints on you are those of your own choosing."*

My breath caught in my throat. The camp of the Warlord, the camp of the dreaded Firelanders. A people who were a total mystery to me, for I had no idea of what my life would be like among them, or what awaited me at the Heart of the Plains. The camp of a man who was risking everything on the chance of building something better. Stronger. Brighter. For both our peoples.

Returning to the camp and Keir was a risk. A wild unknown, for no one could tell if his plans would survive to the dawn, much less work. And there was no way to predict what would happen to any of us if he failed.

There was another aspect to all of this, grand plans and kingdoms aside. I flushed to think of it. For certain, a Daughter of Xy contemplating her duties and obligations was not supposed to think of the touch of a man's hand in the night, or how a simple brush of lips on her neck could raise such a heat in her breast. No, a loyal Daughter of Xy should think only of her duties and obligations, as I had when I knelt in the throne room to surrender myself to slavery.

And yet, what I had thought a claiming, had been a seduction.

What I had thought were chains, were tokens.

What I had thought was pride of possession in a certain pair of blue eyes was . . . the promise of a lifetime?

Hope rose in my breast like a sunrise. There was but one way to find out. That was the only certainty I had. If I took either of the other paths, up to the castle, or out to my lands, I'd never know the answers. Or I could take the biggest risk of all, and open my heart and myself to Keir. Of all the possibilities, of all the paths, it was that one that set my blood afire. A future full of risk and dangers, potential and promise. For him. For me. For us.

I laughed and urged the horse on, and once again it sprang forward with a willingness. Down the rise we went, the horse's hooves churning the soil. We galloped through the gate, without so much as a hail of the guard. I caught a brief glimpse of their expressions as we came back through, and laughed again, certain that they were thinking that I was no rider. I didn't stop until I pulled the horse up outside my stilltent.

Joden was still standing there, and I could see the joy in his eyes as I slid from the saddle. Epor and Isdra ran to me, joy and relief on their faces.

"Thank the skies," Epor spoke as I handed the reins to Joden.

"One more question." I stood straight and looked Joden right in the eye. He grew serious, and nodded for me to continue. "Am I required to bear five children?"

He blinked, confused but then his face cleared. A smile crept back over his broad face. "No."

"Where is he?" I demanded.

Now Joden's whole face lit up, and he pointed past the tents to the practice grounds. I smiled, and turned to go.

"Warprize!" Epor stepped in front of me, his hand out, pleading. "Warprize, please let us to go with you."

Isdra added her voice. "Warprize, it's worth our lives to let you—"

I stopped and turned. "And if I say 'no'?"

Isdra swallowed hard. "We'd obey, Warprize." Epor, his face gray, nodded his obedience as well. Joden just smiled at me.

"Come then," I said as I turned and started to run. Joden laughed behind me, but in a thrice they were beside me, pacing me easily. As I neared Keir's tent, I thought for a minute. I could go back and bathe, find that white shift and be waiting for him barefoot with my hair falling free . . .

No.

He had waited too long.

I had waited too long.

Not one minute more.

The practice ground was a large dirt circle, with the sod removed. Keir was squared off against two men as we came up. There was quite a crowd, including Simus, who was seated on a stool, making insulting comments, and urging them on. I had no idea what lessons were being taught, I only had eyes for one man.

One tall, blue-eyed, sweaty man.

No one noticed as I moved to the edge. I stopped to catch my breath and watched him flow around the other men, using their movements against them. He was in bright chainmail with the black under-padding. He had on a coif, and was using two wooden swords. The men fighting him were using shields and wooden swords. The dust was thick as they shuffled about, trying to flank Keir, but only tripping over themselves. Keir's face was a snarl of concentration, completely focused on his opponents. I could watch for hours. I would watch for hours. But right now I had other things on my mind.

"Keir." I called.

His head swivelled around, homing in on my face at the exact moment one of his opponents was in mid-swing with his wooden sword. It 'thwacked' Keir right in the ass. I winced at the sound. The attacker jumped back, horrified as the watchers laughed, Simus loudest of all. Keir ignored them. He looked worried as he walked over to me, tilting his head to the side a little, lowering his weapons. My heart swelled, and I bounced on the balls of my feet.

"Warprize?"

Once he got close, I grabbed his shoulders, pulled myself up and kissed him. Hard. Keir was caught by surprise, and brought his arms up to embrace me, careful of the weapons in his hands. I laughed against his mouth, then gently bit his lower lip. "I want you." I leaned back to see his face. Stunned, he blinked at me. "Now, my Warlord." I released him, turned, and started walking for our tent. Epor and Isdra moved with me, but kept their distance.

"Warprize?" Keir called after me.

I looked over my shoulder at him, grinned, and started walking faster.

Simus was shouting his laughter, and I heard Keir curse as he started to follow. The warriors were calling, making encouraging noises, and some catcalls. I laughed and kept walking. I could hear chainmail jingling behind me, catching up. I threw a glance back, only to see that he was gaining on me.

I started to run.

I managed to reach the tent first, barely, darting through the flaps. Epor and Isdra stayed outside. I stood by the bed, turned and waited for him. He was a breath behind, breathing hard, dressed in that chainmail and leather outfit. As he advanced on me, it came to me that I didn't really know what to do next.

I needn't have worried. He swept me up and kissed me hard, using his hands to mold me to him. We tumbled onto the bed, Keir falling backwards with me landing on top. The breath left him in a rush, and I pulled back, concerned that I'd hurt him. His expression was so surprised, I started laughing. He looked up into my face, searching for the reason for my actions.

"Mine," I said, staring into those blue eyes. I leaned down, letting my hair fall around his face. "My Warlord." He opened his mouth to speak, and I darted down, kissing him, daring to take control. Only the lack of air forced me to pull back, and we both breathed hard for a moment. My hair made a curtain, sheltering his face. He licked his lips, eyes staring up into mine with a sense of wonder and a hint of disbelief.

"Say it." I bent down, licking his cheek. He tasted of salt and dust. He tasted fantastic. He swallowed hard and cleared his throat. I raised my head and smiled down at him.

"Yours?"

My heart swelled in my chest till I thought it would burst. "Mine. My Warlord. My Keir." I leaned back down, and this time the kiss was a caress, a mutual exploration.

Till my hair got caught in the chainmail links.

Cursing, I let go of his hands to try to get my hair loose. Keir started to snicker at my efforts. He brought his arms around me and started laughing as I struggled with my hair. "My Warprize." He smiled at me as I worked my hair free. "My Warprize."

I carefully caught up my rescued hair and held it away from the evil mail links. I leaned down and whispered in his ear. "Take me, my Warlord."

That wiped the smile right off his face. "Marcus!" he yelled as he rolled, moving me carefully over and onto the bed. Keir reached up to remove the coif from his head.

"Warlord?" Marcus popped in from the back room, surprise evident in his voice.

Keir had tossed the coif to the floor and was working on his belt. "Come help me get this off." Marcus raised his eyebrow, then turned to look at me, lying on my side on the bed.

I smiled at him.

A smile started to creep over Marcus's face. "At once, my Warlord." He helped Keir remove the heavy chain suit and the padding underneath. Finally, Keir stood there in his black leather pants and his black boots. Keir's eyes drilled into mine. I met his gaze head on, unafraid.

Marcus was picking up the various articles of armor and clothing that had been flung around. Keir never looked at him. "Thank you, Marcus. Leave us now."

Marcus bowed himself out, a slight smirk on his face. Keir moved toward the privy enclosure. "Let me clean up . . ."

"No." I sat up, my knees on the edge of the bed. "Come here." He moved forward, standing in front of me. I just looked for a minute, staring into blue eyes. Hesitantly, I put my hands at his waistband. He sucked in a breath at my touch, and I froze, uncertain. His hand covered mine and moved it up his stomach to splay over his chest. I surged up a little, wrapped my arms around his neck and kissed him with all the passion I had. He returned it with fervor, and gently lowered me onto the bed.

I tried to pull him down, to bring his body closer to mine, but he resisted. He hovered over me with concern in those bright blue eyes. "The first time, Lara, it's not always good, it can hurt. I can ask an initiator, someone to teach you—"

I drew in all the air I could. "Only you, Keir. No initiators, no teachers." I lifted my head, moving my lips over his face and chin. "Please."

His eyes dilated in a breath, but still he paused. As he had before, he placed his hand over my heart. "This is not your way, Xylara. Your people's customs—"

I covered his mouth with my fingers. "There's no Xy here, no Plains. There's only you, only me." Concerned, I pulled my hand back. "Unless you do not want—"

He kissed my fingers, then kissed me, removing my hesitation. Gently, he lowered himself to the bed, pulling me close so that we were on our sides, face to face. His other hand rubbed my hip, warming the skin beneath the cloth. His kisses were slow and stirring, and I returned them with a growing hunger.

But a passive role no longer satisfied me. I was curious to know more and I placed my hands on his chest, exploring the expanse of skin and hair. To my delight, I discovered that a stroke of my hand burned his body just as his did mine, if his shivers were any guide. The sparse and curly hair was silky beneath my fingertips. The change in his breathing, the look on his face hinted of the power that lurked within me in the future. But for now, my touch was tentative, tracing faint scars and muscles.

Moving deliberately, he brought his hands under my tunic, and pulled it up and over my head. I flushed and closed my eyes when his hands moved to my breast band. He paused, his fingers resting just under the curves of my breasts. "What's wrong?" he whispered.

"Nothing." I breathed shallowly, conscious of his touch. "It's just that I'm not very . . . ample."

Warm blue eyes laughed at me as his hands moved under the cloth, and warmth surged over me as he cupped my breasts. "They're perfect," he murmured. I arched up, trying to remember to breathe, as he showed me just how perfect they were.

The breast band, our clothes, and the world disappeared. There was only us, and the smoldering desire between us. Every touch brought new discoveries and feelings such as I'd never known before. How could a puff of warm breath over dampened skin produce such sensations? Why did I tingle all over when Keir ran his fingers through my hair to fan it out over the pillows? How could the smallest kiss behind my ear provoke such passion?

I was floating on a sea of pleasure and contentment, melting onto the bed like gold in a fire. Keir raised his head to look at me. "You're sure, Lara?"

"So very sure." I smiled at him.

"Good." He leaned in and kissed me, making a new and urgent demand with his mouth. I responded, recognizing something new in his caress. If I'd been molten gold before, now I was a storm raging through the mountains. I gasped, writhing in my efforts to touch more of him, to feel more, to know more—

I am a healer, wise in the ways of the flesh. How it moves, how it sickens, even how it dies. I knew of the mating process, had heard of the pleasures it affords, thought I knew its effects. None of that prepared me for the reality.

He moved slowly, carefully, driving me mad with the hunger he built in my soul, only to bring me down again to lay in his arms, trembling and achy. I clutched him to me, and begged for more, and he obliged, his soft laughter floating over us as he began again.

Then finally, finally I had him in my arms and in my body and we both froze, staring at one another.

"Lara, are you well?" His breathing was ragged, and I felt his shoulders tremble under my fingers as he held himself above me. "Did I hurt you?"

"Oh, Keir. My Keir." I relaxed, warmed by his hesitation and shifted slightly, only to see the passion flare in his face. He kissed me even as he began to move, and there was joy and pleasure and transcendent light exploding within me and around us and through the very essence of our bonded souls.

I awakened to find myself tucked under a loving arm, my head on Keir's chest. With my eyes closed, I took a deep breath and listened to his heart beat. I felt a deep sense of peace, a sense of belonging. I opened my eyes slightly. From the gleam of the braziers, I knew I had not been asleep long.

Keir's hand was on his chest. I reached over and covered it with mine. His hand was so warm. I pulled it closer. The nails were cut straight across and trimmed close. I turned it over. There were calluses on the palm and fingers, from years of wielding a sword. I ran my fingers over his palm lightly, teasingly. The fingers were long and strong. I smiled and kissed the palm. And then traced the kiss with my tongue.

His fingers flexed quickly, then relaxed. I pulled back a little and blew over the damp spot. I was rewarded with a soft, low moan and followed up with a kiss to his wrist.

Keir chuckled and stroked my head with his other hand. "Was there some potion in your tent that turned the shy kitten into the wildcat?" he murmured.

I moved my head so I could look into his sleepy eyes, soft blue under half-closed lids. "I finally worked up the nerve to ask Joden if you had ever sold a warprize before. That's when he explained the difference. Explained what a warprize is and means. That's when he told me I was free. That, that you were . . ." I stopped. Those half-lidded eyes had opened wide, and blazed diamond bright.

"That I what?" I could feel the tension in his muscles and see the tightness of his jaw.

"That you were asking me to be your mate, your consort." I dropped my eyes and pulled back. Perhaps Joden had been wrong, perhaps I . . .

Keir didn't let me move. He simply held me against him,

resisting my attempt to slip away. I looked up. His eyes had narrowed to slits, his face grim and hard. But his voice was soft and quiet when he spoke. "Lara, what did Xymund tell you before the ceremony?"

I lowered my head to his chest again. His hand soothed my head, separating the strands of hair and letting his fingers run through it. I took a trembling breath and told him what Xymund had said. I explained the meaning of the word 'slave', then repeated what Joden had told me was the meaning of warprize. I stopped, out of breath.

Keir continued to stroke my hair. His voice was still soft when he spoke. "You weren't afraid that night because you were untouched. You thought I was going to rape you."

I looked up, to see hard eyes that held despair as well. I brought my hand to his cheek and left it there as I held his gaze. "I thought you were going to make use of what belonged to you, yes. But you took nothing that was not freely given." His eyes never left mine. "So my fear became that you would take my heart and give me nothing in exchange." I ran my thumb over his lips. "Or worse yet, that you would take my heart and then discard me, like a worn out boot." His arm tightened around me for a moment. "When I heard Joden's words, I knew that you had not been taking. That you had been giving. Giving me time. Giving me your heart."

He admired me, stroking my cheek. "You have such courage."

I blushed and lowered my gaze. Keir lifted my chin with his fingers. "And why does that embarrass you so?"

I turned my head. Keir stroked his fingers over my cheek and down under my ear, caressing my neck. "I love that blush. My wildcat, so very strong and yet so very vulnerable." He kissed my neck, then moved to my collarbone, and started taking little tastes. "When I started the talks, I took your dear brother aside privately and explained everything to him. I wanted him to know that you would be courted with honor and desire." I shivered at the way he said that word. He stopped and looked into my eyes. "Lara, I assumed that bastard had told you . . ." His voice choked. I soothed him with soft touches and kisses. "I was waiting for you to indicate that you were willing. I didn't understand—" He cut himself off, then spoke quietly. "You have my heart, Lara." His voice in my ear filled me with a wondrous sense of the rightness of this man. He placed his forehead against mine.

"My Warlord," I whispered. He took my lips then, kissing me deeply.

We broke apart, and he chuckled. "We best get clean, before we find ourselves stuck to the furs." He got up, and attended to details, padding naked like a large cat around the tent. While I admired him, I wasn't comfortable that way. I pulled the furs up and tucked them under my arms to conceal myself. He returned, bringing me a cloth, and a tray with a sweating pitcher and some pears. "A gift from Marcus." We drank the cold spring water and fed each other slices of pear, content in the silence between us.

Some juice ran down my chin and onto my neck and chest. I wrinkled my nose and smiled at Keir. "I'm going to need a bath in the morning."

Keir darted in, and licked the juice trail with his tongue. I looked at him, startled. He looked back, his eyes dancing. Carefully removing the tray, he placed it on the floor by the bed. Then he pounced, rolling me over onto my back and covering me with his length.

I laughed. "Keir, I am all sticky."

He growled, eyes gleaming in the light. "I am going to get you stickier."

"It's enough to cry challenge on him." Simus growled.

My Warlord had invited Simus and Joden to eat the evening meal with us. Marcus muttered as he delivered the various dishes to the table, but there was a twinkle in his eye that caused me to flush whenever he looked at me.

"No, it's not." Keir helped himself to some of the spicy meat.

"He meant no peace!" Simus thumped his fist on the table, and the dishes rattled. "Telling his people that she is to be a 'thing'."

"Daughters of Xy are born to be given in alliance marriages, Simus." I saved one of the bowls from falling. "I came willingly, to forge a peace."

"To bind partners together for gain? Who is the barbarian, Warprize?" Joden looked at me intently.

"He lies to her, and to his people, and sends men to kill her." Simus clenched his mug. "Challenge and gut him." He was deadly serious.

"We have no proof—" I started, but Keir leapt in.

"He gave you poison."

"In the same way you grant mercy to your wounded."

"No," Keir shook his head. "He knew the truth, Lara. It's not the same."

"What of Iften, then?" I helped myself to the bread. "That lance was full-tipped."

"Eh?" From the looks on their faces, it was clear that Keir had not told them about the marketplace. Keir told them now, in short crisp words, and they both grew quiet, thinking of the implications. Simus sighed heavily. "Well, that changes some well laid plans."

"What plans?" I asked.

"From the beginning, we'd hoped for conquest. The plan was to secure the city and then split the army, with Keir remaining here. I'd return to the Plains, and bring more men in the spring." Simus picked up his mug. "Now, Keir must return to the Heart of the Plains."

"Leaving Simus with no one to watch his back." Keir scowled. "I'll not leave him here with Iften."

"I could stay." Joden's voice was soft.

Simus shook his head violently. Keir raised an eyebrow. "What of your plans to advance to Singer during the snows? Stay here, and it will be another year before you can—"

"He's going." Simus was firm. "I'll not see that dream delayed, Joden."

Joden looked down. "The Elders may not—"

"You've been punished." Simus's dark eyes twinkled as he changed the subject. "Speaking of that, have you started to work on the song?"

Joden nodded.

"Tell us the chorus at least, Joden." Simus gestured with a hand, almost spilling my kavage. "Are we to wait until you perform it to hear it?"

"No." Joden chewed on a chicken leg. "Yes."

"No fair." Simus turned to Keir. "You're the Warlord. Order him to give us a hint."

Keir snorted. "Order a singer?"

Simus leaned toward me, a wicked gleam in those dark eyes. "You're the Warprize. You could . . ." He waggled his eyebrows suggestively.

"If she does," Joden spoke calmly, "the verses will talk about a certain wounded warrior who got fat and lazy as he healed."

Simus looked down at his third plate-full. "I need food to mend. Isn't that right, little healer?"

I looked at him, keeping my face serious. "Simus, the entire army could heal on what you eat."

Keir and Joden roared. Simus tried not to laugh as he objected to my statement.

"What's the ruckus?" Marcus entered with more kavage. Keir and Joden explained over Simus's protests of innocence. "Ah, there's truth in what the Warprize says." Marcus poured for all of us. "Your gut will soon over hang your belt."

"Lara." I looked Marcus straight in the eye. "My name is Lara."

Keir, Simus and Joden all busied themselves with their food. Marcus ignored me.

"Marcus," I sat up very straight, determined to win this point. "I wish to be called 'Lara'."

His one eye flashed at me; Marcus was not a happy man. He put the pot of kavage on the table, bowed and turned to go.

"Marcus, stop." He stopped where he was, but didn't turn to face me. "Marcus, I order—"

Joden choked on his kavage. Simus sucked in a breath between his teeth, and Keir had his hand over his eyes. Apparently, I was about to do something very, very foolish.

Marcus turned on his heel, his one eyebrow arched. "Yes?"

Utter silence from the three men at the table.

"Marcus, it would mean a lot to me if you would call me 'Lara' occasionally."

"I'll think on it." Marcus turned again and left.

Simus sighed. "You're a brave one, little healer."

"He wouldn't hurt me." I protested.

"Gruel. Cold gruel and watery kavage for a month." Keir shuddered. "I've learned the hard way not to cross Marcus."

"Aye to that," Joden said and Simus agreed.

It was late when Simus and Joden left. I stripped and got under the furs, and waited for Keir to return from checking the watch. The braziers gave off their heat and a familiar glow lit the tent.

Keir returned, and I looked up at him with a smile.

He frowned and gave me a look. "We will sleep now, Warprize. You will be sore enough in the morning."

I smiled, reached out my hand, and pulled him into the bed.

Marcus' voice cut through the morning fog. "Your lazy butts best be moving. There's a morning senel. Less than a mark to make ready." I could hear him moving about, readying the privy area. "There's more water warming. You can break your fast at the senel. I've a pitcher of kavage waiting. Shake yourselves now." I heard him move off, but wanted nothing more than to go back to sleep. Keir and I had 'discussed' matters for quite some time.

A hand stroked my warm cheek. I lifted my head and blinked sleepily into his eyes. Keir rolled me over and kissed me. "When you look like that, all drowsy and sweet it's all I can do not to . . ."

"None of that, now." Marcus came back into the room, with more warm water. He went into the privy area.

Keir sighed deeply, then kissed me again. He pulled his head back, just as I started to return the kiss with a rising passion. "None of that, now," he whispered. I smiled at him. He sighed again, and levered himself up and off the bed. "I'd best go first." He looked down at my face as an idea crossed my mind. He glared. "Alone."

I threw him a disgusted look.

Marcus left, and Keir went to clean up. I lay there for a moment, basking in the remaining warmth. Then I arched my back, preparing to stretch . . . and stopped.

Oooo. That hurt.

I must have made a noise, because Keir was next to me in an instant, a towel wrapped around his waist. Water droplets clung to his arms and chest.

"Are you all right?"

I blinked and just admired him. He looked down at me, slowly smiled, and repeated his question. "I'm fine." I smiled at him. Marcus came into the room, and I flushed slightly, adjusting the blanket a bit higher. "My arm's a little sore, that's all."

Keir frowned, then understanding came into his eyes. "Perhaps you should stay in bed today."

I tilted my head and smiled wider. "Only if you stay with me." His eyes flared, and I seemed to see some movement underneath the towel. My smile expanded.

He mock growled and stalked off toward the privy. "Marcus! Send a runner for Gils. I want him to look at her arm." With that, his high and mightiness entered the privy and dropped the flap behind him.

Marcus looked over at me, concerned. "Is it the arm that's hurting?"

I busied myself with the placement of the furs. "No."

Marcus smiled. "Ah." He left, whistling tunelessly as he did so.

After I bathed, Marcus stood over me as Gils changed the bandage and administered fever's foe. The wound was very sore, but looked well. Marcus grunted when Gils was done and whisked him out of the tent. He'd not be allowed to serve this time.

I could hear the men gathering in the main area and tried

to concentrate on putting my hair up and out of my way. Keir
came up behind me and captured my hands. "Leave it down.
Please?" He ran his fingers through the half-formed bun and
shook it out. I sighed as he pulled me up and over to the flap.

Marcus played herald for us, bearing Keir's token, and the
men rose as we made our way to our seats. Trays of food
were brought out and pitchers of kavage were quickly passed
around. I dug in, hungry. Keir sparked conversation, asking
about the status of men, gear and supplies.

I listened as I ate, noting that Keir seemed very satisfied
with the responses. Simus was also asking questions and listening, but while both men seemed to concentrate on the talk,
and the food, I knew their attention was also on Iften, sitting
off to the far side, nursing some kavage. Iften made no move
to join the conversation, but also drew no attention to himself.

Marcus went out for a moment to speak with the guards,
then returned. When he had caught Keir's eye, he spoke. "A
messenger from the castle."

Keir nodded. "I was hoping to hear from Warren. Bring the
messenger in."

The flap parted, and a figure walked in. With the light behind
him, I could not make out his face until he drew nearer. It was
Heath. My face split into a delighted smile. "Heath." I stood
and went over to him, wrapping him in an enthusiastic hug. He
returned it with gusto, then pulled back. As always, his hand
came up to cup my neck and he pulled his forehead to mine.

"Lara. Are you well?" His whisper was fierce and hard, a
contrast to his smiling face.

I nodded, still resting my forehead on his. "Well, very,
very well." I lifted my head and smiled at him. "Come, sit
with me. Eat."

He shook his head, speaking in a low voice. "No. I've a
message to deliver and I don't know how it will be received.
Go. Return to your seat."

I frowned. "Something's wrong." It was there in his eyes.

Heath released me and gave me a slight push. I returned to
my seat, casting a glance at Keir, who had a concerned look
on his face.

Heath advanced another step, and then sank to one knee, bowing before Keir.

"Welcome." Keir indicated that Heath could rise, but Heath did not do so. Keir continued, "Do you bring word from Lord Warren?"

"Warlord, I was sent by Xymund, the King."

Keir gestured for him to continue.

"Warlord, the message I was given was of treachery. Of an attack upon Xymund by Lord Warren as he rode through the city." Keir sat up straight as Heath took a deep breath. "They are not true words, but I will repeat them if you so desire."

Keir and Simus tensed. The men about me stopped their idle talk and stilled, conscious of a new tension.

Heath continued. "Warlord, my true mission was to kill . . ." His voice faltered. ". . . the King told me that upon entrance to the tent he was sure that Lara would approach me and greet me as she is like to do. Upon her approach, I was to strike and kill her."

Keir was feral still, his voice deep and soft and full of menace. "How so? I see no weapon."

"Like so, Warlord." Heath extended his arm, twisted his wrist. A blade the length of a child's hand sprang forth from under his sleeve. It gleamed, sharp and deadly in the light.

The reaction was immediate. The men around me jumped up, some forming a barrier in front of me, the others pulling their weapons and pointing them at Heath. I stood, fearful for his life, but Keir stopped all movement with a gesture of his hand.

"Yet the Warprize is safe, and you are on your knees before me."

Heath nodded and swallowed. With quick movements, he removed the hidden blade from his arm as he spoke, "Xymund swore fealty to you, Warlord, and my oath to Xymund then flows through to you. I would not have this stain on my soul. Lara is as a sister to me, and I could not . . ." His voice cracked under the strain. He threw the mechanism at Keir's feet and sat back on his heels, slumped in sorrow. "Xymund holds my parents as guarantee that I would perform this action. He will kill them if my mission fails."

"Anna and Othur," I looked at Keir, my heart in my throat.

"I fear that he has been touched by the Goddess," Heath continued. "I have no other explanation."

"What does that mean?" Keir looked at me.

"Insane. Mad." My hand rose to my lips. "Heath, he can't be—"

"Lara, he changed the day he swore fealty to the Warlord. After you left, he raved for hours." Heath wiped sweat off his forehead with the heel of his hand. "I swear the defeat did something to him."

"Sit. Sit," Simus spoke, gesturing for everyone to return to their seats. Keir nodded, and everyone sat down. I took a step toward Heath, but a quick glance at Keir showed that it would not be a good idea. Undecided, I hesitated. Keir's jaw was tight, his eyes hard on Heath. I moved to stand behind my Warlord, resting my hand on his shoulder. At my touch, some of the tension left him.

Simus broke the silence. "So the serpent shows his fangs."

Keir nodded. "If his wits have been taken by the winds, how stands the castle? The city walls?"

"Xymund had me escorted to the rise that overlooks your camp. Two watchers remain there, waiting. They will return to Xymund with word of what occurs within your camp." Heath raised his head to meet Keir's eyes. "I believe that once my father and Warren are freed—"

"Warren is held?" Simus leaned forward to ask.

Heath nodded. "He was imprisoned after the Warlord came to the castle."

"What of the city?" Keir asked again, drawing Heath back to the subject.

"Warlord, if Othur and Warren are freed, I believe that the army and the palace guards will listen to them. Xymund is the ordained King, but evidence of his madness grows by the hour."

Keir nodded. With quick words, he translated events for those that didn't speak Xyian. Once done, his eyes dropped to Heath's kneeling form and returned to my language. "Rise, Heath. You have risked much, and spared the Warprize. I will not forget this. Where are your parents held?"

Heath stood. "There are cellars, Warlord, under the kitchens. They are confined there, with the rest of the kitchen staff. Xymund took no risk that word would leak before I arrived here."

Keir nodded and switched tongues again. "Prest, Rafe, you have been to the castle and the kitchens. Pick men to go with us to secure the hostages. Keep the group small. Joden, take charge of the camp. We will make it appear that the Warprize is slain and that the camp is in confusion. But under the cover of that confusion, let men prepare to mount and ride for the castle. Xymund has breeched the peace through his actions, and I will have his head."

I started, squeezing Keir's shoulder. He did not look at me, turning to look at Simus instead. "Simus, I ask that you undertake the protection of the warprize personally. Designate whatever men you need to hold her safe. Once the commotion has started, place the army on alert."

Iften rose at that. "Warlord, it's my place to take charge of the camp, not Joden." He almost spat Joden's name.

Keir almost snarled. "Iften, if you had both feet planted on the earth, were bathed in flames, calling a wind, holding my token, and blessed by rain from the skies, still I would not trust you with my warprize."

Marcus snickered, as did some of the others. Iften turned bright red, but held his tongue.

Keir looked at Heath, and once again switched tongues. "Heath, you will be a part of the rescue. Prest and Rafe speak your language. Stay close to them." Keir covered my hand with his. "The warprize has faith in you. You will be given weapons. But if you should betray us, you are dead. Am I understood?"

"You are, Warlord." Heath bowed his head.

Keir stood. "Talk amongst yourselves, but let no man leave the tent till we have completed our plans." The men moved to obey. Keir turned, and in one quick movement, blocked my view of the tent. He towered over me. I stood my ground and returned his look. He raised his hand and placed a finger against my lips. "Don't," he breathed. "I need you safe, need to know that you are well out of that treacherous dog's hands."

"Keir, he is my brother and lawful king. You can't just kill him without . . ." I paused, torn.

Keir's jaw tightened. "He has betrayed his people. He has broken his oath to me. He has tried to kill you, his blood and kin. His life is forfeit and it will be at my hand. Would you protect him even so?"

"Keir, we do not punish the insane for their actions. You can't—"

"We hold that truth as well, Lara, unless the addled one is dangerous."

"I know." I closed my eyes, and looked away. "But he is of my blood and of the Blood of Xy." I looked up into his eyes, trying to figure out how to explain. Xymund might be a poor ruler, and mad as well, but he was my half-brother, and my father had loved him.

Keir's finger stroked my cheek. "I'm trying to understand, Lara."

"I know." I whispered. "I'm trying to figure it out myself. He threatens Anna and Othur, and this fragile peace between our peoples. Yet—"

"You would have him unharmed." Keir grimaced. "I will try, Lara. But I make no promise."

"Thank you." I smiled.

Keir gave me a knowing look. "You will remain here, Warprize."

"But—"

Keir grabbed my shoulders and gave me a firm shake. "Your oath now, that you will remain in this tent under protection. Or as the sun rises, I swear that I will chain you to a post before I leave."

The fear was there, haunting his blue eyes. I nodded. "Waste no time. Save Anna and Othur. Do what you have to do. I will be here when you return."

Relief flooded his face, and he kissed me, drawing me into

his arms. I went willingly, and clung to him with all the strength I had, afraid for him. Afraid for the peace. He held me for a long moment before turning to the room. "Are we ready?" The men started to gather around him.

I moved to Simus's side, clutched at his arm to get his attention. "Simus, you must go with him." Simus looked down at me, puzzled. "Simus, he must not kill Xymund." I shook his arm to make my point. "Xymund is a sworn king. There must be agreement from the lords, proof that he breeched his oath."

Simus nodded. "Keir knows that, little healer. He will . . ."

"Look at him, Simus."

Simus did. His eyes narrowed as he took in Keir's stance. "Maybe you are right." He smiled down at me. "Leave it to me." Simus moved next to Keir and began to speak. Keir shot me a glance, then turned to argue with Simus.

After a few minutes of debate, a compromise was struck. Simus and Joden would create the confusion in the camp. Under that cover Keir would leave with Prest, Rafe, and Heath to make for the castle kitchens to secure the hostages. Simus and Iften would lead a unit to secure the castle and join with Keir to confront Xymund. Joden would remain behind, taking command of the watch. I would remain safe within the tent, heavily guarded and under my oath not to leave. Epor and Isdra were summoned quickly, to take up a position inside the tent.

With a nod, Keir started all in motion. Voices cried out as if in horror, Keir's voice rising above the others. Warriors started to rush out of the tent and mill about at the entrance, with cries of outrage. The guards outside could be heard to ask questions and to wail in response to the news. Simus strode out, crying for vengeance and calling for mounts.

Prest, Rafe, and Heath stood by the entrance. Heath had been fitted with helm and sword. They waited for Keir, who stood beside me, strapping on his swords. He nodded to them to proceed him and turned to me.

I placed my hand on his heart. The mail shirt he had put on felt cold under my fingers. "Be safe."

He stared down at me, then gently gathered me into his

arms, burying his face in my hair. "I will. I regret this, Lara. He is your blood and kin." He raised his head, and I saw the anger in his eyes.

I nodded. "I know." He nodded as well, released me, and with a swirl of his cape, left the tent. As the flap fell, I saw him speak to Marcus, who was standing just inside.

I stood there, afraid not so much for Keir's physical safety as for the price of Xymund's death. Guilty or not, he was a king, and the local lords who had agreed to the terms of the peace might rise in defiance of his death at the hands of the Warlord. He was also my brother, no matter his mistakes and misjudgments. I did not want to see him harmed. Those thoughts whirled around in my head as I stood there.

Marcus reentered the tent. He shook his head and guided me back to my seat. "Hisself will be fine, Warprize. Fretting does no good." Within moments I found myself wrapped in a thick cloak and drinking warmed wine. Marcus watched me anxiously.

"It's hard to wait," I said quietly, looking into the goblet.

"Aye. I am thinking it takes more courage to be waiting then to be in the thick of things. A lesson I learned when my warrior days ended." Marcus sat at my feet and picked up another goblet for himself. He refilled his cup and mine as well. "You barely ate a thing." He pushed some of the tastier dishes my way. "Eat a bite and I will regale you with tales. Better than a singer, I am."

"Really?" I reached for some bread.

"Aye. Would you like to know how I met Hisself?"

I nodded as I chewed. Marcus continued, "Twas out in the practice grounds. I was training the young ones sword fighting, putting them through their paces, when this wee bit of a lad, all blue eyes and soft curls comes into the circle, dragging a wooden sword behind him." Marcus took a draught. " 'What's this?' says I. 'Wanna fight' says the lad." Marcus grinned. "Hisself too small to wield a sword almost as big as him. 'You're too little,' says I, kneeling down in front of him. Those defiant blue eyes staring back at me. 'Wor-wor.' He says. 'I'm gonna be wor-wor.' " Marcus shook his head.

"I finally had to pick him up and carry him out of the circle to let the others get back to work."

"What did he do?" I mumbled around my food.

Marcus laughed. "Well, I had one unhappy little man on my hands. I sat him next to me on a bench and started talking about the fighting, about the mistakes that they were making, what they did right, what they could have done better. He sat there by me, enthralled, till a thea came looking for him." Marcus looked at me, his eye twinkling. "Hisself took to escaping from the theas every chance he got to come and watch. Drove'em mad." He chuckled as he poured more wine. "When he finally got a sword in his hands, it was as if he had listened and learned from everything he had heard me say. Have no fear for the Warlord's safety, Warprize. He will be well."

As I ate, Marcus kept me diverted with tales of the little boy. But as time passed, and the shadows lengthened, my worries grew. I started to pace in the confines of the tent. Marcus stayed near me, pretending to clean and straighten the area, walking amidst over turned stumps, picking up scattered plates. He even offered to send for Gils so that I could give him a lesson, but I waved him off.

Finally, there was a noise outside. Epor went out, and there was a muted discussion. Finally, Epor lifted the flap. "A messenger has arrived, who speaks only Xyian. I told them to bring him here, since Joden is making rounds."

Marcus nodded. "That is well. I'm thinking the Warprize can't wait a moment longer." Epor dropped the flap, and Marcus chivied me to my usual seat and helped me arrange my cloak. "I'm thinking some wine would not go amiss. Put some color in your cheeks." Marcus swiftly moved to gather up a jug and cup, and was serving me as the messenger walked in, cloaked and hooded. Epor followed, taking his position opposite Isdra.

The messenger threw back his hood. I swallowed, suddenly nervous, to find my half-brother standing before me.

Xymund looked terrible. His eyes were sunken into his head, and his face was haggard and gray. This was not the older half-brother I'd grown up with, or the proud young man I'd seen crowned king. It seemed a stranger stared at me, and for a moment I sat stock-still before I recovered my wits.

"Please sit, brother. You look exhausted." I spoke in Xyian, hoping to put Xymund at his ease. I was determined that this end without bloodshed or harm to anyone. Marcus had taken up his station behind me. I felt comforted by his presence.

Xymund barely took note of him. "You look well, Lara. Slavery agrees with you." His voice was thick and harsh, as if he had been drinking.

I flushed, but did not drop my eyes. "I am not a slave. I am mate and consort to Keir, Warlord. Your Overlord." I sat taller and put my shoulders back, realizing that this man would never again have authority over me. "My position is one of honor, for I am the Warprize."

He sneered. "Another word for whore."

Marcus stiffened next to me.

I looked at the man before me, taking in his exhaustion. Yet, in his eyes I could see a deep hatred of myself and of Keir. My Warlord, who even now was trying to rescue my beloved Anna and Othur and maintain the peace that Xymund was throwing away by his actions. It angered me that Xymund had manipulated us. My loyalties may have been divided before, but they were suddenly clear. I frowned at him, feeling no sympathy for a plight he'd brought upon himself. "I am willing to listen, my brother. But I will not tolerate insults."

He snarled. "Your Warlord is at the castle. He has invaded the place with his men, and they are hunting for me. Warren has turned against me. They are making wild claims that I tried to have you killed."

I took a breath. "Heath . . ."

Xymund glared at me. "Heath is a liar."

I just looked at him. "You have known Heath and his parents since we were children. He does not lie."

Xymund's eyes were wild. His hands clenched and unclenched, forming tight fists. He seemed lost somehow, as if looking into a world I could not see. "You were always the favorite." He looked up, as if to curse the gods. "I thought you were my loyal little sister, who would do her duty and suffer the consequences." He took a step closer. "I go to clean out your room as a dutiful and loving brother should. And what do I find in the toe of your boot?" His hand moved. Marcus tensed behind me. But Xymund simply threw something small toward the dais, where it landed on the first step, by my feet.

Marcus went forward, knelt down and handed it to me.

It was Simus's broach. The black pouncing cat gleamed in the light. It was warm to the touch and my fingers folded around it.

Xymund continued. "You traitor. You wanted the throne for yourself, and betrayed me to my enemies." He almost spat the words at me.

My heart raced in my breast, but I fought to stay calm. "Xymund, I did not betray you. I slipped this off a wounded man because I was afraid that you would kill him outright rather then let him be exchanged."

Xymund was red, a vein in his neck throbbing. "Father adored you. Even when you refused to be an obedient Daughter of Xy. I knew I could surpass you, outshine you as the heir, as a warrior, but you became a healer, and Father was so *proud*."

"He was proud of you as well," I said quietly.

Xymund continued on, spitting in his fury. "Damn them all, they all watched me, waiting for me to fail. Whispering behind my back, that I was a coward, that I panicked. Always my mother's son, never my father's heir." His voice grew shrill. "So I sent Arneath and his men to kill you and any with you. Arneath swore he'd give his life for me, got that fool boy Degnan and hired scum." Xymund paused, breathing heavily.

"And so they died." I was bitter and so sick at heart with disappointment. I'd have wept at the waste, but my anger was stronger. "And in the marketplace? Did you hire them as well?"

"Market?" Xymund paused, "I wanted you dead in their camp, dead in breech of this so called peace. Arneath failed me. I will do what he could not." With one swift move he pulled his sword and advanced on me.

I froze.

Marcus, still at my feet, did not. He sprang forward, pulling two daggers as if from thin air. He took Xymund's charge, catching his blade in the daggers, and stopping him cold.

Xymund swore. Marcus smiled up at him. For a brief moment, they stood there, Xymund towering over the thin and wiry older man. The tableau broke as they pulled away from each other. Xymund tried to move back, stumbling over the stumps and tables, and Marcus was quick to press his advantage. Holding his sword held out before him, Xymund drew a dagger with the other hand, and glared at Marcus with a wild look.

Epor and Isdra leaped forward, weapons out. They circled the combatants to reach my side, followed by the guards from outside, who paused in the entrance, drawn by the noise.

"Xymund, put down your weapons." I moved forward, angry that he would attack Marcus.

Marcus swore and moved between Xymund and myself. "Lara, you idiot, get back."

I stopped where I was, but Epor had other ideas. He pushed me back as he and Isdra interposed between me and the threat.

Marcus held his hands to his sides and gestured for Xymund to come at him.

"A cripple?" Xymund laughed. He lunged in, swinging his sword in a fierce arc. Marcus dodged in, blocked the sword and parried the dagger. Xymund broke away. Marcus danced back. Xymund came in again, thrusting his sword at Marcus's body. But Marcus had already moved, and seeing that Xymund's reach was extended, leaned in and cut him on his cheek.

Xymund jerked back, shocked. Marcus moved to press his advantage, driving him back, away from me.

"Marcus, be careful," I called out, afraid for him. I would have moved toward them, but Epor and Isdra prevented me. "Xymund, in the name of the Goddess, please—"

"I'll kill you, bitch." Xymund howled, like a dog gone mad.

Marcus laughed and smirked at the sweaty and bleeding Xymund. He stopped pressing him and backed away. Marcus struck his chest with his fist, clearly defying Xymund, daring him to attack. What was he thinking? Xymund was bigger and stronger. Why didn't Epor help him?

Xymund glared at Marcus, panting and dripping blood. "I will kill your servant, and kill you where you stand, you miserable whore."

Marcus's face went flat, the one eye narrowing. He'd recognized the word 'whore'. The atmosphere in the tent changed. Marcus was no longer playing, his stance and attitude changing subtly. Xymund seemed to feel it as well. He tightened his grip on his weapons and crouched lower. Suddenly I understood that it was Xymund in deadly danger, not Marcus.

From outside came the sounds of horses, lots of them galloping to a halt outside the tent. Some of the guards by the door stepped out to confront the newcomers.

Still, I pleaded, "Xymund, stop this. Whatever you feel about me, remember the peace. Your oath demands . . ."

Xymund snarled and attacked Marcus viciously. His face was distorted, eyes bulging and mouth twisted. He rushed in, sword slashing at Marcus's face. Marcus parried with a kind of contempt, catching the blades with his daggers, he moved in close and spat in Xymund's face.

Screaming in rage, Xymund reared back and instinctively lifted a forearm to clean his eyes. Marcus saw his chance and took it, striking the sword from Xymund's hand. One dagger dug into Xymund's neck, the tip of the other rested just above his groin.

Xymund froze.

Marcus chuckled. "Warprize, tell this fool to kneel."

Xymund's eyes swung wildly about the room as I repeated the words. "I will not kneel to a servant and a whore." His eyes landed on mine. "I am your king, enthroned and consecrated. You cannot call for my death."

The entire outside wall of the tent fell, revealing Keir, Simus, and his men. Lord Warren was there as well, along with some of the lords. They were all standing and staring at Xymund with hate in their eyes. Keir's voice came, cold and sharp. "I can."

Marcus's grin got sharper and the blade of the dagger moved to press a bit deeper into Xymund's neck. Xymund slowly lowered himself to his knees. Marcus allowed the lower dagger to trail up Xymund's jerkin till the point rested at his heart.

"Marcus," Keir growled. "Don't kill him."

Marcus snorted. "Give me a good reason, Warlord. This pig is not worthy to die on your blade and, with all due respect, the warprize couldn't kill for her nooning if she were starving and there were fowl aplenty." Not for one minute did Marcus relax the blades pressed against Xymund's throat and chest.

"Marcus." My voice cracked. "Marcus, his own people must try him, must find him guilty, must know what he has done . . . Marcus, they must know—otherwise everything Keir wants to achieve will be lost. Please . . ."

Marcus sneered and leaned in on Xymund. "The only thing that saves you now are the words of the Warprize . . . she who is honored before all." Xymund may not have understood the words, but he certainly got their meaning. His eyes blazed hot as Marcus stepped back. Epor and Isdra moved forward, ready to secure the prisoner.

As the tent filled, I turned and smiled at Keir. The stiffness in his back eased, as his eyes passed over me, assuring himself that I was safe. I moved forward, intent only on reaching him.

Unknowingly, I moved closer to Xymund, and into Marcus's blind spot.

With a howl, Xymund jumped to his feet, swept up his dagger and lunged at me. He grabbed my shoulder and I saw his rage, felt his breath hot on my face as his dagger moved toward my stomach.

Keir was there. In one move he threw me backwards to the floor, and stepped between us, securing Xymund's wrist in one hand. The blade was poised between them.

Xymund fought, struggling against the grip, bringing his

other hand up. His face was wild and frightening, the blood oozing from his cheek, splattering Keir's chest as he struggled Keir stood firm. "End this. Now."

Xymund raged, trying with all his might to free his wrist. "No, no! Death to the whore and traitor."

Keir said nothing, merely hooded his eyes. He slowly forced the point of the dagger down and toward Xymund's stomach. Keir's voice grated as he spoke. "For the last time, end this now and save your life."

Xymund shrieked and threw himself at Keir.

Keir shoved the point of the dagger into his stomach.

Xymund's eyes bulged. He still held the hilt. Keir released him and stepped back, turning to sweep me up and away. Epor, Isdra, and Marcus moved toward Xymund. Over their shoulders, I saw Xymund start to buckle, then my view was blocked by Keir as he embraced me.

I resisted, trying to see around him. "Let me go, let me see . . ." Keir was running his hands over me, checking for injury and restraining me at the same time. "Keir, let me try to . . ."

"No." Keir caught me up again, pressing my head to his chest. He rocked me slightly.

I heard a cough come from behind Keir. Simus spoke quietly, "He is dead. What are your instructions, Warlord?"

Keir said nothing. He pulled back and looked at me. I looked into his eyes and tried to smile. He smiled back, but with an overcast of sadness in his eyes. "Remove the body. We will take it to the city and inform the nobles and the people of what has happened." He rubbed his thumb over my lips. "Lara, I . . ." He paused, as if in pain. "Remember that you have my heart."

"Lara!" A shriek filled the air as Anna descended on us, weeping and crying. She hugged me to her bosom. Keir stood and backed away, letting Anna and Othur close. We hugged and embraced in joyful reunion.

Lord Warren approached Keir. "Warlord, who shall now rule in Xymund's stead?"

There was sudden hush, as the Xyians all looked to Keir.

Keir inclined his head. "That's an issue that must be discussed. We'll take up the body and return to the castle. The future of this land, and the Daughter of Xy must be resolved quickly to preserve our peace."

My heart stopped.

I could feel the tension of the room decrease. Warren smiled, and the nobles seemed to relax, moving toward their horses. Anna was fussing, and Othur and Marcus seemed to be sizing each other up. The fears of my people had eased.

Only my fears had intensified.

12

Keir moved swiftly, issuing orders that got everyone moving. Even as Epor and Isdra secured Xymund's body, Keir had Warren sending messages into the city, to rouse the lords and members of the council from their beds and order them to the castle. The confusion of bodies in the tent was organized chaos, with everyone following orders. Some took instruction to guard the camp, others to go to the city with us. Horses were brought to the tent entrance. To my frustration, I only had a moment with Keir before we left. He drew me close, and before I could ask any questions, he kissed me gently, then swept me into his arms. Outside, Lord Warren was mounted, and Keir placed me on the saddle before him. "You'll keep her safe?"

Warren controlled the horse as it shifted under our weight. "With my life."

Keir nodded once and moved to his own horse, calling for everyone to follow to the castle. Warren summoned his men, who surrounded us as a bodyguard. As we moved off behind

Keir's group, not even the sight of poor Anna trying to stay on her horse could ease my anxieties.

I shifted slightly in the saddle. "What happened at the castle?"

Warren spoke in my ear. "When I confronted him with my suspicions, Xymund went into a rage. I thought it was because there seemed to be a plot against you. But he raved, Lara. Like a man possessed." Warren sighed. "He wasn't rational. He screamed that you had betrayed him, yet we knew that he had sold you for the peace. My expression must have given me away, for he immediately ordered me imprisoned."

"Xymund didn't sell me." I explained what I had learned.

Warren grunted in surprise. "A consort? That bodes well."

I pulled my cloak tighter around me. "He shouldn't have killed him."

I felt Warren shake his head. "No, Lara. Keir was right to act. Xymund was mad. I'd known that he was a coward, and an indecisive leader. But his actions made it clear that something wasn't right."

"The lords and the council may not—"

"The Warlord is an honorable man." Warren's voice was firm. "All will be well, Daughter of Xy."

I didn't answer him. Instead, I focused on the group of horsemen ahead of us. I caught a glimpse of a cloaked figure riding near Keir. I also saw Simus and Joden next to Keir, and some kind of discussion was going on, one that didn't please Joden or Simus. All I could do was watch as we approached to the castle, my hands sweating and my heart in my throat.

In the courtyard, we dismounted, in a confusion of people and horses. Keir appeared with Othur. "Warren, take her to the antechamber." He turned and moved off before I could even open my mouth.

Warren hustled me into the castle, where we bumped into Heath, looking worse for wear with a cut on his forehead. "Heath!"

Heath turned, smiling to see me, and moved past the guards to catch me up in a hug. "Thank all the gods. I'd thought for sure that the Warlord wouldn't be in time." Heath grimaced. "Xymund caught sight of me as we rescued the hostages and started screaming. He slipped past us in the confusion. The King's insane, Lara, I swear to you, he's—"

"He's dead." Warren spoke from behind us.

"Dead?" Heath sucked in a breath. "By whose hand?"

Warren took my shoulders firmly. "Join your parents, Heath. They're headed to the throne room." Without ceremony, he moved me on, down the hall and into the antechamber.

With an odd feeling of having done all of this before, I waited before the fire in the antechamber, anxious for news, wondering what Keir was going to do. Warren waited with me, having placed his men at each door. Finally, Keir swept in, alone. "The people are assembled, and we are ready. Warren, take your place in the throne room." Warren bowed, and left with his men. Keir moved closer to me, reaching out and taking me in his arms. He buried his head in my hair, and crushed me to his chest.

"What are you going to do?" I asked softly.

"What's best. What's necessary." He nuzzled me behind my ear, and I shivered at the touch. He drew a deep breath, and then Keir pulled back, brushing my hair back with one hand. I stiffened when a horn sounded in the throne room. Keir stepped back without looking at me, took another deep breath, and headed for the double doors, throwing them open.

The Herald, standing there in full uniform, pounded the floor with his staff three times. "Lords and Ladies, all hail Keir, Warlord of the Plains and Overlord of Xy, and Xylara, Warprize, Daughter of Xy."

Keir paused and held out his hand to me in an oddly formal gesture. I placed my hand over his, and we entered the throne room side by side. The white marble of the throne room gleamed in the light of the torches that ringed it. The lords of the court, and the craftmasters of the city filled the room, as did an even larger number of the Warlord's men. Simus and Joden stood by the thrones. Someone had placed a tall brazier near to the throne, and a fire burned there, the flames dancing on the wood.

Not one to keep a formal pace, Keir strode us across the floor quickly, then settled in the throne with an easy grace.

As I sat, I noticed the wide-eyed, frightened looks of men and women pulled from their homes and beds. None of which eased as Keir rose to speak. "There has been violence done this night, an attack on the Warprize, Xylara, Daughter of Xy." Keir continued to speak over the reaction of the crowd. "She was attacked by Xymund, her half-brother." With a gesture of his hand, he summoned Epor and Isdra. They emerged from the antechamber, bearing the shrouded body, only to dump it before Keir. Epor knelt, and cut the shroud away, displaying the body.

The edges of the crowd drew back, voices raised in outrage and horror. I swallowed hard a few times, fighting back nausea. Keir let the assembly vent for a moment, then held his hand up for silence. "You have been gathered to hear our tales. Judge not, until all has been told. Each shall speak, and swear binding oaths as to the truth of their words." Keir's gaze moved over the group, and I somehow knew he was reading hearts as well as faces. "It is the custom of my people that oaths are sworn under the open sky. But an oath to the flame is just as binding." He gestured to the brazier where the flames leaped, then returned to the throne. "I'll be the first to speak." With that, he wasted no time, summarizing the events of the last few days, starting with the assault in the healing tent. The silence deepened as he was brutally honest about the death of Xymund at his hand.

When Keir finished, Warren stepped forward and told his version. Othur spoke as well, holding a trembling Anna by his side. Heath spoke of Xymund's commands, and the actions he had taken. Simus stepped forward and told of what he had witnessed.

When Marcus stepped forward, my heart almost broke. The small, scarred man, so bold and outspoken in Keir's tent, was clearly uncomfortable. But he stood there, his one eye focused on Keir and spoke with Simus interpreting. There was a tinge of hysterical mirth in the crowd when Marcus gave his honest opinion of Xymund's fighting abilities. At the end, he gave his oath, as the others had done before him.

Finally, Keir turned to me. "Xylara."

My mind blanked as I stared at him. I took a deep breath, and started where he had, at Arneath's attack. As I spoke, I scanned the faces in front of me, seeing an odd mixture of sympathy, trust, and suspicion. My voice stayed calm as I kept my facts in order, trying to remove the emotion from my voice and words. That broke down when I reached the part of Xymund's arrival, and his words to me in the end. I had to look down at that point, focus on my hands, and struggled to complete the tale. Keir's hand moved into my vision and covered mine, giving me strength. I didn't look up, managing to stumble though the last of it, including the oath. There was silence at the end.

Keir withdrew his hand and stood. "Are there any who challenge the truth of these words?"

No one spoke.

"Are there any who challenge my authority to deal with Xymund as I saw fit?"

No one raised their voice.

"This matter is finished."

While the faces in the crowd were still a mixture of doubts, fears, and mistrust, I relaxed slightly, resting against the back of the throne, feeling the tension in my shoulders ease. With no voices raised, I was sure that all would be well.

Keir turned his head, gesturing to Epor and Isdra. "Remove this." Keir focused on the Archbishop Drizen. "Please see to it that the body is given the rites of his faith, with no further ceremony."

"Please," I cleared my throat. "Please have him interred with the royal family, Warlord."

Keir frowned. "He would have killed you."

"His mind was not his own at the end. Please let him lay next to his mother."

Keir gave an abrupt nod. "See to it."

The Archbishop inclined his head.

The crowd was growing restless. Keir gestured to the Herald, who tapped his staff three times in a call for silence. Still, Keir had to raise his voice to be heard. "Would the King's Council step forward?"

The council stepped forward, led by Archbishop Drizen and Lord Marshall Warren.

Keir nodded to each. "We must now consider who will rule the Kingdom of Xy."

My stomach knotted.

"It is right that Xylara, Daughter of the House of Xy take the throne," Keir raised his voice, insuring that he would be heard. "I hereby release my claim of the Warprize and return her to her people."

Stunned, the council gaped like fish. I opened my mouth, but Keir cut us all off. He rose to his feet. "My army will depart in four days. I leave Simus of the Hawk to act as my Overlord. Once we reach the borders of your land, I will send word back, recalling Simus, and releasing Queen Xylara of her oaths of fealty to me. Arrange the coronation with all due speed." With that, he inclined his head to me and extended his hand. I rose and took his hand automatically. Using his advantage, he pulled me forward, then pressed me onto the seat of the high throne.

The cheers exploded from the throats of my people. The entire council began to clap, cheering as well. Keir looked at them, nodded to me, then strode toward the antechamber. I rose to follow, but the council surged forward, to clasp my hand, hug me, and to express their joy.

Overwhelmed, I fell back on the throne, stunned. Warren fought his way to my side, urging people back, and cleared the space in front of me. Amidst the cheers of my people, I rose, and followed Keir into the antechamber.

He was standing by the fireplace when I walked in, facing the door. His face was grim, his eyes on the fire.

I stopped just inside the room. "What are you doing?"

"This Kingdom must be ruled, and you are the blood heir, the logical choice for the throne." He never looked up, didn't turn to face me.

"You have claimed me as Warprize."

"I renounce that claim."

I moved closer, watching the light of the flames dance on his face. The muscle of his jaw was twitching as his jaw clenched. "Renounce the claim?" There was no response. "Renounce me? After we—"

Keir just stood there, watching the flames. "This is your home. These people will keep you safe, safe from attackers, safe from injury, safe from harm." He looked up at me, his eyes bright. I couldn't tell if it was reflected firelight or something else. "Being a Warprize is not safe." He returned to staring at the flames.

"Especially when I've surrendered everything to the Warlord, only to have it flung back in my face!" Goddess, that wasn't true, but I was so hurt the words were out of my mouth before I could think. He'd given me hope and joy so bright it hurt and now he was dousing the flame. I crossed my arms over my chest, suddenly chilled in a way that had nothing to do with the heat of the fire.

Keir didn't respond to my words.

I drew myself up, and stretched out a trembling hand. "Keir, don't do this." I took a step toward him. He jerked back, avoiding my touch. As I stood there, stricken, he seemed to relent. He drew me into his embrace, wrapping his arms around me as if I were a precious treasure. I leaned into his hug, feeling the leather under my cheek and the warmth of his body. He drew a deep breath, held it, and let it out slowly.

As carefully as he had enfolded me, he released me slowly, taking a long step back. Tears in my eyes, I looked up at him, smiling. But his face was just as grim, and to my horror he turned away and went through the door into the hall. I followed, only to find Simus, Joden, Warren and Other standing there. Anna was there as well, with a tray of tea and sweets. Marcus stood off to one side, already wrapped in his cloak.

Keir cleared his throat. "Simus, you will remain here, as my representative. Joden, you will return with me to camp." He spun on his heel to look at me. "Warren, I charge you with

Queen Xylara's security. For her own safety, I forbid her access to my camp. She is to remain safe within the city walls until I depart."

Everyone gaped at him. He turned, and strode away, with Joden and Marcus scrambling behind him. Seized with an outraged fury, I grabbed the tea pot off Anna's tray, and hurled it at Keir's head. It missed, flew into the wall, and shattered into a thousand pieces, spraying tea everywhere.

Keir flinched, but kept moving.

Just as shattered as the pot, I spun on my heels and ran, crying, to my old bedroom.

An hour later, the door opened, and two servants brought in one of the crates from my stilltent. I looked up, still weepy-eyed as they set it down, and bowed themselves out of the room. It didn't take long for me to pry open the rough lid. It contained my herb book, my notebooks, my under things, the vanilla soap and oils, and the white sheath. No note, no comment, no message. I sat on the floor next to it, and wept.

The next morn, I watched from the window as the army packed up and prepared to march, letting the tears flow down my cheeks. I sat by the window all day as the shadows lengthened, and the torches flared up in the darkness. How could he do this? Didn't he want me? I'd heard stories of course, overheard kitchen maids sobbing to Anna about men who'd stolen their virtue and left them crying, alone. Was that it?

I hurt so much, my head, my heart. My sorrow seemed unending and bottomless. Over and over, the events of the past week flicked through my mind. I leaned my cheek against the rough stone and gave in to my despair.

Anna brought in food at regular intervals. I am fairly certain that she begged me to eat something.

Warren came in, with reports and documents that needed my attention. I am sure that some of them were important.

Remn came in, to talk books and the replacement of the stillroom. I am fairly certain that he talked for some time before he left.

Othur came in, and discussed duties and obligations. He talked for quite awhile, till finally I turned and stared at him. He looked into my eyes, sighed, and left.

Heath came in, and stood there for a bit. He walked up behind me, and laid a hand on my shoulder. When I looked up, he smiled. "Follow your heart, my sister." He turned and left the room.

And so I sat, mired in sadness and grief, 'til just after dawn.

Eln entered. With gentle, understanding hands, he pulled me away from the window, and seated me on the bed. He checked me over quietly, with no comment. I closed my puffy eyes and sat silently, my head aching something fierce. Finally, Eln put one finger under my chin and lifted my head. I opened my eyes to see his concerned face, before a strange look flashed over his features.

Eln slapped me.

The blow rocked my head back, and I saw stars. I jumped up, my hand pressed to my face in astonishment, and felt the heat in my cheek. Eln stood there glaring, his face disdainful. "Is this the girl that demanded to become my apprentice? Who healed the enemy in the face of her brother's wrath? Who sacrificed her life for her people?" His mouth pursed, like he had tasted bad wine.

"Eln, I—"

"No excuses. You want something, you work for it, not sulk in your room weeping like a spoiled child. In all honor, either balance the needs of your people and your desires, or accept your responsibilities." He drew himself up. "I am ashamed to claim you as student when you act like this."

The heat that flooded my face had nothing to do with his blow. I bowed my head. "I'm sorry, Master."

"Then do something." Eln swept toward the door. "Bathing would be a good start."

He left me standing there, looking down at my tear-stained tunic and feeling an utter fool. My old master was right. There was more at risk here than my heart, and I was acting like a spoiled child. Embarrassed, I wiped my face, gathered up clean clothes and opened the door to the hall. Two guards stood outside the door, and a chambermaid was sitting against the far wall. She jumped when I opened the door.

"Your Majesty." She curtsied, wobbling a bit as she rose.

I grimaced. "Not very majestic at the moment."

She fixed her eyes on me like a frightened doe.

"I'm going down to the baths. Would you ask Anna to have some food ready for when I'm done? I'll come down to the kitchen."

"I'd bring up a bath for you, Majesty, if you want."

"No, thank you. Just please take my message to Anna."

"Oh, yes, Your Majesty. She'll be so happy." The girl hiked up her skirts and took off.

"Wait!" I called after her. She turned, still moving backwards. "Please ask Othur to join me there?"

"Oh, aye, I'll tell him you want him." She called over her shoulder. "Aye!"

"Make sure you say please!"

I heard her faint 'Aye' as I turned to my guards and looked them over. The younger one shifted uncomfortably. The older one gave me a patient look. "Your Majesty, Lord Marshall Warren's orders are that you are to be protected at all times. Him and the Warlord's orders."

I sighed, but knew this was a lost cause. I nodded to the guards, and started down the corridor.

Scrubbed clean, and with fresh clothes, I sat at the huge table near the hearth in the kitchen, with hot soup and bread before me. The soup was thick with chunks of meat and potatoes. The bread was warm, and Anna was spreading the butter thick with a knife. "Here, child, eat."

My two guards were at the kitchen door, far enough for privacy's sake. Othur sat opposite me, nursing an ale. "Might as well, Lara. She won't rest until you do."

I pulled the bowl close, hoping that the warm food would

ease the pounding in my head. I craved a mug of kavage, but knew better than to ask for it. Besides, it wouldn't taste the same without—

I cut that thought off, and dug into the food.

"I can drizzle the bread with some honey." Anna moved toward the shelves.

"No, Anna, please sit." I tucked a strand of damp hair behind my ear, and kept eating.

Anna finally settled her bulk on the stool next to me, her smile so large it increased the number of her chins. "There's so much to plan, now that you're returned safe and sound to us. A coronation feast, the ceremonies—"

The bread tasted wonderful, and I dipped a piece in the soup as Anna talked about a half dozen things, including preparing my father's old rooms for me. Othur said nothing, just studied his ale, then my face, then returned to his ale again. Eventually, Anna ran out of words and she sat silent, darting looks between Othur and me. Neither of us was willing to speak first, and finally Anna lost her patience. "What is it, child?"

"She doesn't want the crown." Othur rumbled.

"What?"

"Othur," I pleaded. "You've been the seneschal for years, under my father. Can you honestly say it's in the best interest of the kingdom for me to rule?"

Othur frowned. "You are a Daughter of Xy. Your duty requires you to rule your kingdom and rule it well, Xylara. That is what your father would expect of you. Regardless of your personal desires."

"Othur, I never wanted to be queen. I don't have the skills to be queen. My dream was having a school of healing, not to—"

"The events of the last month have frightened the people. They need stability, reassurance that all will be well." Othur's eyes drilled into me. "Your presence on the throne will comfort them. You can learn the skills necessary, given time."

"I—"

"Anything less is a betrayal of your father and your father's father." Othur stood, pushing his stool back. "I'll hear no more of this, My Queen." With that, he walked out of the kitchen.

Anna placed a trembling hand on my arm. "Child, you're home and safe. Where else would you want to be?"

I sighed, and ate more soup.

I left Anna, and went out into the kitchen gardens, then down the path to the great rose briar. My two guards followed like shadows.

I hated to admit it, even to myself, but Othur was right. Father had always said that the price of privilege was responsibility. Like it or not, I was Heir to the Throne of Xy. I had an obligation, one that I could not avoid or ignore or pass to someone else.

The scent of roses grew as I got closer to the briar. Apparently Anna had not yet picked it clean. I picked one of the flowers, and held it to my nose, enjoying the scent, bringing memories of my father. But not just his sickbed. I saw him on the throne, and in council, making decisions, ruling wisely and well. I walked on, lost in my thoughts.

I knew little of politics, little of diplomacy, and the thousand other things one needed to be queen. Maybe Keir's people had a better way, one that depended on proven abilities rather than birth. One thing was certain, at least to me. I'd be an inept ruler. And if I did take the throne, it was highly unlikely that I'd be able to tend a sick person ever again. As warprize, I'd be able to, even encouraged to heal, maybe teach.

I jerked to a stop and stopped breathing. For here in the dimness of the garden, where shadows hid me from prying eyes, I faced the truth.

I wanted Keir.

I wanted Keir more than I wanted to make the sick well, or pass on my skills to others. I wanted Keir more than I wanted to sit on the Throne of Xy and ward my people. I wanted his strength, his touch, his sly sense of humor, his honor and his passion.

I stroked the flower against my warm cheek, feeling the velvet of the petals. Days? Had it only been days? Does the heart count days, or even hours?

I moved over to one of the stone benches, and slumped down. I sounded like one of those horrid old ballads, sung by minstrels to lovesick court maidens with empty heads. Part of me was ashamed to face the truth. A true Daughter of Xy would put aside her desires and serve her people.

With Keir beside me, that service was one that would fill my days with joy and purpose.

Without him, it felt like a cold and joyless burden.

If I'd thought my options limited with Xymund alive, they seemed even more confining now that he was dead. Being the warprize might be a risk, but it held out opportunities I'd never dreamed of.

Keir had made his decision, for reasons I didn't fully understand. Clearly, Anna and Othur would not help me. They seemed to think that they could put everything back the way it was, reassemble the broken teapot and put it back up on the shelf, as if nothing had happened. Except, I didn't want to go back on the shelf and I couldn't believe that my father would have wanted me to be miserable.

There had to be a way.

Anna had housed Simus in the quarters usually used by visiting ambassadors. They were large and spacious, with plenty of room for he and his guard. The rest of his men were housed in one of the barracks. As I was admitted to the outer sitting room, I scanned the faces of the guards, but saw no one familiar.

"Little healer!" Simus's voice boomed out, and I turned to behold him standing there, hands on hips. My smile and laugh burst out spontaneously. He was a vision, dressed in a flowing shirt of white, black trous, a belt of red and a bright blue vest. I'd never seen him in other than armor. His left ear was pierced with five gold hoops of varying sizes, and they glittered every time he moved his head. He grinned at my reaction, and spread his arms wide. "I thought to make your people green with envy at my splendor. Have I succeeded?"

"Beyond your wildest expectations." I chuckled. "Their eyes will pop out of their heads like marbles."

Simus drew himself up proudly, then made a sweeping bow. "Welcome to my chambers, Your Majesty." His Xyian was carefully pronounced. "How may I assist you?"

"Simus, I want to ask your advice about something."

He looked at me carefully, growing serious, and reverted to the language of his people. "I can't promise to assist you, Your Majesty. The Warlord has made his wishes known, and I am bound to obey him."

I rubbed my sweaty palms on my dress, trying to remain calm and controlled. "Simus, I don't understand. Why is he doing this?"

Simus shrugged. "What's to understand? Does one understand the wind or predict the flame?" Simus gestured me to a chair. "There are things you do not know, little healer. Being warprize carries its own dangers. The warrior-priests and the elders will fight Keir tooth and nail over this, and you'd be in the center."

"Do they hate Keir that much?"

Simus's face grew serious. "Ah, that hate lies on both sides, and who is to say whose is the greater? But it matters not. Keir is the Warlord, and his will binds me. You will remain in your kingdom, and be crowned its queen. Once that is accomplished, I will return to the plains, and all will be well."

"Simus—"

He shook his head, setting his earrings glittering in the light. "No. I will not discuss this with you." He gestured toward two chairs by the unlit fireplace. "Come. We will have some of Anna's good cooking and swill this drink called 'ale' and you will tell me of your ceremonies. Tell me what a 'coronation' is and what tasks you are required to perform." He raised a finger in warning. "But I will hear no talk of anything else. Understood?" His eyes were kind but firm.

"Understood."

* * *

Eln opened the backdoor of his clinic, and regarded Heath and me and my four bodyguards with a neutral expression. After a slight pause, he stepped aside. Heath and I slipped past him, into the stillroom, followed by two of the guards. It was a bright, cheery place, with a crackling fire in the hearth, and various potions bubbling in caldrons. I felt myself relax as I breathed in the familiar scents of medicines and tonics. I'd learned my craft here, and it felt like home.

"What's that stink?" Heath asked, screwing up his face.

"A medicine." Eln moved over to the table to stir a pot. He glanced at me with a questioning look. "What brings Your Majesty to my humble clinic?"

"My majesty needs to talk to you. To talk to someone I can trust." I sat on a stool. Heath wandered the room, looking at the various bottles and jars. The two guards remained by the door.

"Trust?" Eln focused on me, at the same time he reached out and slapped Heath's hands away from a jar.

"Trust that you have no preconceived notions of what is best for the kingdom and for me."

Eln gave me a sharp look before turning to Heath. "Scamp, make yourself useful. There's a load of new wood at the back. Go cut it for me. And take those two lummoxes with you."

Heath looked startled. "We're protecting Lara."

Eln snorted. "She's worked in this clinic for many years with no fears. Your muscles are wasted in here when they could be useful. Go. Or I'll set you to chopping herbs and stirring cauldrons."

Heath flashed a grin. "At least we won't be breathing in the stink." He laughed as Eln scowled. The guards chuckled too, as they headed out the door.

"So?" Eln looked me over from head to toe. His face was still neutral.

"Eln, I know what I want. Everyone at the castle is certain that I'm best for the kingdom, and I don't think that's true."

"And?"

I gritted my teeth. Eln was in teacher mode, which was very irritating. "Simus won't talk to me. Othur and Warren have already decided what is best for the kingdom. And I'm not sure of what to do next."

Eln stirred his pot for a moment. "If the kingdom were ill, what would you do?"

"What?"

He shot me a look. "If the kingdom were to somehow stumble into the clinic, weak and ill, what would you do first?"

"I'd ask questions, try to discover what was wrong."

"Such as?"

Impatient, I glared at him. "What is wrong? How are you feeling? Have you urinated today? Have you vomited? How are your bowels?"

Eln kept silent and kept stirring.

"One of the rules you teach us is that before we can start to cure a patient, we must first understand the disease." He nodded, taking a pinch of marjoram and sprinkling it into the pot. I sat for a moment, trying to apply my healing skills to my problem. "I need to know what problems my coronation solves, and see if there's an alternative."

He shrugged. "You need to start thinking."

I rubbed my cheek. "So you said."

"Well, you came up with a punishment for me, I fear." He smiled ruefully. "Seems my newest patient wants me to read *The Epic of Xyson* to her on a daily basis. A fate worse than death."

I sat up, surprised. "Is Atira here?"

"Just so. The Warlord sent her to me, with a pouch of gold. Asked that I see to her, since her healer is no longer available." He held up a hand at my indignant expression. "His words, not mine."

"Where?"

"I put her in the corner room. If you're going back there, take this to her." Eln handed me two mugs of tea. "She asked for kavage, but will have to make do with this for now."

I took the mugs and headed for the corner room. It was one

of the larger ones, with a big fireplace of its own. Behind me, I heard Eln call out the door for one of the guards to fetch water, and for the others to keep chopping. I had to smile as I ducked into the corner room.

Atira lay there, her leg suspended from one of Eln's rigs, his weights pulling it straight. She blinked at me for a moment, then a smile covered her entire face. "Warprize!" She struggled to sit up. "No, no, that's not right." She narrowed her eyes in concentration. "Greetings, Your Majesty." She spoke the words in Xyian. "Did I say it right?"

I set the mugs down and helped her sit up. "You did." Once she was settled, I handed her one of the mugs.

She sipped it, and wrinkled her nose. "If I'd had time, I'd have asked for kavage before they hauled me here. But the Warlord hustled me right out of camp."

"Maybe Simus will share his supply."

She rolled her eyes. "Nay, he'll hoard what he has and use the grounds twice, even if I had a headache that might kill me. Not that I blame him." She looked at me over the rim of the mug. "I only got hints of what happened at the castle. The Warlord said that I was to be cared for here until the leg is healed, then join him on the Plains." Her eyes were bright with curiosity.

I took the hint and summarized what had happened. She listened intently, shaking her head when I reached the end.

Heath stomped in, a load of wood in his arms. "Eln never changes, Lara. Always the task master." He moved to the wood box and dumped his load. As he stood, he flashed a grin at Atira. "How's the leg?"

She frowned, and answered carefully in Xyian. "It is well. Thank you."

Heath laughed. "I don't envy you, stuck here with Eln for the next few weeks."

Atira smiled. "I have this." She held up *The Epic of Xyson* and the reader that I had purchased.

Heath rolled his eyes. "That hoary old thing? There are better books to read."

Atira's eyes got big. "There is more than one?" She looked at me for confirmation.

Heath laughed. "I'll bring you something from the castle that's better than that one." Eln's voice raised from the still-room and Heath grimaced. "Back to work." He gave me an imploring look as he walked to the door. "Please, don't be long."

I laughed at him, then turned back to Atira, switching back to her language. "Will it harm Keir, not to produce a Warprize?"

"Aye." Atira nodded. "The Warlord sent messages when you were claimed. If he can't produce you, the people will say that the Warprize rejected him." She thought for a moment, stroking the cover of the *Epic*. "The Warlord built this army carefully, explaining that we would not receive the usual share of the spoils. Instead, he made agreements to pay his warriors with money or land. If he can't reward the army, he will be shamed. Or worse."

"I don't understand him." I set my mug down and ran my fingers through my hair. "Why is he doing this?" She shrugged. "Atira, Simus said that the warrior-priests and the elders hate Keir as much as he hates them. Why?"

"I don't know all the details. Keir has always been vocal that warrior-priests withhold their magic from those who need them most."

"Magic? They use magic?" My voice squeaked. "There's no such thing, Atira."

"Yet that is what they claim." Atira frowned. "I'm not privy to the ways of warlords, or their councils. I didn't even know that a warlord could renounce a warprize." She shrugged. "But then, I am no singer, to know all the laws and customs."

I blinked. "Joden would know, wouldn't he?"

"Of course."

Keir had taken Joden back to camp, and forbidden me to follow. I chewed my lip, thinking about that for a moment.

"Now." Atira looked at me intently. "You can answer a question for me. I've been thinking about the *Epic*, and listening closely. It speaks of a son 'inheriting' from his father. Does this mean that the son can 'inherit' a thing? Like a horse?"

I nodded. "Yes."

"Can a son 'inherit' power? Status?"

"Or even a throne. Xymund got the throne when my father died."

Atira frowned, thinking. "So a man with no real skill could hold a place of power, without earning it? That is very strange." She sipped her tea, then looked at me. "And with Xymund's death, you take the throne." She paused. "Who takes the throne if you die with no children?"

My eyes widened. Who indeed?

I burst out of the clinic, to find Heath and the guards at work on the firewood. "Heath!"

"Lara?" Heath turned, surprised, as the guards reached for their weapons. "What's wrong?"

"I need to get some maps of the lands that surround us and talk to Remn. And Estoval, and Kalisa, if I can find her." I grabbed my horse's reins and mounted. The guards ran for their mounts.

"The cheesemaker?" Heath stood there, looking like a half-wit, the axe in his hand.

"Yes, the cheesemaker." I urged my horse out the back gate. Heath dropped the axe and ran to his horse. "And Warren. I need to talk to them all, right now."

Heath heaved himself into the saddle. "What's the rush, Lara?"

"The Warlord's army leaves in two days!"

My hands were sweating, my stomach lay in knots, my head ached, and the crown of the Kingdom of Xy was going to fall off my head at any moment. I'd sent messages as soon as I had returned to the castle, and called a Council meeting for ꞌsunset. Since that time, I'd locked myself in my room with maps of the region and considered my options.

The council room was packed, with Simus, Othur, Warren and the council members. All of them staring at me as I sat behind my father's desk. I sat up straight, and kept my hands in my lap. It would make it easier to conceal their shaking. I cleared my throat, and the room settled. "I have called this meeting to discuss the welfare of the Kingdom of Xy." I took a breath to quiet my stomach. "Simus of the Hawk is here as a representative of the Warlord Keir. The Warlord has confirmed that he will relinquish his claims to the Kingdom of Xy once I have been crowned." Simus inclined his head as an acknowledgment. His attendance was important, but even more important was that he didn't understand what I was doing until it was too late.

I smiled at the council members. "Thank you for attending this meeting on such short notice. I wish to apologize for not being prepared to name my council at this time, for I am minded to reduce the size of the council. I regret the delay, but ask your forgiveness during this chaotic period. I would request that you all continue to serve in a temporary capacity, until I have considered and chosen my permanent advisors."

That set the cat among the fowl. I could tell that some hadn't considered my right to name a new or smaller council. Good. I wanted them unsettled and thinking about what my coronation would mean to them.

"First, I feel that I must correct a lie that Xymund told to us and to the people. Let me explain the meaning of the word 'warprize'." I took my time, emphasizing the honor that the title bestowed, and its meaning to those of the Plains. Simus confirmed my words, but I could see limited understanding in their eyes. It didn't matter to me if they thought it was the truth, or an effort to restore my wounded pride. So long as they believed. That chore done, I turned to the important issues. "With the Kingdom returned to the House of Xy, we must consider the needs of our country and its people. While the Warlord has offered assurances that the raiding will not resume during his lifetime, Lord Warren and I have discussed our safety. The knowledge of a female ruler on a throne will spread, and there may be those who will challenge our throne and borders. Our military must be strong enough to deal with these challenges, and that will mean raising taxes for its support."

I cleared my throat and took a sip of water. The headache was still there, pounding fiercely behind my temples. "Which leads me to the next topic that I and my council need to consider. We need to consider any potential alliance marriages and assuring that the royal line continues."

Archbishop Drizen was frowning. Hopefully, he was starting to think about what a royal consort would mean. A man, unknown to them, who would come in and, by simple virtue of my lack of skills, would move into a position of power. Let that idea settle into their understanding.

"We must also prepare in the event that I should die in childbirth or without living issue. The people must be assured that the kingdom will pass into safe and strong hands." I bit my lip, as if in thought. "There are few distant cousins, but they must be considered as potential heirs."

There were definite looks of concern now. They all knew the cousins.

"Would that there was time to discuss some type of trade relations with the Warlord before he left." I turned my head carefully. "Simus, would your people be open to such talks?"

Simus shook his head. "Your Majesty, our people take what they want. The idea of trade is foreign to them. I fear that will not happen." He shrugged. "That is a concept that only a warprize could introduce to the tribes."

"A shame. I liked the colors." I smiled at him. "Especially the purple that you wear today."

Simus arched his eyebrows and smiled, sitting a bit straighter in his chair. I stifled a smile, for Simus out of uniform was a sight to behold. He seemed to prefer gaudy colors, and shone like a peacock among drab pigeons. He preened as the lords and ladies of the council gawked at him. What he missed was the look of greed on Masterweaver

Meris's face. She looked like she would do anything to get the secret of those dyes.

Exactly as I had hoped.

I rose, and everyone rose with me. "We have many hard decisions to make in the coming days. We will meet tomorrow, three hours after dawn, in order to begin this great work. May the Goddess bless us all."

Simus extended his arm, and I took it. The buzz of talk started before we were over the threshold and into the hall. As the doors swung shut, I took the crown off with a sigh. "Simus, do you have any kavage in your chambers?"

Simus laughed. "I do indeed."

13

Anna had assigned Simus servants and they brought hot kavage as we settled into the chairs by the fireplace in his quarters. Even with the flames roaring, there was a chill in the room. I took the offered mug and sipped the bitter liquid carefully. The servants bowed and retreated from the chamber. Simus had a mug of his own, and settled in a chair opposite me. "I swear by the skies that my tent is warmer than this stone castle of yours." He grumbled in his own language.

I nodded and ran a hand through my hair, thankful to be rid of the weight of the crown. It sat on the table next to me, gleaming in the firelight. The taste of kavage was bitter on my tongue, yet soothing. I could almost feel my headache fade with every sip.

"You did well, little healer." Simus leaned back, stretching out his long legs, cupping his mug in two hands. "You showed knowledge and strength."

I stared down into the dark liquid left in my mug. It was time. "Simus, as Queen of Xy, I must obey you as the repre-

sentative of my liege lord, right?" I used his tongue, mindful
of those who might overhear us.

Simus nodded. "Yes, I speak for the Warlord until he releases his claim. You have sworn fealty to him."

"But I haven't sworn, have I?" I looked out of the corner of
my eye.

Simus was puzzled, but he answered my question. "Your
system allows oaths to pass from heir to heir, am I not right?"

I nodded slowly. "Yes, but the oath must be ratified."

Simus shrugged.

Casually, I continued. "And as warprize, Simus?"

"Eh?"

"As warprize, must I obey you?"

Simus tensed. It was a slight movement, involuntary on his
part, but I caught it. He recovered well. "You are no longer
warprize, Your Majesty."

"But if I were?"

"As warprize, you would rank me." He looked at me
closely, but his eyes betrayed nothing. "But you are no longer
claimed as warprize."

I tilted my head and smiled at him over the brim of my
mug. "That's odd."

"Odd?"

"I'm sure that Joden told me that once claimed, only the
elders could confirm or deny my status as warprize."

Simus stared at me, his eyes wide.

I thumped my mug down on the table, hard enough to rat-
tle the crown. "You will tell me now, Simus, and tell me the
truth, with the flames as a witness."

Simus dropped his mug, groaned and dropped his head
into his hands. "Who told you? Keir was sure that—"

I stood, furious. "No one told me the entire truth. I had to
figure it out for myself." I breathed in, trying to maintain my
anger and control my delight. "I must be confirmed as the
warprize by the Council of Elders, yes?"

Simus nodded, head never leaving his hands.

"I remain the warprize until the elders confirm or deny me,

yes?" I pressed him hard. I was rewarded with a muffled 'yes'. I pressed on. "Keir can't change my status once he claims me, can he?"

"No."

"As warprize, I answer only to my chosen warlord and I haven't yet formally chosen a warlord, have I? That's why he denied me access to the camp, so I couldn't talk to Marcus or Joden, isn't it?"

Simus moaned.

"Look at me." He didn't move. "Look at me, Simus."

Dropping his hands, he collapsed back in his chair and looked at me. "Lara, please—"

I drew myself up. "As warprize,—"

Simus held up a hand, palm out. "You rank me, little healer." He dropped his hand down, and leaned forward slightly. "Keir is trying to do what is best for you and this land. Your kingdom needs you and there are things that you will face as warprize, obstacles that—"

"Never asking if there might be alternatives!" I was furious, practically spitting. "Without considering my thoughts on the matter!"

"Lara—"

"Enough, Simus." I lifted my chin. "Hear now the will of the warprize."

He sagged in his chair. "I will hear and obey, warprize." He looked up, pained and yet with a gleam of mischief in his eyes. "Can we at least have more kavage before you order me to thwart Keir's plans?"

I smiled, and sat back down, feeling strangely exhilarated, my headache gone. I was going to make this work, find a way to balance the interests of my kingdom and my heart.

Keir had been right. The best part of being a queen and a warprize is getting exactly what you want.

Once again I faced the council over my father's desk, my hands sweating, my stomach cramping, and the crown of the Kingdom of Xy about to fall off my head at any moment. I put my hands face down on the maps spread out over the desk, and tried to remain calm, for this day would see either the birth or the death of my hopes. "My councilors, I thank you for joining me this morning. I have something that I wish to announce before we begin our deliberations."

This was no group of sleepy lords, craftmasters, and clergy—half-awake from being roused from their beds. These men and women faced me alert and ready, each with their own agenda to be considered. They'd all come, with the exception of Lord Durst. He still lay abed, recovering from his wound. I'd tried to blunt the edge with an offering of tea and sweet pastries, but mere food would not be enough. Othur had a chair off to the side, not technically part of the council, but as Seneschal he'd been invited to councils by my father. Xymund had removed the privilege, but I had restored it the day before. Warren was sitting next to Simus, whose tunic and trous were the color of gold. He looked relaxed and opulent, with the onyx brooch of the cat gleaming on his collar.

I pulled my eyes from the brooch, and cleared my throat to continue. "I believe that it is in the best interests of this kingdom if I go with the warlord as the warprize."

I'd stunned them. Taking full advantage, I continued. "Our joy at my return must quickly give way to the hard reality of this kingdom's situation." I held up my hands as Othur and the Archbishop both tried to interrupt. "I will state my case, then I will answer your challenges and questions." I drew in a breath. "There are no potential alliance marriages that would be acceptable to the council or to me, one of the reasons that Xymund didn't contract my marriage." There were none. I had poured over the damn map for hours, checking the status of the neighboring monarchs. The only one that might be a potential ally was five years old and had a regent.

"There are no nobles within the kingdom that would be suitable for me to take as consort." This was trickier, since there were a few that I could marry. But I was certain that the political infighting would prevent anyone from becoming attractive in the entire council's eyes.

"If I should pass to the Goddess without a living heir, the

throne would descend to my cousins." I cleared my throat. No need to go any further, since they knew of the cousins. "The combination of a lack of an heir and a lack of a potential spouse is a fatal one."

They sat there, focused on me. The only encouragement I saw was in Simus's eyes. I stiffened my resolve, hoped that the crown would stay on, and continued, "Our army has been weakened, and there will be attempts on our borders, especially with an inexperienced woman on the throne." I glanced at Warren, but his expression told me nothing. "To strengthen the army will take time, men, and an increase of taxes and tithes. That will be especially hard, since there has been little trade with other kingdoms since the war, and no new routes since my father's time." Remn, Estoval, and Kalisa had all confirmed that fact for me.

"A union between the Warlord and myself provides answers to these problems. We would have an alliance, bound by marriage." The Archbishop coughed, but I ignored him. "Bound by marriage. I am certain that our union would be fruitful, and Simus of the Hawk has confirmed that my firstborn could be raised as a Son of Xy, and designated as the heir to the throne."

"By taking my place as warprize, I would be able to promote trade between our peoples, opening up potential markets for us, and bringing in new trade goods. By taking my place as warprize, I will insure that the Warlord will provide men to aid in our security. When our more aggressive neighbors hear of this alliance, they'll be slow to challenge a warlord. That would reduce the need for increasing taxes and tithes." I wasn't going to let them off the hook completely on that issue. The Kingdom needed money.

"I'll listen to your arguments and answer your challenges. If any has a better idea to serve the needs of the kingdom, let them speak. I must stress that time is of the essence. If the Warlord returns to his people without the Warprize at his side, our opportunity will be gone. And he departs soon."

They were on their feet in seconds, talking at the top of

their lungs. Othur pressed his lips together in a thin line. Warren looked thoughtful. Archbishop Drizen looked apoplectic.

I let them stew for a while, not so much listening to any one voice, but trying to catch the general tone. I'd diagnosed my patient, now all I had to do was convince the patient that the treatment would work, no matter how bad the taste.

I put my shoulders back, called the room to order and called on Lord Warren to speak first. By all rights, it would have been better to have gone about this slowly, persuasively, and tactfully, approaching the councillors individually. I had time for none of that. If this were to happen, it had to happen quickly.

Step by step I took them through my reasoning. We poured over the maps of the surrounding kingdoms, and scrutinized the potential marriages in agonizing detail. Of the six potential rulers, three were already married, with heirs. One was a woman. One was age five, and the last one had a streak of madness that ran through the male side of the family. To my astonishment, there were advocates for this alliance, until they were silenced by their peers.

A marriage with one of the local nobility caused a great deal of ruckus. There were a few second sons that might have qualified, except that many of the lords hated one another. I sat back in my chair and let them have at it. Simus was having a wonderful time, although his command of Xyian was not strong enough to follow all of the rapid cursing and swearing. I happened to catch Othur staring at me at one point. I tried to catch his eye, but he looked away. Finally, I had to take a stand and stop the discussion. It was getting no where and we were losing time.

The discussion about potential heirs was very short. Everyone knew my cousins and no one wanted to see them on the throne of Xy.

It was during the discussion on taxes and tithes that I got my first indication that I had support. Lord Warren stood and held up a hand. "I believe that Xylara is right. If she claims the title of Warprize, it will bring more good than harm to the Kingdom of Xy." Warren looked around the room, then focused on Othur. "I've dealt with the Warlord first hand, and I know that he is a man on whom we can depend. I say that we should support the Daughter of Xy in her decision." He took a seat as the members of the council talked among themselves.

Masterweaver Meris popped up. "The merchants support this decision as well." She popped back down. Thank the Goddess for mercantile instincts. We weren't going to have to debate the benefits of expanded trade. The way Meris kept eyeing Simus, I'd had no doubt she'd support me.

"Well, I'm against it." The Archbishop rose ponderously from his chair. "We are talking about binding a Daughter of Xy to little more than a barbarian, and a heathen barbarian at that. Goddess forbid."

Having anticipated this argument, I rose from my chair. "Perhaps now would be a good time to speak privately and refresh ourselves."

The servants brought in fresh drinks and offered mugs of soup and warm bread. I circled the room, talking to each councilor for a moment, smiling at each one, and made sure that I ended up at the side of the Archbishop. Deacon Browdus stood at his side. "Devoted One." I sat next to him. "May I speak with you privately?"

"Of course, Daughter of Xy." The Archbishop lowered himself in the chair next to me, adjusting his robes. Deacon Browdus took up his usual position, just behind the Archbishop, a stern frown on his face.

"Devoted One, before we go much further with our council, I feel that I must draw your attention to the sleeping arrangements while I was in the Warlord's camp."

"Sleeping arrangements?" Drizen's voice lowered to a whisper. "Where did you sleep?"

I waited until he was mid-sip with his tea. "In the Warlord's bed, Devoted One."

He choked on the tea, splattering his vestments. Wide-eyed, he waved off the Deacon's assistance, and mopped at his robes with a cloth. "Child, what are you saying?"

"I'm saying that while in the camp of the Warlord, I slept in the Warlord's bed, Devoted One."

"Oh, my poor child." His face flushed.

"Devoted One, I have wished to discuss this matter with you, for it troubles me greatly."

"Child, I—" Archbishop Drizen shifted in his chair as his face grew redder. "There's no need to share the details—"

"My thanks for your willingness to spare me, Devoted One, but I feel that you must know the truth."

"T-truth?" Beads of sweat were forming on his forehead as he set down his tea, and let his eyes dart around the room, searching for an escape.

"I am no longer a virgin, Devoted One." I took a sip of tea to give him time to absorb the information.

"Really?" he squeaked. Deacon Browdus's face was pinched up and his eyes were bugged out.

"Yes, Devoted One." I looked him straight in the eye. "A foreign prince might have a problem accepting that."

The poor man blushed deeper. "I'm certain that allowances would be made, Daughter of Xy."

"Alas, Devoted One, not everyone is as forgiving as you." Since during the last sermon I attended he had discussed that very point in great detail, I was sure he'd see it as a difficulty.

"It could pose a problem, my child." He sucked in air, and let it out slowly. "I'm encouraged that the Warlord seems to respect our traditions."

I inclined my head. "During my short time with his people, it seemed that they were tolerant of our beliefs." I rose from my chair. "My thanks, Devoted One. Your words have brought me comfort."

He looked relieved and confused at the same time. "You are always welcome to confide in me, Xylara."

I moved toward the window, anxious to check that Keir was still here. Simus had assured me that he wouldn't move any earlier than stated, but my heart feared otherwise. A quick glance out the window told me that they were making preparations, but they were still there.

Othur moved up next to me, mug in hand. We stood for a moment in uncomfortable silence. "Othur—"

"Lara—"

We both chuckled, but Othur shook his head when I tried to speak. "No. Me first." He lifted a hand to tug on one of my curls. "You are like a daughter to Anna and me, Lara. Don't fault us for wanting to protect you."

Tears filled my eyes. "I don't want to hurt you," I whispered.

Othur turned to look out the window. "I've thought long and hard about this, Lara. Have to admit that I prayed about it was well. Tried to imagine what your father would say. When you removed that brooch from Simus's cloak, you were trying to save a life. A worthy goal. But kings and queens must look beyond the individual and work for the benefit of the people and the land as a whole." He turned back to me. "You'd learn to be a great queen, Lara, but you would be miserable and lose a part of your soul in the process. The day would come when you'd make the right decision, but the weight of it would haunt you forever, haunted by the lives you sacrificed rather than rejoicing in the lives you saved. You are of the Blood, but I can't wish that fate on you. Even more, it's hard to admit that our chick has grown wings." He considered my face with a wry smile. "Your arguments make good sense, Lara." He sighed, and looked out the window. "This is what you want?" He gave me a sideways glance. "Or rather, who you want?"

I nodded, then put my hand up to make sure the crown stayed straight.

"And who will rule in your stead, Daughter of Xy?" There was no condemnation in his eyes, just honest concern. "Have you thought that far ahead?"

I smiled at him, my heart feeling a bit lighter. "Are you familiar with *The Epic of Xyson?*"

He grunted. "Yes, but I was hoping you wouldn't remember." His tired eyes sparkled with a touch of his old humor. "Very well. You have my support, Warprize." He nodded toward the group behind us. "And you'll have their support

once they settle down. Make an excuse to leave the room for
a bit, and let Warren and I talk to them."

Simus came up to us at that point, limping slightly, mug in
one hand, a plate of Anna's tarts in the other. "Try one of
these."

Othur and I each took one. One bite, and I knew where the
bitterest opponent of my plan lay. I looked up into Simus's
dark eyes ruefully. "Apparently I have angered the cook."

Simus nodded.

"Word must have gotten down to the kitchens." Othur
dropped his tart back onto the plate. "You'd better go talk to
her."

"She's your wife."

Othur arched an eyebrow. "You're the Daughter of Xy, and
Warprize. This is one duty that you cannot abrogate."

I couldn't argue with that.

As usual, the castle kitchen was hot, overcrowded, and cluttered. The staff seemed particularly frantic, and I'd heard
Anna berating a maid for breaking a dish before I'd even entered the room. She was scolding everyone, standing in the
center of the kitchen, wielding her wooden spoon, her apron
covered in food stains. I eased in the door, and stood for a
moment, just watching her. She was upset, and taking it out
on everyone in sight.

One of the servants noticed me and said something to
Anna. She stiffened and jerked her head around, setting her
chins to jiggling. I withstood the scorching by lifting my
chin. She scowled. "Food not to your liking, eh, missy?"

"Anna—"

"Here now, keep turning that spit!" Anna cursed at the
young boy who was turning the meat. She turned back to me,
her face hard. "Rumor has it that you're wanting to follow after that barbarian."

"Anna—"

Her face changed in an instant, crumpling before my eyes.

"Why? Tell me that? He let you go, gave you back to us. Why would you want to go?" She collapsed onto one of the stools, which creaked in protest. The room went silent, as everyone stared.

I gestured for the servants to leave, and they filed out, after taking the various meats and stews off the fires. Once the room was empty, I went to Anna, who still sobbed, and put my arms around her. I lay my head atop hers, and let her cry.

Othur came in. He knelt before her and rubbed her knees with his large hands. "Anna."

She sniffed, her face red and tear-streaked. Othur reached into a pocket and handed her a large white handkerchief. She took it and blew her nose. "We just got her back, safe and well, why can't she stay?" Anna sobbed, her chins wobbling. "There's no reason for her to leave."

I lifted my head and took a breath, but Othur took one of Anna's hands in his own. With the other, he pulled me down to kneel next to him. "Anna, my love, look at her."

Anna looked at me with reddened eyes.

"Anna, the eyrie's open and our chick has flown. The truth is that she wants to go."

"Truly?" Anna squinted at me and frowned. Something she saw made her eyes widen. "You've lost your heart to that barbarian, haven't you?"

My eyes filled, and I tried to smile and nod at her at the same time.

"Besides which," Othur spoke softly, "she's convinced me and the entire Council that it's in the best interest of the Kingdom that she go."

"Well." Anna pulled her hands free and mopped her eyes with her apron. "Just so you know, whoever sits on the throne will not get one bite of food from my kitchen worth eating."

Othur sighed heavily. "A hard thing to be starved to death by your own wife."

"Eh?"

"Anna, I am going to name Othur Warden of the Kingdom of Xy. He will rule in my stead while I am with the Warlord."

"Please say that you will feed me, lady wife." Othur stood and hugged her, as she burst out crying all over again.

The morning of Keir's departure dawned bright and clear. As the sun left the horizon, the front runners of the Warlord's army moved out, scouting the way for the bulk of the army to follow. Simus and I watched from the walls, wrapped in cloaks.

"He will kill me, you know," Simus spoke morosely.

I glanced at him from under my hood. "No, Simus. The blame will rest on me. Keir won't hold you responsible."

Simus snorted. "It's not Keir I'm worried about, Warprize. It's Joden. He will be furious that he missed seeing this. At least let me send a messenger—"

"No. I'll not risk Keir getting wind of what I intend to do. If it's Joden you're worried about, then send him a letter and describe it to him. But wait awhile. This might not work."

"A letter?" Simus rolled his eyes. "Warprize, I can't—"

"You tell your words to someone, and they write them down for you."

"Ah." Simus looked pleased.

I continued my watch out over the valley. "How long before they leave?"

"Keir usually sends the scouts out two hours before the army moves." I turned and smiled at Simus, who just shook his head, his gold earring swaying in his ear. "Warprize, they will sing of this for a thousand years."

I just smiled and headed down off the battlements. The guards bowed to me as I moved quickly back into the castle and headed for the throne room.

It was one of the fastest coronations in the history of the Kingdom of Xy, shorn of its ceremony and pomp. We'd gathered the nobles, merchants, and the entire palace staff as witnesses.

Once I was officially Queen of Xy, Simus came forth, and

I knelt before him and repeated all of the oaths that Xymund had made for the peace.

I then summoned Othur forth, and in a ceremony pulled directly from *The Epic of Xyson* made him Warden of Xy during my absence.

The public announcement of my decision was harder, for the people were nervous as to its wisdom. Funny that they had been fairly confident when I'd surrendered myself into a form of slavery. Now that I was fighting for something I wanted, they weren't so sure of themselves. But I'd made sure that the discussions in the Council chamber had been made public knowledge, and there was no outward resistence to my plans.

As I made my private goodbyes to Othur, Anna and Warren outside the great double doors, Simus stood close with the reins of our horses. Warren had a frown on his face. "Lara, what if the Warlord will not accept you back? What then?"

I took a deep breath and mounted my horse, thankful that no one else had asked this question. It was one that had weighed heavily on my mind. "I'll deal with it if and when it happens, Warren. Not before."

With that, we turned our horses toward the gate and left the castle.

So it was that Simus and I were on the rise that overlooked the road when Keir's army began to move. The road stretched for long miles down the valley to eventually reach the plains. A well-worn path, it was trampled dirt for miles and miles. The day was clear and crisp, with a slight breeze. It would be cold when the sun sank behind the mountains.

With distant cries, the army began to pass in front of us, with the leaders in the forefront. I spotted Iften and Joden, but my eyes locked on Keir. He was astride his horse, dressed in black, hard to miss with his scarlet cape. He rode at the lead, eyes to the front. Joden had obviously seen us, he surged forward and spoke to Keir. But Keir passed without turning his head, without a glance.

Simus chuckled. "He's showing off."

"How so?"

"Moving out at a trot. Normally the army moves at a walk."

"To save the horses."

Simus laughed. "No, to save our asses. Trotting's hard on the rider. He's trying to impress. They'll slow once they are out of sight."

It took some time for the entire army to pass by, but at last the stream of soldiers and equipment ended. While we couldn't see them, Simus had assured me that the rear guard had stayed behind. They'd wait for about an hour, then spread out, checking for pursuit, reporting back to Keir on a regular basis. I was counting on that last part.

When the last man passed the fork in the road, I dismounted, and removed my cloak and shoes.

"This is dangerous, Lara." Simus frowned. "You'll be alone on the road, with no protection. At least let me follow at a distance to watch over you."

"No, Simus, I forbid it." I shivered in the white shift and crammed the cloak and shoes into the saddlebags. "Your people love a grand gesture, and this certainly qualifies." I handed Simus the reins. "The Warlord has claimed me. I will take nothing except from his hands. I just wish I knew how he will take this." After all, I had his heart, he'd said so himself.

"Would that I could offer you assurances, but all I know for certain is that he will be furious." Simus sighed, then flashed a grin. "So will Joden. Tell him I will send my words. Be well, Warprize."

"Be well, Simus." I turned and walked away, down the road, following the army.

We were still within sight of the city walls, and I could hear a faint cheer as I started down the road. Word had spread of my intentions, and there was a crowd along the walls, watching me go. Othur, Warren, and Simus would take good care of the kingdom, of that I was sure. I was not sure how this grand gesture of mine would be received.

I could see the army moving away up ahead, the cloud of dust still visible. The road was pounded dirt and cool beneath my feet. I walked carefully, trying to avoid the sharper stones and keeping my pace deliberate, not hurried. I had a long way to go before I caught up, and would need my strength. The breeze picked up, cut through my white sheath and blew my hair around my head. I'd left it down, deliberately trying to look as I had looked that night.

I tried to keep my thoughts still and quiet, but I had little success. With every step I imagined Keir's anger when he realized what I had done. My head was filled with mental images of being whipped at a post, or just trampled under the hoofs of his horse. I bit my lip as a stray stone cut into my foot. Best I start watching where I walked, instead of thinking about what might happen. I tried to stay in the clear parts of the road, avoiding horse dung. Perhaps going barefoot had not been the wisest choice.

The sky was a vibrant orange when I finally heard the thunder of hooves behind me. I didn't turn, just continued to walk at a steady pace. For a brief moment, I feared that Simus or Othur had sent troops after me. But instead, as Simus had predicted, the first of the rear scouts moved past me at a gallop, their horses veering around me. One looked back, and let out a yelp of surprise. He pulled on the reins so hard his horse reared, legs splayed in its effort to stop. The other scout, hearing the noise, pulled his sword, and turned off the road, arcing back to me.

I ignored them and kept walking.

The first scout came up on horseback. "Warprize?" he asked, looking horrified. I looked up to see Tant, the warrior that had been whipped for falling asleep on watch.

The other scout came up, scanning for danger. He glanced at his partner. "That's the Warprize?"

Tant swung down from his horse, to stand beside me. "Warprize, what are you doing here? Where is your escort?"

I walked past him. "I am returning to the Warlord's side." I kept moving. They followed, Tant leading his horse, the other remaining in the saddle.

"Warprize, please mount, and we will take you to the Warlord." Tant's voice came over my shoulder. "There's really no need for you to walk."

"She's barefoot." The other observed.

I kept moving, looking forward. "My Warlord has claimed me. I will take nothing except from his hands."

Tant came along side, and he gulped. "Warprize, the army will not rest for at least another two marks. It'll be some time before you reach him, and I can't allow . . ." I glared at him and he did not complete the sentence. He stopped dead, and I heard curses muttered behind me. I just kept walking, determined to continue on. There was an argument going on behind me.

"You go tell the Warlord."

"No, I'll stay with her, you go tell the Warlord."

The argument continued, then the same voice snarled. "Pluck hairs, then. Short hair goes."

After a moment there was a snort of triumph and then the mounted scout was galloping off toward the army. Tant caught up with me, his voice pleading. "Warprize, please, take my boots and cloak. You're cold, and your feet are bleeding."

In point of fact, they burned like flames. "No." I kept walking.

Muttering something, Tant raised his hands to the sky as he walked beside me. I wasn't sure if it was a prayer or curse, but I distinctly heard "Why me?" I was tired, my feet hurt, and I wasn't going to listen to his whining on top of it all. "Return to your duties."

"With all due respect, Warprize, I will not." Tant caught up again, his horse protesting at being jerked forward. "If you'll not take my help, at the least, I'll guard you."

"You disobey the Warprize?" I looked at him.

"Yes, if that's the choice." He twisted the reins in his hands. "The way the Warlord's been stomping around like a crazed ehat, snapping and snarling at any that come near, I'll disobey you. Better a punishment at your hands then death at the Warlord's."

I nodded, faced forward and kept walking. But my heart was a bit lighter. Snapping and snarling, was he? Like an ehat, eh?

Of course, I still didn't know what an ehat was.

It seemed like hours before there was a commotion ahead of us. A cloud of dust betrayed the horsemen coming hard and fast up the road. My self-appointed guard faded back as Keir came thundering into view, galloping his horse, his scarlet cloak flaring behind him. There were a few more men behind him. I stopped and stood where I was, waiting.

Keir reared his horse to a stop in front of me. The animal towered over me, and I could hear its harsh breathing. I kept my eyes down, on the road.

"What in the name of all the elements do you think you are doing?" Keir thundered.

"Following my Warlord." I kept my voice steady.

"You have sworn fealty to me, to hold these lands." He moved his horse, circling me. I could feel the heat of his gaze on my neck, and shivered at the bite in his words.

"The queen may have so sworn, the warprize has not." I lifted my eyes as his horse moved in front of me. His face was distorted with rage. I swallowed hard, but continued. "The warprize follows the warlord."

The horse moved to circle me again. "I'll have you taken back to the castle."

"That just means that I will have to walk this all over again."

Keir brought the horse around again to face me. "Not if you're chained to your throne," he snarled.

Joden coughed from the side of the road, where he sat on his horse. Marcus was beside him, mounted as well, wrapped in his familiar cloak. Keir whipped his head around. "What?"

Joden shrugged. "Well, it occurs to me that the army is marching away from us as we speak."

Marcus piped up. "And when your high and mightiness is finished hollering, ya might notice that she is bleeding."

Keir's head whipped around, and his nostrils flared as he raked me with his glance. I tried not to fidget under his glare. He cursed. "Ride with Marcus. We will see to your feet, and return you to the castle." He turned his horse away from me.

"No."

"What!" Keir jerked his horse's head around, and the animal snorted in protest.

I looked up. "My Warlord is sworn to care for me. I will take nothing except at his hands."

Joden started laughing at that. "Oh, what a song this will make!"

Keir cursed again, dismounted and stalked over to me. I clasped my hands tight together as he moved into my space, coming as close as he could without touching me. I closed my eyes and trembled, craving his warmth and touch. He stood there for a moment, breathing.

Breathing in the scent of the vanilla that I had rubbed into my hair and skin.

If this didn't work there would be no need for chains. I was certain that if we parted again, a part of me would simply die. I opened my eyes and stared up into his, where his anger raged unabated. Hope died in my breast. This wasn't going to work.

I swallowed hard, and went to my knees before him there on the road.

I didn't make it. At the first hint of what I was about to do, he swept his cloak off and wrapped it about my shoulders. Then picking me up, he cradled me in his arms, and headed for his horse. "Joden," he barked.

Joden dismounted, and handed his reins to Marcus. Keir handed me off to him, then turned to his own horse. Joden smiled at me, his round face almost split by his wide smile. "Oh, Lara, what a song I will make of this!" He kept his voice down, as Keir brought his horse in close. I bit my lip, afraid that Joden was speaking too soon.

Joden lifted me up to Keir, who cradled me in his arms. Joden's voice rang out loudly. "I return your warprize, Warlord."

Keir shot him an angry look, but said nothing. He turned his horse toward the army, and we set off. I noticed that Tant had made himself scarce. He was no where to be seen.

As we rode, I worked a hand free and lifted it to Keir's cheek. I could feel his jaw clenching under my hand.

"The Council of Xy agreed that I would serve the kingdom better as warprize."

The muscles of his jaw moved under my fingers, but he said nothing.

"I made Othur Warden of Xy. He will take good care of my people and the land."

Keir stared straight ahead, controlling the horse as we rejoined the army. The cloak had fallen to my shoulders, and I heard the warriors react as they saw my hair whipping about in the wind.

I kept talking, murmuring my words softly. "This is what I want, Keir."

He didn't look at me. "Marcus! Find Gils and figure out where they stored the medicines. Have him come and tend her. And find her some clothes and shoes."

"Aye, Warlord." Marcus moved off, but Keir still didn't look at me.

I tried again. "You have only to hear my heartbeat to know that each beat is for you."

He did not respond. I swallowed hard. "For us."

No response.

Nothing.

I closed my eyes and pulled back my hand, afraid that I had lost.

A finger under my chin forced my head up, and I opened my eyes to find him gazing down at me. Those blue eyes were suspiciously bright, with a trace of humor as he bent his head to whisper against my lips.

"Forever."

A preview of the next novel of

Keir and Xylara

BY ELIZABETH A. VAUGHAN

Coming in 2006 from Tor Romance

1

"Bloodmoss! That's bloodmoss, Marcus!" I leaned over, try-ing to get a better look. I was positive that the grubby little plant I was seeing passing under the hooves of the horse was the legendary herb. "Let me down!"

The horse we were riding danced as my weight shifted and Marcus tightened up the reins. "If you don't stop wiggling, you're gonna tumble off, and embarrass Hisself and me." Marcus groused as the horse pranced under us.

I tightened my grip on his waist. "If you let me ride by my-self, this wouldn't be a problem."

"You can't ride worth a damn, and your feet are still ill. Now sit still! How would it look, the Warprize sprawled in the dirt?"

"Marcus, I am a Master Healer and my feet are healing fine."

"You know from nothing," Marcus growled. "I will judge if the Warprize is fit to walk."

I settled back, frustrated. While I might be Xylara, Master Healer, Daughter of the House of Xy, Queen of Xy, Warprize of Keir of the Tribe of the Cat, Warlord of the Plains but as far as Marcus was concerned I was little more than an unruly child. I sighed, and leaned my head on the back of his shoulder. "I can ride just fine."

Marcus snorted. "About as well as you tend your own feet."

Therein lay one of my problems. When I'd made the decision to follow the Warlord's army, I'd done so in the same garb I'd worn for the original claiming ceremony. Since tradition required that the Warprize accept nothing except from the hand of the Warlord, I had walked barefoot behind the army for some time before Keir had discovered what I was doing and reclaimed me. Following my Warlord, challenging his decision, had been the best choice, both for us and for our peoples.

Choosing to walk barefoot had not been quite so clever.

Joden, in training as a Singer, said that by choosing to honor the traditions of the Plains, I had made a powerful statement, one that would ring in the songs he was crafting. Marcus had arched his one eyebrow over his remaining eye, and inquired if the fact that my feet had sickened afterwards would in the first verse or the second.

I straightened slowly, craning my neck to look around, careful not to disturb the horse this time. We were at the center of the Firelander Army, returning to the Plains. Not that Keir's people called themselves 'Firelanders'. That was a term my people used. They used 'of the Plains' which sounded awkward to my ears. In my thoughts, at least, they remained the Firelanders. Of course, I no longer add 'cursed' or 'evil' or thought that they belched fire. I still had hopes of seeing a blue one, though. There were brown ones, and black ones, and some even had a yellow tinge to their skin. Who knew what wonders awaited me on the Plains?

Marcu and I were surrounded by horses and riders, which spilled out beyond the road as we moved. Keir had ordered that I travel at the center of this moving mass of warriors and horses. Even so, I knew that my guards would not be far away. Rafe and Prest were ahead of us. "Rafe!"

Marcus jerked his head beneath his cloak, and muttered.

Fall was upon us, but the day was fine, and the sun warm on our backs. Regardless, Marcus rode cloaked, wrapped well lest the skies be offended by his scars. Yet another aspect of these people that I didn't understand.

Rafe turned and waved, and he and Prest slowed their mounts so that we could catch up with them. Marcus grumbled, but maneuvered his mount between them.

"Rafe, see that plant?" I tried to point it out to him as we moved.

"Plant?" Rafe looked in confusion at the ground. "Warprize . . ."

"The pale one; the one that looks like moss, but its buttercolored."

Rafe shrugged. "Wouldn't it be easier to pick it yourself?"

I rolled my eyes in frustration. "Marcus won't stop!"

Rafe let his laughter ring out, then Prest reached over and grabbed the halter of our horse. Marcus exclaimed bitterly, but Prest guided us out of the crush, and off to the side where he pulled the horses to a stop.

I started to wiggle off, but Marcus would have none of it. "You are to stay off those feet, you are."

"Marcus-"

Rafe swung down off his horse. "Point it out to me, Warprize and I'll get you handfuls."

Epor and Isdra came up besides us. "Problem?" Isdra asked.

"Herself wants to be picking weeds." Marcus grumbled.

"Bloodmoss." I corrected him. "That's the one, Rafe. Let me see."

Epor snickered slightly as Rafe bent to the task of getting the plants. I noticed that Isdra gave him an amused look and reached over to nudge his leg. He caught her hand, and raised it to his lips. I look away, embarrassed at such a display.

Rafe held up a handful of leaves and plants, their torn roots tangling. "Which one, Warprize?"

I heard a pounding of hooves behind us, even as I reached for the plants. Marcus heaved a sigh. "That'll be the youngin'."

It was Gils, all right, riding his horse at breakneck speed along the army, grinning like a madman. It cheered me to see his simple pleasure in racing his horse like the wind. Marcus grumbled, bu the others smiled and made room as Gils galloped to my side.

"Cadr came to see me, Warprize! To ask for help with a bad boil." He smiled broadly at me, his curly red hair dancing in the breeze, his words spilling out. "I told him that I would ask you, that I had to consult with my Master."

I grinned back at him, the young Firelander that had declared himself my apprentice. While Keir had decreed that he had to keep his place as a warrior for now, his secondary duties were to act as my helper. At least until we reached the Heart of the Plains. I'd used every spare minute to give him lessons. "Good. With any luck I can show you how to lance it. But first, Gils, remember what I told you about bloodmoss?" Gils nodded, but I didn't give him time to answer. I grabbed the soft yellow leaves out of Rafe's hands, scattering the rest. "It's there, right there, Gils. Get some for me."

The army continued past as he swung down to join Rafe in picking the plants. The others had gone on alert, something I doubt they were even aware of, moving their horses to encircle us. Even though we were traveling in the center of the Warlord's army, their instincts were to safeguard. There was no danger in being left behind, since the army was moving at a walk, and was spread out over what seemed to me to be miles.

"Prest, do you have any ehat leather to spare?" Epor asked.

"Yes." Prest cast a look over his shoulder. "You have a need?"

"The handle of my club needs rewrapping."

"He fancies ehat for the grip." Isdra explained.

"Would take a piece the size of an ehat to wrap that fool weapon of yours." Marcus groused.

I glanced over at Epor, who had his club fastened to his back in some kind of harness. It was a long thick piece of wood, half again as long as my arm, with metal studs along the length of the top. "What's wrong with his weapon?"

Rafe popped up next to my leg, bloodmoss in two hands. "Marcus doesn't approve, Warprize."

Marcus grunted. "Too slow and unwieldy."

"For you," Epor responded, as if this were an old argument. "I prefer a weapon where if I hit the enemy, the enemy goes down and stays down." Epor gave me a saucy grin and a wink.

I gave Rafe a look, and he laughed at my confusion. "Warprize, a club is a two-handed weapon, best used by a big man with strength in his arms and chest. Like Epor or Prest."

"Not you?" I asked.

Rafe shook his head. "I'm one for speed. Quicker with a sword or dagger. Isdra, Gils or I would strike twice for every one of Epor's blows." His eyebrows danced as he gave Marcus a quick glance. "Or once for every three blows from Marcus with those daggers of his."

Epor laughed, his blond hair gleaming in the sun. "Ah, but in need, even you or Isdra could use it two-handed."

Rafe nodded. "Maybe. If I was desperate."

"Or insane." Isdra added.

Prest dismounted, and dug through his packs, pulling out a fold of dark leather. He handed it to Epor, who nodded his thanks. "I'll replace it, Prest, after the next ehat hunt."

"What exactly is a—"

Gils popped up and handed me a bunch of leaves, laughing up at me. "How much of this you want?"

I smiled at him. "As much as I can get, Gils. Do you remember what it can do?"

He gave me a scornful look. "I's know, Warprize." He bent to his task, his voice taking on a chanting tone. "Bloodmoss is for packing wounds. It grows at the site of great battles. It will not bind to the flesh, will not stick in the scabs. It seems to aid healing, fighting infection and closing the wound. It absorbs as much blood as it can, and when you are done with it you should scatter it about, for the plant will use the blood to take root and grow." He stood, his hands full of more leaves.

Marcus groaned. "A blood-sucking plant. More knowledge than I need."

I was pleased. But Gils's memory had never been a problem in his lessons. It was the practical application of the information that was the problem. My feet had been a good example. It's one thing to talk about cleaning and treating an infected wound. It's another to work on a wiggling patient who couldn't help but jerk her feet at every touch. Finally, in frustration Marcus had me lay on my stomach, and he and Keir held my feet as Gils cleaned them. The boy had done the best he could, but the right foot had become infected. An angry, red, and puss-filled wound, which the poor lad had to clean out with an angry and worried Keir hanging over his shoulder.

I leaned forward, holding my hand in front of Marcus's face. "It's wonderful, Marcus. Give me your knife and I'll show you how it works."

"Skies above." Marcus jerked his head back and the horse danced beneath us. "It's more like you'll cut your hand off. Not with my knife!"

Isdra laughed, and moved her horse closer. "Show me, Warprize." She pulled her knife and sliced deep into the meat beneath her thumb. Blood welled up quickly.

I took the leaves and twisted them, crushing their fibers. A strong scent of mold rose into my nostrils. "Take this and press it to the cut."

Isdra wiped her blade clean on her trous and sheathed it, then used her fingers to press the mass to the cut. The leaves turned color almost immediately as it drank up the blood, changing to a pale green. Gils craned his head to see, and Isdra lowered her hand to let him get a good look. At my nod, she pulled the leaves away. The skin was healed, with only an angry red line left to show she'd been hurt. Isdra held her hand up to show the others, and let the used leaves fall to the ground.

Prest and Rafe were clearly impressed, and Rafe started to gather the crop in earnest. Gils knelt, staring at the bloody leaves intently. I watched for a minute, then smiled. "Gils, I don't think it will take root while you watch."

"Oh." He was clearly disappointed as he started to gather more.

"And what do we have to be careful of when we use this plant?" I asked him gently.

He frowned a bit, then his face cleared. "Not to use it on a dirty wound. It will seal the dirt inside, if you are not careful." He bit his lip. "I could not have used it on your feet."

Marcus grunted at that. "Does it have to be fresh?"

"I was told that it works just as well dried, just not quite so quickly."

"I can think of other uses." Isdra smiled slyly. "It would be handy at moon times. Would it grow on the Plains?"

I flushed even as I shrugged. She spoke so casually about something that wasn't discussed out loud by my people.

Epor had dismounted, and was looking at the leaves he was holding. His horse nosed his hand, but threw its head up when he offered it the leaves. "Would it work on a horse?"

"Why is it always about horses with you people?" I snapped, suddenly irritated.

There was an uncomfortable silence. The surprised looks on their faces made my pique vanish. I looked down at Marcus's back and mumbled. "I don't know."

Gils, bless his youth, was oblivious. "How much will you want, Warprize?" His arms were filled with his pickings.

"As much as we can take." I looked around, amazed to see that the little plant was spread through the grass as far as I could see. "Two handfuls in each warrior's kit would be useful in case of injury."

Gils quickly handed out his crop, making sure that each had at least two handfuls. Even Marcus took a supply. Gils placed his own in his saddlebags and then mounted. "I'll pass the word, Warprize. Two-handfuls"

"Tell them to dry it well, Gils." I called after him as he galloped off. "We'll see to Cadr once we stop for the night."

Rafe mounted up as well, and Marcus headed us back toward the army at a more sedate walk. "Hisself will not like his warriors stopping to pick posies."

"They all have to pass water at some point, don't they?" I pointed out.

Rafe laughed, but Marcus just grunted.

As we returned to our position in the flowing mass of warriors, Marcus was careful to thread his way back into the direct center. Rafe and Prest rode ahead of us a little ways, and Epor and Isdra faded behind us. They didn't really try to maintain any kind of positions, since there were warriors all around us. I shifted, trying to get comfortable, and tried not to sigh in Marcus's ear.

Marcus must have heard me, for he cleared his throat. "Epor meant no offense, Warprize."

"I know, Marcus."

I yawned, tired now that the excitement was over. It had been a brief change from the monotony of the days since Keir had taken me up on his horse and re-claimed me as his Warprize. I fingered the leaves that I still held in my hand. Eln would be so pleased to hear that bloodmoss thrived in this area. I could send him a plant with the next messenger, dig it up, roots and all, and wrap it in wet cloth. Even his dour face would crack with a smile at the sight. I'd laugh to see it—except that I wouldn't be there.

Suddenly, it all seemed too much. A flood of sickness rose up in my body, a sickness of the heart for which there was no cure. I was all to familiar with this feeling, for I was sick for my home, for the castle and the people that I'd left behind in Water's Fall. For Anna's stew and Heath's teasing, and my old room with its four familiar stone walls. I sighed again, trying not to feel sorry for myself and failing.

"You've not been yourself, Warprize." Marcus had his head turned, and I could just see his nose and lips under the hood of the cloak. His voice dropped to a low gentle tone. "You're not eating, and I'm thinking that you're not sleeping either."

I watched the ground pass below us. "I'm fine."

"Are you pregnant?"

I dropped my head onto his back and groaned. "Marcus . . ."

"It's a fair question." Marcus replied. "Our women take precautions in the field, but you Xyians have such strange ways . . ."

"I am not pregnant." I growled. I didn't want to think about that, although he was right. I hadn't taken any precautions.

My courses were due any day. But the idea of being pregnant raised issues that I didn't want to consider.

"Then what is wrong, Lara?"

The fact that he was using my name told me that he was worried. I opened my mouth, but the truth would not come. "I'm fine, Marcus. Truly."

He snorted. "As you say, Warprize." He stiffened in the saddle, and I knew that I had upset him. This scarred little man had come to mean a great deal to me within a short period of time. He was fiercely loyal to his Warlord, and I was included in that loyalty. I wasn't sure that was by virtue of my own self, or that fact that I was Keir's chosen Warprize. Regardless, how could I confide my worries and fears to him? He already held Xyians in contempt on general principals. My fretful complaints could only heap wood on that fire.

I settled for an obvious question. "When do you think we'll stop for the night?"

"A few hours yet, Warprize. Hisself will keep us moving until we lose the light."

"Why is he in such a hurry?"

"Hisself has his reasons. You're to be confirmed when we reach the Heart of the Plains, and the sooner the better." Marcus's tone was a clear indication that the topic was now settled.

I looked about for a different distraction, and caught a glimpse of Epor reaching over to tug on Isdra's braid. "Epor seems sweet on Isdra."

"Eh?" Marcus growled. "Sweet? What means this?"

I floundered for the unfamiliar words. "That he cares for her."

There was an unnatural pause. I leaned forward. "Marcus?"

"They are bonded." He spoke grudgingly, almost as if the words caused him pain. "Do you not see the ear spirals?"

"Bonded? Is that the same as married?" I twisted about, trying to get a better look at their ears, but Marcus had apparently grown weary of me.

"Ask Epor. Or Isdra." His tone was curt and he whistled, somehow catching Prest's attention. Prest raised a hand, and started to move back toward us. Because I was a burden on the horse, I was traded off every hour so as not to tire any one animal. The elements forbid that a horse be over-tried. I was starting to feel like a package in a trading caravan.

Marcus spoke as Prest moved into position. 'Joden is a good man, Lara, valued for his wisdom. He is heard in senel, although he holds no rank, and even by the Elders when he appears before their councils. He will make a great Singer once he is recognized as such."

Prest drew closer, preparing to transfer me to his horse. I was trying to figure out what Marcus was trying to say.

"If you can't confide in anyone else, you can confide in a Singer. Words spoken to a Singer are held to his heart, where they can not be pried free. Talk to Joden, Lara. Please."

With that, they transferred me to Prest's horse without breaking stride, and Marcus faded back and away into the crowd.

Prest is a full head taller then Marcus and easily twice as broad. I rather dreaded riding with him, since I could not see over his shoulders. Which meant that my stomach would be upset by the time I left his horse.

Prest also isn't much of a talker, which left me free to dwell on my miseries. If Atira were here, I might be able to confide in her, but she'd been left in Water's Fall, under the care of Eln. Her leg would heal true, but the break would not let her travel. Even surrounded by thousands of warriors, I felt terribly alone. Keir had been absent now for two days, and part of me feared he'd decided that this Warprize no longer interested him. Maybe I could talk to Joden, confide in him. Joden had helped me so much when I'd been taken to the camp. He'd been the one to figure out that I'd been lied to by Xymund, my late half-brother. But I felt so very stupid and silly. Like a spoiled child with a broken toy.

Just how could I tell anyone how miserable I was? Fire-landers already had a fairly low opinion of soft city folk, and if I started complaining it would only reinforce their ideas.

It wasn't so bad when Keir was with me. For some reason I could sleep in his presence. Well, truth be told, I could sleep in his arms. But he had duties and had to travel from one end of his army to the other, and it spread out for miles. So there were some nights when he wasn't in our shelter, and I had not seen him at all for the last two days.

Firelanders could sleep in the saddle. If I tried that, I got sick. Firelanders, in the saddle, could repair tack, or sharpen blades or argue or, Goddess help me, talk.

Which was another thing. We had horses in Xy. I'd been taught to ride as a child, and have ridden many times. But in the city I rarely bothered. By the time a groom had saddled one for me, I could be half way to where I was going. You had to worry about tying them to things and leaving them for long periods. I'd never been really enamored of the beasts; they were a form of transportation and not much more.

But I'd learned fast that Firelanders had relationships with their animals. Horses were treated like small children, acknowledged and admired. One of the worst insults imaginable was 'bracnect', which meant 'killer of foals'. Now that I knew what the word meant, I was more careful in how I used it.

And just like proud parents are wont to do, they talk about horses. Constantly. Obsessively. They'd discuss the details of ears and mane and gaits until I wanted to scream. They have seventeen words for a male horse and can talk for HOURS about saddles. They love to modify saddles with hooks and protrusions and supports, and talk out that the advantages and disadvantages. Their world is very dependant on their animals and its fascinating for about the first day. After that, I tired quickly of horses and horse talk.

And that was another thing. All this talk was out in the open where everyone could hear. They have no sense of modesty or privacy that I could see. I'd had one rider come up, and start to discuss the state of his bowels without a qualm, in the middle of a moving mass of warriors. You couldn't really talk to anyone without being over-heard.

So here I was, Warprize to the Warlord of the Plains, acclaimed before my people and his, praised and admired for my willingness to journey to a new and strange place, to be a bridge between his people and mine. What would they think, to find out that I was sick to my stomach, hungry, exhausted, dirty, and alone and certain that the Warlord had lost interest in me?